Book One -

DiAngelo's GUN

DANNY LEE JONES

Editing, Layout, and Cover Design by Sheila R. Boyd, EdD, sheilaraeboyd@ gmail.com.

Dedicated to

my family and friends

who were a constant source of inspiration to me in taking an idea through to the completion of this novel.

Table of Contents

Chapter 1

I turned from a sound sleep; I heard pans rattling in the kitchen. I could almost smell the breakfast of my childhood. A smell of bacon filled my nose. Before I knew it, I was lost in the memories of my childhood—ones that I hadn't thought of in years . . . ones that I had locked far in the back of my mind as I started a new life. It was a time when it was impossible to look to the future and too hurtful to look back. This particular warm morning reminded me of my first day of third grade.

Mom hurried around the kitchen cooking Pa's breakfast while at the same time washing my face and taking quick breaks to turn the bacon. I wondered if her apron was for keeping food off her clothes or really for use as a washcloth to wet and clean my sleepy eyes and face.

Mom was a short woman with tired eyes. She seemed so old to me. I guess I didn't realize that she was only 36, but life had not been so good to her. Her hair was auburn, and her green eyes made her look like a cat.

Mom plopped Pa's filled plate on the table, grabbed my hand, and hurriedly led me to the sink. I stepped up on the stepstool so she could finish cleaning me up to get me ready for school.

I looked over at Pa. He was eating his food but still kept his eyes on me. I always hated it when he would stare at me with those coal-black eyes. It seemed as though they would go through my heart and straight to the bottom of my stomach.

Mom started getting her things gathered up for the day when she turned and said, "Oh, Lord! I almost forgot to feed my baby!"

I was still standing on the stepstool. Her words caused me to cringe at her reference to me as "the baby."

With one foot hooked under the stepstool, she deftly pulled me—stepstool and all—up to the counter. She placed a plate of food in front of me, and I ate as she finished getting herself ready.

Now, as I look back, I think she kept me as far away from Pa as possible. He was a mean and hateful man with the hearts of seven demons mixed within him.

I prayed over the food that Mom gave me and started eating.

Pa mumbled something, but the only part I heard was, "Is your food good?"

I said, "Yes, sir."

I heard Pa say, "Food *I* bought . . . and look who's eating it."

I couldn't keep myself from saying, "No, sir. This is food Mom brought from Aunt Hadie's Grill last night."

Before I knew what was happening, Pa was on his feet. He grabbed me and was about to whip me, but Mom came just in time . . . like so many times before.

Pa glared at me as he sternly advised, "Better stop that back-talking, or I will give you something to remember."

With that, I watched as he turned to walk out the door.

Mom spoke up, "Hank, I will be late this evening. Hadie has a meeting; I need to get the supper food going."

All she got for an answer was a slamming door, and he was gone.

Mom grabbed my hand as she said, "Baby, try and not make Pa mad."

I answered, "Well, it's not hard to make him mad; he's *always* mad."

Soon, we started on our walk toward the school. For conversation, Mom asked me, "Are you ready for your new school year?"

I replied, "No, Mom. This is the first year that Mikie and I won't be in the same class. I don't even want to go to school."

Mikie was my cousin . . . and my very best friend. He was two months younger than me, and we were as close as grapes on a vine.

Mom said, "Well, you better get used to being without Mikie; they're not going to be putting you both in the same room every year. The way you two carry on, it's a wonder they haven't separated you before now."

"But, Mom," I said in protest. "I can't think without him. We are like twins, folks say. He is my reason for doing so good in school."

We continued walking in silence. The heat pounded down upon us. It was the same road we had walked since I could remember . . . the dirt road that lead down to Aunt Hadie's Grill, where there was a filling station, as well. Uncle Marco took care of the filling station, while Aunt Hadie took care of feeding the folks who came into the grill. Uncle Marco and Aunt Hadie's house was built onto the grill, so they didn't have far to walk to get to work.

Mom worked at the grill with Aunt Hadie. However, most of the time the two were huddled together at the end of the counter whispering things back and forth just like Mikie and I did at the other end.

The Kentucky sun seemed hotter this year for some reason, and I told Mom, "I'm thirsty."

"We'll be there in a few minutes," Mom answered.

I always walked on the left of Mom for some reason . . . I guess it was because she always had something she carried in her right hand. Most of the time it was some sewing or something that needed to be washed because while she worked at the grill, she also did our clothes.

"Hey, Mom," I quipped, "there's Mr. Creek! Look!" I pointed at an older man puttering around in his front yard.

"Hush, boy!"

However, before I heard her "Hush!" I had already yelled out his name.

"Mr. Creek, how are you today? You better get that grass cut; it's going to grow over your house!" I challenged.

He stood up and smiled at me. "Boy, you sure know how to talk."

"Mr. Creek, may I have a glass of water? I'm so thirsty."

"Sure," he readily replied. "I will get it for you."

Mom squeezed my hand so hard, I said, "Mom, stop! You're going to squeeze my hand off, and the folks will be calling me 'No Hand.'"

This made my mom laugh. She always loved to laugh with me.

"Boy, you are my joy. You're the one thing in life I did right."

By this time, Mr. Creek was back with a tall glass of water. I drank like a horse that had just run a race.

Mr. Creek remarked, "Boy, don't they give you water at home?"

Mom stepped in and answered, "Yes, we have plenty of water." She looked at him with her green eyes and continued, "Good day, Mr. Creek."

I added, "See you tomorrow, buddy."

We walked on.

Mom said, "See, that's what I mean. You always got something to say, even before you think. That's what makes your pa so mad at you all the time."

"He don't like me is all, Mom. He never has liked me."

"Boy, who's been telling you such things?"

"No one. When someone hates you, you can feel it in your heart."

I was glad to finally see Aunt Hadie's Grill appear from the road. I couldn't wait to see Mikie. It felt like a long time since I'd seen him, even though it had only been since yesterday.

As we entered the grill, Mom said, "Morning, Hadie."

"Morning, Dean," Hadie responded.

I asked, "Where's he at? Where is Mikie?"

Aunt Hadie answered, "He says he's not going to school today."

I walked through the grill and went straight to his room. He had a bed, a chair, and his own desk in his room. When I got there, he was sitting on the bed with the very same shirt and jeans on that I had on. I guess it was because every time Aunt Hadie bought Mikie something, she got the same for me . . . as if we were really twins.

"Mikie, you look like someone took your breakfast and fed it to the dogs."

"I ain't going to school. They're trying to tear us apart, and I ain't having it!" he answered with a streak of stubbornness in his voice.

"Mikie, they're going to put you in jail if you don't go, so I will make us a deal: you and I will always be best friends and first cousins."

Mikie smiled. "You are my cousin two times."

I never really knew what he meant when he said that, and I would always just let it go.

"So, is it a deal?" I continued. "I will walk you to your class and come get you. Then we will ride the bus together like always. It will be okay, Mikie. It is the way it has to be this year."

*****

The more things change, it seems they stay the same. We hadn't been on the bus for more than a few minutes when the thorn in my and Mikie's sides appeared. There he was—the devil himself—but he was called Todd. He had always given Mikie trouble, calling him names and pushing him. Today was no different than past years. He called Mikie a "Whop" and a "Greaser." I was not sure what the names meant, but I knew Pa had called Uncle Marco that a few times at the supper table, and Mom would just give him a stare.

I said to Todd, "You better leave us alone, and go back to your seat."

Mikie was always the quiet one . . . like Uncle Marco. He had a lot to say, but he always kept it in until we were alone. Then he would let it all come out.

Mikie was a bit shorter than me, and his hair was not as dark. Mom called the color of my hair jet-black. I was a tad bit tanner than Mikie, and he was more of a scrawny kid with lots of curl to his hair. My hair was wavy, but not curly. We were all each other had.

We took the lunches that Aunt Hadie had made us. The kids always said we were too good to eat school lunch, but Uncle Marco was firm about it: we were not to eat the food from school. He was always on us to eat right foods that would turn us into good men, strong men.

After a few years of eating with them in their house, I could not take too much of the red sauce Aunt Hadie would make for Uncle Marco. It was spicy and would make me belch. Sometimes it felt like it was about to come right back up.

If I was going to stay overnight at Mikie's house, Mom would always bake some cornbread and put it in my brown food bag. She made sure I had a change of clothes, as well. I would be all set for a free night away from home and away from Pa.

As we got off the bus, Todd got one more joke in. "Here come the Greasers."

We just kept walking, my head held high, and Mikie's held toward the ground.

"If you don't look up, I am going to slap you in the head myself!" I warned Mikie.

With this, my friend and my first cousin held his head up, and he smiled . . . the first one I had seen so far that day.

"You sure know how to take care of me and make me smile, Rocco," Mikie offered.

It wasn't long before the rest of the kids gathered by the school door to go in for their first day of school for the new school year. As we walked in, I could feel in my heart that Mikie was about to burst out crying.

I could not hug my friend because Mom and Aunt Hadie had taught us that boys didn't hug each other. Life is funny sometimes. We are taught in church to love one another; but when we do, we get in trouble for hugging.

Mikie and I worked out a secret code: when we felt like hugging, we would squint our eyes real tightly; and we would know the love from our hearts was going to each other. He needed one of those so, when he turned, I gave it all I had. When I opened my eyes, he had faded in with the other kids. That fast, my friend and my cousin was gone away from me. My soul was lonely, and a huge part of me was gone. Third grade was about to be the worst day of my life.

As I walked on, I could see Todd with his big head bobbing about a foot above the rest of us. He was going into Mr. Ball's room. Well, if anyone had to put up with him, I was glad it was going to be me. This way Mikie could get a break from the name-calling. I was stronger and could put Todd in his place.

I went in and picked a seat as far away from Todd as I could, and everyone seemed to be looking for Mikie: they didn't sit in the seat next to me. Mr. Ball came in, set his bag down, and greeted us.

"Hi!" he started. "I have some very special things for us to do this year. I will teach you how to be smart and delightful students."

I thought to myself, "It's gonna take a lot of teaching to make Todd into a nice person!"

The knock on the door stopped Mr. Ball from continuing his welcome speech. He walked to the door to see who it was. It was Mrs. Parsons, the other third grade teacher. She whispered something into Mr. Ball's ear, and he nodded. She stepped aside; and with a loving shove, she sent Mikie into the room and motioned for Todd to come with her.

Mikie started to go to Todd's chair, so I coughed to signal him to come and sit next to me. The smiles that stole across our faces was as if Santa had come and left us all good things . . . things that our hearts had been wanting all summer long. It was the way that God had made it; it was a gift much bigger than Santa could have brought. It was sent from the highest Heaven. No, third grade wasn't going to be so bad; third grade was going to be great!

As Mr. Ball talked and handed out books to the students, I wondered how long it would be before it would be time for lunch. I squirmed as I tried to get through the time until I could sit and ask Mikie how he got to come to my class. Every time he would turn to me, that smile made my heart feel good. We might have been poor, but we had each other.

Finally, the lunch bell rang. We went on our way out to the tree in the schoolyard where we always sat and ate our lunch. I would sit one way, and Mikie sat the other way in case Todd tried to sneak up on us. That way we would be able to get him.

We hadn't even reached our tree when Todd, red-faced as all get out, slammed his bag down and came running.

"Those Greasers had this fixed so they could be in the same class, and I don't even get to be with one of 'em."

Todd then grabbed Mikie's neck, pushed him down, and kicked him. Suddenly, I was like a crazy man. I grabbed his leg and made him fall, and the fight was on.

I grabbed for his throat and choked him as I shouted, "You better never touch Mikie again!"

After that, all I could hear was Mikie yelling, "You're gonna kill him! Please stop!"

When I finally came back to this world, Todd was white and gasping for air. Mikie had my arms, pulling me away from Todd. I felt another hand take a hold of me—a stronger, firmer hand. It almost cut into my bones it had me so tight.

Mr. Ball said, "Boy, what are you trying to do? Kill him?"

"No, if I wanted to kill him, I would have gotten him last year."

All the anger in me from Pa and the world had done its damage. I had so much anger in me that day that I took it all out on Todd.

Mr. Ball herded me into the schoolhouse. "If you're going to kill him, you're gonna have to do it off school grounds," he commanded. "I don't like him, either; and I have seen him aggravating you and your friend."

"Cousin," I corrected him.

"Well, your cousin, then," Mr. Ball replied. "But I can't let you all fight like this."

"Then tell him to leave us alone. We just want to come and learn and not be stupid."

"Okay, Rocco. Here's the deal. If you tell Todd you're sorry, I will let it go; but you had better let this be the last time."

"You want *me* to say I'm sorry for something I didn't start?" I asked incredulously. "Mom always tells us not to start trouble; but if it finds me, I should take care of me and Mikie. I was doing just that. Now, I am gonna be hungry because dinner is almost over with."

"You mean lunch, don't you, Rocco?"

"No, I mean dinner; and I am gonna be a bear if I don't get some food in my belly."

With that, Mr. Ball took me back to the playground and let me eat dinner—or lunch—whatever he wanted to call it. Mikie stayed with me for the few minutes before the bell rang. I sat and finished my dinner thinking of how I was going to say I was sorry for something I wasn't sorry for.

I went back inside and, before returning to the classroom, I stopped to wash the sweat and dirt from my hands from tussling on the ground with Todd. I looked over at Mr. Ball, who, with a stern look on his face, raised his eyebrows questioningly at me. Suddenly, he smiled, and I knew right then that it was going to be a good year. I sat down and looked over at Mikie. He squinted his eyes really hard, and I knew he was grateful once again that I had saved his life.

The three o'clock bell rang, and one had never seen so much movement in their life! We walked at a steady pace to get on the bus. I headed right to the back. I guessed everyone knew not to even try to sit with me. Mikie dragged along as usual, and there were about four kids in front of him.

Todd trudged along behind Mikie and finally sat down one seat in front of us, across the row. I patted Todd's shoulder.

"Todd, you okay?"

"Shut up!" he snarled.

"Todd, I am sorry. I didn't mean to hurt you. I was just angry the way you keep treating Mikie. Let's be friends."

"Forget about it," Todd hissed.

I knew in my heart that Todd really didn't hate me; it was Mikie whom he didn't like. For some reason, since first grade, he had had a dislike for Mikie and was determined to make life hell for us both.

I tried to think of good things like Brother Wallace at church said. He told us to try to love everyone, but Todd was sure a hard one to love.

Pa was another one. It was hard to love someone who was always angry, always mad, waiting to give me a hard way to go. Pa was so full of hate, but he was good to Mom. That's all that mattered.

I wondered if he ever wanted me. Maybe he never wanted a kid. Maybe he just wanted Mom and himself alone. The only time I saw him happy was when they were alone on the porch.

I tried to talk about all this with Mikie, but he held a different kind of faith. He was Catholic. Mom and I went to a little church down the road from Aunt Hadie's Grill. They taught us to love and not to steal. They taught us from the Bible. We would sing and clap our hands to the fast music. Brother Wallace played the guitar and stomped his feet. Some of the folks danced around their seats and yelled, "Praise God!" Sometimes I wondered that if the music stopped, would they stop dancing? However, most of the time, they continued to holler even when the music stopped.

One time I went with Mikie and Uncle Marco to their church. Mikie did the cross thing before he sat down, like he does right before he eats.

Uncle Marco's mom's name was Mrs. Liza. She was nice; and every time she hugged Mikie, she motioned for me to come and hug her, also. She was a tiny thing. She wrapped her hair in a net, all in a ball. It was hard for her to live here. She only knew the language from her country, and the only one who knew how to talk to her in her language was Marco. He would tell us what she said when she spoke to us.

One night I had to go potty, and only a nightlight was on. Mrs. Liza sat at the big table. All I could see was lots of hair. She had her hands over her face, and she was crying. I went to her. In her hands, she had a long chain of beads with a cross on it. Even though I could not speak to her, she always had eyes of love for Mikie and me. I could feel her love as much as I could feel Pa's hate. I patted her shoulder. She turned to me and smiled. I wiped the tears from her face and rubbed her head. We sat for what seemed all night, and I held her hand till she was done crying. Then she clasped her hands together and laid her head sideways on them. I knew Mrs. Liza was telling me it was time for us to go to bed. She grabbed my face between her hands and kissed the top of my head as she mumbled something. She was then off to bed.

*****

As the bus came to a stop the next day, I knew we were getting close to home. We were the second stop on the route. I had to wake up Mikie, who had already fallen asleep, and get our books together to get ready to get off. As the bus rolled to a stop, I saw Mom and Aunt Hadie in front of the grill, waiting for us. I elbowed Mikie to get moving. On our way out, Todd held his big, ol', fat feet out; and Mikie found them. Down he went.

As Mikie gathered his stuff back up, I whispered to Todd, "Tomorrow is another day, and I will get you again for that."

As we walked toward our moms, I could see them talking back and forth; and I could see how proud they were of us.

"Well, young men, how did school go? We see you guys made it without each other."

We turned and looked at each other and cracked up laughing.

I answered, "Mikie is in my class; they said he could. We're heading inside to do our homework."

Mom replied, "Don't think you're fooling us; we know you don't have homework on your first day; but go ahead. I have to work late; and Aunt Hadie has a meeting to go to, remember? And I don't want you in Uncle Marco's way. Take off your school clothes. I brought you a change of clothes. They're in Mikie's room."

"Yes, Ma'am, Momma Dean."

Again, a smile came to my dear Mom's face; and we were off.

"Okay, Mikie, spit it out," I demanded. "How did you get to come into Mr. Ball's room?"

"It was easier than one, two, three, Rocco. I bent over and pretended that I was sick. When the teacher asked what was wrong, I told her I always got sick and threw up whenever I am not near Rocco in school. I told her all year was gonna be like this. She said, 'Come with me,' and I thought she was taking me to the restroom. She took me to Mr. Ball's class, instead."

"Dang, Mikie, you are smarter than I thought. I think most of the time you just play dumb."

We squinted at each other.

Mikie said, "This is the best birthday gift I could ask for."

I acted like I didn't hear, but I knew his birthday was in one week. Mom said they were having a party for him and that I was going to get to spend the night. I loved when Uncle Marco had a party; there was lots of music and things to do. Mikie and I would laugh and never know there was a bad thing in the world.

I had been saving all summer to buy Mikie a good birthday gift. Every year he bought me something nice, and I wanted to get him a real gift this year.

We changed clothes and headed for his backyard.

"Rocco, do you ever think of death?"

"Death? No, I never think of death, Mikie. I was born only eight years ago!"

"I wish your pa was dead. I wish he would just go away and leave you alone so you and Aunt Dean could come and live with us forever and that he would never hurt you again. I heard my dad say if your pa ever hits you, he was gonna kill him. He said one hair on your head is worth a thousand of his."

"Mikie, listen to me. We should not wish bad things on anyone . . . not Pa, Todd, or anyone . . . so, don't wish things on my pa. He's a mean thing, but he's the only pa I got."

"You're my cousin two times, Rocco."

"No, boy, I keep telling you I am your first cousin—not your second. Now, start saying it right."

"Rocco! Mikie! Come on!" I heard Mom yell from the back of the grill.

I said to Mikie, "Must be your mom is home, and it's time for us to go."

As we walked to the front of the grill, I saw Pa sitting in his car and Mom standing next to it. Aunt Hadie was on the sidewalk in front of the grill staring at them as we walked up.

"Boy, come here and give Hadie a kiss goodnight."

She kissed me and gave me a bear hug like I had never had before. We got into the car. As I looked around, I saw Mikie still looking at us as we drove away. I waved and squinted my eyes.

Pa said, "Turn around right, and sit in your seat. Stop acting like they're the only ones in the world."

"Yes, sir."

"Hank," my mom broke in, "I need to stop by the store and pick up a few things real fast."

As we reached Lewis' small store, I jumped out before Pa could instruct me to stay in the car with him. I beat Mom to the store and went on in.

"Hi, Mrs. Sadie. How are you today?" I greeted the cashier.

"I am good, and yourself?"

"I am good, also . . . top of the world." I stopped for a minute before turning back to her. "I was wondering something. Has my friend, Mikie, been in here looking at anything?"

"Yes, matter of fact, he has been on his mom to buy him this camping knife. It's the one with the red handle with a spoon and some other stuff on it. Come here, and I will show you."

As Mrs. Sadie walked me to a display case in the front of the store, I saw Mom looking at me, watching to see what I was about to do. Sometimes I think Mom didn't like that I loved Mikie so much. Maybe she thought I loved him more than her . . . but it was like he was my *brother*, and she was my mom.

"How much for the knife?" I asked Mrs. Sadie.

"Well, for you, maybe $19.99."

"Will you take $18 even?"

"For you I will, since you did such a good job beating that boy, Todd, today at school. Don't care too much for him or his family myself."

I felt the air go out of my body. Chills ran all over my chest and legs. I knew Mom was right behind me hearing all this.

"Yes, Ma'am, I will have it, please."

I reached down into my pocket and brought out a handful of $1 bills. I had earned the money from Mom and Aunt Hadie doing things around the yard, helping take out the grease from the grill, and sweeping. Most of the time it was while Mikie slept or was busy with Uncle Marco.

I slowly counted out 18 single dollars.

Mrs. Sadie talked to Mom on the other side of me, "Mrs. Dean, how have you been?"

"Fine, thanks, Sadie. I've been busy working that grill for my sister and taking care of this knucklehead," she answered as she patted my head; but I knew that pat was going to be a bit harder after she got me to the car.

I said, "Mrs. Sadie, does this knife come with some wrap?"

"You mean, you got it for less . . . and now you want me to wrap it?"

"Yes, please."

Mom piped up, "It's okay, Sadie. I will wrap it for him. See if he has enough money for some butt salve; he's gonna need it."

As we walked out of the store, Mom sat down on a window seat on the front of the store and just looked at me.

"You got in a fight your first day of school?"

"Yes, Ma'am."

"What did I tell you about that, boy?"

"Mom!"

"Don't 'Mom' me! I don't want you fighting and carrying on, acting like the rest of the kids."

"But, Mom, he hit Mikie and pushed him down."

Mom just shook her head.

"Mikie can take care of himself; he is as old as you are."

"No, he's two months younger, and he's little. I have to watch out for him."

"Rocco, don't say anything in the car about it; we will talk tomorrow."

We gathered our bags again and headed to the car. I saw Pa had that old, mean look again. I got in and sat straight ahead like he always told me to sit, and we were off.

As soon as I got into the house, I kicked those dumb, tight shoes off and headed for bed.

Lying there, I thought to myself, "Lord, please make the rest of third grade easier than today, and keep your angels over me and Mom."

Chapter 2

Still warm in the mornings, about the second week of school Mom and I were again walking the road as we did every morning.

"Rocco, I don't want you fighting anymore," Mom started. "I want you to tell the teachers or me when Todd acts up."

"Well, he always does it when there's no one around and I don't have time to stop and get a teacher. Most of the time he already has Mikie and me on the ground."

"Well, be a good boy. Do it for Mom, and be good."

"Yes, Mom."

As we came up to Mr. Creek's, I did not see him outside. All these years he always waited pretty close to the road to say 'Hello' to me. His house was big and had a porch that wrapped all the way around it.

"Mom, do you reckon I ought to check on him?"

"No, Rocco. We do not have time this morning."

"Well, I think I am gonna make some time and go see if my friend, Mr. Creek, is all right."

"Rocco, hurry up. Go check, and do not do a lot of talking . . . I mean it."

I ran down through the ditch and climbed back up the other side to Mr. Creek's yard. I went up to the house, yelling before I got to the door.

"Mr. Creek, you here? Mr. Creek, it's me . . . Rocco. You okay?"

I heard him hacking and coughing, and I went on in. There he sat at his kitchen table with his head in his hands.

"Mr. Creek, are you okay?"

"Yes, boy, I am okay. Just got this cough and cannot shed it."

"Your face is all red. I think I had better go get my mom."

Mr. Creek answered simply, "No."

"Mr. Creek, she will know what to do for you; she will make you better."

"No, boy, don't bother her; just go on, and I will see you after school . . . I promise."

As I walked off, I was worried about my friend. He had a bad cough. He could barely get air going. His house was clean as a pin, and everything was in a certain place; but there was a feeling of loneliness. I pushed the screen door open as I saw Mom waving to me to hurry and come on. I got to her as fast as I could, and we started walking again toward Aunt Hadie's.

"Is he dead?" Mom asked.

"Mom, no, he ain't dead. He has a cough."

"Well, it's a good thing it's all it is."

"Mom, you know Mr. Creek is my friend. Why do you say things like that?"

"You have too many friends," Mom replied.

"Mom, I don't think I should leave him alone like this. He ain't got nobody to be with him. I don't feel right in my heart leaving him."

Mom was silent. I guess she thought if she did not talk, I would let it go.

I pulled my hand from hers and said, "Mom, I am talking to you!"

"Boy, you better hush and get walking, or we are both going to be late."

As we got to the grill, Aunt Hadie greeted us. "Dean, is everything all right?" she asked Mom.

"Yes, Hadie. Mr. Know-it-all here has to check on the whole town before we can get to your house."

I said, "Good morning, Aunt Hadie."

"Hi, boy. How are you?"

"I'm fine. Aunt Hadie, do you got any food left in there . . . like some scrambled eggs and taters . . . maybe a few biscuits and jelly?"

Aunt Hadie replied, "Boy, you ain't going to eat all that food!"

"It's not for *me* . . . I am going to take it back to Mr. Creek. He is sick, and Mom won't let me tend to him."

"Well, I don't blame her. You get in here and eat . . . and wash those hands!"

My hands *were* dirty from climbing in and out of the ditch at Mr. Creek's house. I did not know how I was going to do it, but I was at least going to get my friend something to eat.

While Mikie and I were at the counter, I grabbed my plate and put a lot of Mikie's food on it.

He complained, "Hey, that's mine!"

"It will be okay, Mikie. You got your lunch, and you can have mine. I ain't going to school; and before school, you will be fine."

I never missed a day of school before, mainly because Mom had to work and I never wanted to leave Mikie to have to watch out for himself. However, this time I had no choice.

I wrapped up the food with some foil and put it down in my shirt. When the bus came, Mom and Aunt Hadie were talking. When Mikie boarded the bus, I went in front of it, crossed the busy street, and trotted right back up the road to Mr. Creek's. I planned ahead that when the bus came at three o'clock, I would do the same trick and get in with the other kids. It would look like I got off the bus with them.

The road seemed longer without Mom to keep me company. I walked to the side so no one would see me and cars would not hit me. I was well on my way and over the little hill when I saw Pa's car. It was flying. I wondered if he would kill me and Mom would never find me. I jumped into the weeds on the side of the road and waited until he passed and then a few more minutes in case he came back. After I saw that he was nowhere around, I took off running as fast as I could. I did not climb the ditch this time; I went to the driveway and went up that way.

"Mr. Creek . . . it is me, Mr. Creek; I'm back."

I went in, and he was still in the same chair and looked like he had not moved an inch in my absence.

"Boy, what are you doing back?" he quietly demanded.

"I brought you some food. I am going to take care of you today."

Mr. Creek just shook his head.

"Now, here are some eggs and bacon from Aunt Hadie's Grill. You want some milk with this?"

Mr. Creek did not have the strength to talk. He simply pointed at the cabinet. I got a glass and poured Mr. Creek some milk out of a pitcher. I got a fork for him out of the sink and washed it. Mr. Creek took to eating like a dog that hadn't eaten in days. He drank his milk.

"Boy, I sure do thank you; you saved my life."

"Shucks! I did not; you just needed someone to love you for a bit. We all just need to be loved."

A big tear came to his eye, and I pretended I didn't see him. Mikie didn't like for me to see him cry, so I figured it was the same for Mr. Creek. All guys just want to cry by themselves.

Mr. Creek wobblingly stood up.

"Boy, let's go to the porch and sit for a spell and think what we're gonna do to get you back to school."

"Mr. Creek, you got a back porch?"

"Sure, why?"

"You reckon we can sit there and figure?"

"Why, boy? What is wrong?"

"Well, I saw Pa go by in his car; and I do not want him coming back and seeing me sitting here."

Mr. Creek shuffled to the back porch and sat down. The porch overlooked land as far as I could see. There was not a single tree all the way back, maybe an acre or so.

"Boy, did your Pa ever hit you? Is that what you're afraid of?"

"One time he did. He hit me right here."

I showed him right above my ear.

"And Pa's ol', nasty finger poked me in the eye and made me cry quiet," I continued.

"Made you cry quiet?" Mr. Creek repeated.

"Yes. That is when you cry but there is no huffing and puffing. It is a heart cry; you hurt more in the heart, and the tears come quietly. But one time Mom whipped me, and it was a whooping cry. It hurt in a different way, and you cry in a different way."

After a short silence, I continued. "It is so peaceful here, Mr. Creek. I could sit here and really rest. Sometimes my head gets so full and tired from thinking about everyone, wondering and worrying if they're okay . . . wondering if the bad man will get them and take them away from me."

"Boy, who is the bad man?"

"I don't know, yet. Mom says he gets all bad kids. That is why I have to behave and do what is right . . . or the bad man will get me."

"Well, boy, if the bad man ever comes near you, you run to me; and I will save you. I will shoot him in the head, and he won't ever bother you again."

"Do you promise, Mr. Creek?"

"Yes, boy, I do. I would never let anyone hurt you."

"Yes, sir."

"I think I am going to bring you my supper every day that Aunt Hadie makes for me. I will make you really better."

"Boy, look at me. You already made me better. I think I feel like a teenager. Now, we have to find a way to get you in the schoolhouse so you won't get a whooping from your mom."

"I am gonna run by the bus when it comes at three o'clock and get with Mikie. They won't ever know I wasn't in school."

"Well, since I don't drive, I think you're gonna have to do that; but you have to promise you will never do this again."

"Well, it scared me when I came by and you weren't by the road, Mr. Creek. I walked up to see you and make sure you were okay."

"Boy, it's the same way with me. I get up and get going just so I can see you by the road and make sure you are okay."

"I am always okay, Mr. Creek. I have angels and Mom watching over me. One time Mom told Pa if he ever made me cry quiet again, she would get her chicken skillet and melt enough fat to fry three chickens, boil it until it was frying hot, and throw it on him."

"Good Lord alive! I believe Miss Dean would do just that."

"Mr. Creek, I was born in that house up there. I don't feel like it's home. I feel at home at Mikie's house."

"Boy, you weren't born up there. You moved there when you were about a year old. I remember you well . . . the nicest boy . . . behaved well and listened to your mom . . . as good as gold. By the time you were two, she was walking you to work with her."

"Are you sure, Mr. Creek?"

"Yes, I'm sure."

"I could swear Mom told me I was born up there . . . maybe not."

After thinking on that a moment, I abruptly changed the subject, "We're going to have a party for my cousin, Mikie. He's my first cousin, and it's going to be the best party ever! We're going to sing and dance and be happy!"

"Well, good," Mr. Creek responded.

"Do you want to come, Mr. Creek?"

"Where?"

"To Mikie's party."

"I don't know him."

"He knows you, Mr. Creek. I tell him every day about you and how you come to the road to say 'Hi' to me."

"When I used to drive, I would stop down there and gas up. I like your Uncle Marco. He was always nice and always wanted to buy my old car."

As an afterthought, Mr. Creek added, "Why doesn't this Mikie kid ever go to *your* house, Rocco?"

"Because of Pa. Everything bad is because of Pa. Aunt Hadie would never let Mikie come over. I have to stay the night over to his house, and then I spend most of it worrying about my mom . . . worrying if he is gonna be mean to her or if he would ever hit her and all that stuff."

"Boy, you sure know how to talk."

"That's what Mom always says to me, Mr. Creek."

I continued to sit on the glider swing; and before I knew it, I was sound asleep. The morning sun and the peaceful view of cleared land had me resting my eyes. The breeze played with my hair and brought the smell of fall flowers to my nostrils. The next thing I knew, I was lying on a pillow wondering what time it was.

I heard Mr. Creek's voice, "Boy, I was about to wake you up. It's time for you to go back and get with Mikie."

I leaned forward and stretched my arms and back. It was the most peaceful place in the world on Mr. Creek's back porch where I felt safe. Pa and the bad man could not get me. Mr. Creek had watched over me while I slept, and I didn't have to keep waking myself up to see if the bad man might be there.

"Mr. Creek, remember your promise. If the bad man gets after me, I am running down the hill to get you."

"You always remember that, boy. You come get Mr. Creek, and I will save you from the bad man."

I walked fast to the big road, crossed while there was no traffic, and got by the church. When I heard the bus coming to a stop, I jumped out. I went into the group of kids getting off the bus, found Mikie, and walked over to the grill. I could tell Mikie was still mad that I did not go to school, so I talked about being at Mr. Creek's house and how he was feeling better.

"Todd didn't bother me today. I think he knew I was worried about you, Rocco, so he left me alone," Mikie said.

"Mikie, I love you; you are my best friend . . . also, your cousin."

Mikie smiled at me.

We got to the grill, and Mom and Aunt Hadie had coupons strewed all over the counter, looking to see on what items they could save money. We got our kisses, and we went through the grill to Mikie's house.

Uncle Marco stopped us, "My mother would like to talk to you boys."

We both looked at him like he had lost his mind. He started to laugh and added, "I will tell you what she has to say."

We went to Mrs. Liza's bedroom. She was sitting regally in a chair. She had two birthday gifts for Mikie in her lap. I kind of held back so he could have time with his grandmother. She patted her hands like so many times before and held them outward for me to come to her, also. She motioned for us to sit on the floor before her as if we were her two loyal subjects.

Marco began interpreting her words as she spoke, "I have a gift for each of you two boys," she stated.

She handed one gift to me and one to Mikie. We looked at each other and then started opening the boxes. They were the nicest rings I had ever seen in my life.

"Just alike," Marco said after Mrs. Liza said something in Italian.

I looked into Mrs. Liza's eyes as she continued to speak. I heard Marco's voice telling us what she was saying: "You boys need to love each other and be good men. These rings will save your lives one day."

She gave us time to further admire the rings before continuing, "My husband was a very important man in Italy. When he died, he left these rings for his two sons, Marco and Ray. I never gave them to my sons. I could never feel in my heart that there was a bond between them. It would have torn my family apart.

"But there is a bond between you two," she went on. "I have watched you and seen the love of a brother . . . a love from the heart. What these rings will bring you could never tear you apart. Never take them off; never give them to anyone. For the day that you do, your safety will be gone."

She kissed the rings and placed them on our fingers and then kissed our heads. It was almost as if she had cast a spell on us. We looked up at Marco to see if he was going to say anything else. We got up off the floor and went to Mikie's room.

We were quiet only for about three minutes. We looked at each other and squinted our eyes. However, it was not a heart squint; it was more like a "we're scared" squint.

The rings were gold and each had a red garnet stone set in them. There were birds flying on each side of the ring. Right to the tee, our rings were alike; they were identical.

"What a birthday gift!" Mikie said as he screwed up his face in frustration. "I wanted a knife. Instead, I got a dumb ring."

"No, it's not dumb," I responded. "It can be our secret ring. They will keep our hearts close to each other. If we ever get in trouble, we can send our ring to the other. No matter where you are, I can come find you; no matter how far I am, I will always find you, Mikie.

"We already have our eye squints . . . and now a pair of

rings. The world—not *anyone*—can ever tear us apart," Mikie added. "We are more than cousins; we are brothers."

Mikie and I talked for a few more minutes. I finally heard my mom yell for me to come.

"Mikie, I don't see Pa, so I think we have to walk home again." I turned to my mom and said, "Mom, do you think I can take some food for Mr. Creek until he gets on his feet?"

Mom looked to Hadie, and she said, "Okay, but only a few days until he gets up and going."

"Aunt Hadie, I am sure there is a place in Heaven for you."

"Rocco, where do you get all this talk from? I have never known of an eight-year-old to talk so much Bible . . . and trying to help so many folks."

"I have to be good or the bad man will get me . . . right, Mom?"

Aunt Hadie almost fell out. "Dean, why are you telling him such things?"

"He is mixed up," Mom answered. "I said there are bad men out there in the world."

"Well, stop scaring him. No wonder he can't sleep well. When he is down here, he is up and down all night checking the doors and looking around waiting for someone any minute to come in and get him."

Hadie made up two plates. I put them down in a box. We said our goodbyes.

I went back to Mikie and whispered, "I am going to school tomorrow, buddy. I will see you in the morning."

I turned to go back to my mom and kissed my ring.

Mom saw me and asked, "What do you have? Hadie, what's he got?"

Mikie and I both held out our hands. Aunt Hadie looked

at our fingers and saw the matching rings that Mrs. Liza had given us.

She took to screaming, "Marco, come here! Look what your mother did to our son. Look what she did to Rocco. Take 'em off, boys; take 'em off *now*!"

Mikie and I looked at each other as if Aunt Hadie had lost her mind.

I said, "We can't. She told us to never take them off or we would be unprotected."

Whatever it was that had Aunt Hadie in a tailspin, she looked over to Mom and demanded, "Dean, make them take 'em off, please."

Hadie wrung her hands, then began throwing things around. Mom started to cry quiet and just looked at me and Mikie in despair.

Uncle Marco suddenly stepped in. "Mother had her mind set on it," he quietly responded. "She insisted that Mikie and Rocco be the leaders of the family one day."

"Don't worry, Aunt Hadie," I quipped. "I will take care of you and Mom always . . . and Uncle Marco, also . . . me and Mikie are gonna be good men. We will show you. I will never let you go hungry . . . and Mom won't have to work when I get older."

This did not seem to help as Aunt Hadie and Mom stood by the counter whispering something while Uncle Marco stood by us boys. There was a lot of crying going on over there.

Mikie looked at me. "Maybe we should just give them back. Maybe that will help."

Mom and Aunt Hadie turned and looked at us fearfully.

"What, boy?" Aunt Hadie asked of Mikie.

"Me and Mikie want to talk to you," I answered. "We will give the rings back. We didn't mean to hurt you. We don't want you crying. Here are our rings. We don't want them if it's gonna hurt you."

Uncle Marco went to the ladies and began quietly talking to them. When the talking was finished, our moms said we could wear the rings . . . we could keep them. Little did we know that the rings were just a symbol of what was about to come into our lives. It was far bigger than any ring; it is what the rings meant.

On our way home it was quiet. It seemed miles up that road that night; but before I knew it, I was at Mr. Creek's house, going up his driveway. He was on the porch.

"Hey, boy," Mr. Creek greeted me. "How are you?"

"I am okay. I didn't get caught not going to school today." I smiled at Mr. Creek. "Here is some supper. Aunt Hadie made two plates up: one for me and one for you. I can't take to talking; I have to get home. You sleep well, and I will see you in the morning, Mr. Creek. Goodnight."

As I got back down the driveway to Mom, I saw him wave at her. She nodded her head back at him, and we walked off.

We continued our walk home. When we arrived, we went into the house; and Mom got Pa's supper ready. I had forgotten where I was with all the excitement of the day, and without thinking I set my plate of food at Pa's table.

When he saw it, he growled, "Get that, and eat at the counter."

Mom put Pa's food on the table. When she got my drink, she set her plate next to mine at the counter, also.

"What are you doing, Dean?" he inquired.

“Hank, if the boy can’t eat at the table like a person—like our son—then I am not welcome at your table, either.”

A surprised look stole across his face.

“Okay. Sit over here . . . and bring him with you.”

Not much else was said at the table; it didn’t have to be said. I wasn’t welcome there. After supper, I got up, cleaned my plate off and put it in the sink. I looked at my spot on the counter and thought it would have been better to eat there.

“Rocco, we are having dessert out on the porch tonight,” Mom said.

“Yes, Mom,” I answered and walked outside.

I could see a light still burning at Mr. Creek’s house on down the road. I thought to myself that I hoped he was all right. I thought back about the day.

Pa came out and took his place on the porch. He nodded in my direction.

“Rocco, where did you get that ring? Who gave it to you?”

“Mrs. Liza,” I responded.

“Let me see it!”

“No. I can’t take it off, Pa.”

“I don’t think she gave it to you. I think you stole it!”

“No, sir! I don’t steal! Brother Wallace told us it’s bad to steal, and it will give us a ticket straight to hell.”

“Give me that ring right now!” Pa sternly demanded.

“No, I can’t!”

Before I knew what happened, I felt a pain in the back of my head as I went flying off the porch toward the chopping block where Pa always kept his axe for splitting wood. I tried putting my hands out to cushion the blow I was anticipating, but the chopping block and my head made contact before I could manage to soften the shock.

I heard Mom scream. It felt like warm water flowing all over me. Everything went silent, and I could not hear anything for a while. I simply lay there. It was peaceful, like when I was lying on Mr. Creek's back porch swing.

I finally heard Mom say as if she was far from me, "Baby, hold on. Hold on. Do it for Mom. Fight and be a strong boy. Don't leave Mom."

I heard sirens coming closer.

Then I heard Mr. Creek's voice, "Who did this? Who did this to the boy?"

Mom kept asking if I could hear her. I did hear her, but I couldn't tell her.

She held my hand as she continued saying, "Baby, please stay with Mom."

I gave a grip as hard as I could. I wanted my dear mom to know I was okay. I felt the warmest feeling in my heart . . . and the light was as strong as hundreds of lightning bugs on the darkest night. I heard cars pull in; Mom must have given Mr. Creek the number to get a hold of Aunt Hadie.

Suddenly, someone was picking me up. I felt my neck go backward.

Someone screamed, "His neck is broke!"

They put me into an ambulance, and the loud sirens made my head hurt badly. That was the last thing I remembered that night.

The next day I could see a man standing in the room where I was lying. He was the only thing I could see. The man was tall, and he just stood there, not talking to anyone. I couldn't make out where I had seen him before. I knew he was a good man, but I didn't think I had ever talked to him.

I could hear Mom talking to Hadie. Mom sat by my bed holding my hand like when we walked down the road.

I heard the doctor say to Mom, "We have to get the swelling down or he could die."

Mom answered, "He's not going to die. He told me. He squeezed my hand."

The doctor left.

"Baby, you have to fight harder. Do it for Mom. Come back, and show the world."

As hard as I tried, I could not move. I couldn't tell Mom I would be all right.

I heard Aunt Hadie say, "Dean, what are you going to do? Where can we send him to be safe when he gets better?"

The man standing in the room walked closer to me, but still did not speak. He walked a few steps more, stopped, and looked at me. As he got closer, I could see he was something other than a doctor. He had a light around him; he glowed like the fireflies.

When he reached my bed, he touched my head, looked down at me, and said, "Now, go back."

At that moment I could move. Whatever had held my eyes closed was removed, and I could open them. I had to adjust my eyes to the light which became the only thing I could see, and my head hurt badly. Mom sat, talking to Aunt Hadie.

"Mom," I spoke.

I could tell my mom was crying quiet. She just looked at me.

"Boy, you scared me to death! What took you so long to get back here?"

I took her hands and put them on my eyes.

"What's wrong, Rocco? Tell Mom," she pleaded. "Hadie, go get the doctor."

"I can't see you, Mom. I can't see through the light; it's too bright. What happened to me, Mom?"

"You fell off the porch, right onto the chopping block. You knocked yourself out," she explained.

"Did I miss Mikie's birthday party?"

"Son, you have been here for weeks; you were close to death."

"Mom, did you give Mikie his knife . . . and tend to Mr. Creek?"

"I have been right here with you. I never went home. I couldn't go back to that house. Your aunt brought me clothes and sat here with me a bit each day."

"Mrs. Dean, you're gonna have to move so I can check him," the doctor said as he moved between her and me.

"Yes, sir," she politely answered as she quickly moved out of her chair.

"Turn off the light," the doctor instructed.

He began shining his small light back and forth into my eyes. The doctor finally finished his exam of me and left. I could see figures of folks standing over by Mom. As long as the lights were off, I could see folks well. I could see Uncle Marco standing where the tall man previously had stood. I could make out Aunt Hadie and Mr. Creek. I smiled at him.

"Mr. Creek, how did you get here? You can't drive!"

He smiled back at me and said, "I can drive good enough to go to your uncle's station and hitch a ride to come here and see about you."

All in this one room were the folks who loved me the most:

Mom, Aunt Hadie, Uncle Marco, and Mr. Creek. Around the corner came Brother Wallace with Mikie.

"Mikie, come here. Mr. Creek, this is my best friend and cousin. This is Mikie." After the introduction, I looked sternly at Mikie. "Mikie, what took you so long to come and see me?"

Mikie started to cry.

Marco walked over and put his arm around him and explained, "Mikie, he's okay. Look at him. He's talking non-stop. Rocco is better."

Mikie inched his way to me, and this time there was no squinting; he hugged me for all he was worth. My heart was fixed.

"What happened, Rocco?" Mikie finally found his voice. "How did this happen?"

"Mom says I fell off the porch."

"Rocco, you never fall; it's always me falling. I don't think you fell. Tell me and Father what really happened."

"I can't remember nothing," I replied. "I fell off the porch."

Mom stepped in and said, "I think he's tired now. He needs to rest."

Everyone started hugging me and telling me they were glad I was back to the land of the living.

When Marco hugged me, he whispered into my ear, "I will get whoever done this to you, Rocco. I promise you that."

After everyone left, Mom still sat by my bed, humming and rocking back and forth. I knew something was on her mind.

"Mom, are you okay?"

"Yes, my baby is back. I am fine as pure gold."

"Mom, stop rocking; you're making my head hurt more. What did the doctor say? When can I go home?"

"Well, he said you need better doctors . . . city doctors. I am going to figure it out, so don't you worry."

"I don't need any more doctors; I want to go home and be with Mikie and go to school. I promise I won't talk too much."

"Baby, it's not that," she said. "I love when you talk. I have missed you so bad. You know what I say to you . . . you are the best thing I have ever done with my life; you are the best thing that ever happened to me."

"Mom, everyone is gone. Tell me what happened."

"Okay. You promise me not to speak of this to no one?"

"Yes, Mom. I promise."

"When you were on the porch, I saw a man come around the side of the house. He went right by Pa and kicked you right off the porch. You fell against the chopping block."

I studied Mom's expression. Something was killing her inside. She was crying quiet as she told me what happened.

"That's why you need to stay here a few more days until they get the bad man who did this. You will need to see city doctors so you can be well."

"Will you watch out for Mikie and Mr. Creek for me . . . and take him his supper every day?"

"I will," my mom answered. "I will do it for you, I promise. Now, you rest . . . and no more worries about the bad man. He can never find you again."

Chapter 3

It was about 10 o'clock in the morning, and the nurse was dressing the wound on my head. I wondered why Mom hadn't come to help get me ready for my home going.

"What clothes do you want to put on?" the nurse inquired.

"I will try my new overalls and this loose shirt. I hope the shoes won't hurt."

"Well, look at you. How sweet," the nurse offered as a compliment.

I didn't feel sweet. I wanted to hurry up and get home so I could see if Mikie had learned anything with his new knife, but these folks were taking their sweet time getting me ready to go home.

"Brother Wallace, what are you doing here?" I asked as my preacher walked into my room.

"Your mom asked if I could come pick you up and take you to your aunt's house. She will meet us there," he replied with a broad, friendly smile on his face.

The nurse broke in, "What do you want me to do with these clothes?"

She held in her hands a bundle of what looked like bloody rags. They were the clothes I had on when I had come to the hospital.

Brother Wallace spoke up, "Bag 'em."

I said, "No! I don't want them. Burn them; tear them up; throw them away . . . I don't care what you do with them, but I don't want them."

"Well, look who's back," Brother Wallace responded. "Mr. Yakkie! All that big talk from a young'un like you."

"I am sorry, Brother Wallace."

"It's okay. I am glad to see you with your spirit back!"

The nurse helped me move to a chair with wheels. She pushed me to the elevator, which we rode to the first floor. She and Brother Wallace helped me into Brother Wallace's truck, and we began our trip to Aunt Hadie's house.

"Rocco?" Brother Wallace started.

"Yes, sir?"

"Will you do me a favor?"

"Sure, I will. You are my preacher."

"Will you always remember one thing: God loves you and will always be your best friend."

Brother Wallace glanced at me sideways to be sure I was listening.

He continued, "When things get hard and you can't understand, remember this, and talk to your friend. He will never leave you. Always think with your heart. Never hurt folks, and you will be fine."

"So, you are telling me that God has to be my best friend? What about Mikie?"

"Rocco, folks will come and go in your life; but God will always be there for you."

"Well, you just passed the road. We are going to the grill, remember?" I reminded Brother Wallace.

"Oh, yeah, I guess I forgot."

As we pulled in, I saw lots of folks in the grill. There was a great big, white car; it looked like a funeral car.

As the truck rolled to a stop and I got ready to ease myself out, Brother Wallace said, "Boy, remember what I told you; and remember the things I taught you."

"I will, Brother."

And before I knew it, he was gone.

Folks helped me walk into the grill, and there were folks all around waiting for me . . . some I didn't even know. I looked around for Mom, but she wasn't there. Aunt Hadie made me sit down while folks came to me and expressed their well wishes. I didn't like it without my mom. Mikie was over at the counter with Uncle Marco, and everyone was looking at me.

Something was building in my throat . . . a big ball of hurt. When I complained of it to Aunt Hadie, she dismissed it with a "Rocco, you will be fine."

"I want my mom. Where is she?" I asked of her.

"She will be here. She went to get you something for your trip."

"What trip?" I asked her with panic edging my voice.

"You have to see more doctors," Aunt Hadie answered matter-of-factly.

The ball of hurt grew bigger. I couldn't figure out why Mikie wouldn't come to me; he just kept looking at me, also.

Mom finally arrived. She came in with an armful of stuff, sat it on the counter, then came and kissed me. She grabbed my hand, and we went to Mikie's room to talk in private.

"Baby, you know how much Mom loves you; but I have to look out for you and do what's best for you. Right now, I can't keep you safe. You have to go with Mikie's cousin. He will take you to a place called Michigan, and there will be better doctors for you there. When I can make it safe for you to come home, I will come and get you. You remember that. I *will* come and get you! You are my son, and I will always love you."

About this time, the big ball of hurt tore loose. I took to crying, and no matter how close Mom tucked me in her arms, the hurt continued to grow. My head started to hurt.

Suddenly the door flew open. Mikie ran in.

"Stop it! You're stop hurting him! Stop making him cry! I hate you! I hate all of you!" he raged.

Mikie cried as hard as I was crying. Folks stood in the doorway looking at us. I looked at Mom through my tears, pleading with her with my eyes. She pushed the folks out and left Mikie and me alone.

"I am gonna kill the bad man," Mikie said solemnly. "I am."

I couldn't stop crying long enough to tell him that we were to love, not hate.

With my best friend I got my things together, and we went back to the grill. I told all the folks goodbye.

Mom gave me a surprise: cornbread. Whenever things went wrong, her cornbread seemed to make it better. I noticed the cornbread was on Mom's favorite plate.

She realized I noticed the plate and said, "Keep this safe until I come for you. Keep Mom's plate safe."

"I will, Mom. I will."

As she walked me out the door of the grill, a tall man opened the door to the long, white car. There was a person in the back.

He got out and said, "Hi." He was no more than 17 years old. He had dark hair like mine and was tall and thin. His white t-shirt and leather jacket made him look like a thug to me. His jeans were tight, and his shoes were polished. I did not understand the way he was dressed.

"Hi," he repeated. "My name is DiAngelo. I am going to take you to my mom in Michigan. She will see that you are well taken care of with the doctors."

Uncle Marco quickly walked up to DiAngelo. He took hold of DiAngelo's arm and pulled him close.

I heard Uncle Marco quietly—but firmly—tell DiAngelo, "Watch him; and if anything happens to him, I will kill you."

As I got into the big white car, my mom reached in as she was crying quiet. She hugged me one last time. I turned to see that all the folks were standing around, crying quiet, watching me. I looked over, and Mikie was buried into Uncle Marco's belly. I started to go to him, but DiAngelo grabbed my arm and said, "Leave him be."

Before I knew it, the door was shut; and all my folks were out of sight. As I settled back in my seat, I noticed the prettiest girl I had ever seen in my life was sitting across from me.

Suddenly a thought came to me.

"Stop! Stop the car! I forgot to say goodbye to Mr. Creek."

DiAngelo responded, "No, we're not stopping anywhere."

"You better stop this car, or I am going to jump. I mean it!"

"Where does this man live?" the driver asked.

"Turn around. It is the road right there, Church Street," I answered.

As the driver pulled the car into a driveway to turn around, it seemed it took forever to back it out onto the busy road. When the driver did get a chance to back out, the car took up both lanes to turn.

We finally pulled into Mr. Creek's driveway. He was on the porch. I got out; and before I knew it, I was crying again.

"Mr. Creek, can I live with you? I will be good. I promise. I won't talk too much. Please, don't let them take me. I don't know these folks. Can I?" I pleaded my case to Mr. Creek.

When Mr. Creek didn't immediately respond, I looked up at him. He was crying as hard as I was.

"Boy, you have to go and see more doctors. Stay there until we can get the bad man. We will make it fast. I promise. Then you will be sitting right here with me."

Mr. Creek hugged me and walked me back to the car.

"Wipe your face, boy. Don't let those northerners see you cry. Be strong. Be strong."

"I will. Get the bad man; and hurry, Mr. Creek, so I can come home."

As I got back into the car, I looked at DiAngelo and said, "Thanks."

"Thanks for what?" he asked.

"For letting me see Mr. Creek before I left."

"Whatever," was his only response.

I looked once again at the girl across from me. She was pretty. Her skin was smooth and tan, not from the sun. She had the whitest teeth I had ever seen.

"What is your name?" I asked her.

She looked at DiAngelo as if to ask him if it was okay to talk to me.

Finally, she said, "My name is Evett. And you are Rocco."

"Yes. That sure is a pretty name; I don't think I ever heard that name before."

"Thank you," she responded.

"DiAngelo, how far to this city, Michigan?" I asked as I turned to look at him.

"Stupid, Michigan is not a city; it's a *state*."

"Well, look who's calling someone stupid. You look like you don't have a mom to dress you, and you dress like a clown."

"Shut up, or I will choke you with those dumb-looking bandages on your head!"

"You better not. I heard Uncle Marco tell you if anything happens to me, he would kill you. You better write that down in case you forget it."

"Just shut up, Rocco."

A few minutes of silence was all I could stand.

With a smile, I pressed DiAngelo, "Do you like my overalls? Aunt Hadie bought 'em for me."

"Yeah, they're nifty for an eight-year-old with bandages on his head. You look like a southern mummy."

He laughed so hard at his own joke that he almost coughed up a lung. As I sat and sized him up, I realized if I tore into him, he could whip me bad . . . more or less if he set me out on the road, I wouldn't know how to get back home.

"I got an idea," DiAngelo said with sudden enthusiasm. "Why don't we play Quiet Mouse, and see who can go the longest without talking."

"I have a better idea!" I responded. "Why don't you play Quiet Mouse by yourself, and let Evett and me talk?"

This time, *I* laughed.

DiAngelo had a pillow on his side of the big car. He laid his head down on it and was soon asleep. Evett took his legs and laid him all the way out on the big seat and came over to sit on my side of the car.

"I hope we get home before my parents get back in town."

"Why?" I inquired.

"They think I spent the weekend at my girlfriend's house. Instead, DiAngelo wanted me to come with him to pick you up."

"Oh, so you sneaked off?" I quizzed her.

"Well, yeah, kind of."

"Your mom is gonna whoop you bad."

"No, she is not."

"Yup, she is."

"No, she is not. She will probably be drunk and passed out and not even know if I am home or not."

"Oh, she drinks the devil's juice," I commiserated with her. "That's too bad."

After a few seconds of silence, I asked, "So, are you his girlfriend?"

"Yes, I am."

"Sorry, to hear that. He is a mean one, he is."

"No, we're just tired; and he is cranky. We drove all the way down here, and we only got there a few minutes before you came home from the hospital. We have hardly even had time to take a shower, and now we are back on the road again."

"Did you see Mikie?" I asked her.

"Yes. He is DiAngelo's cousin."

"Mine, too," I added. "My mom is Aunt Hadie's blood sister."

"What does that mean, Rocco?"

"It means they are full-blooded sisters, and Mikie is also my best friend."

"Rocco, can you do me a favor?" Evett inquired.

"Sure."

"Do not make fun of DiAngelo's clothes. Many people make fun of the way he dresses, and it makes him mad. My parents do not like him or the way he dresses, either."

"Well, he *does* look like a thug, but I will not make fun again for you."

She smiled her white smile and said, "Thank you."

Just about then, DiAngelo rolled over and turned himself right off the seat and onto the floor of the car.

It struck me funny, and I said, "Looks like he needs a car seat for babies."

"Dear Lord," DiAngelo responded. "I bet you have not shut your mouth for one minute, have you?"

"No, and you better not say that again!"

"I had better not say what? 'Dear Lord'?"

"You want us to get hit with lightning or something worse?"

"Okay, boys, be nice," Evett interjected.

"Yes, Evett," I answered with a smirk on my face.

DiAngelo turned to Evett. "Do you want to stop and get something to eat?"

I pulled out the cornbread my mom had given me. I offered some to Evett. DiAngelo suddenly snatched it out of my hand and threw it out the window.

"We do not eat cornbread. If you are going to be one of us, then you do not eat cornbread, either," he stated.

"Why did you do that to him?" Evett asked DiAngelo incredulously. "Don't you think his day has been bad enough that you have to treat him like that?"

She looked at me. "Rocco, are you all right?"

I didn't know if I was in shock or ready to kill him. I was silent for a few seconds.

Then I hissed, “You had no right to do that. That was my mom’s favorite plate, and she told me to keep it safe until she came and got me. I was only trying to be your friend and give you some of my food. One day you will pay for breaking my mom’s favorite plate. One day you will need something, and I will pass you by like I don’t even know you. As it is written, so shall it be.”

“Look,” Evett began, “you hurt him bad. Now, say you’re sorry. I mean it. You better say you’re sorry.”

“It’s okay. He doesn’t have to. I wrote it down; I wrote it in my soul,” I told Evett. “One day, Angelo.”

“Stop calling me Angelo. My name is *Di*Angelo.”

“Why? Don’t you like it?” I taunted him. “Good! Today your new name starts; this will be your payback for throwing my cornbread and my mom’s favorite plate out the window. Evett, I thought you said after his nap he would be better. If anything, he is worse! Can he play Quiet Mouse again?”

It seemed I had gone from one hell with Pa to another one with this DiAngelo guy.

“Rocco?” Evett broke through a silence of several minutes.

“Yes, Miss Evett?”

“Do you think we should keep a secret?”

“About what?”

“About me coming down with DiAngelo to pick you up. It seems the closer we get to Michigan, the more scared I get.”

“Are you rethinking about getting a whooping?”

DiAngelo piped up, “No one had better ever touch her.”

“Well, it looks like someone ought to teach you a few things, buddy. Your pa needed to give you a few more whoopings and put the fear of God in you.”

DiAngelo looked at me with eyes of someone who had never been told anything about the church ways.

"Little Buckaroo, are you a preacher?" he asked me.

"No. Brother Wallace, my preacher, taught me well the ways . . . the *right* ways."

"I will make you a deal," DiAngelo offered.

"What kind o' deal?"

"If you do not tell anyone that Evett came with me, I will let you use the phone."

"I have my own money to call from a pay phone. Uncle Marco said I could call collect. What else you got?" I tried to bargain for more.

"I think I'm gonna like you, after all," DiAngelo said with a grin.

"I think I am *not* going to like you. You have a mean spirit in you."

DiAngelo looked down a bit and then said, "What if I shoot you now and you won't have to worry about it?"

"Then I will scream from Heaven, 'Evett was with us'; and you will get in trouble," I retorted.

"Do you want Evett to get a whooping?"

"Nope."

"Then it's a deal?"

"Not so fast . . ." I interjected. "Where is the phone? I will think of something else later."

Evett smiled and said, "DiAngelo is just like you in a way. Look at him. He has hair like yours, eyes, and the same stubborn ways."

She looked to DiAngelo as she said, "He could pass for your little brother."

"No thanks. I do not need any little brother tagging behind me, telling on me everything I do."

"Stop getting so worked up," I responded. "You give me a headache, Angelo. Now, where is that phone?"

"Where is the phone . . . what?"

"Please, where is the phone?" I repeated.

DiAngelo pulled a phone out of a box that sat in the middle of the seat.

"Number, please," he said to me with a question in his expression.

"Funny," I answered. "Just call Aunt Hadie's Grill."

DiAngelo pulled out a book, looked up the number, dialed it, and handed me the phone.

"Aunt Hadie's Grill," came a voice from the other end of the line.

"Aunt Hadie, it's me. Is Mom still there?"

"You don't have to yell!" DiAngelo remarked.

"Yeah, she is over here still. How are you, boy?" Aunt Hadie asked.

"I am okay. I want to come home soon as I can."

"Well, okay. Let me get Dean for you."

As she went to get my mom, I looked at DiAngelo and said, "I am telling on you for breaking her favorite plate."

"Baby, is that you?" my mom's voice came across.

"Yes, Mom. I called to say 'Hi' and see how you are."

The silence on the phone overtook my heart and soul.

"I am good, baby, but I sure do miss you."

"I miss you, also, Mom."

"Rocco, where are you now?"

"Hang on, Mom. I will ask." After verifying our location with the driver of the big white car, I continued, "Mom, the driver said we are somewhere in Ohio. Mom, did you get Mr. Creek something to eat for supper?"

"Yes, I went home, got some clothes, and gave him some food."

"You ain't staying at home, Mom?"

"No, it hurts me to stay were my baby got hurt so bad. I am staying at Hadie's for a while."

"Mom, Angelo says I can talk to Mikie. But before I do, I have to tell you something. You know I was carrying your plate. I dropped it. I am sorry, Mom."

"It's okay, Rocco. You are more important than any ol' plate."

"Mom, I promise when I get bigger, I am going to buy you a whole new set of plates, and all of them are going to match."

"Okay, baby. I am going to get Mikie for you. I love you a bushel and a peck and a hug around the neck."

She went to get Mikie.

"Rocco, how are you?" came Mikie's voice across the phone.

"I am okay, but I miss you and Mom."

"Guess what, Rocco? Mr. Creek and Father are out looking for the bad man who hurt you. They said as soon as they get him and you see the doctors, you can come home."

"Really? They must miss me, too. Did you learn anything with your knife yet?"

"I haven't wanted to use it until you get home."

"Mikie, go ahead and learn to use it; and I will learn from you when I get home. And, Mikie, tell Todd that this is a bad time for me and my folks and that he better not try anything while I am gone or he will pay when I *do* get home. You got all that?"

"Yes, Rocco. I will tell him if he gets on me . . . or I might tell him before he gets started. That way maybe we can have peace."

"Good."

It seemed like a few minutes without either one of us saying anything, but I couldn't talk . . . there was a lump in my throat. Besides, I didn't want to cry in front of Evett or Angelo.

"Mikie, I better get going. I am on their car phone, and I did not have to use my own change to call."

Still there was no sound from Mikie.

"Mikie, are you there?"

"Yes."

I knew my friend, my cousin, was crying.

"Mikie, don't cry. You know things all work together if you try and be a good person. Like Mrs. Liza says, we have a bond. No matter how many miles I am from you, I will always be your best friend."

"You will always be my cousin two times," Mikie answered.

"Okay, Mikie. I love you. Goodnight."

"Goodnight, Rocco."

DiAngelo took the phone and hung it back up.

"Rocco, are you okay? Rocco!" Evett insisted.

"I reckon I am."

Suddenly, Evett was at my side, hugging me as I cried.

"Shhhh. It's okay. It's going to be okay."

DiAngelo said, "Come here."

I didn't know if he was gonna smack me or tell me to shut up. I moved to his side of the car and sat next to him.

"Wipe your eyes and blow that big nose."

He handed me a handkerchief.

"You know, I am your friend, also. I know we got started on the wrong foot, but we can be friends. Since my cousin is your cousin, maybe we can be kinda like cousins, also," DiAngelo offered.

I sat there, and for the first time I think I liked this boy. For the first time, I saw a side of him—a good side—that I only thought was in my folks in Kentucky.

"Angelo, don't take me up to Michigan and leave me. I don't know anyone. I am scared. What is your mom like? What is your pa like?"

"Well, my mother is different. She stays at home and does not go anywhere. She thinks people are talking about her and looking at her. She says my father has ruined her reputation.

"My father has been in Italy for about seven or eight years, so I can't really say what he is like. I was young, but I remember him being all-knowing and uptight.

"It looks like we are all that each other has in Michigan, so we need to tend to each other and love each other."

With that, the three of us put our hands together and made a deal: we would be there for each other.

"It really is like having a little brother that I never had. I always wanted a younger brother," DiAngelo added. "Do you ever think you can love me like you love Mikie?"

"I love Mikie," I answered, "like I love myself . . . probably even more."

"Really?" DiAngelo asked.

"Yes. Him and Mom . . . they are the only ones I have in the world who love me and understand me. They are the best folks in the world."

DiAngelo looked at me. "Come here," he said.

I scooted closer to him, and he hugged me. It was the first hug I ever got from anyone from the north.

"I am sorry for being mean to you . . . and I am sorry you got hurt," DiAngelo said. "I understand you fell off the porch."

"No, Angelo. That is not true. I say that because Mom told me to."

"What happened to you, then?"

"A bad man got me and kicked me in the neck. Now it's got to heal slowly. I have some pressure on the brain . . . maybe a tumor. Mom said I was coming up here to get it looked at by the city doctors. When I flew off the porch, I hit the chopping block, which made it worse. The ambulance came and took me away to the hospital."

DiAngelo responded, "Dear Lord."

"Yes, Jesus."

"What did you just say?" DiAngelo asked.

"You said 'Dear Lord,' so I said 'Yes, Jesus.'"

"I thought you were praying," DiAngelo answered. "Rocco, you are gonna have to let me be the older friend. It's time for you to rest and be taken care of. You need to be a kid and play and have fun . . . and not be so serious. You let Evett and I do all the worrying."

"Okay, but could you worry about getting us some food? The cornbread was all I had."

DiAngelo laughed like I had never heard anyone laugh. He held his head back and let it roar; it was as if it came from the bottom of his belly and went out like a lion.

"Am I going to sleep on the couch when I get to your house?" I inquired.

"No. We have a great big house with lots of room for you.

You will be in a room next to mine so I can watch you. There is a bathroom in between our bedrooms."

"I thought your mom was gonna tend to me."

"No, she is busy taking care of her mother. My father asked if I would watch you and take you to the doctors, and I said 'Yes.' But I didn't know it was going to be such a big job!"

"Angelo, I won't give no trouble. I will be good and listen. You'll see."

"Buckaroo, I was kidding. I know you are a good boy."

I didn't know how to handle DiAngelo's teasing. I guess from living with Pa's always pushing me away, it would take time for me to get used to DiAngelo. It would take time for me to love anyone else besides Mom and Mikie.

DiAngelo spoke up, "Michigan! Thank God."

"Amen," I responded.

"Rocco, you really need to stop that."

"Okay, I will. What do I need to stop?" Without missing a beat, I changed the subject, "Evett?"

"Yes, Rocco?"

"I won't tell anyone that you were with us."

"Thank you, Rocco. I appreciate it," she answered.

It wasn't long until we were in a place called Holland. We pulled up to Evett's home. It was a big, two-story house with bushes growing in front. DiAngelo and Evett got quiet for a few minutes. They were whispering and holding hands, so I turned my head and looked out the window.

"Rocco, what are you doing?"

"I am hiding my face so you all can kiss. Are you going to kiss the girl or not?" I pressed.

"Well, since you are telling me to kiss Miss Evett, I guess I had better."

He reached over, kissed the pretty girl, and said, "Evett, I really do love you."

She smiled and said, "I know you do . . . and I love you. I just hope it is enough."

The driver let her out of the car, and we were on our way.

"Rocco, are you ready for this?"

"No, I don't like new places that I haven't slept at before."

"It's okay," DiAngelo said, trying to sooth my fears. "Everyone is already sleeping. It is 10:30. We will just quietly go upstairs and go to sleep."

The car turned into the driveway of the biggest house I had ever seen in my life. There was a gate. The driver pushed a button to open the gate, and he drove down a long drive and pulled in front of the house. It not only had one door; it had two. The house was wide and had lots of lights burning. The driver got out and let us out. I waited to get my suitcase that Hadie let me borrow in which to bring my clothes.

DiAngelo spoke, "It's okay. Mr. Scott will bring in your suitcase. No one will steal it."

Chapter 4

As we went into the house, there was a big room with no furniture. There were two sets of stairs, but they met together in the middle of the second floor.

"That is our side to the right," DiAngelo explained as he pointed. "The side to the left is my mother's and grandmother's side."

DiAngelo turned around and looked at me looking at the grandeur of the house.

"What are you doing?" he questioned.

"I am about to take off my shoes so I won't track that clean floor."

DiAngelo let out one of those loud laughs, and I tucked in behind him.

"What's wrong?" he asked in alarm.

"You're gonna wake up everyone, and we're gonna get thrown out!"

I looked up at the second floor again. A woman stood there, staring down at us. She was tall and dark-headed with beady eyes.

DiAngelo greeted her, "Hello, beautiful."

"Don't 'beautiful' me! Did you take that girl with you?"

DiAngelo smiled. "What girl, Mother?"

"Evett's parents called about an hour ago and wondered if we'd seen her. You're just like your father . . . always trying to embarrass me."

As she came down the stairs, she walked over to give DiAngelo a kiss.

She stared at me and said, "What do you have here?"

"Mother, this is Rocco. Rocco, this is my mother."

"Glad to meet you," I answered and reached out for her hand.

"You can call me Mrs. Faye."

"Yes, Ma'am."

"Well, you are a polite, little guy. Anyway, how are your aunt and uncle?"

At the same time, DiAngelo and I started to talk. We looked at each other, and I nodded my head to let DiAngelo talk first.

"They are fine," he said. "They said to tell you 'Hi' and that they send their love."

"I bet they did," her coarse voice added a touch of bitterness. "Did you get to see your fraternal grandmother?"

"Yes, she was there."

I knew they were talking about Mrs. Liza; and I was waiting for her to say something bad . . . I was gonna get her. Instead, she only let out a "Hmmm."

"So, Rocco, was a girl with DiAngelo when he picked you up?" she asked as she averted her eyes from DiAngelo and fixed them upon me.

"Mrs. Faye, I have a note from my mom that she sent you."

"I will take it," DiAngelo said. "I will be looking after you and making sure you get to the doctors and all that."

"What happened to his head?" Mrs. Faye inquired as her attention was diverted away from the subject of Evett.

"Long story, Mother; and I really need to get him some food and get him to bed. It has been a long day for him."

"Damn, you have become quite the little father," Mrs. Faye observed.

"He needs me to look out for him, and I need him," DiAngelo responded.

"Okay, boys, I am going back to bed. I will see you in the morning."

"Goodnight, Mrs. Faye," I threw out.

"Goodnight . . . uhhhhh . . ."

"Rocco. Rocco is his name, Mother."

I followed DiAngelo into the kitchen where we discovered some leftovers. DiAngelo made the best heated-up cheeseburger I ever ate. He also put out something called chips. He drank a soda; I had some milk. We didn't talk while we ate. I guess we were both tired and really just wanted to go to bed. We finished up. I went to the sink with my plate and started to rinse it like I was taught at home.

"Just leave it; the help will get it cleaned up," DiAngelo instructed me.

I don't know if I was too tired to argue with him or if I liked more the idea of not having to do it. DiAngelo simply set his plate on the counter. I followed suit.

"Come on. I will show you upstairs," he motioned to me as he talked.

As we climbed the stairs, I looked around at all the stuff sitting on tables and the big pictures hanging on the walls.

"Hey! There's Uncle Marco," I spoke out.

DiAngelo looked and said, "No, that is my father."

"Oh, his name is Ray."

"Rocco, how did you know that?"

"Mrs. Liza told me about him and Uncle Marco."

"Oh, you speak Italian?" DiAngelo quizzed.

"No, Uncle Marco would tell me what Mrs. Liza was saying as she talked."

The floors upstairs were carpeted, and it felt as though there was about a foot of padding under it. When I walked across it, my feet sank into it.

"This is my room," DiAngelo explained as he opened a door.

I followed him inside. He had a great big bed, a dresser, and his own desk. There were posters on his wall of girls and NASCAR stuff, along with a few football posters.

He walked over to the bathroom.

"Buckaroo, you better hit the toilet and not pee on the seat."

"I won't, Angelo," I answered before continuing. "Hush before you get us in trouble."

"Trouble . . . why?"

"You are being too loud."

DiAngelo screamed, "No I am not!"

I quickly covered my ears, and it made him laugh one of his silly laughs.

"See, no one can hear us over here. I scream all the time," DiAngelo added.

"Someone might have you locked up for being crazy if you scream like that," I pointed out.

"When do we have to change the bandages on your head?" DiAngelo inquired.

"Before we go to the doctor's. When am I going?"

"I will call our family doctor in the morning. We will see him first and then go from there. But maybe we should look at your head and make sure the wound is clean. Sit here on the bed and let me see."

DiAngelo started to unwrap my bandages. There was still some pulling which made my neck hurt.

"Ouch, dummy!"

"Oh, I am sorry," DiAngelo quickly apologized. "Did it hurt?"

"A bit . . . it hurt a bit."

As he got closer to having the bandages unwrapped from around my head, the pressure disappeared.

When DiAngelo came to the last of the bandages, he exclaimed, "Dear Lord."

"Yes, Jesus," I responded.

DiAngelo stepped back and rolled his eyes at me.

"You were not supposed to do that again."

"Is it bad, Angelo?"

"Rocco, you haven't seen it yet?"

"No."

DiAngelo walked to the bathroom and brought back a mirror.

"Are you ready?" he asked simply.

He held up the mirror for me. There were big, black bruises all over my forehead.

"Angelo, I look like a prune."

"Well, Buckaroo, I would try and make you feel better; but you *do* look like a prune. Where is your clean wrap?"

"It's in my bag. I will get it."

"No," DiAngelo placed a hand on my shoulder as he spoke. "Sit still and don't move."

Soon he came back and went to wrapping my head in a clean bandage.

"Let me see the back of your head," DiAngelo said.

DiAngelo helped me take off my shirt.

"Oh, my God, Rocco. Your back is black and blue, also."

It's okay, Angelo. It only hurts a bit, and that's only when I lie on it. I have taken to sleeping on my side. It will heal."

"Are you sure you didn't see anyone? You didn't see who did this to you?"

"Yeah, I did, Angelo."

Just then the phone rang. It was Miss Evett.

"Did you get into a lot of trouble?" I heard DiAngelo ask. "Did they believe you? . . . Good . . . Okay, I have to talk to Rocco about something. I love you, and sleep well."

DiAngelo hung up the phone.

He went right back into our conversation as though nothing had interrupted it.

"Who was it, Rocco? Who did this?"

"The bad man."

"Rocco, you *have* to tell me . . . I mean right *now*."

"I can't tell you, Angelo. Uncle Marco and Mr. Creek are gonna get him. You're making my head hurt now. Leave me alone."

"Okay, okay. Let's get your pjs on and get you ready for bed."

DiAngelo took me to my room. There were two big beds and a dresser, a desk, and a window that reached over the entire wall.

"My room is bigger than yours. I have two beds. When they come to get me, Mikie can sleep over there in that one."

"Where are Evett and I going to sleep?" DiAngelo inquired.

"Are you two married?"

"No, we're not."

"Then she has to sleep in your room, and you have to sleep with us," I instructed him.

"You sure know how to make me happy. Life is just great now. I have a girlfriend who loves me and a buckaroo . . . who could ask for more?"

DiAngelo jerked up onto the bed the big suitcase that Mr. Scott, the driver, had previously deposited in my bedroom. He rummaged around in it and pulled my nightshirt out.

"We will unpack tomorrow," he suggested.

DiAngelo got out my toothbrush.

Mom had left a note in the bag: "Don't forget to brush your teeth every night and in the morning, also."

"Yes, Mom," I said out loud as I smiled.

DiAngelo reached out and hugged me under his arm.

"After we see the doctor, what if I take you home to see your Mom?"

"When?" I answered excitedly.

"Maybe this Friday. If you're good and tell the doctor where it hurts and everything—don't hide anything—they can help get you better."

DiAngelo then walked me to my bed and pulled down the covers.

"Get in," he said gently.

The sheets were nice and clean as though Mom had just washed them and hung them out on the line. I could smell the country air on them.

"Rocco, do you want the window open or shut?"

"No, we have to lock them. Did you lock the front door? Did you lock everything?" I nervously asked in rapid succession.

DiAngelo sat on the edge of the bed.

"Rocco, you don't have to be scared here. No one can climb this high to your window. There are big dogs out in the yard; they would chew up anyone if they came on the property. We have guards who watch night and day. No one can hurt you here. You are safe from the bad man. I think that's why your mom sent you here."

"You reckon, Angelo?"

"Yeah, I reckon," he laughed. "Goodnight, Buckaroo."

"Night, Angelo."

I went right to sleep and went to dreaming of the country air and sitting on Mr. Creek's porch. Some folks count sheep, but I thought about the time when I was so sleepy and rested while Mr. Creek stood guard over me.

I can remember that night like it was yesterday: the way the wind blew the curtains and how DiAngelo left on a little light in the bathroom for me. I could see him sleeping in the other room. It was so real as if I was on the outside of my body standing guard over myself, but I thought I was sleeping. I looked over and saw a man in a hat standing there just like Pa.

"Bad man, bad man, bad man, bad man!"

I screamed for all I was worth for someone to come help me, pointing to the man who was trying to get me.

"Rocco, wake up! Wake up!"

"Get 'im. He's there!" I screamed. "Bad man!"

Someone grabbed me; and when they did, I guess I passed out. When I came to, DiAngelo was wiping my head with a cloth soaked in cold water.

"Did you get him? Did you get him?" I frantically asked him.

"Rocco, shhhh. Stay still. You ripped your bandages off, and we have to fix them again."

I looked over. Mrs. Faye was standing there, looking at me. Her arms were crossed, and she was shaking.

"Your mom needs a sweater," I told DiAngelo.

"No, I'm okay. I heard you screaming and came to see what happened."

"I don't know. I was sleeping, Mrs. Faye."

I looked at DiAngelo. "What happened to your face? It has blood on it. Did the bad man get you?"

"No, but a very strong eight-year-old got me."

"Who? Me?"

"Yes. You were having a bad dream and screaming. I tried to wake you up, and you tore into me like a cat."

"I'm sorry. I will pack up and go home tomorrow. I didn't mean to hurt you."

Mrs. Faye spoke, "Yes, his clothes are still packed. We can send him back tomorrow."

"Mother, go to bed. He is not going anywhere until I take him to the doctor's like Father said, and . . ."

"And what?" Mrs. Faye pressed.

"Until I can be sure he is safe and no one will hurt him, he is not going anywhere."

"Well, keep him quiet . . . and no more screaming!"

With that, Mrs. Faye left.

"I told you we were gonna get kicked out, Angelo."

"No, we're not. This house belonged to my grandfather, and he left it to my father and Uncle Marco. No one can throw us out."

"Mrs. Liza's husband owned this house?" I inquired.

"Sure did . . . and the house in Italy, as well. My family is very rich and powerful. I will not let anyone hurt you."

DiAngelo wrapped up my head once again and gave me some water. I drank it and lay back down. He walked over to the other bed and cleared it off.

"What are you doing? Are you scared, too?" I questioned.

"Yes, Buckaroo, I think I will sleep in this bed so you can keep me safe," he said as he smiled.

"Reckon I can yell louder than you. I woke your mom up."

"She will get over it. Tomorrow is a new day, and we will have fun. We will get you to the doctor and get you better."

DiAngelo left the bigger light on in the bathroom this time. I faced him and could see he was there in case the bad man came back.

That night I slept without a worry and dreamed only of good things. DiAngelo stood guard like an angel and let me sleep. I seemed to wake up peaceful and rested. I turned over to look at DiAngelo. He was snoring and making sounds like a whistle from his bed. I wondered what the day would bring and if the doctor would hurry up and fix my head so I could go home.

The wind blew in through the window but it was a nice, warm breeze. In Kentucky when the wind blew, it meant cold weather was on our doorstep. In the summer, we prayed for the colder wind to blow. The heat was hot and nauseous at home . . . not like the heat in the north. Uncle Marco put an air conditioning unit in the grill so the customers could stay cool. It seemed like it was the busiest time of the year in the grill.

I wondered how long this boy could sleep; it was already 7 a.m. I wanted something to eat. However, I remembered what Miss Evett said about DiAngelo when he was tired, and I didn't want him waking up grumpy.

I walked to the window and pulled back the curtain to look out. The view was breath-taking. There was a lake bigger than any I had ever seen . . . so big that one couldn't see the other side. There were boats going up and down the lake; some had ropes used for pulling folks. I stood there for what seemed like forever, taking it all in.

I heard DiAngelo move from the other bed and turn over.

"Hey, you. Angelo, you going to sleep your life away?"

"No, just the day. Go back to sleep."

"We can't. You got to get up and call the doctor, remember? I need to get fixed so I can go home."

"Are you going to miss Evett and me?" he questioned sleepily.

"Nope."

"You're not going to miss us?"

"Nope. I am going to take you back home with me and keep you all."

DiAngelo went to laughing that silly laugh again. Every time he did it, it would make me smile for some reason.

"Is Miss Evett coming over here today? I need to ask her something."

"What?" DiAngelo asked.

"Is your name Miss Evett?"

"If you tell me what you want to ask her, I will have you some breakfast cooked."

"Hey, Angelo, I am hungry for real. I been sitting here waiting for your lazy butt to get up and get going."

"Buckaroo, how about some cereal and toast? Or how about some fried eggs, bacon, and a biscuit with gravy?

"No taters!" I interjected.

"No taters, it is."

With that he jumped up out of bed and ran to the bathroom and shut the door. I heard water running. In a few minutes he came out. He had on the same clothes that he wore yesterday.

"Stinky, you put on the same clothes as yesterday," I observed aloud.

"No, they're not. They're just like those . . . but these are *fresh* ones."

"You wear the same thing every day . . . never any change of colors?"

"Nope. Just a t-shirt and some jeans."

"I think I better not wear jeans to the doctor. I should wear my church pants and shirt."

"Okay, but you have to shower, Stinky, and get ready for breakfast," DiAngelo prompted.

"Shower?"

"Yes, Rocco . . . shower."

"No, Mom draws me a tubful of water. I don't know how to take a shower."

"Man, are you joking?"

"Here, I will show you, Angelo."

I walked to the bathroom and started for the handle in the shower.

"Wait, Buckaroo!"

"I got it, Angelo!"

I quickly turned the handle, and water came down all over my head. I learned real fast what a shower was.

"I tried to tell you to wait," DiAngelo complained.

"Now I am going to get in trouble. I don't have any more bandages. That was the last one."

"Well, it's okay. We will go see Dr. Bill this morning and let him take a look-see."

I looked mean at him, and then I laughed.

"So, since you're all wet, how about I get you a washcloth and you just clean up. Deal?"

"Deal," I responded.

DiAngelo pulled both doors to the bathroom shut, and I went to washing my hands and feet. I got into my clothes and knocked on his door, but he never came. I went into my room and sat on the bed. I had put on my new dress shirt that Aunt Hadie bought me along with some tan britches. Mom had bought me some dark brown, patent leather shoes at a garage sale . . . almost new. I combed my hair real nice, and I was ready to go.

Finally, DiAngelo knocked on my bedroom door and asked, "What are you doing?"

"I am waiting for you to come get me."

"You don't have to wait. Just come on downstairs. Mother and Grandmother are waiting on you so we can eat."

"I am gonna look like a prune for a long time. You got me wet, and now everyone is gonna look at me."

"If you hurry, I will take you to see Miss Evett on our way and show her how nice you look."

"Okay, deal." I jumped up and said, "Let's go!"

We walked down the stairs. When we got to the bottom, I held back.

"It's okay. Come on," encouraged DiAngelo.

We walked in, and Mrs. Faye was fixing her mom's chair and putting a napkin on her lap. The table was long and empty. DiAngelo sat at the right of his mom, and her mother was at the left. I sat next to DiAngelo. There was a whole lot of room left to sit about 10 more folks. We needed this table when Uncle Marco had one of his parties.

"Good morning, DiAngelo."

"I already told you good morning, Mother."

"I meant for you to say good morning to your grandmother."

"Good morning, Grandmother."

She nodded at DiAngelo and then looked at me. "Good morning, little man."

"Good morning, Ma'am," I responded. "How are you today?"

"I'm fine. Was that you screaming last night?"

"Yes, Ma'am, I think it was. Angelo said I had a bad dream."

"Mother, eat your breakfast before it gets cold," Mrs. Faye broke in.

DiAngelo's grandmother had a bowl of oatmeal and was stirring it, but I don't think I saw her take a bite.

"Ma'am, you want some of my breakfast?"

Before she could answer, Mrs. Faye answered, "No, she doesn't want any of your breakfast; she has to eat her own."

"But I don't think she likes it," I said. "I think she is hungry."

I walked over and put my plate down in front of her. "Here, Ma'am, I am not that hungry."

I traded her water for my orange juice.

"That will kill her. She is on a very strict diet, and we have to watch what she eats," Mrs. Faye tried to explain.

"Well, at her age, I think she can eat what she wants and go to be with God on a full belly," I retorted.

Mrs. Faye gasped as she looked over at her mom and saw how she was shoveling the food into her mouth. She dipped one of her . . . or should I say one of *my* . . . biscuits in her tea. She looked over at me and winked.

"Boy, what is your name?" she asked.

"Rocco," I answered simply.

"Thank you for your kindness. I think they are trying to starve me. These eggs are the best I ever had."

"Thank Angelo," I said. "He made them."

"No, I didn't make them," DiAngelo answered.

His mom said, "Don't look at me; I don't cook," as everyone's head turned in her direction.

"Well, someone made them," I said.

"We have a lady who cooks for us. Her name is Miss Maria."

"Oh, well, we have to make sure we thank her," DiAngelo's grandmother remarked.

I looked at Mrs. Faye's mom. "What is your name, Ma'am?"

"My name is Sandra, but you may call me Grandmother, also."

"No, he may not," Mrs. Faye suddenly insisted.

"I can call you Mrs. Sandra. If you need me for anything, just yell," I offered.

Mrs. Faye looked meanly at me and said, "I am sure that my mother knows my name; and if she needs anything, *I* will get it for her."

"Well, remember she don't like oatmeal."

DiAngelo let one of his laughs escape, and so did his grandmother. This time I did more than just smile; I laughed out loud myself . . . laughing at their laughter.

"Well, Buckaroo, we better get going if we're going to see the doctor," DiAngelo remarked.

"I thought his appointment was at 10:00," Mrs. Faye said.

"It is, Mother, but I want to show him around."

DiAngelo turned and stared at me as if to say, "Shut up."

I guess he didn't want his mom to know we were going to see Evett. He grabbed his keys, and we walked to the door. I turned around and said goodbye to Mrs. Faye and Mrs. Sandra.

"Goodbye," Mrs. Sandra answered. "You come and see me when you get back."

"I will," I promised.

As DiAngelo and I went outside, I could feel that warm wind again. DiAngelo was walking fast.

"Well, come on, Buckaroo!" he prompted.

"I was waiting for the car."

"No, I am going to drive my truck."

"Oh, do you have a license?" I quizzed.

"I guess you are a cop now," DiAngelo snipped. "Yes, I have a license."

"Well, I was just asking. Mom said never go with someone who doesn't have a license."

DiAngelo walked into a long, low building. I followed. He got into a nice, shiny, black truck. It was clean, and the wheels were chrome. I got in, as well.

"Buckle up," DiAngelo instructed me.

"I can't. It hurts my neck and head."

"Well, here."

DiAngelo buckled just the one for my lap. As he pulled out of the building, he jerked the truck and made it jump. He went really fast, all the way to the gate.

"Shit, I'm sorry. Did I hurt your head?"

"Yes."

I smiled then and gave him a sideways glance.

"Buckaroo, was that a lie?"

"No, a teasing. You can play and be teasing and lie, but if you look at someone in the face and not be teasing, then that's a lie."

"Oh, I see."

"Angelo?"

"Yes, Buckaroo?"

"Don't tell Miss Evett that I had a bad dream last night."

"Why?"

"I don't want her to think I am a baby; I am eight years old."

"Well, you *are* a baby."

"No, I'm not!" I said adamantly.

"Well, if you're not a baby, then stop acting like one and tell me who beat you."

"I didn't see anyone. I was looking at my ring."

"How can someone just sneak up on you like that? Okay, I'm gonna teach you how to fight before I send you back . . . and how to shoot a gun . . . and how to be tough."

"We are to turn the other cheek and not live in fighting ways. A boy at school named Todd is getting bigger and bigger. He is always bothering Mikie and me. Soon Mikie and I will have to whip him, but I don't like to fight."

"Neither do I, Rocco, but sometimes you have to protect yourself."

"I think you're right, Angelo."

"Really?"

"Yes, I counted on Mom and Mr. Creek to protect me, and they didn't. Mom should have let me eat at the kitchen counter."

"What do you mean?" DiAngelo pressed.

"I would eat at the kitchen counter, and Mom and Pa would eat at the table . . . and everything was okay. But Mom wanted me to eat with them. I think that is why he was mad that day."

"Buckaroo, you never got to sit at the table and eat?"

"Are you going to be mad if I say 'No'? I don't want you to be mad."

"Yes, I am going to be mad . . . but not at *you*. I am going to be mad at your pa!"

"What good does being mad do? Sometimes, we have to just go on and take the hits that life gives us."

"Rocco, see that is what I mean . . . right there. It's okay to be mad. You don't have to be so grown up. You act older than I am."

"Besides Mikie, all my folks are grown up. They teach me the ways; they teach me from their mistakes so I won't make the same ones. When we get home, you will see. You will learn the ways, also."

"Okay, two things here," DiAngelo started to explain. One, I'm not going to move to Kentucky. Two, I am not learning their ways; my ways are just fine . . . but I will teach you to protect yourself before I take you back."

"Are you tired of me already, Angelo?"

"No, not at all, Buckaroo. I just want you to be yourself and not the way they tell you to be."

"I don't know any other way; all I know is the folks and

their ways. I didn't know there was any other way. Do you think I should call Mom and tell her to come and get me?"

"Damn it!"

"What, Angelo?"

"I went and said it wrong."

"Well, maybe we should play Quiet Mouse until you figure it out. So, tell me 1-2-3 Quiet Mouse."

"I don't want to play."

"You lose, Angelo."

"My father said he has to work and can't be here this summer again. I was going to Italy, but I am not sure about that now."

"Are you afraid?" I asked him.

"No. Why would I be afraid?"

"Because you haven't seen him in so long. It would be like going somewhere you never been . . . somewhere with strangers. Maybe his ideas aren't like yours. Maybe his ways are not like yours. You would have to work hard at trying to be like him. What if he doesn't understand why you dress like this? What would you say?"

"I would say, 'This is me. If you don't like it, too bad.'"

"Then I would say the same to you. Checkmate!"

DiAngelo started laughing as we stopped in front of Miss Evett's house.

"What are you laughing at?" Evett asked approaching DiAngelo's truck as we pulled up in front of her house.

"Good morning, dear. Rocco just gave me a lesson of a lifetime, and I played right into his hands."

DiAngelo leaned out the window and gave Evett a kiss.

"Doesn't Rocco look nice?" he asked her.

"He sure does. Rocco, you sure clean up nice."

“Thank you, Evett. Did you get whooped last night?”

“No,” she answered. “My parents called my friend’s house, and I told them I was at another friend’s house.”

“Ohhhh,” I let out.

“What, Rocco?”

“If you tell one lie, you gonna have to tell another and then another and keep lying to cover your lies.”

DiAngelo laughed, “I guess we both learned a life lesson this morning . . . and from an eight-year-old!”

Evett just squinted her eyes halfway and stared at Rocco.

Chapter 5

"Miss Evett, can I talk to you?"

"Sure."

"Not by 'Big Ears.' Over there," I said as I pointed to a tree.

I got out of the truck, and we went over by a big tree in her front yard.

"Could you do me a favor?"

"Sure, Rocco."

"I want a pair of jeans and a white t-shirt just like him," I explained as I nodded in DiAngelo's direction. "And some shoes, too."

"Dear Lord. Why?"

"Everyone makes him feel bad, and so did I. I think if there were two of us wearing the same thing, maybe folks wouldn't make fun of him."

"You are such a good, little guy; I have never seen such a big heart," Evett responded.

"I have my own money, see?"

"Well, what if I tell him we're going shopping after your doctor's appointment and see what he says?"

"Okay, deal."

We walked back to the truck, and I got in. DiAngelo looked at me.

"Are you trying to steal my girl?"

I simply smiled back at him.

"Hey, I want to take him shopping after he gets done with the doctor," Evett said. "We will only be gone for a little while, and I will drop him back off at your house."

"Okay, but I have to get him to Dr. Bill's office. We're cutting it close. Bye, baby. Love you."

Evett looked over at me and winked. "See you afterwards."

"Okay," I answered.

We made it to the doctor's office with time to spare. DiAngelo signed me in. We sat there for a few minutes, and they finally called my name. I got up, but DiAngelo stayed seated.

"Come on, Meathead," I said to him.

DiAngelo laid down his magazine, and we went in together.

When the doctor came in, I saw he was tall and had brown hair, a mustache, and a goatee. His eyes shined with friendliness. He looked down at me and smiled.

"Well, Mr. Rocco, you must be someone special. They moved a lot of appointments to get you in today."

"I think Angelo here wants me to hurry up and go back home."

"Hey, I didn't say that," DiAngelo lamented.

The doctor nodded his head at what I held in my hands.

"What do you have there? Are those for me?"

"These are the papers Mom said to give you from the doctor down home. Here are some pictures of my head."

"Okay. Good! I will go look at the pictures and read the letter. I will be right back."

"Why did you say that to him?" DiAngelo asked as he knocked me with his elbow.

"What?"

"That I wanted you to go back home? I never said that. I couldn't care less if you stayed here forever. I am starting to get used to you. I can see why you have so many friends in Kentucky, and I can see why your mom loves you so much."

"Your mom loves you the same way, Angelo."

"Well, I don't know about that."

"Sure, she does. It's in all moms to love us and tend to us. They never stop loving. It's the pas who are hateful. Uncle Marco is a good pa. He does things with Mikie; and everywhere Mikie goes, he has to tell Uncle Marco to see if it's okay and safe. He plays with both of us; and sometimes when I spend the night there, he lays on the floor and talks with us. He tells us stories of his country and how things were when he was growing up and everything."

"Does he talk about my father?" DiAngelo inquired.

"No. Mrs. Liza does, though. She said he was once a good man, also . . . like Uncle Marco."

The doctor walked back in.

"Okay, we have some good news." He sat down as he continued speaking, "Your neck is not broken, but it has a whiplash. We can fix that. The not-so-good news is you have three broken ribs, and your skull has a fracture and may give us some trouble in the future. For now, we wait till more of the swelling goes down and take more x-rays and see what we can see. Now, a few questions: has there been any forgetfulness?"

"No."

"Yes, there has, Dr. Bill," interjected DiAngelo. "He is forgetting a lot of things."

"Such as?"

"Can we talk outside?" DiAngelo suggested.

"Certainly."

Dr. Bill and DiAngelo went out, and I went over to stand by the door so I could hear what they were saying.

I heard DiAngelo's voice, "He has forgotten who did this to him."

"Wait," I heard the doctor say, "someone did this to him? The reports say that he fell off his porch."

It was quiet for a minute when I could hear nothing.

Then DiAngelo continued, "I think that someone did this to him, and he is forgetting who it was."

"He could have blocked it out," the doctor commented.

"Can you look at his back, also?" DiAngelo asked.

"Sure."

I hurried to get back onto the examining table, but not in time. Dr. Bill, followed closely by DiAngelo, walked in as I was climbing up.

"Buckaroo, were you listening at the door?"

"Kinda," I sheepishly answered.

"You little eavesdropper."

"Okay, I need to check your eyes and nose and some other things," Dr. Bill started.

"Don't forget my back," I reminded him as I looked over at DiAngelo.

They both laughed. The doctor pulled up my shirt.

"Wow!"

As he started feeling over my back and pushing here and there, the pain shot to my head.

"Well, more bad news," he said. "I need to have a picture of his back, and the other hospital didn't take one."

"Can I go home now?" I insisted.

"In a few minutes," the doctor answered.

DiAngelo said, "No, he can't."

The doctor looked at DiAngelo with a quizzical look.

"He means can he go back to his home in Kentucky," DiAngelo explained.

The doctor relaxed. "Oh, no . . . no traveling for a few days . . . maybe weeks. We have to get you better."

Then looking at DiAngelo, the doctor handed him a paper.

"Take this over to Grand Rapids. They will take you right in for the x-ray. Bring it back to me today so we can see it," he instructed.

Turning back to me, the doctor asked, "Any problems sleeping?"

"No," I answered shortly.

"Yes, he does," interjected DiAngelo once again. "He has bad dreams."

"I have some samples of a medication I want you to give him one hour before he is to go to sleep. What time does he usually go to sleep?" the doctor inquired.

"When Angelo stops snoring!" I quipped.

"I don't snore," DiAngelo defended himself.

"Hmmm," I retorted.

So, we were off to Grand Rapids to the hospital for an x-ray.

I reminded DiAngelo, "We have to hurry; Evett is taking me shopping."

"Dang, I forgot," DiAngelo responded.

"Maybe the doctor should have checked you out. You are forgetful."

"Rocco, don't be fresh with me."

"I am just being me," I said as I smiled broadly at him. "Your nana ate my food, and I am hungry."

"My what?"

"Your nana is your grandmother."

"Well, we will stop for lunch after the x-ray is done."

When we arrived at the hospital, DiAngelo once again signed me in. The lady at the window asked for a permission slip.

"Call Dr. Bill. He can confirm this for you," DiAngelo explained.

"One moment," she answered.

Finally, a nurse called my name.

DiAngelo said, "That is you."

He grabbed my hand and led me to the nurse, whom we followed down a hall into a room.

"Angelo, I am sick of these hospitals."

"You better get used to them; until you are 100% better, we will be seeing a lot of them."

"Yuck!" I exclaimed.

"Here is a gown," the nurse offered. Change into it, and we will take your speedy, all-important x-rays," she added, rather sarcastically.

DiAngelo pressed her, "What is your problem?"

"Oh, there has been a rush placed on his x-rays by the head of radiology. They're to be taken, developed, and sent with you to Holland. I guess it is all about who you know," she added flippantly.

I asked the nurse, "Do you want my dress pants—to fold them?"

"No! I'm not your servant!" she bit back.

DiAngelo broke in, "Throw 'em here."

He held out his hands to catch them. I threw them to him, and my money fell out.

"Angelo," I cried out in alarm. "Get my money!"

"Buckaroo, you're a dollar man. *You* can buy lunch."

"I can't," I started explaining. "I have to save it to get home."

"You know we can't go this Friday, right?"

"Angelo, you said we could."

"But the doctor said he would see how your new x-rays go."

"Okay," the nurse instructed. "Lie down; and in a few minutes, you will slide in and go through the tunnel."

It took a while to go all the way through the tunnel. Finally, she helped me off the table.

"Give me my pants, Angelo. You better not have taken my dollars."

DiAngelo laughed, "I have a lot of those. I don't need yours."

"Okay then . . . *you* buy lunch!"

By the time I was dressed, the nurse was back with the x-rays, and we left. DiAngelo drove really fast again to get back to Dr. Bill. He forgot about lunch.

When Dr. Bill had finished looking at them, he said, "DiAngelo, I need to speak with you."

This time the doctor took him somewhere else because I didn't hear anything by the door. When they returned, they both stared at me.

"Rocco?" the doctor started.

"Yeah?"

"We have to put a special thing on your back up to your neck. Your back has been fractured, also. I am afraid that it will push into your spine and make you not be able to walk. It is more serious than any of us thought," the doctor explained.

"Well, can I walk with this thing on?"

The doctor smiled, "Sure . . . but it will keep you straight and make things go back into place."

"Okay, I will have one, please. How much is it?" I inquired of him.

"I have an extra one I can let you borrow at no charge."

"Okay, I will keep it nice and bring it back."

I had to unbutton my pants and take off my shirt once again. The doctor put a type of jacket on me, and it went to my neck just like he said it would. Like DiAngelo's truck, it buckled around my waist.

"You didn't say it was this heavy. Will my clothes fit over it?" I worried.

"Sure, they will," the doctor responded. "You will get used to it. It has weights in it, and your back will grow stronger again."

When we were finally ready to leave, I held out my hand to Dr. Bill.

"Well, nice meeting you, Dr. Bill."

We shook hands, and we were off for DiAngelo's home.

"Damn, this makes me feel like a mummy for real," I complained to DiAngelo.

"You had better not cuss. Just because I do doesn't mean you can." DiAngelo paused a moment, then continued speaking, "Are you going to feel like shopping after all this today?"

"Yes, for a bit."

DiAngelo finally remembered lunch, and we went to find something to eat. After eating, we went right to Evett's house; and, like before, she met us outside.

"What took so long? I was getting worried," she said. She

stopped short as she finally saw me. "What's he got on?" she asked, looking to DiAngelo for the answer.

"It's a Superman costume. Doesn't it look nice?" I piped up.

"Actually, yes, it looks very nice," she diplomatically answered. "Did you bring me one?"

I smiled as I answered, "No, because you are Wonder Woman."

She laughed.

"Well, let's go, Superman, so we can find the best deals."

DiAngelo gave Evett a lot of money to shop with.

"I got my own money," I informed them.

"Well, you were so good and strong at Dr. Bill's place, I want to treat you," DiAngelo offered.

"Don't argue, Rocco. We can shop all day with this," Evett responded.

"He can't stay out long. He needs a nap, Evett. It was hard over there. Okay?"

I got out of the truck.

"Go straight home," I instructed DiAngelo. "I will be there soon . . . and don't drive fast!"

"It's okay, Rocco. I will be there when you get home. Have fun with Evett, Buckaroo. When you get home, I have a surprise for you."

We got into Evett's little car that looked more like an egg, and we were off. We went to a place called a mall, and there were lots and lots of folks there.

The first store we went into didn't have jeans like DiAngelo's, so we went to the next one. There, we found the jeans on a fake man. In fact, his entire outfit was exactly like DiAngelo's.

"Well, I guess we found out where DiAngelo shops," Evett observed.

"Evett, do you think Angelo really likes me?"

"Who?" she quizzed.

"Angelo."

"Rocco, I have not seen him so happy. He goes from me to you. Most of the time, when he gets to my house, he is a drag and always depressed. Now, he is talking and laughing. I think he really does like you."

"I hope so," I responded.

We bought my clothes a bit bigger so they could fit over the brace. Evett then took me to a hair-cutting place, and I got a haircut. She showed the girl a picture of DiAngelo and instructed her to cut my hair just like his. When the lady got done with my hair, she turned me around. It almost scared me to see that I was a little DiAngelo; I looked just like him.

"Oh, my goodness!" was all Evett could say.

We got into her car again and started to the house. She kept looking at me, but not saying anything . . . just looking.

"What's wrong?" I finally asked her.

"Nothing," she answered simply.

"Something is wrong or you wouldn't keep looking at me like that."

"It's just I can't get over how much you look like him."

"I know," I agreed. "It scared me, also . . . but I hope I don't snore like he does."

After a brief silence, a thought popped into my head.

"Miss Evett, you know his mom does not like me . . . Mrs. Faye?"

"Honey, Mrs. Faye doesn't like anyone. She doesn't even like herself. She is an unhappy woman with no character."

"Her mom seems real nice . . . Mrs. Sandra."

"You have talked to her?" Evett asked.

"Yes, I gave her my breakfast because she was hungry. She wants me to come see her after I get home. I didn't even know she could talk at first."

When we pulled into the drive, the gate didn't open. Evett buzzed it.

"Who is it?" a voice came over the intercom.

"DiAngelo, open the gate."

"Who is it?" he repeated the question.

I screamed, "It's Superman and Wonder Woman. Now, open the damn gate!"

Evett stared at me with round eyes.

"What has he been teaching you?"

Matter-of-factly, I answered, "Damn and ass. I think that's it."

The gate came open, cutting our conversation short. We drove to the house. The dogs were there, so I wouldn't get out.

"Let's go," Evett prompted.

"No."

"What's wrong?"

"They're gonna eat me!"

"Who told you that? They won't hurt you. They know me."

"But they don't know me!"

"Come on and get out," she pushed.

"No!"

DiAngelo yelled out from the door, "Come on."

"No! You come get me. The dogs are gonna eat me."

Evett accused DiAngelo, "Did you tell him that?"

"Yes, but only the bad man gets ate by the dogs."

Evett went up to the door.

I heard her tell DiAngelo, "Stop scaring him."

"I had to tell him about the dogs last night so he could sleep," DiAngelo lamented.

"Just go get him," Evett commanded with exasperation in her voice.

DiAngelo came to Evett's car. When he took the handle and opened it, I got out and stood behind him.

He looked at me and said, "Oh, shit!"

"What? Are they coming? Are the dogs coming?" I almost yelled.

"No, it's that you look just like me."

"Well, if we don't get into the house, we will both be dog meat."

The brace made me walk like I was a cripple. When we got inside, however, there was a party going on. Mrs. Faye and her mother had on hats and were blowing horns. When I turned and looked at DiAngelo's mom, she almost lost her breath from gasping so hard.

DiAngelo exclaimed, "Happy day! We all look like Uncle Marco."

Mrs. Sandra said, "Yes, happy day!"

We went into the dining room. There was cake, presents, and streamers. It was a surprise party for me . . . but I think I surprised all of them the most.

We sat down to the table. Evett was on one side of me, and DiAngelo was on the other. His mom sat at the head of the table, and Mrs. Sandra had been placed by herself across the table.

I smiled at Mrs. Sandra and waved, emphasizing the great span between us.

"Angelo?" I said rather timidly.

"What?" he answered gruffly.

"Can I go sit with Mrs. Sandra? She doesn't have anyone to talk to."

DiAngelo nodded his head.

I went over and sat next to Mrs. Sandra and said, "Hi. I am back. Did you get some lunch?"

"Yes. I had some soup and a few crackers."

"I will give you some more of my food tonight. I already had a big lunch, and at the mall I had a warm pretzel."

From across the table DiAngelo looked at me. "Do you have any change left?"

I looked at Evett, and she smiled at DiAngelo sweetly.

"No," she answered, "we spent every penny of it to get him to look like you."

Looking back at me, DiAngelo asked, "Why did you want to dress like me?"

"I want to be just like you. I want everyone to know I am proud to be your friend; but I think if we are gonna dress like this, I know how to save us some money."

DiAngelo's expression softened. "How's that, Buckaroo?"

"We can go to the Goodwill store and buy some jeans and white t-shirts a whole lot cheaper than they charged me at the mall."

DiAngelo let out one of those darned laughs and almost tore the roof off. His mom gasped for air again.

Mrs. Sandra spoke up, "Faye?"

"Yes, Mother?"

"I think you need to remember where you came from. You act like you are above the Goodwill store. You started school in clothes that I bought from there. I sent you to school dressed in clean and ironed clothes from there."

"Mother?" DiAngelo asked as if he wasn't believing what he was hearing.

Everyone turned to look at Mrs. Faye.

"No, not *my* mother," DiAngelo said.

"Yes, *your* mother!" Mrs. Sandra said emphatically. "We came to this country poor, and your grandfather worked for a milling factory," she began, looking at DiAngelo. "He worked his fingers to the bone to take care of us, and I am proud of him. Yes, you better believe I bought Faye's clothes from Goodwill and took them home, washed them, bleached them . . . and she looked and acted like everyone else."

Everyone sat in shock, not only at the story Mrs. Sandra had just laid out, but also at the fact that Mrs. Sandra had spoken so many words at one time.

I quickly added, "The Goodwill store had good deals, if you ask me. See these shoes right here?"

I raised one leg into the air and wiggled my foot around so that everyone might see my shoe.

"These shoes cost Mom 75 cents, and . . ." I drew out, "she could take what she saved on the shoes to keep me in socks!"

Evett spoke up, "Your mother is a bright woman, a frugal woman."

"No," I responded, "we're Southern Baptist."

Everyone burst out laughing. I couldn't figure it out, but this time Mrs. Faye was laughing right along with everyone. I was glad to see that everyone was happy.

"Rocco?" Mrs. Faye said.

"Yes, Ma'am," I answered.

"What did the doctor say? When can you go home?"

"Mother," DiAngelo interrupted, "Rocco has to be in his

Superman brace for a while. Dr. Bill thinks it would be best for him not to travel at this time."

"Angelo," I said, "when do you start school?"

"I don't go to school, Buckaroo. I study at home and have a tutor who comes here and teaches me."

"Where is my school gonna be?" I inquired.

"I haven't really thought about that."

Mrs. Sandra spoke up, "He can be taught, as well, here at home. Everything will work itself out."

I started to laugh, but I noticed no one else in the room was laughing.

Mrs. Faye looked at me. "What are you laughing about, Rocco?"

"Angelo and me gonna be in the same room. Wait till I tell Mikie this."

"And why is this so funny?" Mrs. Faye pressed.

"You're a tall man," Rocco started, looking at DiAngelo, "and you are gonna be in a small man's class. Everyone will think you didn't pass about six grades."

I think they got it then, and everyone started to laugh with me.

"His sense of humor is refreshing to me," Mrs. Sandra observed.

Just then the help, Miss Maria, started bringing supper out. It was cooked in the red sauce . . . and more red sauce. I thought I would fall out if anyone cooked with more red sauce! It made my stomach hurt.

"Mrs. Sandra, I hope you are hungry." I said, looking at her. "You can eat my supper. I should have had Evett stop to the dollar store and fetch me some stuff."

"Buckaroo, what could you possibly need from there?"

"Some chicken and dumplings!" I said emphatically.

"What?"

"Angelo, it's good. I will make you some."

"No, thank you," he answered.

"I would like some," Mrs. Sandra said as she looked straight at me with a twinkle in her eye.

"That is enough talk about this silliness," Mrs. Faye inserted. "Everyone eat what is set before them and . . . Mother, you would do well not to tell stories about the old days. We are in the here and now."

"Reckon without the old days none of us would be here and now," I couldn't help but say. "We had to come from somewhere."

"DiAngelo, will you shut him up?" Mrs. Faye insisted.

DiAngelo could see his mom was getting pretty upset. He put his finger up to his mouth, looking at me, then started to eat. I sat there for a bit and messed with the rabbit food.

"Uncle Marco made Mikie and me eat this salad stuff sometimes, but I liked mine with a lot of dressing soaked in it," I tentatively offered.

"Are you going to eat, Rocco?" DiAngelo asked rather quietly.

"No, I can't."

"Well, how about some garlic toast?"

"Nope, makes me belch, also. All this room and no one can't get no food. It's a shame."

DiAngelo's mother suddenly slammed down her fork and yelled for Miss Maria.

"Clear the table! Clear it now!"

Miss Maria rapidly started to take up the plates, so Mrs. Sandra tried to hurry to eat.

I slowed her down by saying, "It's okay."

Miss Maria started to take her plate, so I said, "No, she is still eating."

"Take it!" Mrs. Faye demanded.

"No!" I responded.

I grabbed Miss Maria's hands away from Mrs. Sandra's plate.

"She is still eating!" I insisted.

It was a standoff. Miss Maria stood there looking at DiAngelo's mom, who was looking at me with a mean and hateful look.

"She has to eat to be strong. Uncle Marco says folks don't eat enough to stay strong and healthy," I said, trying to break the stalemate.

"Very well," Mrs. Faye said as she somewhat relaxed back into her chair.

Mrs. Sandra continued eating. It was quiet until she finished, and I was thinking of how I was ever going to win Mrs. Faye's liking. She was a tough one, but I was sure I could teach her the right ways. I was certain she just didn't have patience for her mom, and I could help her with Mrs. Sandra. I knew how to tend to folks; I could get her up and . . . well, like I did for Mr. Creek.

"Who wants presents?" DiAngelo announced.

"Dang, I don't know why you are so nice to me, Angelo. All I did was go to the doctor's."

"You were so good and made me proud of you," DiAngelo answered.

Miss Evett was quiet through most of supper, and I thought I had better pay her some attention.

So, I looked over at her and said, “Wonder Woman did a good job today finding my clothes and getting me a haircut, didn’t she?”

I could see DiAngelo and her holding hands under the table. I knew DiAngelo loved this young lady, and so did I.

“She sure did,” DiAngelo piped up. “She made us twins!”

He rubbed her back as he spoke, then got up to get my presents.

DiAngelo set the gifts in front of me, but set one aside from the rest. He handed me one after another. I really liked the chain for my wrist. It was nice and shiny. The next present was a ring.

“Dang,” I responded. “Angelo wants to marry me; he gave me a ring.”

Everyone started laughing.

“No,” DiAngelo answered, “I just want you to look nice when we find your kind of church.”

“That won’t be hard; just listen for the folks.”

“What, Rocco?” DiAngelo screwed up his face as he questioned me.

“They will be singing loud and shouting!” I responded.

“Dear Lord,” Mrs. Faye said from the end of the table.

“Amen,” I said.

“Don’t do that, Buckaroo. You promised.”

The last gift I opened slowly. It was the present DiAngelo had set to the side. It was heavy. After I got it open, I saw a brown case. It had birds on it and a hunting dog engraved in the top of it.

“Open it! Hurry!” DiAngelo pressed, nodding his head at the brown case.

I opened the case . . . there lay the prettiest gun I had ever seen.

"A gun . . . a real gun," was all I could say.

"A gun to protect yourself. I am going to teach you how to use it. I am going to make sure you are always safe when you go back home," DiAngelo explained.

"I am gonna shoot Todd in the leg when he comes after me and Mikie."

"No, no! It is for when real bad men come to get you . . . not just for when you are in a little fight. It's to save your life. Do you understand?"

"Yes, I think so."

Evett spoke up, "Maybe this wasn't such a good gift."

"No," I countered, "Angelo means if it's a little problem, not to use it; but if the bad man tries to get me, I can use it."

"Yes, exactly! That's it! That's what I mean. You did understand," DiAngelo said with pride in his voice.

DiAngelo was so happy that I understood what he meant. I could feel what he was saying and, therefore, knew what he meant. He was the first one since Mikie with whom I could do that. They would say one thing but mean another. I would have to think the way they did, or I would always be mixed up.

"Well, I hate to stop the party, but I need to get going. I have school tomorrow . . . my last year!" Evett announced as she stood up from the table.

"You get to graduate this year, Miss Evett?" I asked.

"Sure do."

"You will be needing a party of your own! Are you and Angelo getting married then?"

"Dreadful!" Mrs. Faye blurted.

Evett looked at Mrs. Faye as she said evenly, "I think it's a possibility if DiAngelo behaves himself."

"He will. I will make him behave!" I announced. "You are going to be welcome in this family and bring babies and love him forever. Maybe you can cook something besides red sauce when I come to visit."

With that, Mrs. Faye stood up and went to take Mrs. Sandra back upstairs, but Mrs. Sandra resisted.

"I will be up in a few minutes," Mrs. Sandra said.

"Walk your grandmother up when she is ready," Mrs. Faye instructed DiAngelo before she turned and walked out of the room.

I yelled after Evett as she walked toward the front door, "Thanks for shopping for me and coming to my party!"

I ran after her.

Breathlessly I added, "I think I need one more thing if you don't mind taking me to another store after school tomorrow."

"I can take you," DiAngelo answered.

"But then we won't get to see Evett tomorrow," I countered.

"Oh, I get it. You made a shopping partner so we can see her."

"Yes."

"Well, we're going to swim and lay out in the sun after school tomorrow, so we will see her."

"Okay."

With that DiAngelo finished walking Evett to the door and kissed her goodnight. This time it was a longer kiss, and then they walked together outside.

"Mrs. Sandra, did you get enough to eat?" I asked her as I returned to the dining room.

"I sure did. Marco has had a lot to do with you, hasn't he?" she surmised out loud.

"Yeah," I answered. "I love Uncle Marco."

I really did love Uncle Marco. He was kind and loving. He had the quickest, prettiest smile I had ever seen.

"Yes . . . salt of the earth . . . I love him, also," Mrs. Sandra said quietly. "Did you know him and Faye used to date?"

"No, never heard that. I sure can't see that. Uncle Marco has so much life to him, and Mrs. Faye doesn't like anyone."

"She loved Marco very much and has been acting hateful like this ever since she broke his heart years ago."

"How did she marry Ray? I understand he was the not-so-good son to Mrs. Liza."

"You're right, Rocco. He was a thug; and Marco was just the opposite. He was as good as Ray was bad. Marco and Faye were childhood sweethearts. They were to get married. Ray came home from being away," she continued. "When my Faye was coming home from being out with Marco, Ray got her and kissed her and had his way with her. I always taught her to save her body for her husband and that she had to marry the first man she was with. So, she broke Marco's heart and married Ray. Nine months later, DiAngelo was born. Marco went away; and the next thing we heard, he was getting married to some girl in the south."

"That would have been Aunt Hadie, my mom's sister," I said thoughtfully.

"Yes."

"Where did this guy, Ray, go, Mrs. Sandra?"

"About nine years ago, him and Faye couldn't stand it anymore. The fighting was awful; and since we don't believe in divorce, he went away to see his mother and brother in

Kentucky. He stayed there for a few months and then went to Italy to run some of his father's businesses. We have not seen him since."

"Poor Mrs. Faye, poor Angelo, and poor Mrs. Liza. She hasn't seen him, either."

I heard the front door slam. DiAngelo came into the big dining room.

"Grandmother, are you ready to go upstairs?" he asked her.

"Yes. Rocco and I were just talking about the good ol' *bad* days."

"Mrs. Sandra," I started before she could leave for upstairs, "I have a surprise for you tomorrow."

"You're such a sweet boy . . . such a loving boy."

"Goodnight, Mrs. Sandra."

"Goodnight."

She grabbed one of Angelo's arms, and he led her away.

Chapter 6

DiAngelo and I went outside to the backyard. It was a long yard that stretched to the edge of the beach bordering the big lake. The border fence went right into the water.

"Rocco, can you keep a secret?" DiAngelo asked.

"Nope," I stated, teasingly. I laughed as I added, "Sure, I can."

He reached into his pocket and pulled out some cigarettes.

"You gonna smoke those stinky things?" I asked him.

"Yes."

"What's the secret you want me to keep?"

DiAngelo looked over at me and said, "Don't tell Mother and Evett that I smoke."

"I don't have to; they can smell you!"

There was a log on the beach. I sat down on it, and it almost flipped me over.

"What are you doing?" DiAngelo asked me.

"Sitting down. You want to?"

DiAngelo sat down on the log with me, and we just sat there and looked at the waves on the lake while the big, orange ball of a sun started going down.

"Michigan sure is pretty," I observed out loud. "All this water puts you to sleep."

"Damn it!"

"What, Angelo?" I asked, alarmed.

"I forgot your medicine the doctor told me to give you."

"What was it for, again?"

"To help you sleep."

"If you sleep in the other bed in my room, I think I might sleep, okay?"

"Well, Buckaroo, let's try the medicine *and* I will sleep in your room."

"Well, that way I can make sure you are okay, Angelo."

"You can make sure *I* am okay?"

"Yes."

"Okay, deal, Buckaroo."

"Angelo, what time is it?"

"Almost 6:30."

"Do you want to get Mr. Scott to take us to the dollar store so I can get Mrs. Sandra's surprise?" I inquired.

"Sure, but I will drive," DiAngelo answered.

"Damn."

"What? You don't like my driving?"

"No, you go too fast. You're gonna get us both to Heaven before our time."

"Aww, there is no Heaven."

"What do you mean there's no Heaven?" I asked incredulously. "That's where the Father is. That's where His Son, Jesus, is."

"No, they just say that so you will behave and be the way they want you to be."

I thought on that, but I didn't know what to say; I didn't know what to do.

I looked back at DiAngelo and said, "We better play Quiet Mouse on that till I can think."

I sat there a few minutes longer and suddenly said, "See that sky? See the water? See that tree over there?"

"Of course."

"Can you make them, Angelo?"

"No, I can't make any of them."

"That's what makes God bigger and better than any of us. He made all this and rested on Saturday," I said as I waved my arm over the expanse of the view. "My God can do something more than you; He is bigger than you."

"Where did God go when I was sick and didn't have my father here?"

"He was here; He was loving you through your mom. See, Angelo, that's what I mean: if we are good to folks and love them, no matter who or what they are, it is like God loving them through us."

"Do you love me, Rocco?"

"Yes . . . and Miss Evett, also!"

"Will you always love me and be my friend . . . even when I am bad?"

"I will always love you and be your friend and tell you when you are being bad. I will still love you . . . kinda like Mom: even though I get a streak of meanness in me, she is still my mom; and she keeps on loving me."

I stood to get up, but I couldn't: the brace had me weighed down.

"Angelo, help me up. Help me get up."

"Damn," DiAngelo responded. "You're gonna be just like Grandmother: always having to get you up and walk with you."

"What's that over there?" I asked as I pointed to a small building at the end of a dock out over the water.

"It's called a boathouse. We keep the ski boat in there and some other stuff." After a short pause, DiAngelo started again, "We better get going if we are gonna beat the store before closing time."

We were off to the store. DiAngelo was unusually quiet.

"Are you okay, Angelo?"

"Yes, why?"

"You are not talking."

"I am used to being by myself. Besides Evett, I stick to myself."

"Well, it's too quiet for me. Tell me what you were just thinking."

"I was thinking how much I love Evett, and it hurts when she is not here with me."

"But you have me here with you . . . till we can see her again tomorrow."

"I sure do, Buckaroo, and I love having a good friend like you."

In a short time, we pulled into the dollar store. I could slide out of the truck pretty easily; it was when my feet hit the ground that it would hurt my back.

"Ouch!" I exclaimed as pain shot from my back, up my neck, and to my head.

"What's wrong, Rocco?" DiAngelo questioned with a hint of alarm in his voice.

"I hit the ground too hard, but I am okay."

We went into the store, and the cashier greeted us with a "Good evening."

I motioned to DiAngelo, "This way, Angelo."

"How do you know?"

"These stores are all alike. Everything is in the same place at these stores, and they carry the same things."

"Buckaroo, you sure are a smart one!"

As we approached the back of the store, DiAngelo pressed, "Rocco, what are you doing here?"

"I'm cooking cheap." After spotting the cans of chicken and dumplings, I added, "I reckon I better get two cans of these. Angelo, grab two cans of that chicken in a can."

DiAngelo handed me two cans of tuna.

Just as I took them from him, I said, "Nope, these are tuna; we need the blue cans with the chicken on it."

"Rocco, can you read?" he quizzed me.

"Well, I know a chicken from a fish; I guess that's all I need to know. Mikie does all the reading for me."

I continued looking around.

"Now, we need some cream of chicken soup . . . two cans of that, also. Let's see . . ." I said as I looked over the cart to see if everything I needed was there. "Oh, cranberry sauce," I mentioned as I looked at DiAngelo for him to reach it for me.

The cranberry sauce was on the top shelf, so DiAngelo got it down for me and put it in the cart.

"We have to get that cranberry sauce cold one hour before supper. Remind me of that tomorrow," I instructed DiAngelo.

DiAngelo asked, "What are dumplings, anyway?"

"Goodness, you sure don't know a lot! Dumplings are biscuit dough dropped into beans or chicken and cooked. Mom makes 'em great. We have this when we are in a hurry."

"Rocco, you had to do the cooking at your house?"

"No, I would watch Mom from my counter and learn. Mom said, 'Watch; you might have to cook for yourself one day.'"

My face clouded at the memory of that counter.

"That damn counter," I simply stated.

"What are you saying, Rocco?"

"I hate that kitchen counter . . . even though it kept me safe and away from Pa. Mom was watching out for me."

"Anyway," DiAngelo said, "do you have all you need?"

"Look!" I exclaimed.

"What?" DiAngelo answered, matching the excitement in my voice.

"A box of cornbread mix!"

"Yeah, so?"

"We never had this at our store. I guess 'cause folks knew how to make it up real fast. Let's get some."

I placed two boxes into the cart.

"Angelo, you got any kick-in?"

"What is kick-in, Rocco?"

"Kick-in money to buy this stuff with me."

He never did answer; he just hugged me to his side real close, and then we were off with the two extra boxes of cornbread mix, as well.

We got home pretty fast, and I was glad. The day had been long, and it was past my 8:00 bedtime. We went straight upstairs and lay on the beds talking small talk. DiAngelo opened the big door on the dresser, and there was a tv.

"Dang, Angelo! This is for lazy folks: lying in the bed, watching the tv. We have one at Uncle Marco's, also, but it's in the living room."

DiAngelo went and got me a glass of water and gave me one pill, just like the doctor said. I took the pill, swallowed it, and drank every bit of the water. I lay and looked at the tv, but I was thinking about Mom and Mikie. With that window open, giving me fresh, warm, Michigan air, it didn't take me long to fall right to sleep.

*****

I woke up feeling kinda light-headed and sick to my stomach. I didn't hear or see DiAngelo anywhere. I wondered what today would bring and what I could see in Michigan. I thought of Mikie and Mom and wondered what they were having for breakfast. I am sure it was better than the one I was fixin' to have. I wondered if there was such a thing as red sauce on eggs; if not, I hope they didn't think of it.

"Buckaroo, are you going to wake up?"

"I *am* awake, Angelo."

"Well, everyone is downstairs waiting on you."

"Why? What time is it?"

"Eleven o'clock."

"Dang, Angelo, why did you let me sleep so long? Half the day is gone already."

"It's okay. You needed the rest. Now, get up, or I will throw you out of that bed."

"Don't! You will hurt my head, and I will have to go back to the hospital."

"Funny guy," DiAngelo remarked. "I will put a pillow on the floor and throw you on it!"

"Why are you so awake? *You're* the sleepyhead!"

"Rocco, remember you had that pill last night. It made you sleep 14 hours."

I got up and started to the shower. I felt off-balance, as if the floor was coming up to me. Just about that time, DiAngelo caught me and sat me back down on the bed.

"Buckaroo, are you okay?"

"Yeah. I need some water so I can wake up."

DiAngelo helped me to the bathroom and pulled the doors shut. I washed my face. It made me feel better. I turned on the water like DiAngelo showed me; but when I tried to get in, the water was burning hot. I jumped out really fast and turned it down before trying again.

When I finished and was drying off, DiAngelo knocked on the door.

"Don't forget your Superman brace," he reminded me.

"Okay, I won't."

I finished getting dressed and combed my hair. I thought about the last week and how it seemed to fly by. Where in life was I going? When was Mom going to come and get me? And then I thought how I would miss DiAngelo and Evett when I left here.

"Rocco, are you coming down? Are you okay?" DiAngelo spoke through the door.

"Yeah, hang on. I am coming right out."

As we walked together toward the stairs, I looked down. It was as if there were 100 of them.

"Rocco, hang onto the banister and my arm so you don't fall," DiAngelo offered.

We arrived at the dining room.

Mrs. Faye spoke up gruffly, "Stop carrying him and sit down."

"I'm not carrying him, Mother. I think he had too much medicine."

"Good morning, Mrs. Sandra," I said.

"Good morning, Rocco," Mrs. Sandra said cheerily. "Bring him here, DiAngelo. Let me check on him."

"He's fine, Mother," Mrs. Faye said brusquely. "Are we going to eat sometime today?"

DiAngelo walked me over to his grandmother. She felt my head and cheeks.

"He is hot and flashy," she spoke matter-of-factly. "I think you need to call for the doctor, DiAngelo."

"He is fine. He didn't eat his dinner last night, and then he took the medicine. He just has to get used to it," Mrs. Faye offered impatiently.

DiAngelo responded, "I think Grandmother is right; I am worried about him."

I looked at DiAngelo.

"Don't worry, Angelo. I am okay."

Mrs. Sandra tried to perk me up.

"I have a surprise for you, Rocco. I will be ordering our food; so, anything we want to eat, we can have."

I said, "No red sauce?"

"Not, if we don't want it."

"I have a surprise for you, too, Mrs. Sandra."

"That's what you told me last night," she responded with an expectant edge to her voice.

"I did? I don't remember that."

DiAngelo broke in, "Buckaroo, are you up to reading lessons today?"

"Sure, I am, Angelo!"

With disdain showing in her words, Mrs. Sandra sat up straighter in her chair and said, "Look what you and that doctor have done to him: he has lost his smile; he has lost his joy."

"No, the world didn't give it, and the world can't take my joy," I answered.

"Good boy," Mrs. Sandra said. "I ordered toast, some potatoes, and eggs."

"He doesn't like taters," DiAngelo said, looking smugly at Mrs. Sandra.

"I do, too, Angelo!"

"Well, you didn't want any yesterday, Rocco."

"That was yesterday; I like to put some change in my life every day."

DiAngelo smiled and winked at me.

Miss Maria came with the food, placed it on the table, and said, "Good morning, Mr. Rocco."

"Good morning, Miss Maria. I need to speak with you in a bit, okay?"

"Sure," Miss Maria responded. "Come find me in the kitchen when you finish eating."

Everyone started to eat; but the smell of the food made me nauseous, so I just sat there trying not to look at it.

"Rocco, eat your food," Mrs. Faye prompted.

"I can't, Mrs. Faye."

"Eat your food," she insisted again. "It will make you feel better."

"Yes, my mother should know all about tranquilizers and their side effects. She has taken her share of them." DiAngelo's voice dripped with sarcasm.

It was as if my head was moving involuntarily with my breathing . . . back and forth, back and forth.

"Could you wrap this up for me so I can eat it later?" Rocco inquired.

"Sure, we can," Mrs. Sandra quickly responded.

"If you're done, let's go to the study and get started making you the best reader in Kentucky," DiAngelo suggested.

Mrs. Faye threw out, "That won't be hard since most of them can't read or write."

"I go to school! I am in Mr. Ball's class. I am right up there with everyone else. I am not stupid, Mrs. Faye!"

"No, honey, you're not," Mrs. Sandra soothed. "You are as smart as you want to be."

"That's what Uncle Marco says."

"Uncle Marco . . . Uncle Marco . . . I am sick of hearing that!" Mrs. Faye spoke in a sing-song manner.

"Can we give her one of my pills?" I offered. "Maybe she will be nicer."

DiAngelo laughed and got up.

"Buckaroo, let's go read."

"Bye, Mrs. Sandra. I will see you soon after I read."

"Okay, boy."

DiAngelo and I went into the study. It had a big, red cherry desk, a couch, and a few upholstered chairs.

I looked up and said, pointing at a very large portrait on the wall, "How did you get that?"

"What?" DiAngelo answered.

"The picture of that man."

DiAngelo looked in the direction of where I was pointing and said, "That is my grandfather."

"No, it's not; he is my angel."

"What are you talking about, Rocco?"

"When I was in the hospital, I couldn't tell Mom anything. I was unconscious or something like that. He was in the room, and light was all around him. I couldn't open my eyes, but I could see him. He got closer and closer to me until I could see him. He touched my head and said, 'Go back.' Then the things that held my eyes closed were gone, and I could open them. I talked to Mom after that, and I was fine."

"Sometimes you scare me," DiAngelo said with a worried look on his face.

"No, really, this is my man; he is my angel . . . amen and amen."

"I am going to call Father and get to the bottom of all this. There's a lot he is not telling me all the way from Italy."

I said, "There's something wrong."

With concern in his voice, DiAngelo responded, "What?"

"There's something wrong at home . . . I can feel it. I can feel it in my soul."

"Buckaroo, it's the medicine. It's got you all confused."

Suddenly, the phone rang, and I heard someone coming toward us.

I said. "I hear death steps."

"Stop it, Rocco!"

Miss Maria came into the study.

"Mr. DiAngelo, phone call from Kentucky for you and Mr. Rocco. They want to talk to you first."

She handed the phone to DiAngelo, and he said, "Thank you, Miss Maria."

"Good morning. Yes. Yes, he is here with me," DiAngelo spoke into the phone. "Oh, I am sorry to hear that."

As DiAngelo talked, he stared at me as hard as I was staring at him.

"Yes, Ma'am. No, I will tell him right away. We will call you back in a minute. Goodbye."

"Hey, didn't they want to talk to me?" I protested.

"Rocco, let's sit down."

"Spit it out, Angelo! What's wrong?"

"Well, you know Mr. Creek and Uncle Marco were out looking for the bad man?"

"Yes."

"Well, Mr. Creek . . . he got sick from being out, and he has passed away."

"He went home and didn't even say goodbye? Shame on you, Mr. Creek."

"Rocco, I mean he died this morning."

"I know what you mean, Angelo. We gonna read now?"

"No, I want you to talk to me."

"About what?"

"Well, are you okay?"

"Sure, I am okay . . . a bit hungry now."

DiAngelo just sat there staring at me.

"Rocco, do you even know what death is?"

"Yup. It means Mr. Creek went back to the Father where he came from."

"Rocco, are you going to cry or not? Stop acting like you're all grown up."

"I will cry Friday when we are down there at the burial."

"How did you know that his services were Friday?" DiAngelo asked, puzzled.

"Three days pass from today. Mom didn't want to tell me, so she had you tell me. I have to go talk to Miss Maria about how to get supper ready for Mrs. Sandra and me this evening."

"Rocco, come here."

"What, Angelo? I got to speak to Miss Maria about supper."

DiAngelo put his arms around me and said, "Mr. Creek was your friend; it's okay to hurt."

"I can't."

"Why?"

"If I let it go, it will all come out, and we will have a mess. I have to keep going . . . do you understand, Angelo? I have to not let it get me."

"Okay, but we have to make a call back to your mom."

"I wish you could have met my friend. He loved me, and now he's gone."

We went to the kitchen, and Miss Maria looked up from her work.

"Mr. Rocco, what are we going to cook this evening?"

"We're gonna cook Mrs. Sandra some chicken and dumplings and some cornbread."

I pulled out all the cans and started opening them. Under my direction, Miss Maria mixed the canned chicken and dumplings with the cream of chicken soup. Then we added two cans of chicken so it would be nice and thick.

"Don't forget to put your cranberry sauce in there," DiAngelo prompted, nodding his head toward the thick mixture.

Everybody has jokes, it seems.

"It doesn't go in there . . . you eat it on the side," I corrected him.

Smiling, he said, "Oh, yeah, you told me to remind you to chill it. That's what you said." He laughed.

DiAngelo then looked at Miss Maria, "You better stick to Mother's menu for the rest of them. This will be for us."

"Oh, you got a smell of it, and now you want some?" she teased.

"Well, I want to try it since you worked so hard, slaving over the stove."

"Go ahead and make fun, but you don't get seconds," she

laughingly responded. "Now, to the cornbread. I have muffin pans we can use."

"No, no! We need an iron skillet. You got one of those?" I quickly inserted.

"Yes," Miss Maria said. "I make baked beans in it."

"I wonder where Mr. Creek's going-home party is gonna be," I stated.

"Party?"

"Yes, Angelo! It's a party to send him to Jesus. I hope it is at White Plains Church so you can meet the folks."

"I'm not going to a funeral," DiAngelo stated matter-of-factly.

"Yes, you are," I said adamantly. "I need you to protect me while I go and pay my respects to my friend . . . so the bad man won't get me."

"He wouldn't try to get you at a time like this. There will be too many people around."

"Are you going to take that chance with me?"

"No, Buckaroo. I will go with you; I will protect you."

"We will leave at night on Thursday and get there before the going-home party," I started planning out loud.

"Wait, Rocco. We will do it my way."

I looked over to him and said, "I hope your way don't get us killed."

*****

Miss Evett came the following day, and we went swimming and lay in the sun for the better part of it. It turned into a nice afternoon, although DiAngelo kept asking me if I was okay. It got on my nerves, and Evett kept hugging on me.

"You bring my man back safe, okay, Rocco?" she asked me.

"I will. We are gonna take DiAngelo's gun and my new gun; and if the bad man comes to get me, we are gonna shoot him. I am tired of this man . . . who I don't even know . . . ruining my life."

"I think dinner is ready. We should go and see," DiAngelo offered as the sun got low in the sky.

We got dressed, and back to the dining room we went. I sat next to my friend, Mrs. Sandra; and Evett sat next to DiAngelo. Mrs. Faye sat at her spot at the head of the table.

"Mrs. Sandra, are you ready for your surprise?"

"Yes!" she said with enthusiasm and a sparkle in her eye.

Miss Maria started serving the supper. The others were having ravioli. Then she returned to the kitchen and brought out our supper.

Mrs. Faye remarked, "Two meals served at one setting. I have never seen such a mess. He is lucky to be getting one meal under my roof!"

As Miss Maria set down our food, the smell of my mom's kitchen filled the big dining room; and everyone was looking at our plates and watched us about to dig in.

"Oh, my boy, this looks to be the best food I have had in a long time . . . and look here! We have some cornbread, also!"

"Yes, they sell it in boxes now," I answered.

Mrs. Sandra said, "I have a good recipe for cornbread that I haven't used in years. I would have made you some cornbread if I had known you wanted some."

"Well, I am sure that if the bad man doesn't get me Friday, there will be a next time. We will have you cook the cornbread next time. I am sure it will be better than this."

"Where are you going Friday?" Mrs. Sandra asked.

DiAngelo answered, "Rocco's friend in Kentucky died this morning. He and I are going to the going-home party."

"Dear Lord, my son is talking like him now. You mean the funeral?" Mrs. Faye wanted to know.

Mrs. Sandra looked at me and said, "Faye?"

"Yes, Mother."

"I want you to listen to me reeeaaaal good," she started as she drew out the word for emphasis. "I am your mother, and I have raised you with all my heart. I taught you to be a good woman, a kind woman. If I hear you talk down to this boy one more time, I am going to slap your face . . . do you understand me?"

Mrs. Sandra's eyes never left my face as she spoke to her daughter.

"Yes, Mother," Mrs. Faye contritely answered.

"Now, I am the eldest in this house. I will be treated as such. Do you understand me, DiAngelo?"

"Yes, Grandmother," he likewise quietly answered.

"As far as you talking like this boy, I pray that you get some of his and Marco's manners." After a short pause, Mrs. Sandra took her eyes off me and announced, "Now, let's eat before this food gets cold!"

"Mrs. Sandra, pass some of that cranberry sauce in front of you; and quit trying to eat it all," I playfully scolded her.

Everyone laughed. The ice was broken.

DiAngelo said, "I think I will have some of that, also, if Grandmother and Rocco will just share some of their supper."

"Me, too!" Evett joined in enthusiastically.

It made me feel good in my soul to see them eat some down-home food and all of them laughing and talking. I wanted good times and free times at supper . . . not like the ones at home.

“I made enough for your lunch tomorrow, Mrs. Sandra, in case you want some leftovers . . . and if it’s okay with Mrs. Faye,” I said while looking at Mrs. Faye from the corner of my eye.

“Yes, it is fine with me; and I might try a bowl of it, as well,” she favorably responded.

Slowly, I was warming Mrs. Faye’s heart . . . or she was afraid her mom might really slap her. One or the other, she was stepping off her high horse.

“I am not taking that medicine tonight, Angelo,” I announced to him later.

“Well, maybe half,” he said, trying a compromise.

“I have to be thinking clear for our trip, so maybe smaller than half,” I suggested.

“I will be praying for you both for a safe return,” Mrs. Sandra offered.

“Thank you, Mrs. Sandra, but if they get the bad man, I might not be coming back.”

“You will be back; my family needs you. You are an angel sent from Heaven to fix my family.”

“That’s what Mrs. Liza says. She says me and Mikie will be the ones to keep her family together . . . and now Angelo!” I enthusiastically added.

“Don’t put me in that mess,” DiAngelo protested. “This is a dysfunctional family. Evett and I are going to get married and take cover.”

“You and Evett are my family now. Mrs. Sandra and Mrs. Faye are even my family, and we will all love one another and take care of each other. We will step on our past hurts. It will make us taller for the future. We will be tall, strong men who take care of our folks. You will see: if we put our two families together and stick together, no one can ever hurt us. We won't give the devil a chance to come in between us. We will be as strong as ever."

Mrs. Sandra piped up, "Love has divided us, but a greater love is going to bring us back together."

"I am still trying to find out how he knew someone died this morning even before the phone call came in," DiAngelo brought up.

"Did you hear them, boy?" Mrs. Sandra quizzed.

I sat and was quiet because I didn't want to scare DiAngelo with any more talk.

He answered Mrs. Sandra, "Rocco heard death steps. Then we got the call. It scared me."

"I heard then, too," Mrs. Sandra announced.

"Great! Now, there are two of them!" DiAngelo remarked.

Evett elbowed his side to hush him up.

"I am going to tell my mom I am not coming," I declared.

"Why is that, Buckaroo?" DiAngelo quizzed with a hint of alarm in his voice.

"I don't want anyone knowing that I am coming."

"Oh, so you want to surprise them?"

"No, I want the bad man to know that I was there right under his nose, and he didn't get me. I will take care of my folks down home, and we will be home Saturday morning if all goes well."

Chapter 7

Wednesday morning came bright and early.

I was getting ready for breakfast when DiAngelo came up the stairs and asked, "Are you ready?"

"Ready for what?"

"We are going to see some country before we go to Kentucky . . . like a trip—just you and me."

"We aren't supposed to leave until tomorrow night."

"We can do anything we want. I am DiAngelo, and you are Buckaroo."

"Where are we gonna lay our head down tonight and tomorrow night?" I wondered out loud.

"Don't worry about it; I got it all taken care of."

"Let's see . . . I only have $17 left for our gas home. Here," I said as I held out the bills toward DiAngelo.

DiAngelo took the money and some change I offered, laid it on the headboard of my bed and said, "I have all we need."

"Angelo, I sure thank God for you. Is Mr. Scott ready for our trip?"

"Nope. I don't want to take the car. I am going to drive . . . just you and me."

I took a step closer to DiAngelo.

"I have my gun in my turtle book bag," I whispered.

He whispered back, "I have mine in my bag, also." He gave me a wink.

We finished packing, went down the stairs, and headed out the front door.

"Just a minute, boy," Mrs. Sandra called out.

"Mrs. Sandra, I was hoping to see you before I left. I wanted to give you a hug and say that I really like you."

"Boy, you will be back; I know it, and I know it in my heart."

I gave my sweet Mrs. Sandra a goodbye hug and smiled at Mrs. Faye.

"We will be back," I announced.

"Rocco?" Mrs. Faye said.

"Yes, Mrs. Faye?"

"I want you to wear this; it will keep you safe."

She handed me a necklace like Mrs. Liza had . . . with all the beads on it and a cross. She kissed my head and gave her own son a kiss on his cheek. We were off.

After giving DiAngelo the forty questions on whether he remembered this or that, it got quiet in the truck for a bit.

DiAngelo finally said, "Are you sleeping over there?"

"Nope, I am thinking."

"What are you thinking about?"

"I am thinking maybe I don't want to go, Angelo."

"Why not, Rocco?"

"What if he gets me? I mean, what if he really gets me and kills me this time? Maybe this is not so good of an idea. I'm sure Mr. Creek won't be mad if I miss his going-home party. Maybe we can just send flowers; maybe Mom already sent them for me."

The words tumbled out of my mouth.

"Calm down, Buckaroo. I promise with all my heart that the bad man is not going to get you."

"I'm gonna hold you to that. If you let him get me, I am never going to talk to you again."

DiAngelo said something that made me know it was going to be all right: "Deal, Buckaroo?"

"Deal," I said.

"Okay, enough of this. We have two days of fun before we get there."

"Where are we going?" I quizzed.

"Up here a few more miles. You will see."

Finally, DiAngelo pulled into a big parking lot filled with a lot of cars . . . red ones and others of every color.

"Get ready. We are at Cedar Point," DiAngelo announced.

We walked through a big gate, and DiAngelo gave them some money to let us in. As we walked in, I could see it was a fair—or a carnival—the biggest one I had ever seen. There were rides, food, and lots and lots of folks. They were all smiling and having fun. We waited in a line; and when it came to our turn, we got in a small car and were pulled way high. Then, like a car out of control, it went down rails as fast as lightning and took us into a pool of water. Then the car came to a stop, and we got off. What fun it was! We were soaking wet, but the sun dried us off really fast.

"Are you hungry?" DiAngelo prompted.

"No, I think I don't feel so good."

"Damn it!"

"What, Angelo?"

"I forgot about your head and back; I just wanted you to have some fun. I messed up everything."

"Fun? Are you kidding? This is the best time I ever had,

and I am going to get another turn on that one," I answered, nodding toward the wet car ride.

"Are you sure?" DiAngelo pressed.

I really wasn't sure, but I didn't want to hurt his feelings.

"We should have brought Evett; she would be crazy about these rides, also," I suggested.

"Nope. No Evett, no Mr. Scott, not Mother, or anyone . . . just you and me."

"You got your cigarettes wet. Now, what are you going to do?" I laughingly pointed out to DiAngelo.

"I am going to buy some more and blow that stinky smoke on you," he prodded.

"Better not, Angelo!"

"Hey, want some cotton candy?" inquired DiAngelo, changing the subject.

"I had that before. I want one of those heated pretzels. Do you think they have those here?" I wanted to know.

"Yes, over there next to the hot dogs."

"Wait! I want a hot dog, instead."

"Let's get both of them," he offered.

"We better not get greedy, Angelo."

"We better be greedy; this is our time. We can do whatever we want."

"We can?"

"Yes."

"Then, give me one of those cigarettes; I want to smoke."

"Well, maybe not *anything* we want. What if your mom smells it on you?"

"I am gonna shower before two days are up! I ain't no stinky."

DiAngelo laughed.

"No, Buckaroo, no cigarettes for you."

So, we got our hot dogs and pretzels, sat at a table in the sun, and ate.

"Reckon we should put on some shorts; it's getting hot," I suggested.

"No."

"Why not, Angelo?"

"I can't wear shorts; I have a red mark on my leg . . . a birthmark."

"I've got a whole headful of marks. You think I am gonna let that stop me from anything? Why, hell, no! I think you are a baby, Angelo."

"No, I'm not."

"Yes, you are."

"No, I'm not," he said, more emphatically than the first time. "I just don't want anyone to see it."

"Baby," I taunted. "Letting something keep you from something you want."

We went on a few more rides. As dusk approached, we left the big park. On the way, DiAngelo smoked a cigarette. He handed it to me.

"Here, take just one draw; and I hope it makes you sick."

It didn't make me sick, but I coughed up a lung when it went down.

"It ain't so bad," I boldly remarked.

I took another puff. I had been watching him and how he would puff and blow it out.

"Okay, that's enough," he said.

I smiled at him and said, "Selfish."

I refused to give him back the cigarette and continued smoking it.

A lady walked past us and remarked, "Boys, throw that cigarette down."

"No, Ma'am. I am smoking like my friend. It's *our* time; we can do anything we want."

"Okay, Rocco, throw it down; we have to get in the truck."

We both had on our jeans and white t-shirts . . . and smoking cigarettes. It must have really been a sight for folks looking at us. I think that day built a bond between him and me. I think he knew it would. I think DiAngelo Pettrachini knew what he was doing that day. I loved my new friend as much as I loved Mikie and Mom.

"Where are we going now?" I asked as we climbed back into the truck.

"Back on the road a little way. I want to show you something."

We arrived at a town called Cincinnati and then over a way to Louisville.

"Damn, we're in Kentucky already! You sure drive fast," I observed out loud.

"You better not say those words while we are down here," DiAngelo cautioned me.

We pulled into a nice hotel. We went in, and DiAngelo told the man behind a counter that we needed a room with one bed and "just the floor for him" as he nodded in my direction.

"I ain't no dog! I am not sleeping on the floor!"

DiAngelo laughed as he said to the man, "Well, then give us two beds since he is a baby."

"No," I countered. "Give us one bed, and *he* can sleep on the floor."

The man seemed to enjoy our bantering.

"Why don't you *both* sleep on the floor?" the man suggested. "Cheaper that way."

"Okay, deal," DiAngelo responded, smiling and looking at me.

"No, I am not sleeping on the floor! My head will hurt."

"Oh, yeah, that's right," he conceded. "We'll need two beds, then."

"What happened to your head, little guy?" the man inquired.

"He hit me," I answered as I pointed at DiAngelo.

The man looked at Angelo suddenly and wondered if the teasing had now become real.

"No, I didn't!" DiAngelo insisted.

The man looked at me; and I smiled and shook my head, letting him know I was just teasing.

"Room 110, and I better not hear this guy screaming from the hits," he said, looking at DiAngelo with a smile.

"I think we better give you at least a half pill so you can sleep well tonight. Tomorrow is a big day."

"Nope. I have to think clear."

DiAngelo went into the bathroom and came out in his boxer shorts.

"See, isn't it ugly?" DiAngelo asked, pointing at the red birthmark on his calf.

"Is that all there is? A little, red spot and you're a baby over that? Angelo, don't you know anything? A person is to be looked at for their heart—what kind of person they are—not by what they have or what they look like. Be proud of your leg. It was something that didn't kill you. Let it make you stronger."

I thought he was just being funny when he said, "Amen, Brother Buckaroo."

The next day we got up, showered, and were on the road by 10 a.m.

"Where are we going next?" I questioned.

"To win some money; we are going horse racing."

When we arrived, DiAngelo told me to pick a horse. From the book, I picked a horse named My Darling. DiAngelo was on his way to put one last bet at the window.

"Bet $10 on the damn thing!" I blurted out.

I heard someone say that at a race before, so I felt smart repeating it. DiAngelo turned and looked at me with his brow crinkled up.

When DiAngelo returned to where we were sitting, he gave me a ticket and said, "Good luck!"

"What number is my horse?" I asked.

"Your horse is seven."

"Lucky seven, come on," I yelled.

The race started, and my horse was near the middle of the pack.

I shouted, "Geddy-up, My Darling!"

Out of nowhere, My Darling took to running and won the race before any of them even got near the finish line.

When I turned and looked at DiAngelo, his face was strange as he quietly told me, "You won."

"I know!" I loudly responded. "Now, go get my damn money!"

When DiAngelo returned, he had a fistful of money.

I said, "They gave us too much money; they were only supposed to give us our $10 back, right?"

"You won almost $700, Buckaroo! If I had known how you betted, I would have let you pick them all."

"Too late," I answered. "Everyone is leaving."

He put my money in my new wallet that he had given me before we left home and said, "Now, you have $717 with the money you have at home."

I thought about the words, "at home." It sure did seem like a home . . . a home with no loud arguing and no hitting. I have to say, I did like eating at the table with the other folks; I didn't miss eating at my counter.

*****

"Let's go ahead and go further down the road. We can stay at a hotel in a nearby town," suggested DiAngelo.

"Well, it is only 3 o'clock; if we get home, we can go to Uncle Marco's by five and I can see my mom and Mikie. Deal?"

"Deal, but I might drop you off and go back into town, get a hotel room, and just go with you in the morning."

"No, Angelo. You promised to stay with me."

"Well, your Uncle Marco might not have enough room for me."

"We always have enough room. You are my friend. I will sleep with Mikie and his stinky feet; you can have his bed. You can't be far from me . . . no more than a few minutes without me seeing you," I whined.

"You are really scared, aren't you?"

"He snuck right up on me without Pa or me even knowing. He is a tricky man," I tried to explain.

I looked out the window and saw Kentucky for the first time during the daytime. I had never seen much of Kentucky except our hometown. I thought how I might like the water, trees, and that warm wind in Michigan better.

"Angelo, Michigan is prettier than Kentucky, right?"

"Well, some people like different things," he responded.

"I like living with you."

DiAngelo turned to look at me.

"Really, Rocco? Do you?"

"Yes, I do. If I had a wish, I would wish Mikie, you, and me could live in the same town in Michigan."

"I'm glad you said that."

"Angelo, you don't like Kentucky?"

"I am mad at Kentucky right now for all the things that happened to you here."

"I have had some good times here," I countered, "mainly when Mom and me would go to Aunt Hadie's."

"I can see why you always liked to get out of that house and go to Hadie's."

"Hey, look! We're in Madisonville. I went there with Aunt Hadie and Uncle Marco. Next town is Earlington, and then Nortonville, and then to Mikie's! Yaaaayyyy!" I screamed.

"You sure love my cousin."

"Yes, we are like twins; and now with you, we are like triplets."

"Boy, you are silly. I am older than you and Mikie."

"So. You are my best friend, also. Now, I have two best friends; and we will always be good to one another and be family."

We continued to drive.

"Hey, Angelo, stop there at the Ideal Mart, and we will get some more cigarettes."

"You're not smoking any more cigarettes; do you hear me?" DiAngelo said somewhat gruffly.

"Yes, sir, Mr. Angelo; but we can get one of those frozen sodas. I will pay. Remember, I got $700."

"All right, then," DiAngelo said as he pulled in.

I looked around to make sure Pa wasn't anywhere around.

"Get your gun, Angelo."

"We don't need it here, Rocco."

"Yes, we do."

"Hey, look! There's Brother Wallace," I said as I pointed in his direction. "Hi, Brother Wallace!"

"Boy, what are you doing here?"

"I come for Mr. Creek's going-home party. Is it going to be at your church?"

"Yes, but I don't think it is wise for you to come back so soon."

"I wouldn't miss Mr. Creek's party for nothing."

"You knew him better than anyone the folks say."

"Yes," I answered, "he was my friend. His land connects to Pa's land, and every time I would go over to the line, he would bring me some candy. Every morning he would come to the road and say 'Hi' to me before school."

"Well," Brother Wallace continued, "I might be calling on you tomorrow to say some things about him since I didn't know him and he didn't go to church anywhere."

Brother Wallace then looked over to DiAngelo and said, "Do *not* let this boy out of your sight."

"Excuse me, Brother Wallace. Can I speak to you for a few minutes?" DiAngelo questioned.

"Sure, you can. Rocco, go get us one of those frozen cokes, but come right back."

"Ok," I responded.

"And some candy!" DiAngelo added.

"See, that's what I mean," Brother Wallace said, pointing

at Rocco's back as he disappeared into the mart. "You let him go by himself. It is not safe for him to be here."

"Who is trying to hurt him? Who could hurt such a good and loving soul? He's only a kid," DiAngelo replied.

"Listen, I will tell you this much: Rocco is one of us. I have taught that boy since he was big enough to sit. He learned well the ways. More than half the town has been out looking for the man who hurt him. We will take care of this our way."

DiAngelo said, "An eye for an eye and a tooth for a tooth?"

"We appreciate you taking care of him for a while until they get the job done. Once again," Brother Wallace emphasized, "don't let him out of your sight."

"Do you really think he is at this much risk?"

"Yes, and when you get to Marco's house, pull your truck behind the house and take the plates off the truck so he will not see Michigan plates. This is a small place, and folks talk. Don't let anyone see him until tomorrow; then, take him to the church and get right back out of town with him."

"You love him, also, don't you?"

"We all love that boy. He has taught us how to love and be loved. We have learned more from him than ten preachers could have taught us. In his childlike ways, he taught us how to be good folks."

Rocco emerged from the mart and approached DiAngelo and Brother Wallace.

"Get in the truck, Rocco," DiAngelo instructed.

"Okay, Boss."

I rolled down the window and yelled, "Brother Wallace, I will see you tomorrow."

"Be a good boy. Listen to this man, and do what he says."

"I will, Brother Wallace."

DiAngelo got in the truck and rummaged around in his bag. He pulled out his gun and lay it on the seat next to him.

"Get on the floor, Rocco."

"No, I'm not a dog!"

"Get on the floor so the bad man won't see you."

"Oh, okay," I responded, deciding that was a good enough reason to get on the floor.

It was only about another seven miles to the grill. When we pulled in, DiAngelo parked behind the garage.

"Stay here," he instructed me.

DiAngelo went to the back of the truck and removed the Michigan plates. He motioned for me to get out, and we went on into the house.

"Mikie! Mikie!" I called out.

I went to his room, but he wasn't there. DiAngelo wouldn't let me go into the grill.

"I'm sure Hadie is really busy; we don't want to interrupt her," he gave as an excuse.

"My mom's out there, and I want to see her," I demanded.

Just then, DiAngelo grabbed me by the arm and gruffly walked me to the half-open door between the house and the grill. I stood behind the door and looked into the grill from the space next to the door's hinges. I saw my mom and Aunt Hadie at the counter. Mom was wiping it down and picking up some dishes and putting them in a tub. There was Mikie at a table doing his homework and tapping his pencil as he always did.

"Damn! That gets on my nerves when he does that," I whispered, without really knowing why I was whispering.

DiAngelo coughed, and Mom turned and saw him. She stared at him for a moment. He motioned for her to come.

Mom started crying before she even got to the door. Once she got into the house, DiAngelo shut the door so no one could see us. Mom grabbed me in her arms and hugged me so hard I thought I was gonna scream from the pain. When she backed off, she saw my head without the bandages and cried even harder.

DiAngelo tapped my mom on her back and motioned with his head for us to go deeper into the house away from the door. He carried his gun at all times now, it seemed. The three of us went into the living room.

Mom kept her voice to a whisper, "Boy, you *did* come. I am so glad to see you. Mom missed you so bad, I couldn't hardly breathe."

"I know, Mom. Me, also."

I could tell DiAngelo was nervous. He kept looking out the windows from the living room door.

He asked, "Where's Marco?"

"He is in the garage," Mom answered. "You can go get him."

"No," DiAngelo responded, "*you* go so I can watch over him."

Mom stood up, kissed my head, and said, "DiAngelo, thanks for taking such good care of my Rocco."

Then off she went to find Uncle Marco. Mom soon returned with him. He was red in the face.

"What are you doing here?" he demanded of DiAngelo.

"He insisted on coming."

"I trusted you to take care of him, and you have brought him right back to the place where he got hurt."

"I didn't think he was in that much danger."

"That's right, DiAngelo. You didn't think! Now, get back

in that truck; and go back where you came from until we can make it safe for him."

"No!" I suddenly demanded. "I am staying until tomorrow!"

"Dean, go tell Hadie I said to close the grill up; and don't say anything more. She will know what I mean. Don't tell anyone the boy is here . . . not even Mikie . . . *especially* Mikie! DiAngelo, pull the truck into the garage," Marco barked the orders.

"I took off the plates, Uncle Marco."

"Well, Mr. Smarty, no one in this part of the country has a big city truck like that. It is a flashing sign that says, 'The boy is back in town; come and kill him.'"

DiAngelo ran out of the house.

Mrs. Liza walked by just then and looked into the living room. When she saw me, she hurriedly came to me and kissed my face and head and hugged on me.

Marco hushed her and said, "My mother says she missed you and prayed every day for you."

With that, I pulled out the necklace that Mrs. Faye had given me and showed it to her.

Mrs. Liza was on one side of me, and Mom was on the other; I felt safe. No one could ever hurt me again.

I looked as DiAngelo came back in the house after moving his truck. He looked at his grandmother.

"Come here, Angelo," I said to him.

He walked up to me.

"Come down here to my level. Don't stand over her; she doesn't like that."

DiAngelo bent down on his knees. I looked up at Uncle Marco.

"Uncle Marco, please tell Mrs. Liza this is my friend, Angelo. He can't speak Italian, either, but he has been good to me and watched over me while I was away."

Uncle Marco began translating what I had said, but she kept her eyes riveted on DiAngelo.

"Mrs. Liza," I continued, "he is a good man. He takes care of his mother and grandmother, Mrs. Sandra. You can be proud of him."

Mrs. Liza then spoke something to Uncle Marco. Uncle Marco translated her words that were for DiAngelo.

"She says you look like her Ray and her husband, your grandfather."

With that, she pulled DiAngelo close as she hugged and patted him on his back.

"Uncle Marco," I started, "tell Mrs. Liza I seen a picture of her husband in the big house in Michigan, and he was the same man I saw in the light who made me better and told me to go back to Mom."

As Uncle Marco translated what I had said, Mrs. Liza started crying. She then said a few words through her tears.

"She wants to thank you," Uncle Marco said, looking at me, "for telling her. She has been praying for years that he is in the right place, and now her heart is at peace."

Mom sat there, taking it all in without saying a word. Aunt Hadie came in and had the biggest smile on her face when she saw me.

"Boy, give your Aunt Hadie a hug!"

I got up and went to her.

As I hugged her, she stroked my face and said, "Look, Dean. He's home . . . our boy is home!" She turned to her husband, "Marco, the grill is closed, like you said. Mikie is getting washed up, and he will be in here in a few minutes."

When Mikie came into the room, he just stood there, looking at me . . . not talking, just looking. He started crying, and I went to my friend. I didn't care who was there; I hugged him for all I was worth. We cried and hugged for a long time, and the folks just let us talk without any interruptions.

Chapter 8

After a while, I said, "Angelo, come here. This is Mikie, my other best friend. I know you two are cousins, but I want you to know each other . . . *really* know each other like I know you both."

"Buckaroo has told me so much about you . . . so much I didn't know."

Mikie looked at me and said, "Why does he call you Buckaroo?"

"It's my nickname," I explained.

In his own way, he was sizing up DiAngelo, trying to see if he wanted to like him or not.

"Mikie is a part of our family. Remember what Mrs. Liza said . . . that we are to take care of the folks—you and I."

With that, Mikie shook DiAngelo's hand.

Without skipping a beat and looking at the gun DiAngelo had tucked in his belt, Mikie added, "And where did you get that gun?"

"I have lots of them at home in Michigan."

"I got one, too, Mikie! It's in my bag," I blurted.

"So," Mikie responded, trying to sound important, "I got my knife. If *he* comes around, I will stab him in the head!"

"Show Angelo your knife, Mikie," I prompted.

He reached in his pocket, and it opened before he got it all the way out.

"Dang, Mikie! That was good!" I commended him.

"I learnt it and kept trying until I got it right; but, look . . . I cut my fingers a few times." After putting his knife back away, Mikie looked at me.

"Rocco, it's sad about Mr. Creek; he was a good man like you said. He hung out with us after they took you away in that long car," he said as he looked accusingly at DiAngelo.

"He kept me safe from the bad man; he was one of us, Mikie," I explained.

It was getting dark outside, and they pulled the shades so no one could see us inside. Aunt Hadie and Mom returned to the grill to fix supper. Me, Mikie, and DiAngelo were on the couch, while Uncle Marco walked the floors. Mrs. Liza sat in her chair; she had the biggest smile, seeing the three of us getting along so well.

Mom came in and kissed me again and again. Uncle Marco told her that maybe she should call that lawyer and get some "stuff" taken care of tonight after supper and "get those papers signed."

DiAngelo quizzed, "What papers?"

Uncle Marco cut him off, "None of your business."

"If it concerns him," DiAngelo started, nodding toward me, "it *is* my business."

"Remember, you only have the boy until it is safe for his return. This is family business," Uncle Marco stated rather tersely.

I had never seen Uncle Marco rude a day of his life. I couldn't understand his attitude toward DiAngelo.

"Uncle Marco," I started, "Angelo is family. He is good to me, watches over me, and takes me to the doctor's. Please don't be rude to him. Do it for me, please."

"Well, what I meant is that it is private," Uncle Marco said much kinder.

Supper was up, so we all went to the table. They pulled a few of the little grill tables together to make one, big table. We had all kinds of food, some with red sauce and some without. Mom had made me her special cornbread, sat it in front of me, and smiled as she went on placing food on the tables. She was singing, "My baby's home; my baby's home."

Mikie whispered, "This is the first time since you left that she has been happy. She has been moping and crying quiet; and every time I say your name, she cries. Mom told me not to say 'Rocco' too much, but she is glad you're home now. We all are," he added as he squinted his eyes at me.

Mom sat next to me, and Mikie sat on the other side. I wondered where DiAngelo was going to sit. I couldn't leave him by himself.

"Damn!" I said to myself as I tried to figure out the seating puzzle.

"Rocco, what did you just say?"

My mom was staring at me incredulously with one raised eyebrow.

Uncle Marco said, "Figures."

And everyone's head turned toward DiAngelo.

"He didn't teach it to me!" I cried out. "The lady in the kitchen who does the cooking said it when she burnt her hand!"

I swallowed hard, wondering if they would believe that.

After supper, someone knocked on the door. I had never seen so many folks jump up all at once. One had a rifle; one had a pistol; and Mikie had his knife out . . . all ready for my defense. Uncle Marco went to the door.

"Who is it?" he shouted through the door.

DiAngelo was on the other side of the door from Uncle Marco with his pistol ready to shoot.

"Who is it?" Uncle Marco shouted again, louder.

"Mr. Pettrachini, it is Darryl . . . Darryl Hamson."

Uncle Marco relaxed and opened the door as DiAngelo quickly put away his gun and Mikie snapped his knife shut and slid it back into his pocket.

"Hi, Mr. Hamson," Uncle Marco said in a much friendlier tone. "Come on in," he added as he opened the door wide.

Mr. Hamson stepped inside the door, and everyone let out a combined sigh of relief.

Uncle Marco led Mr. Hamson to the little office where he took care of the bills and stuff like that. Then he came back and got Mom and me.

I said, "Angelo, come on."

DiAngelo had already sat back down and continued sitting, looking at Uncle Marco questioningly.

"Very well," Uncle Marco conceded. "Come on," he said to DiAngelo.

As we all went into the office, Mr. Hamson spoke, "Well, is this Rocco?"

My mom said, "Yes, this is my son."

"I just need you to sign a few papers; then we will be done, and I will be on my way," Mr. Hamson offered. Looking at me, he said, "You came all the way back from Michigan for Mr. Creek's funeral?"

"Yes, sir," I answered politely.

"Well, he seems to have taken quite a liking to you. He wanted you to have his house and his land."

"Who . . . me?" I asked.

"Yes, and there are some moneys that will be transferred to your account in Michigan."

"Dang! I won $700 today, and now Mr. Creek left me some more!" I exclaimed.

"Where did you get $700 from?" quizzed Uncle Marco.

"We went to the horse races . . . Angelo and me."

Uncle Marco glared at DiAngelo.

"He saw the track and wanted to go," DiAngelo offered lamely.

"I bet he did," Uncle Marco answered.

"Anyway," Mr. Hamson interrupted, "the house and the land are worth a hefty amount. I assume you want to sell it. I have an offer for it already."

"I can't sell it!" I piped up. "Mr. Creek isn't gone even for a week. How do you think that would make him feel?"

"Who wants to buy it?" Uncle Marco curiously inquired.

"Coal's Chapel Mining," Mr. Hamson responded.

"I suppose they want to mine it, then," Uncle Marco responded.

"A mining company tearing up Mr. Creek's land and tearing down his house?" I objected. "No way! I ain't gonna have it! Mom, tell him 'No'!"

Mom simply stated, "My son doesn't want to sell right now. We might have to live there one day."

I perked up.

"Honest, Mom? Do you want to live there, Mom?" I asked excitedly. "You and me will live in Mr. Creek's house, and Pa can live in his own house." After a short pause, I suddenly added, "Where is Pa anyway? I thought he would have been here, also, to see me."

"Well, you know he never comes down here. It's always me and you who come to see Hadie," Mom offered.

"He's probably running around in that car of his, wasting gas," I added.

Mom answered, "He might be."

DiAngelo spoke up, "Could I interrupt?"

"Sure, Angelo, you can speak."

"Well, it seems this could be a lifetime change for Rocco," DiAngelo started. "I mean, if he sells, he could have the money to do with what he wanted. I am not sure what that would be, but at least he would have a future and could go to school and things like that."

Mom responded, "Yes, you are right, DiAngelo." She looked at me. "You can have what I could not give you: an education and not have to work those mines and hurt yourself; you could have an easier life."

"But it's Mr. Creek's house," I complained. "I don't know; I don't feel right in my soul."

"I have a letter from Mr. Creek to you," Mr. Hamson broke in. "He wrote it in the hospital and made me promise to give it to you."

"Ha! I knew he wouldn't leave without saying goodbye. I take it back."

"Take back what, boy?" asked Mr. Hamson.

"I shamed him for not saying goodbye when the call came that he had passed."

Uncle Marco handed me the letter. I, in turn, handed the letter to DiAngelo.

"Can you read it for me?"

DiAngelo began,

"Dear Boy,

I wanted to tell you a few things before I leave this old world. I wanted to thank you for being my friend and always putting up with me. In my last years you have made me a happy man, giving me a reason for getting up each morning to see that you were okay. I always enjoyed seeing you go to school, walking along with your ma. I wanted to thank you for feeding me when I was hungry and couldn't tend to myself."

"Stop!" I interrupted DiAngelo. "Don't say no more; I don't want to hear any more."

I cried loudly into DiAngelo's side.

"Mr. Creek is really gone; I won't see him no more," I said as I sniffled hard.

Mom grabbed me to herself.

"Boy, we will see Mr. Creek again . . . when we get to Heaven."

As she continued to hold me, she told DiAngelo to finish the letter.

DiAngelo picked up where he left off,

"All I have to give to you is this house and land that my pa left to me and a little pocket change. I wish you well and want to thank you for sitting on the back porch with me. It made me feel like I really had a family. Boy, I want you to sell this place and go away. Your Uncle Marco and me couldn't get our hands on the bad man. I want you to be safe. Sell it;

start over somewhere else, and take care of your mom. Be good, and I will see you on the other side.

Love,
Mr. Creek"

By this time, I was a sobbing, heartbroken child who had just lost his friend.

"If I sell this house, I won't have a place when they get the bad man. I want to keep it," I tried to explain.

"Well," Mr. Hamson started, "you could lease the land to the mining company. They are willing to lease that land if you don't want to sell it and pay you royalties from the coal they get. You would probably make more money that way, anyhow."

DiAngelo piped up, "If he leased the land, would he be able to still keep the house?"

"Yes," the lawyer answered.

"And you'd make them keep their trucks off the grass?" I added. "Mr. Creek always had nice grass, didn't he, Mom?"

"He sure did, boy," she answered. Turning to Mr. Hamson, she asked, "How much land is there?"

"Approximately 250 acres."

"Okay," Mom responded. After thinking a minute, she resumed, "Here's what we will do: you run the trucks along the line where my husband's land and Mr. Creek's land meet. Leave ten of those acres around the house untouched."

Before she could say more, I interrupted, "But, Mom, the line between Pa's land and Mr. Creek's land runs right in front of Pa's front door. That will drive him crazy . . . his front yard ain't big enough to whip a cat!"

Mom said, "I know," as she smiled knowingly.

Mr. Hamson continued with his explanation, "They are willing to pay $4 a ton on everything they pull out of there. That's a lot of money!"

"How many tons in a truckload, Uncle Marco?" I asked.

"About 40."

"If they will settle for $6 a ton, they can have the coal."

I don't know why I was being greedy or why I even said that; it just kind of came out. However, then I remembered DiAngelo telling me on the way down to Kentucky that this was our trip, so we could be greedy.

Mr. Hamson used Uncle Marco's phone to call someone. He talked quietly in the corner of the room, so we kept talking until he hung up and returned to us.

"Six dollars a ton, it is. You are quite the little businessman," he said to me.

I looked at DiAngelo and said, "Yes or no?"

"Yes!"

"Mom, how about you?"

"Yes."

"Uncle Marco?"

When there was no response, I repeated a little louder, "Uncle Marco?"

Quietly he replied, "The money will need to be set up where no one can get it. It has to be cleared through his mother or by me before anyone can get at it other than a small amount to take care of him."

All nodded their heads in agreement.

Mr. Hamson grinned. "Okay. Yes, then?"

"Deal!" I told the man, and we shook on it.

I signed some papers, and Mr. Hamson asked to where

should he send the royalty money and where the rest of the money from Mr. Creek should be sent.

Uncle Marco suggested, “There should be two different accounts: one for the mining royalties and one for his inheritance from Mr. Creek that he can have open access to.”

Mr. Hamson cleared his throat.

“I said it’s only pocket change from Mr. Creek,” he began.

The man opened a folder and looked at a paper.

“Your pocket change amounts to over $200,000,” Mr. Hamson further explained.

I didn’t know how much money that was, but from the look on Mom’s face I figured it was a whole lot.

“Who’s gonna get Mr. Creek’s clock on the mantel?” I wanted to know. “It chimes pretty songs on the hour.”

“All the furnishings go with the house . . . it is all yours,” Mr. Hamson said as he smiled at me.

Mr. Hamson dangled a key on a gold keychain in front of me.

“Take it,” he said, nodding at me. “It’s the key to your house.”

Turning to my mom, Mr. Hamson said, “Mrs. Dean, as far as your divorce goes, the judge has granted you a decree of divorcement on the grounds of abandonment. You will receive no alimony or child support as we don’t know where he is. His house and land have been turned over to your name, and as of 12:00 noon today, you are no longer married to Mr. Hank Brooks.”

“Thank God” and “Goodbye, Pa” was all I could think to say. Mom hugged me.

“You’re not upset?” she pressed me.

"No, Mom. Uncle Marco has been more of a dad to me . . . the way a *real* dad is supposed to be."

Uncle Marco simply looked at me, tears flowing down his face.

"Well, that is all my business here for now. Good luck to you all," Mr. Hamson said.

"All this talk of money and divorce has made me want some milk," I announced.

"Baby, I will get it for you," Mom offered and went to get it.

"Where are we gonna sleep tonight?" I asked DiAngelo.

Uncle Marco answered, "All of us in the living room so I can watch over everyone."

"DiAngelo and I will stay awake and watch while you and Mikie get some sleep," he added, looking at me.

"Mikie! I have to go see Mikie!" I exclaimed, suddenly full of excitement at seeing my best friend.

The next few hours Mikie and I talked, hugged, squinted at each other, laughed . . . I couldn't wait to tell him what Mr. Creek had done. Aunt Hadie gave us some pie, and DiAngelo seemed to fit right in with the two of us.

Mrs. Liza slept on the couch. Mom had made us up beds on the floor. Mikie and I were next to each other, and Aunt Hadie and Mom were over on the other side of the room, whispering as much as Mikie and I were. DiAngelo and Uncle Marco kept us safe all in one room.

Finally, we all went to sleep, one-by-one. Just before I drifted off, I felt Mom holding my hand and kissing it.

"My baby's home. Thank you, God," she whispered.

*****

Mikie woke up before me and nudged my side.

"Wake up, Rocco. I have to talk to you."

"Okay, I am awake, Mikie."

"What are you wearing on your back? Why do you have that thing on?"

I had gotten hot in the night and took my shirt off. I had forgotten I even had the brace on.

"It's to help make my back stronger. When that bad man beat me, he made my back go crooked, but Dr. Bill said it will straighten out. This brace will help it."

"I wish I could catch him and kill him so you can come back and stay home," Mikie offered.

"Mikie, can I ask something of you?"

"Sure, Rocco . . . anything."

"Can you please try and love Angelo? I know he dresses funny to us, but he has a really big heart. He is a good man. He has a girlfriend; her name is Evett. If I have to go back to Michigan, when you and Uncle Marco come to get me to bring me back here, you can meet her. She is pretty as can be and friendly. Angelo loves her a whole lot . . . but do this for me. He has a hard life, also; with all the money he has, he still needs a friend," I explained.

"Well, Rocco, you are the best friend to have. I will always love you no matter where you go. I will always have one bestest friend."

I looked over at DiAngelo. He looked very tired and cranky.

"Are you awake, Angelo?"

"Yes, Buckaroo. If I even thought about sleeping, Marco would wake me up."

"I will have someone make you some food; maybe you will feel better."

As I left the room, I heard DiAngelo scream, "No! Get back in here!"

I ran back to the living room.

"What's wrong?" I responded as I flung out my arms for emphasis.

DiAngelo relaxed. "You are to stay with me, in my sight. Mikie, go get his mom for him so I can keep an eye on him."

Earlier, Uncle Marco had gone to take a shower. He returned, dressed in his nice clothes, and Aunt Hadie and Mom were all dressed for the party.

Mom said, "Sleepyheads, come and eat. Then you can wash up for the funeral."

Everyone ate; then the three of us went upstairs and took to getting washed up.

I remarked, "See, Angelo, I told you we don't have any shower downstairs."

"Buckaroo, I see you were telling the truth."

"Angelo, can I show Mikie your birthmark?"

"No, hush, Rocco!" DiAngelo blurted, somewhat embarrassed.

After a pause, Mikie's curiosity got the best of him.

"Where does he have a birthmark? Let me see," Mikie pressed.

I pulled up the leg of DiAngelo's jeans to expose his birthmark.

"Look, Mikie, it's a red circle like a full moon," I explained.

"Sure is, Rocco. He has a full moon on his leg."

DiAngelo gruffly pushed his pant leg back down in place.

"Okay, if you knuckleheads are done looking, get out of here so I can finish getting dressed. Buckaroo, you stay right outside the door so I know where you are."

"You're knucklehead number one," I announced as I pushed Mikie on his shoulder, "and I am knucklehead number two . . . and Angelo is knucklehead number three."

Mikie and I laughed and went out of the bathroom to stand outside the door while DiAngelo finished getting ready. We then went back to the dining room, all of us happy as could be.

"This is a great day for Mr. Creek's going-home party. The sky is blue, and the sun is out," I remarked.

"It is hot as hell!" DiAngelo responded.

The folks looked at him.

Aunt Hadie said, "We hope you don't find out."

When we were about to leave, I noticed how beautiful the sun shone in the sky.

"I think I am gonna walk over there," I said.

DiAngelo piped up, "No, you're not, Rocco!"

"It's only right across the field, Angelo."

"So, I will drive you over there. Can I use a car, Uncle Marco?" DiAngelo asked him.

"Yes, take the blue one; and I will drive Mikie and the women with me. As soon as it's over, I want you to get Rocco in your truck and get out of town!"

"No worries about that. Ten minutes after the party, I am out of here with Rocco."

Mom heard the conversation and got a sad face.

"Come on, this is a happy day. No sad faces, Mom. Okay?" I asked her.

"Okay, baby."

She made a half-hearted attempt to smile.

We went to our respective cars and soon pulled into the churchyard. They all circled around me as we walked in. Half the town was there for Mr. Creek's party. I went to the front and sat in my old seat. Mom sat next to me, and DiAngelo sat in the seat directly in back of me.

I turned around to him and said, "Are you okay?"

"Yes, I sure am."

"You got it?" I eyed him knowingly.

He patted his shirt and said, "Right here, Buckaroo. I have it right here."

I didn't say anything but wondered what the bad man was gonna be doing while DiAngelo unbuttoned his shirt to pull out the gun.

Suddenly, Brother Wallace was at the front of the church.

"Let's pray," he started.

He prayed a prayer of welcoming and said, "Amen." After a short pause, he continued, "I did not have the pleasure of knowing Mr. Creek but I want to thank God for watching over Rocco on his return and pray that Mr. DiAngelo will continue to keep a safe eye over him. I'm going to ask Rocco to come up and tell us about Mr. Creek."

Brother Wallace stepped aside and motioned for me to stand where he had been standing. I laid down the hymnal I had been holding and went up to the spot Brother Wallace indicated.

"Hi," I began. "I want to tell you all that Mr. Creek was a good man. He didn't come to church but he had a good heart. He watched over me. He never said that he believed; but with the heart he had, I know down in my soul Mr. Creek knew Jesus . . . and that's all that matters, Amen!"

The church responded together, "Amen!"

I continued, "We were friends, and he always helped look after me in a way that God sends angels to do."

I felt my throat getting dry and crackly. The pain building, I looked at DiAngelo, Mom, and Mikie, and the rest of the folks.

"Would it be all right if I sing a song to my friend?" I asked Brother Wallace.

"Please, do," he prompted.

Sister Linda was already at the piano, so I said, "One day I will see Mr. Creek and talk to him again. One day we will understand it."

With that, I started to sing, "Tempted and tried, we're oft made to wonder . . . we'll understand it all by and by."

By the time I was in the middle of the second verse of the song, folks everywhere were crying and yelling, "Amen!"

"We'll understand it all by and by," I came to the end of the song.

My voice seemed so deep. It carried all over the church. People cried and waved their hankies back and forth in the air.

I looked over at DiAngelo; he was smiling ear-to-ear. Mom was standing on her feet praising God. Aunt Hadie was shouting, and Brother Wallace took to walking around while he played his guitar along with the piano.

So, I just continued, singing the same tune, "We'll understand it all by and by. Gonna see Mr. Creek in the by and by."

Finally, I didn't need to sing anymore. It was all out of me. The piano stopped, and the folks were saying, "That's right! That's right!" and wiping their eyes.

I went back to my seat and sat down. I was sweating something awful. DiAngelo patted me on the back.

Brother Wallace went back to his spot and said "I guess we know where Brother Creek is; the Lord had His way. I just want to say if a boy can be this strong and say that one day we will understand it by and by, let us learn from him and be strong, good folks, Amen!"

The folks started filing past Mr. Creek's casket.

As I walked by, I said, "Bye, Mr. Creek. I loved you, also."

Linda played "Amazing Grace" while six men carried Mr. Creek's casket away.

On our way out of the church, the folks talked and greeted me. Mom and DiAngelo surrounded me as we walked to the car.

On the way back to the grill, DiAngelo said, "Buckaroo, I didn't know you could sing."

"Yes, I think so."

"Well, you do a real good job! You have some good lungs in that little body."

"At home, I always had to sing quiet . . . in my head."

"Why?" DiAngelo wanted to know.

"So I wouldn't make Pa mad."

"Your pa is an ass!"

"Well, he might not be my pa no more. I have to ask mom about that, seeing she divorced him."

"Good riddance!" DiAngelo responded.

We got to the grill. Folks were eating. Some folks went to the graveyard to say goodbye to Mr. Creek. They wouldn't let me go. They didn't want me out in the open, but it was okay since I had already said my goodbyes.

"Well, we're packed up and ready to leave," DiAngelo announced.

"Rocco," my mom began, "you listen to DiAngelo and his mom and grandmother. You behave until I can come and get you. Do what the doctor says and make Mom proud."

"I will, Mom."

"You remember Mom loves you more than life; and when you get back, we will move into Mr. Creek's house and live happily ever after. Do you, by chance, know how many bedrooms his house has?"

"No, Mom, I don't; but even if it has only one bedroom and a couch, it will be enough."

"I know, baby," she said as she cried quiet. "Now, you go on and call Mom when you get up there."

"I will," I promised.

She hugged me and kissed me all over, and to DiAngelo, she said, "Take him."

Aunt Hadie and all the folks hugged me while Mikie waited in line.

When I hugged him, I cried quiet and said, "Buddy, you watch those fingers; and don't cut them off!"

We hugged some more, and he said, "I will see you soon."

DiAngelo grabbed my hand and led me to his truck.

"Are you okay, Buckaroo?"

"Yeah, but I am tired of saying 'Goodbye.' It ought not be this way."

"I know, but I am happy that I get to keep you for a while longer."

"Oh, damn!" I stated.

"What, Rocco? What's wrong?"

"Can you take me to Mr. Creek's house?"

"Well, I think it is your house, so it should be okay," DiAngelo answered.

"I just want to get my clock Mr. Creek left me."

"With all he left you, and you are worried about the clock? I don't get it."

"It is to remember him by . . . money and houses are nice, but I want his clock."

"Okay, deal," DiAngelo responded.

We pulled up in Mr. Creek's driveway, and I told DiAngelo I would be right back.

I jumped out with my turtle book bag, ran to the door, and without thinking yelled, "Mr. Creek?"

I said to myself, "Dummy. Mr. Creek isn't here; he's in Heaven."

Chapter 9

I opened the door and went in. There it was: the prettiest clock I had ever seen. It sat right in the middle of the mantel. It was shiny and made of the nicest wood. The old key with which to wind it lay near it.

It seemed even lonelier now—this house without Mr. Creek—but I felt sure when Mom and I moved in, Mom would liven up the place. Before I got the clock, I wanted to see the rest of the house. All I had ever seen was the living room and the kitchen where I tended to Mr. Creek. I went into the kitchen. There was a door to the dining room. It had an archway opening.

"Oh, nice, Mr. Creek," I whispered.

I went into the dining room, and suddenly someone grabbed my arm. I screamed for dear life.

When I finally was able to stop screaming, my pa seethed, "Shut up, or I will kill you."

"Pa, what are you doing in Mr. Creek's house?"

"I knew you would come and try to steal something. I know your kind, so I have been waiting for you."

"Why? Did you miss me, Pa?" I ventured to ask him. "I missed you a bit."

"No, I didn't miss you. I came to finish the job that I

started. Since I lost your mom over beating you like I did, you are gonna die this time!"

"You are the one who beat me and pushed me off the porch? *You* are the bad man? Why, Pa? Why did you do that? I never did anything to you. I loved you and tried to behave and not talk so much. Why would you want to hurt me like that? You are my pa!"

The words tumbled out of my mouth in a torrent.

"I am not your pa! Stop saying that! You were just luggage I had to accept because I loved your mom. I wanted her to give you to Hadie and Marco, but she wouldn't hear of it. I wanted it to be just her and me and *our* kids, but she could never give me any kids. When she had you, she couldn't have any more children. Your birth made her barren. You are a waste of space in this world, and I am going to make you pay for me losing your mom!"

His anger built like so many times before. I saw it building, little by little. Finally, he pushed me to the floor.

"Pa, you better thank God in Heaven that Mom is down at Aunt Hadie's Grill 'cause she would boil some grease and throw it on you for hitting me."

"Shut up, you Italian bastard!"

"I'm not Italian! Uncle Marco and Mikie are . . . and his family up north."

"That's your family, too!" Pa spat out. "Marco's brother, Ray, is your father; and he didn't want you, either . . . *none* of us wanted you. We wanted your mom. I was just the kind one who took you in."

"Kind one? You say you were the 'kind one'? The way you treated me . . . that was kind? Making me eat at the counter was kind? I was always afraid to speak, always afraid of you, not want to make you mad. You were kind, all right. I am glad Mom divorced you. Her and I are gonna live in this house. Now leave, Pa!"

Pa's face got red as a plum, and he smacked me across the face. Pain shot through my neck and head. My hearing dulled, and my vision blurred.

"The only place you are going to live is in the cemetery!" I barely heard him say.

Pa pulled out his knife. I couldn't move. My legs seemed frozen as my eyes locked on his and my vision cleared to see the knife.

Pa gritted his teeth, and he drooled as he started snarling like a rabid dog. As he drew his arm back to thrust the knife into me, I heard a shot! It made my ears ring. Then there was another shot. Pa fell sideways to the floor. From two wounds in his upper body, blood poured out onto Mr. Creek's floor. The red pool crept toward me.

"Rocco, get up! Get up! Go in the kitchen and get out of here!"

I tried to talk to DiAngelo, but I couldn't get my mouth to work. Suddenly, I felt DiAngelo picking me up by the brace and setting me on my feet. I was shaking, and then I peed my britches.

"Stop it!" I yelled at DiAngelo. "Stop it! That is my pa!"

DiAngelo put his arms around me and drew me to him.

"Rocco, I'm here."

He continued to hold me close as I started sobbing. I don't know why I cried . . . the bad man was gone. I guess I cried because this was the only pa I knew, and now he was gone.

DiAngelo softly spoke, "Let's go in here."

He guided me to the living room and sat me on the couch. He dialed Mr. Creek's phone.

"Better get up to Mr. Creek's house *now*!"

He hung up.

"I'm glad he didn't break my clock, Angelo," was the last thing I remembered as I passed out.

When I came to, my mom was washing my face with cold water.

"Baby, I am sorry; I am sorry. Did he hurt Mom's baby?"

I pushed away her hand as I answered, "He hurt me more than you will ever know. He hurt me more this time than when he put me in the hospital."

Mom looked at me curiously.

"Did your pa hit you?"

"Just one, but then he cut me; he cut me bad."

"Where, baby? I don't see a cut. Show Mom. Show Mom where he cut you."

I pointed to my heart.

"You lied to me, Mom. *He* is the bad man, and he is the one who hurt me before. You said the bad man hurt me. You were protecting him; you were hiding him away so he could get away from Uncle Marco and Mr. Creek, weren't you, Mom?"

"No! No, listen to Mom," she lamely offered.

"No, I don't want to hear any more of your lies!" I shouted.

Uncle Marco came in, followed by DiAngelo.

"Boy, don't you speak to your mom like that!" Marco admonished.

"Why not? She is a liar . . . and so are *you*, Uncle Marco!" I sobbed. "He wasn't my pa!"

The tears continued flowing. I cried loudly, but still tried to talk.

"Mom, you said he was my pa; but Marco's *brother* is my *real* pa. He said I was an Italian bastard and that even Ray didn't want me. No one wants me! He told me! I made you not be able to have any more babies. He was gonna cut my throat!"

By this time, I was sobbing and yelling as loudly as I possibly could as the anger flowed from my mouth.

"Angelo, take me to the grill so I can get Mikie. I am leaving, and I am never coming back here. You can have this damn house and all the money! I am going home with Angelo . . . me, Mikie, and Angelo."

Uncle Marco stepped in, "That's enough!"

"Let the boy speak; let him get it out of his system. I deserve it all. I *did* lie to him . . . but only to make him safe," I heard my mom's voice say.

"She worked like a dog for you," Uncle Marco reprimanded.

"And made me eat like a dog for years . . . not worthy to even eat with them!"

Uncle Marco stared at me.

"Tell him, Mom. He doesn't believe me. Tell him! Tell him how it was at Pa's house. Tell it all . . . you better tell him!"

Mom sobbed along with me. She put her face in her hands.

Her muffled voice came out from behind her hands as she said, "It's true."

"Tell him more, Mom . . . that if Aunt Hadie didn't send food home, I didn't eat . . . how he would eat and not let me have food. Tell him more . . . tell him . . . how he tried to get me all the time and slap on me. Even times when you weren't there to stop him, he hit on me and told me I better not tell my mom."

As Mom cried, Uncle Marco paced back and forth, wringing his hands.

"Angelo," I started, "did you know I was your brother? Or did you lie to me, also? Were you a part of this? Is that why you've been kind to me?"

When DiAngelo didn't immediately answer, I shouted, "Tell me now! Damn it! I mean it . . . you better tell me and not lie! Everyone knew, didn't you? 'Keep him safe, but keep the bastard hid.' Is that it . . . just like Pa said?" I demanded. "At least as mean and hateful as Pa was, he told me the truth."

"No, Buckaroo," DiAngelo quietly started. "I didn't know. I am surprised as you are. I loved you for you . . . but I love you more now."

DiAngelo came and stood in front of me, looking at me in my eyes.

"I will always look after you and take care of you. You are my brother, and I promise as God is my witness, that I will never let anyone hurt you again."

DiAngelo grabbed me by my brace and shoved me toward my mom. I sat next to her and took her hand in mine.

"I am sorry, Mom. I know I hurt you . . . but you hurt me, also," I started in a shaky voice.

She looked at me as I continued, "Reckon we can let bygones be bygones?"

Mom turned to me and said, "Yes, one day you will know the truth and understand why Mom lied. Ray didn't want us. Later, I found out he was still married. He said he loved me and wanted to marry me. Then we had you. He left about four months after you were born, and we haven't seen him since. So, when Pa came along and said he wanted to marry me, I said, 'Yes.'

"A boy needs a pa; he promised he would be good to you. I never wanted to tell you he wasn't your pa; I just didn't want you to think your own pa didn't want you. So, I tried to make up for it by being a good mom. I guess I failed."

"You are a good mom to me . . . always loving me when Pa hated me . . . always taking care of me," I responded.

Maybe in time you will forgive me and want me to be your mom again," she said as she cried quiet.

"You will always be my mom. I just hurt right now, and it feels really bad. Maybe I will go one day and meet this Ray guy, finish learning to read, and come home. Then we can live happily ever after. I have a teacher who comes to the house, and he is gonna teach me and Angelo at the same time. Reckon that would be okay?"

"You promise you won't forget me way up there?"

"I promise."

Angelo took a picture of me hugging my dear mom.

"Where did you all put Pa? Are you sure he is dead?" I suddenly wondered.

"Yes, boy, he is dead . . . dead as a door nail," Uncle Marco answered.

"Mom, we have to clean up Mr. Creek's floor. Pa bled all over the place, and it will stain that nice, wood floor."

"We already did it," DiAngelo said.

"Mom, do you want to see the house?" I inquired.

I grabbed my mom's hand, and we went through the kitchen.

She remarked, "I am gonna cook for my baby in here someday."

We tiptoed around the place where Pa had laid in his own blood and died.

"Look, Mom, two big bedrooms and a bathroom . . . and everything is nice and clean! I want you to see something."

I took my mom and showed her the back porch with the swing and the great view of the land.

"Reckon we can rest here sometimes?" I asked her.

Mom grabbed me gently around the shoulders and said, "It will be great when you get home. We will rest here all day long and sleep well at night."

We went back inside. Mom took to looking in the kitchen cabinets. There was the set of dishes just like the one DiAngelo had broken when he had thrown it out the car window with the cornbread.

"Look, Mom! They match your plate . . . your favorite plate!"

She shut the cupboard door and said quietly, "Yes, I see."

We walked back to the living room. I picked up my clock and pushed its key deep into my jeans pocket. Then I kissed my mom goodbye one more time.

"I will be back," I told her.

I gave my mom the key to our new home and got back in DiAngelo's truck. We left for Michigan.

*****

We sat quietly in the truck. Not much had been said. It was getting darker, and the lights made my eyes tired. I wondered how DiAngelo was doing since he was the one who had stayed up all night with Uncle Marco, watching over us. So much was going on in my mind; I didn't even want to think about today and all that had happened.

"Angelo?" I started.

"Yes, Rocco?"

"Can I do something nice for you?"

"Sure. One million dollars would be nice."

"Pull over to one of those motel rooms. Let's get a good night's sleep and start from scratch in the morning, deal?"

"Okay," he nodded. "That sounds like a good idea."

It was Friday, and we told the girls in Michigan that we would be home Saturday morning. I didn't think it was a lie but I was still wondering if we should call home and let them know. We checked in at the desk. DiAngelo started to hand the man at the counter a credit card.

I grabbed my wallet and said, "Here," handing the entire wallet to DiAngelo.

"Buckaroo is buying?" he asked quizzically.

"Sure, but don't let him have it all," I said as I nodded to the man.

DiAngelo counted out the proper amount of money, gave it to the man, and handed the wallet back to me. We went to our room.

"Buckaroo, that shower felt like $100," he commented a few minutes later.

I could still smell the gunpowder in my nose, as well as the smell of blood. I was really going to enjoy a long, hot shower.

As I got out of the shower, I noticed DiAngelo was sitting up against the headboard, watching tv. He looked up.

"Feel better?" he asked.

"Yeah, I reckon."

I went and lay down on the bed while he continued to watch tv.

"What are you staring at, Rocco?" DiAngelo asked as he turned and looked at me.

"You."

He smiled and said, "Why?"

After a long silence, DiAngelo pushed, "Boy, what's on your mind?"

"Something's different with you. I can't say what it is. I don't know you," I finally answered.

"What do you mean, Rocco?"

"Well, I know Angelo, my friend; but now, you are Angelo, my brother. I can't explain it."

"I know; I can't explain it, either," DiAngelo answered, "so maybe we better talk about something else until we know what to say."

"Maybe we better make a pact," I offered. "Maybe we better never tell anyone about Pa. What if the police come and get you?"

"Oh, my Lord!" DiAngelo suddenly sat up and exclaimed. "I hadn't even thought about that!"

"What if you go to jail?" I pondered.

"I won't. No one can ever find his body. We hid it," DiAngelo answered as he relaxed back against the headboard again.

"How did you know to come into the house?" I quizzed.

"You were gone too long, so I got out of the truck and looked through the window. I opened the door. I heard you talking, and then I saw him smack you. I had to wait until he backed up to get a clear shot. I am sorry I didn't get in there sooner."

"Then he might not have told me the truth. I wouldn't know I was really your brother. I am mad at Mikie, though."

"Why, Rocco?"

"He knew all this time; he kept telling me that I was his cousin *two* times. I didn't know what he meant. I just thought he was mixed up. He was trying to tell me I was his cousin on both his mother's and his father's sides."

"Well, don't be too mad; at least he was trying to tell you."

"Maybe we should keep a lot of this hushed from *your* mom, also," I added.

"Oh, believe me," DiAngelo responded, "I am just as mad as you are! Father has a lot of explaining to do to both of us."

"Are you mad at me because I am your brother?"

DiAngelo turned off the tv so we could talk.

"Now, I am going to do this right this time. I am happy you are my brother. Nothing could make me happier . . . but all these lies and hidden secrets are uncalled for. Father should have told me the truth when I first came and got you. Not only did he leave me, but he also left you in a worse shape. He talks of taking responsibility . . . well, look at *him*: he left two families in the wind and went about his business. He might even have a third family in Italy."

"More brothers? I wonder if they look like us," I speculated out loud.

DiAngelo let out one of those laughs that I hadn't heard in a few days. I guessed it was time for one. One can be sad only so long until they either laugh or cry.

"Let's do something fun. Want to?" I suggested.

"Like what, Rocco? It's getting late; and I am really tired."

"Let's call Evett and talk to her; I will pay for the call."

"Buckaroo, you are going to spend all your money."

"So? Mr. Creek gave it to me; I can spend *some* of it."

"Okay," he relented.

DiAngelo dialed the number and handed me the phone first.

"Hello, Miss Evett," I said.

"Rocco, where are you guys? I have been worried not hearing from you!"

"We couldn't drive anymore; we had to stop and let Angelo get some sleep. He is a baby. How are you, Evett?"

"I am good, and I can't wait to see you guys. Where is DiAngelo?"

"He is here. I will let you talk to him. Goodnight, Evett."

"Goodnight, Rocco," Evett answered.

I handed the phone to DiAngelo and listened to his side of the conversation.

"Hi, Babe," DiAngelo started. "No, I will explain when I get home . . . No, he is fine; and not a hair on his head is harmed . . . We're just outside of Cincinnati . . . I do miss you bad . . . Well, you can't go; you have to finish school. Your parents only care about themselves." He took a breath before he excitedly added, "I got it! You can come and live at my house and finish school; then we can decide what we're going to do . . . No, she won't care. I won't take no for an answer; you *have* to finish high school. Rocco and me can bunk together in his room, and you can have my room. It will be a blast! . . . We'll talk to them about it . . . Okay, honey, I love you."

I looked at DiAngelo and repeated what he said, "Night, honey, I love you," and laughed.

"Shut up," DiAngelo said teasingly. "What are you doing, listening to me talk on the phone to my girlfriend?"

DiAngelo then grabbed me, tickled me, and then said, "I love you, Brother."

I didn't know how to act with all this love from my new brother. It felt strange.

"Dang, Angelo, if I knew you were going to get this much better, I would have called Evett hours ago."

DiAngelo laughed.

"I miss her, and it hurts when she's not around."

"Now, she's always going to be around: the three of us in the same house with Mrs. Sandra and your mom," I observed

"While she is at school, I will teach you to read better and count money. You will be as smart as you are handsome."

"You are just saying I am handsome because I look just like you," I said as I smiled at him.

"You don't look *just* like me; I am better looking than you, Rocco," he taunted.

"Angelo, I am handsome. Evett told me so when I was getting my haircut."

"Oh, she did, did she?"

"Yes!"

"Well, I guess if Evett said it, then it is true. Okay, Rocco, turn your bedside lamp off, and go to sleep."

"Okay. Goodnight, my new brother who is *not* handsomer than me . . . but who I love more than anything in the world."

"Even more than cornbread?" DiAngelo countered.

"Don't push it, Angelo. Goodnight."

*****

"Wake up, my tall brother. We have to get going. I have to get ready for school. I have to learn everything I can. I have missed two weeks of school already, and I need to learn to read and write and . . . well, everything! I am going to be the smartest man in the world. I am going to be a businessman like your father. I am going to keep calling him *your* father; I don't want your mom to know I know, Angelo. Until he is ready to tell everyone, just like you and I share secrets, it is up to him to tell. Deal?"

"Deal, Rocco . . . but you said all that without taking a breath. I really think you have some great lungs. Sing for me."

"What?"

"Sing me a song so I can wake up," DiAngelo pressed.

"I can't sing you a song; I only know how to sing low."

"You sang great yesterday. I might put you in Hollywood lights one day and make some good money."

"I think you are teasing and making fun of me."

"Never, Buckaroo," DiAngelo said solemnly. "I would never make fun of you."

"I am going to learn how to talk like you . . . not like I do. Your mom calls me a hillbilly child who has no teaching, but I know all the ways."

"Yes, you do; and I am going to help you learn. Then you will have both, the ways that are right and book teaching, as well."

"Reckon your father will like me if I try hard and learn how to read and become smarter?"

"Listen, Rocco," DiAngelo started, "don't get it in your mind that you need to change for him. Just be yourself. Everyone loves you."

"But I want him to be proud to be my pa."

"I learned a long time ago he is . . ." DiAngelo's voice trailed off.

"He is what?" Rocco pushed.

"He is a man that is involved in himself; he needs only himself."

"Well, September is almost gone, and Christmas time is gonna be here soon. So, I want to be ready in case he comes home."

"Angelo, let's talk about Evett moving in," DiAngelo attempted to change the subject.

"Yeah! Do you want me to sleep on the couch?"

"No, why would I want that? It's *your* bedroom that I am moving into. It's nice of you to let me share your room."

"I didn't say you could; you just said you *were*," I said with mock grievance in my voice.

DiAngelo tore up laughing and said, "Well, maybe I should have asked you. May I sleep in the other bed in your bedroom?"

"Nope!" I answered.

"Please?" DiAngelo turned on the charm.

We both smiled and let it go.

DiAngelo drove straight through to Michigan, and we arrived home around 7 p.m. Supper was almost ready; we got to the dining room on time for a change. Mrs. Sandra and Mrs. Faye were getting ready to start eating.

"Wait on us! We're here on time," DiAngelo announced as we came through the front door and laid our things down for the moment on the foyer floor. I carefully set Mr. Creek's clock on the floor next to my bag.

Mrs. Sandra smiled and said, "We wouldn't think of eating without you two. Rocco, I have a steak and potatoes ordered for you."

DiAngelo remarked, "Steak . . . yum!"

"You don't get any, Angelo. It's for me and Mrs. Sandra. You can eat some s'getti."

"I don't want s'getti; I want what you and Grandmother are having," DiAngelo whined. "S'getti gives me a bellyache."

DiAngelo went to mock crying. We both tore up laughing.

Mrs. Faye said, "I am going to teach you two dinner manners."

Mrs. Sandra said, chuckling, "I like it when they cut up and have fun. It's been a long time since I've heard laughter in this house. Do you remember when DiAngelo would throw food from his plate, and we would end up wearing more than we ate?"

"I did not, Grandmother, did I?" DiAngelo protested.

"You sure did and ran up and down the stairs with your mom running after you, trying to keep up with you. It was great! Faye, do you remember how his hair would flow as he ran?"

"Yes," Mrs. Faye answered, "and try to run away to the beach every time the door was open. I remember it all."

"That's funny!" I laughed. Then in the same breath, I added, "And can Evett move in with us?"

Everyone suddenly stopped talking and laughing and stared at me as if on cue.

"What?" they all said in unison.

Then the vote came in: "No . . . yes . . . why?"

"Angelo, tell them the truth how you love this girl and how her parents are moving to Greece. She wants to finish school before you two get married. It's not that hard."

"Where will she be sleeping?" Mrs. Sandra inquired.

"In Angelo's bedroom. He can sleep in my room. Anyway, that's the only way I would agree to it; they're not married, and there won't be no kissing after the lights go off. Right, Angelo? You promised."

I looked at DiAngelo to jump in any time.

DiAngelo looked around the table as he simply said, "Right, I promised."

"And I got some money to help feed her, Mrs. Faye. This way, I figured if she don't like Angelo, it's better to know now than later."

"I think this boy has heard this conversation before," Mrs. Sandra said.

"Yes, but I don't know from where. So, do we have a deal?"

"Yes, yes, I guess so," Mrs. Faye finally responded.

"Okay, it's three yeses and a guess . . . so, good! Let's eat!" I said with enthusiasm.

Chapter 10

"Supper was grand, Mrs. Sandra," I offered as we finished eating and Miss Maria set to gathering the dishes. "I appreciate the kindness. Did I sound northern just then?" I prompted.

"Yes, you sure did, boy."

"Were your taters good, also?" DiAngelo asked me.

"They're *potatoes*, Angelo, not taters anymore. I am grown up."

"I don't want you to grow up and talk northern; I want you to stay just like you are, my Buckaroo."

DiAngelo continued, "You should have heard Rocco sing at the funeral. He had everyone in tears, and I bet it carried all over town."

"Who? Rocco?" Mrs. Sandra asked.

"Yes, Grandmother, and there was a lady there playing the piano."

"That was Sister Linda," I added.

"Yes, but he won't sing anymore. I wanted him to sing on the way home but he wouldn't."

"Why not, Rocco?" Mrs. Sandra asked.

"Because he is a baby," DiAngelo answered, with a hint of taunt in his voice.

"No, I am not, Angelo."

"I will play something on the piano if you will sing, Rocco," Mrs. Sandra offered.

"Mother, you haven't played that thing in years," Mrs. Faye said pointedly.

We all filed into the piano room.

"It is nice in here; I haven't seen this room before," I observed.

"Well, we all have a sitting space in our bedrooms; so, we just never come in here," Mrs. Faye explained.

Mrs. Sandra played some random music on the piano.

When she hit a D chord, I said, "There . . . right there."

I started to sing "He Will Never Leave Me Alone" real low.

"Here, boy," Mrs. Sandra started. "Let's try it here; don't be afraid to let it carry."

"Sing loud?" I asked.

"Yes."

I started over again. I sang it in the higher key. Miss Maria and Mr. Scott came in and sat down to listen, also. Mrs. Faye started crying quiet.

It felt peaceful in my soul. I had a home where folks loved me and even wanted to hear me sing loud. When I ended the song, everyone was looking at me.

"Where did you learn to sing?" Mrs. Sandra quietly asked me.

"When I was working in Pa's garden . . . just Mom and me . . . she would let me sing loud and tell me the words. I would sing with her," I responded.

Mrs. Faye said, "I have never heard such beautiful singing in my life."

Mrs. Sandra reached for me. I sat on the bench with her.

I looked at her and said, "This is what you played?"

I played the entire song back to her on the piano without singing it.

"When did you learn that?" she asked in astonishment.

"When you were playing it, I heard it in my head. Did I do badly? I won't do it again."

Mrs. Faye said, "You come in here and play anything you hear in your head from now on. This can be your room."

Suddenly I had an idea.

"Mrs. Faye, can I put Mr. Creek's clock in this room? It's such a fine clock. It would look really nice on that table there," I suggested, pointing to said table.

"Of course, Rocco. I believe it will look very nice there."

DiAngelo spoke up, "Mother, we had better have him evaluated. How can someone hear a song one time and sing it and play it? No offence, Grandmother, but his was better."

"No offence taken. This is our angel sent to help us."

It was almost bedtime, so DiAngelo said, "Buckaroo, we had better get you some good rest after all you have been through."

"I am fine, and I want to start school tomorrow. I want to be the best reader in the world. I am going to be rich and take care of you and Mrs. Faye forever, like you have taken care of me."

"You have taken care of us more than we have you," DiAngelo answered. "We will use Father's money, so everything is great . . . and by the way, thanks for getting Mother to let Evett stay here."

"On the way home when you thought I was sleeping, I was really thinking how I could get them to let Miss Evett come and live here. I made the words up, but it wasn't a lie . . . you better not kiss after the lights go off."

"Okay, I won't . . . but remember, we sleep with the lights on."

"Oooohhh, you slept with that girl!"

"Don't tell anyone, Rocco."

"I won't, but you are going to have a baby if you sleep with a girl."

"Well, we didn't do everything."

"Everything?"

"Well, you have to do '*everything*' in order to have a baby, so we left some stuff out."

"Better get married if you are ever going to do 'everything.'"

"Okay, deal," DiAngelo laughed.

Sometime in the night I heard DiAngelo whisper, "Buckaroo. Buckaroo."

"What, Angelo?"

"I can't sleep. You want to go with me?"

"Sure!" I answered as I jumped right up. "Where are we going?"

"I just need some air. Let's go for a ride."

I stayed in my nightshirt and just put on my shoes. I surmised DiAngelo must not have planned on getting out of the truck because he left his shorts on, seeing he was funny about his birthmark and all.

It seemed DiAngelo simply drove aimlessly around, turning here, turning there.

"How come you can't sleep, Angelo?" I asked.

"I was thinking about everything in Kentucky and how things ended. You don't hate me, do you?"

"Hate you?" I asked incredulously. "Hate you? No, never! You mean because you shot Pa with your gun?"

"Well, that and for taking you away, again."

"No. I need to stay with you for a while until I cannot feel bad at Mom and Uncle Marco. How can I be mad at my only brother? We are gonna be brothers forever . . . you and me."

"Promise?"

"I promise with everything!"

"I have to go to the bank tomorrow and set up your accounts so you can have your money sent to you. Also, I thought I told you not to tell anyone about your money. At supper you said you had some money to help feed Evett."

"Oops," I said as I threw my hand up over my mouth. "I forgot; I just like to share."

"Well, let's keep using Father's money as long as we can and save yours for when you get older and want to go to college."

"Want some pretzels . . . the warm kind?" I asked DiAngelo, hoping to change the subject.

"We can't get them tonight, Buckaroo. Everything is closed."

"Well, are you sleepy yet?"

"Nope."

"Okay. I will sing for you when we get back home if you go to sleep."

"Will you sing loud?" he asked, concern edging his voice.

"Nope. A sleep song has to be nice and peaceful like when I was a baby and Mom would sing to me."

"You remember that?" DiAngelo asked.

"Yes, I can; and she would rock me on Aunt Hadie's porch swing a lot of the time."

"I want to see something," DiAngelo announced.

He turned on the radio. We heard part of a pretty song before he suddenly turned the radio back off.

"Sing that one," DiAngelo said.

"Okay," I answered; and I did.

"Here's another one. Listen to it and then sing it." He turned the radio back on for a few seconds and turned it back off.

"I can't," I told DiAngelo.

"Why? What happened, Rocco?"

"I don't like rock and roll music; it makes my head hurt."

"Oh, I'm sorry," he laughed.

DiAngelo decided to change the subject.

"Evett's mom and dad are having movers come and pack for them Friday and store their things in storage. Evett is going to be able to stay with us until she goes to college next summer."

"Good," I simply responded.

"Are you happy about that?"

"Yes; if you are, then I am. We are happy brothers. Evett likes me, and I will watch out for her like I do for you."

That week was full of eating, reading, more eating, and more reading. We liked our mealtime. When all of us got together, we would laugh and talk as we ate. Then we would each go to our parts of the house again. I couldn't figure out what was missing, though. I always had an empty feeling in my heart.

Friday came, and we helped Evett move her things into DiAngelo's bedroom and move DiAngelo's things over to my room.

"Evett?" I said.

"Yes, Rocco?"

"You sure got a lot of things for one person."

DiAngelo spoke up, "Girls have more than we do, Rocco. They have to look pretty all the time, and they have make-up and all that stuff . . . hair curlers and more clothes than the mall has."

"I can't carry no more. Tell Mr. Scott to come and help us," I complained. "He is bigger and stronger than me."

"Okay, Buckaroo. I think you are getting used to the help now. Would you like him to cook you some taters, also?"

"Shut up, Angelo," I retorted. "I didn't say that; did I, Evett?"

"No, you didn't, Rocco," she sweetly answered. Turning to DiAngelo, she scolded, "Stop teasing him, DiAngelo."

I looked over and smiled mockingly at my brother.

"You little brat!" DiAngelo exclaimed. "Did you see that, Evett? He has you eating out of his hand; he got you to scold me and then laughed at me."

"Well, he is my Buckaroo, too," she answered as she bent over and hugged me.

"Let's let Mr. Scott carry this stuff in and go get some air. Want to?" DiAngelo suggested.

As we readied for bed that night, I asked DiAngelo, "Which bed do you want?"

"I will take the one I have been sleeping in."

"Why are you afraid of the dark, Buckaroo, and need the bathroom night light on?"

"I am not afraid," I responded.

"Well, you sure act like it."

As we lay down in our beds, DiAngelo whispered, "Rocco, can you hear me?"

"Yes, I can hear you."

"I talked to Father today, and he said he can come home for Christmas; he wants to see you."

"Why are you lying?" I pressed DiAngelo.

"What? Rocco, it is not nice to say that."

"You are lying," I answered. "He may have said he is coming home for Christmas, but he didn't say he wanted to see me. I know you just want me to feel welcomed by him, but we can never lie to each other. Promise?"

"Are you mad at me, Rocco?"

"No, I know you did it from your heart, but we are all each other has. We have to be honest even if it hurts."

"Why do you think Father doesn't want to see you?"

"Because if he wanted to see me, when you came and brought me here, he would have come then. I think he is worried of how he is going to get out of the web that he has woven for himself."

"Father doesn't work like that; he doesn't care. He doesn't think or explain any of his actions. He does what he wants to, no matter whom it hurts," DiAngelo explained.

"So, I have you, Mrs. Faye, Evett, Mrs. Sandra, Mrs. Liza, and all my folks to love me . . . so what if he doesn't love me?"

"Well, he is only going to be here for a few days; and then he will be gone. We can then go back to being happy."

"Angelo, I am going to be happy while he is here. We should not change anything . . . like you told me: I am going to be me."

"Okay, I will also. Deal?"

"Deal!"

"Night, Rocco."

"Night, Angelo. I love you."

"Will you two shut up and go to sleep?" Evett yelled from her room.

"Yes, Evett," DiAngelo answered.

"Yes, Evett," I repeated.

We giggled and went to sleep.

*****

"Angelo, get up! I am tired of you sleeping all the time; you sleep the whole day away," I complained.

Weeks had come and gone since Evett moved in, and I was ready for summer and for her to go to college. Every day she came home from school, she was tired. She was getting heavier. Most of the time she and DiAngelo yelled at each other. He was mostly in a bad mood all the time.

"What are you talking about, Rocco?" DiAngelo sleepily answered. "Since you moved in, I have not slept past 10 a.m. When you get up, you think everyone should get up with you."

"Then go back to sleep, and go to hell!" I angrily retorted.

"What did you say?"

"Well, Evett says it to you all the time: 'Go to hell, and stop being mean.' I am telling Mrs. Faye."

"Well, I am sure she is awake. Go tell her now; and tell her to feed your little butt, and let me sleep."

I went into the bathroom and slammed the door. I looked into Evett's room through the other bathroom door; she was still in bed.

"Good morning, Rocco," she said.

"Well, it was a good morning until Grumpy over there started his hatefulness."

"Well, he is just tired," she tried to put me off.

"You always say that when he is being mean and rude: 'He's tired,' 'He's tired.'"

"I will make you a deal," Evett offered. "We will let him sleep and just you and I will go Christmas shopping today and leave his mean butt here. Deal?"

"Deal!" I answered.

I shut her door to the bathroom. I took a shower. When I got my clothes out of the dresser in the bedroom, I slammed the drawers, also.

On my way back to the bathroom, I said, "Ha, ha. I am going with Evett to the mall, and you can't go."

He didn't even argue or say anything funny; he simply turned over, put his pillow over his head, and ignored me. That made me madder than all get out. I went back into the bathroom, got the pail out from under the sink, and filled it with water. I went into the bedroom, yanked his pillow from his head, and drowned him. He came out of that bed faster than a tornado in July. When he did, I ran down the stairs because I knew he was just as mad as I was.

"Damn it, Rocco, you little ass! Get back up here!" DiAngelo yelled from our bedroom.

"No! Leave me alone!"

He was almost on my tail when I ran into the dining room and to the other side of the table.

"What's going on?" Mrs. Sandra asked.

"He's being mean!" I yelled out as I pointed in the direction of DiAngelo.

"You better get up there and clean that mess up now!" DiAngelo seethed at me from the opposite side of the table.

"No! You clean it up!" I yelled back.

DiAngelo started for me again, and I ran to the other end of the long dining room table.

"Stop running, Rocco. I mean it!" DiAngelo demanded angrily.

"No! Mrs. Faye, tell him to stop!"

"I am going to stop when I whip you. No wonder your pa was always hitting on you."

We both stopped in our tracks. I simply walked back up the stairs and into the bathroom. I shut the door, almost in DiAngelo's face and locked it.

"Rocco!" DiAngelo said from the other side of the bathroom door. "I am sorry. Open up the door. I didn't mean it, I swear."

Evett came into our bedroom and stood a few steps from DiAngelo.

"What did you do, DiAngelo?" Evett demanded.

"Nothing. Mind your own business," he spat out at her.

"Rocco, please, I am sorry. I didn't mean to say it. Come on out," DiAngelo urged.

I just sat there on the toilet and wondered if I did make Pa whip on me.

"Move, DiAngelo," I heard Mrs. Faye say on the other side of the door. "Rocco, let me in. It's Mrs. Faye. I won't let him in, I promise."

I unlocked the bathroom door and let her in.

"Sweetheart, he didn't mean it; he was just mad. Are you okay?" Mrs. Faye asked me as she put a hand on my shoulder and looked me in the eye.

"No, Angelo has been in this mood for a long time now."

Mrs. Faye pointed to Evett's room but didn't say her name,

as if to say she knew Evett was the reason for DiAngelo's bad mood.

"I am not talking to him anymore for the whole day. He can just leave me alone. I am sleeping in my piano room on the couch. He snores, anyways. Go tell him to go downstairs till I can pack my bag and move into the piano room."

"Okay, I will," Mrs. Faye answered, "but he is going to be hurt."

"So what?" I responded. "He hurt me. I never made my pa hit on me; he just hit me for meanness . . . for nothing! Angelo said he would never let anyone hurt me again, and he is the one doing the hurting. He lied."

"Well, Rocco," Mrs. Faye started, "sometimes people say things when they're mad that they really don't mean."

"Really, Mrs. Faye?"

"Yes, dear."

"Go ask him if he meant it," I prompted her.

"Okay. I will be right back."

When Mrs. Faye returned, she said "Open sesame."

I let her in.

"No, he didn't mean it for real, and he wants to know if you want to go for a ride with him."

"Where are we going?" I inquired.

"I don't know; but I think you better go because he was crying, and DiAngelo never cries. Maybe you can go tend to him."

As I look back on it, I think Mrs. Faye used reverse psychology on me. She knew I was a caregiver to the needy. She told me that DiAngelo needed a friend and a brother right then.

I said "Okay" and went into my bedroom and got my warm coat and boots on.

"Miss Evett, I can't go to the mall right now. I will be back in a bit, okay?"

"Okay, Rocco," she answered. "I will see you when you get back."

I went downstairs. DiAngelo was already out getting his truck heated up. When he blew his horn, I would know to go out. The northern weather had me chilled all the time. Mrs. Sandra or Mrs. Faye would bundle me up and send me out once the truck was running and warm.

"Okay, now you two be good boys, make up, and come back friends again," Mrs. Sandra commanded.

"I will," I answered somewhat contritely.

I think DiAngelo knew my weakness was that truck. I wanted to go everywhere he went, and it was easier for him to talk without Evett and the ladies around . . . just him and me.

"Get in! Are you okay?" DiAngelo asked.

"Yes."

"Are you mad at me?"

"Yes."

"Well, you shouldn't have thrown water on me; it was cold. It got the bed all wet!"

"Well, you shouldn't have not argued with me," I responded.

"Not argued . . . what?" he screwed up his face in puzzlement.

"You didn't even care enough to argue. You are always ignoring me. You covered your head, and it made me mad inside."

"Oh, is Buckaroo a bit jealous?"

"You never play with me or talk to me anymore since Evett came to stay with us. You're no fun."

"Well, to tell you the truth, I have been really bummed about some things."

"So . . . I don't take it out on you. I haven't seen my mom or Mikie for three months, and I miss them!"

"If I tell you something, no one can know . . . it's our secret, okay?"

"Okay."

"Evett and I are going to have a baby."

"You did '*everything*'?"

"I guess so," he said as he smiled at me.

"Are you going to get married to that girl?"

"Well, I want to be able to make a good living for her, but she has to wait until February until she is 18. By then she will be six months pregnant."

"Good thing her mom and dad are in Greece," I said.

"I know, but we haven't told Mother or Grandmother, yet. That is why we have been arguing. Every time I start to tell them I get nervous; and it won't come out."

"She isn't going to college?"

"Well, we're not sure, yet; she wants to."

"Who is going to watch the baby?" I inquired. "If she does go to college, you don't wake up until the day is almost over."

"I know," DiAngelo answered. "I am trying to figure all this stuff out, and it keeps getting bigger and bigger in my head . . . but I know one thing: I won't hide from my responsibility like Father did with you. I am going to be a good dad and love the baby as much as I do Evett."

"Angelo, you better get a job."

"That's another thing. I asked Father for a loan to buy a carwash. He said he would think about it and let me know."

"Get it from Mrs. Liza; she is loaded with money, so Mikie says."

"Hey, there's an idea! I can borrow it from Grandmother Liza if Father will not give it to me."

"Now, what else has been on your mind?" I insisted.

"Nothing . . . isn't that enough? About to have a baby and get married with no job and a girlfriend who is already cranky seven days a week. I am sorry for what I said to you this morning," he added as he started to cry.

"Angelo, you better pull this truck over if you're going to cry so you don't wreck us, okay?"

"Yes," he simply answered.

He pulled over and sat for a time with his head resting on the steering wheel, crying quiet.

"You know the good Lord never gives us more than we can bear. Maybe you should do some talking to Him and see what He tells you, but I think it will get better for you," I suggested. "Show me the carwash. Can I work for you in the summer?"

"Hold up a few! It's only if Father will give me the loan. He is supposed to call me back tonight."

"Well, let's drive by it and see it together."

I was expecting to see one with stalls where one sprayed their car off and go, but it was a drive-thru kind. DiAngelo started his truck through. The water splashed really hard on the window, and I ducked. It looked like it would come through the window.

"This is a cool thing," I exclaimed. "Why is he selling it?"

"He is retiring and going south to Florida."

"Well, it's a nice one, but I have to go and get Evett and go to the mall."

"So, I hear you are running away from home to live in your piano room," DiAngelo said.

"Yes."

"Well, I wish you wouldn't. I can't sleep without you over in the next bed. What if I have bad dreams?"

"You will snore them away," I teased. "But if you are really scared, I will stay and watch over you."

"Promise?" DiAngelo asked.

"I promise."

*****

When we got back home, Evett drove herself and me in DiAngelo's truck because it was already warmed up.

"Evett, will you take me to the carwash that Angelo wants to buy?"

"Why?" she inquired. "He said he already showed it to you."

"I want to see it again, please."

Evett pulled to the side of the carwash. I told her to stay in the truck; I would be right back.

"Hi, is the owner here who is retiring?" I asked the first person I saw.

"Yes, Mr. Thompson is here . . . just a minute," the man said.

A tall man with silver hair came out from a small office.

"Yes, young man, can I help you?"

"You have a warmer place to talk? I am getting wet here."

He smiled broadly and said, "Sure, come this way."

We went back into his small office. There was a desk with a chair on each side.

"You going to Florida?" I asked.

"Yes, I can't take this cold weather anymore."

"I know, sir. I'm from Kentucky; and the chill gets in my bones, and I shake and shake."

"Me, too," he responded.

"So, how much do you want for this place?" I said, getting down to business.

"I'm asking $145,000."

"Will you take $125,000?"

"If someone had that in their hand, I would take that, as cold as it is today."

"Who pays these folks who work here?" I pressed.

"I do," he answered.

"Can you also pay them for two months after the sale just to give me time to get someone to run this place for me?"

Mr. Thompson straightened his back, starting to resist the offer.

"Well, that will take it down to me making about $123,000 on the deal. One day the land behind the carwash will be worth more than that."

"But we are talking about here and now. I hear it's fixin' to get colder outside," I countered in my most business-like demeanor.

Mr. Thompson laughed.

"You drive a tough bargain there, boy! Is this some kind of joke?" Mr. Thompson pressed, looking around to see if there were any adults close by.

"No, sir. Business is business—no joking allowed."

Mr. Thompson's eyes took on a strange look as he said

accusingly, "Son, how did you get here, and who put you up to this joke?"

"My friend, Evett, brought me. She is waiting outside for me in the truck. She doesn't know what I am doing. It's for my brother . . . I mean, my *friend*, DiAngelo. I need you to tell him the place has been sold if he comes around and asks you about it. It's gonna be his Christmas gift."

Mr. Thompson rubbed his chin, thinking, while I sat motionless and quiet. I waited, barely breathing.

"Okay," he drew out, still not knowing if he should trust that the whole thing was not a joke, "$125,000, and I pay the workers for two months. I really need to get to Florida, so I'll agree to the deal."

"Okay, go get your car warmed up and follow me."

"Where do you think we are going, young man?"

"To the bank to get you some money!"

"A loan?" he quizzed.

"No, sir. You tell the man at the bank what we agreed to, okay? And we will take over the first of January. Then we will pay the folks ourselves, starting in March. Is that right?"

"Yes," Mr. Thompson agreed, still acting somewhat puzzled.

"Angelo can come and learn from you for a few weeks?"

"Certainly, I can do that."

"Then it's a deal! Thank you, sir."

We walked out and went up to Evett still in the truck.

"Hi. My name is Mr. Thompson," he said as he held out his hand to Evett.

She shook his hand and said, "I have heard a lot about you; my fiancée wants to buy your business."

"Oh, I'm sorry," Mr. Thompson tried to sound seriously saddened. "It's not for sale."

Evett pointed at a For Sale sign in front of the carwash as she stated "But the sign is still up."

"Well, this man right here just stole it at a better deal than DiAngelo was willing to pay," Mr. Thompson explained as he kept a hand on my shoulder.

"I better get in the truck," I announced. "I am cold!"

I got in and instructed Evett, "Now, we have to stick to our side of the deal and go get him some money. He will sign some papers at the bank, so hurry before he gets chilled to the bone, also."

"Well, okay," Evett answered, "but I think DiAngelo is going to really be mad."

"Who cares?" I questioned flippantly.

Chapter 11

The three of us went to the bank, and Mr. Thompson signed a temporary Bill of Sale and signed the carwash over to DiAngelo Pettrachini with all the stipulations to which we had agreed. The man to whom we talked had it typed out and notarized.

"Okay," Mr. Thompson started when the dealings had concluded, "thanks, you all."

"Nice meeting you, Mr. Thompson. Good luck in Florida," I added.

I looked back to the bank man and instructed him to keep my money safe. Evett laughed a fake laugh and patted me on the head.

I looked up at Evett as I said, "I have to remember to tell Angelo to minus this much from my account because he said if I bounce a check, I will go to jail."

We got home, and I couldn't wait to tell DiAngelo about his Christmas gift; but I wanted to wait until suppertime and surprise him.

"Where is Miss Maria?" I inquired as I entered the front door.

"She is in the kitchen," Mrs. Faye replied.

"Miss Maria, I need you," I told her as I went into the kitchen.

"Yes, sir?"

"Can you bake a cake . . . a fast one for supper?"

"Yes. What kind?"

"Any kind will do. I have to get busy."

"Yes, sir."

I went to my bedroom and started to wrap the carwash papers in gift wrap but then wondered what would happen if he accidently ripped them up as he opened the gift.

"I better not do that," I thought to myself. "Maybe I just need to put them in an envelope."

"Hey, Buckaroo, what are you doing?" DiAngelo said as he came into the bedroom.

"Get! I am wrapping some things," I told him.

"Let me see."

"I said, 'Get!'" I repeated.

"If you let me see, I will have them make some taters for you," DiAngelo bargained.

"Angelo, I ain't got time for play right now. I am busy. Now, hush and get!" I turned my head toward the bathroom as I screamed, "Evett, come here!"

Evett ran into the bedroom.

"Yes, Rocco. What's wrong?"

"Can I talk to you?"

"Sure. About what?"

"Away from 'Big Ears' Angelo. We can go to the piano room."

I grabbed up the papers; and Evett and I went downstairs, leaving DiAngelo in the bedroom.

"I want to help my brother . . . and I know he told you we are brothers, didn't he?"

"Well, I figured it out when we went to the mall and got

your haircut. You look too much like him not to be brothers," she confessed.

"Then he told you?" I pushed.

"Yes."

"I want to help him. I am going to tell Mrs. Faye and Mrs. Sandra that you two are getting married."

"Maybe another time, Rocco."

"No, tonight! He has been worried about how he is going to support you and the baby."

"He told you about the baby?"

"Yes, but I had to drag it out of him."

"I know he is going to have to tell them sooner or later; I am getting bigger by the minute!"

"So, can I help tell? I will slide it in and make it all okay . . . if it is okay with you."

Evett smiled and said, "I believe if anyone can make it okay, it would be you."

"I love you, Evett. We will always be a family."

I rushed around the house getting myself ready for supper. I had my gift wrapped in an envelope, which I put inside my shirt so DiAngelo wouldn't see it. I told Evett she couldn't tell him, and everything was going as planned . . . or so I thought.

"Mr. DiAngelo, your father is on the phone," Miss Maria's voice broke into my thoughts.

"I will take it in my room, Miss Maria."

DiAngelo went upstairs and got on the phone. It was only but a few minutes when I heard a bang and then another bang, slamming of doors, and a lot of yelling. I ran upstairs to check on DiAngelo.

"Are you okay?" I asked with alarm.

"No, I am not okay," he snapped at me.

"What happened?"

"That was Father, and he said he couldn't see his way to get a loan from his company to lend me anything. It doesn't matter anyway. I called Mr. Thompson, and he said the carwash has been sold; that I waited too long. Father is the one who waited too long! I have never asked him for anything, and just when I ate my pride and asked, he says 'No,'" DiAngelo ranted as he paced the room in anger. "Well, forget him! I am going to make it on my own. Evett and I are going to get married one way or the other."

"Supper is ready, Angelo." I said quietly. "Let's go wash up before we're late."

"Evett, I love you!" he screamed as loud as he could. "I am going to marry you in February."

If he wanted his mom to hear that, I am sure she did. God in Heaven heard it.

"Angelo, why are you screaming?" I asked, trying to calm him down. "Don't you know if it was meant to be, it would have been?"

DiAngelo just stared at me. He continued to stare, having no answer to my question.

"Let's go have supper, and everything will be okay," I suggested.

This was not how I had planned supper out, but I guess sometimes things work themselves out without help from me. We walked into the dining room, and Evett looked at Mrs. Faye and Mrs. Sandra as she went to her seat.

DiAngelo spoke first, "Mother, I cannot stand that man you're married to."

"You mean your father?"

"Don't try to be funny right now; that man is an ass."

"I am so glad I didn't have to tell you that and that you learned it all on your own . . . so, let's eat!" she smugly responded.

Mrs. Sandra looked at DiAngelo and Evett on their side of the table.

"So, who's getting married in February?" she asked.

"Evett and I are going to city hall and get married in February; and Rocco is going to be my best man," DiAngelo announced matter-of-factly.

"I am?" I asked, surprised.

"Yes! Mother, I would really advise you to divorce Father on grounds of stupidity. I can't believe that man!"

"Angelo?" I asked.

"What, Rocco?"

"Can you do me a favor and shut up? I am hungry!"

I think Mrs. Faye was getting a kick out of seeing DiAngelo hate his pa. She had a great big, I-told-you-so smile on her face.

"So, he kicked you while you were down?" Mrs. Faye threw at DiAngelo.

"Mother, I wanted to buy a business and marry Evett. We're going to have a baby."

Her smile slowly dissolved from her face.

"A what?" she asked, almost unbelievingly.

"A baby. I love Evett, and we're going to get married. I am damn going to be a better father to my son than he is. Look at us . . . I haven't seen him in eight years, and Rocco has never even met him."

The whole table—even Miss Maria—stopped in their tracks.

"What are you talking about, DiAngelo?"

"Oh, nothing, Mother."

"I asked you a question: what are you talking about?" Mrs. Faye insisted.

DiAngelo looked at me and said, "I am sorry, Rocco. I have to tell my mother now."

"Go ahead; I don't care. I don't like him anyway."

"Rocco is Father's son, also."

Mrs. Faye turned and looked at me, then at DiAngelo, then back at me.

"Oh, my God," she blurted. "I thought he was really Marco's son."

DiAngelo responded, "Marco's?"

"I would like that," I inserted. "Wouldn't that be nice, Mrs. Sandra? I like Uncle Marco; he is a good pa."

"Mother, are you mad?" DiAngelo dared to ask.

"Hell, yes, I am mad! I am watching over one of his illegitimate children. Your father told me Rocco was Marco's love child."

"Well, now you can divorce him, Mother, on grounds of adultery," DiAngelo suggested.

"Do you hate me, Mrs. Faye, because I am his bastard?" I ventured.

"Oh dear, I am sorry. No, I don't hate you. I just don't understand why he would lie about having such a lovely child."

"He doesn't know I am lovely; I haven't seen him since I was four months old."

"That bastard!" Mrs. Faye exclaimed, bringing her fist down onto the table.

"Maybe I should eat in the piano room if you all are gonna call names like that," I said.

"Tell me everything, DiAngelo . . . right now," Mrs. Faye commanded.

"Well, he left us, went to Kentucky to see his mother and his brother, Marco, and met Rocco's mom. He said he loved her and wanted to marry her, and they had Rocco. They found out, I guess through Marco, that he was still married. That's when he went to Italy."

"So, he ran out on them, also," Mrs. Faye commented.

"Yes."

"And then my pa married Mom and took us to hell," I added.

"Poor boy," Mrs. Sandra offered as she put her arm around me. "We love you."

"You're not mad 'cause I am a bastard? That's what Pa called me the last time," I answered.

"Last time . . . what, boy?" Mrs. Sandra prompted.

"The last time he beat me."

I looked over at DiAngelo, and he was looking at me with the shut-up look.

"And, what? Go ahead and tell Mrs. Sandra," she pressed.

"And told me I was not his son."

"Rocco, don't you ever call yourself that again, do you hear me? A bastard is an unwanted child, and I love you like I do my own son; you are wanted from head to toe. I will always love you, and I am not mad at you. I am mad at your father!"

"Well, I don't think I like him, either, so we will tell him to go back home when he gets here next week," I suggested.

DiAngelo broke in, "That's the other thing, Mother."

"Just how many things are you hiding, DiAngelo?" Mrs. Faye asked.

"He is coming to Michigan for business and will be here for a few days."

"Where is he staying? I want to talk to my dear husband."

"Mother, he is staying here."

"He can't sleep with me," I piped up, "so I guess he is going to sleep in my piano room."

Everyone started to laugh.

Mrs. Faye then spoke, "Let me get this all right in my head: you're getting married in February and having a baby, and Rocco is your real brother, and your father is coming to Michigan next week."

"The good with the bad, just like Brother Wallace says," I expounded.

"What an exciting dinner!" Mrs. Sandra exclaimed.

Mrs. Faye said, "Miss Maria, can you bring some wine? We're going to have to get some more seats for mealtime if our family keeps growing!" She paused, then looked at Mrs. Sandra and added, "Mother, a baby . . . I'm going to get a grandchild to love on and hold and cherish."

"Yes, and I am going to be a great-grandmother, Faye. See, I told you the boy was going to help us," Mrs. Sandra answered.

"Anyone want some cake?" I asked loudly.

"Where does he put all this food?" DiAngelo asked no one in particular.

"Shut up, Angelo, and have some cake. Folks need to eat so they can be strong. Uncle Marco says so."

"Here, the wine first," Mrs. Faye suggested.

We all got a glass of wine that Miss Maria had poured.

Mrs. Faye held hers up and said, "I am glad I am me and I am free. Now, I have moved from the past into the future, thanks to this little guy here. And to my other son, DiAngelo, I give my blessing for your marriage and wish you the best life ever. And to Evett, I thank you for the gift of grandchildren. Welcome to our family."

I hurried up and added, "Wait . . . and long live Mrs. Sandra!"

"Yes, and long live my mother," Mrs. Faye repeated, "and thank you, Mother, for being with me through these bad years. Thank you for helping me from day to day." Mrs. Faye started to cry and added, "I love you all."

We hit our glasses together and drank the wine.

"What a night!" Evett said.

"Wait! One more gift!" I announced.

Miss Maria brought out the cake.

I continued, "Angelo, I love you; and now I can love you as my big brother because everyone knows. I can love you in front of everyone. This is your Christmas gift and wedding gift, all in one."

"What is it, Buckaroo?" DiAngelo asked as he reached out to accept the envelope.

"A job," I simply answered as I walked around the table and stood by my brother's side as he started to open the gift.

"A job?" he laughed.

He slid the papers out of the envelope and began reading the bank papers. As he read, my brother cried quiet, and I held onto him. The rest of them wondered what was going on.

Finally, DiAngelo looked up and said, "Looks like my brother got me a job. He bought my carwash for me."

Mrs. Sandra and Mrs. Faye started talking over one another, "What? How did you do that?"

"Evett took me to the carwash. I went in and told the man I wanted to buy it for my friend."

"Buckaroo, how did you get it at this price?" DiAngelo wanted to know.

"I just told him it was going to get colder and he better be leaving for Florida before he got chilled."

"Mother," DiAngelo started, "look at this."

He passed her the deed to the carwash.

"He even got the old guy to pay the workers for two months until I get on my feet with the business," DiAngelo explained.

Mrs. Sandra asked, "How did you learn to haggle like that?"

"I know that word," I answered. "Aunt Hadie did it when she bought the grill. And then I got Mikie's knife for $18 instead of $19."

DiAngelo continued with apparent pride for me in his voice, "He got the carwash for $20,000 less than the asking price! I love, you Buckaroo, but I am going to pay every penny back, I promise."

"I am going to have to take him with me when we go for baby furniture and clothes," Mrs. Faye said, "to see if he can get me some deals, also."

DiAngelo remarked, "Mother, you haven't been out of this house in eight years."

"I think it's time me and my mother go and see what is going on out there. Come on, ladies, we have a wedding to get ready for and a baby shower to prepare for."

They got up and went toward the piano room.

I screamed at their backs, "Don't mess up my piano room!"

DiAngelo and I sat at the table and looked at each other for several minutes . . . no talking, just looking.

"Cat got your tongue?" I finally asked DiAngelo.

"Yes, I think he does, and he won't let go."

"Then, don't say anything except that you like your new carwash." After a short pause, I added, "I can come work with you in the summer and keep you making money because I can talk to the folks and make them come back."

DiAngelo grabbed me and hugged me hard to the point of almost causing me pain in my back.

"You can never know how much I love you," he said to me. "You are the goodness that the world looks for; you are the love we never knew. You have changed our lives, one-by-one, bringing us back to a place of innocence and making us feel good again."

"I bet you want some cake now and eat it, too," I said as I smiled at my new brother.

The girls were still in the piano room talking about all the girlie stuff . . . wedding, babies, parties, showers, etc.

I said to DiAngelo, "it's only 7 p.m. You want to go see your carwash . . . just you and me?"

"Tonight?"

"Well, I don't see why not; you own it. Mr. Thompson said you could come, work, and learn the business before he leaves. So, by January you will know everything about it."

As the two of us drove toward the carwash, DiAngelo spoke up, "I am kind of scared. It is only a few months before I have to pay the people myself, buy the supplies . . . and everything!"

"Well, you big baby," I started. "You are two months ahead if you just eat green beans and taters and don't spend what you make now. Save it and pay the folks with that. We can live off your Father's money until then. I still have some left, don't I . . . from Mr. Creek's money?"

"Yes, you have more in there, and I don't know how much coal money you have. They haven't sent a statement yet for the last quarter earnings. So, who knows how much coal they have been pulling from there? But you can't spend any more money from your bank account; that is for your college fund."

As we pulled into the carwash, I said, "Look, Angelo! See, we're already making money! There's a line for folks to get in and get their cars washed."

"Yes, the salt from the roads will keep us busy enough in the winter to pay for things, and everyone likes a shiny car in the summertime."

"I think we can mine the few acres behind the carwash," I suggested.

"What?"

"Mr. Thompson said the land back there one day will be worth more than what we paid for the carwash."

"Did he really say that?" DiAngelo wanted to know.

"Yes! Now, let's go meet the folks."

"We don't know them, Rocco."

"There's only one way to get to know them, and that is to jaw with them."

"Do what?"

"To run our jaws to them . . . talk, Angelo! Don't you know anything?"

We went in.

A man greeted us, "Can I help you?"

"Yes," I answered. "This is DiAngelo, and I am Rocco. We bought this place today. What is your name?"

"Lewis."

"Well, that's a nice name . . . easy to remember. This is my brother, DiAngelo; and he will be working with you all come Monday."

"Really?" Lewis couldn't hide his surprise.

Lewis shook DiAngelo's hand.

"Nice to meet you, Lewis," DiAngelo finally spoke.

It got quiet for a little bit until Lewis said, "I see already who does most of the talking in the family."

DiAngelo laughingly responded, "Yes, we can't get a word in edgewise when Rocco talks; we just stay quiet."

"Want to show him around, Lewis?" I asked.

"Sure," he answered. "Tipper, I am off for a few minutes; watch things."

"Gotcha!" Tipper answered.

I stayed where I was and watched until the last car was done being washed.

I yelled out to the man called Tipper, "Hey, Tipper, come here. Where are you from?"

Tipper quickly walked up to me.

"I am from Kentucky."

"Really? I am, too!"

"What part of Kentucky?" Tipper asked me.

"White Plains."

"Heck, I am from south of there about an hour . . . town called Hopkinsville."

"No way! I've been there."

"Dang, I haven't been home in about 12 years."

"Shame on you," I playfully scolded him. "I know your mom must really be missing you."

"Well, I call home I reckon every two weeks, but she is aching to see me."

"My mom, also. I have to get home soon and see her and

Mikie, my cousin, and all the folks. You waiting until spring to go back?"

"Nope. Soon as Christmas is over with, we are going down . . . maybe starting out Christmas night," Tipper explained.

"Really? I hope I get to go soon. I need some good cooking; I am hungry for it . . . you know, some beans, fried taters, and some cornbread."

Tipper took to laughing.

"Boy, you just made my day. But you forgot about the cut-up onions in the beans, though."

"I didn't think there was any other way to eat them. My mom makes the best soup beans in Kentucky. She slow cooks them all day, lets them steam, and lets all the gas out of them."

"Yeah, my mom does the same," Tipper responded. "Good Lord, it's a small world."

"Angelo!" I called out. "Come here."

"Yes, Buckaroo?"

"This is Tipper. He is from Hopkinsville from down home."

"Nice to meet you," DiAngelo said as he shook Tipper's hand.

"Tipper," I started, "my brother here is gonna be starting here Monday with you all. You better take good care of him or I am coming back, and you know what that means."

"I sure do, Rocco. We will take good care of him and teach him everything."

"By the way, Tipper, did you find a church up here like ours down home?" I pressed.

"I sure did. Over here on 37th Street they have a preacher from Tennessee, and he's hot on fire."

"Tell my brother where it is, and I will be right back."

I left DiAngelo to get the location of the church while I went and stood by the blowers where it was warm from their drying off the last few cars.

"Rocco, what are you doing?" DiAngelo asked as he walked up to me.

"I am warming up; I got a chill."

"Well, we better get you home and warmed up. Guys, I have to get him home. It was good meeting you, and I will see you bright and early Monday morning."

"Not too bright and early," Tipper responded. "We start at 9 a.m. and stop at 7 p.m. in the winter."

"Okay. See you guys then," DiAngelo answered.

We got into DiAngelo's cold truck and went home.

*****

"Goodness, boy, you're shaking like a wet dog. Get those wet clothes off and get warmed up," Mrs. Sandra instructed me as soon as we walked in the door.

"Yes, Mrs. Sandra. Angelo threw me in the water at the carwash."

"DiAngelo, what did you do that for?"

"Grandmother, he is fibbing. I didn't do that. He is trying to pull jokes." DiAngelo responded. "Where is Mother and Evett?"

"They left and went to the mall."

"Mother did?" DiAngelo asked, surprised.

"Yes, she is all happy about everything and says her new life started tonight."

"Grandmother, while Rocco is upstairs changing clothes, can I talk to you?"

"Yes."

"Do you really think he is an angel?" he asked her.

"I think sometimes God uses different things to get our attention, and this child has won the hearts of everyone he comes in contact with. He is a warm soul in a cold world."

"We really have to watch him around your father; I remember him as being cold and starchy and self-centered."

"I remember him the same way, DiAngelo. We will keep an eye on Rocco. You and I will make sure he feels all the love he needs right now. You know his strength comes from the kindness and love he receives."

"I don't understand, Grandmother."

"DiAngelo, he is like a pitcher of milk. If you pour it out without refilling, it will soon be an empty pitcher."

"I get it; he is a vessel, and even he can run dry."

"So, we will refill him with more love," Mrs. Sandra added. "Then he will keep pouring and never run dry."

"Did you need me to walk you up, Grandmother?"

"No, I am staying up until the girls get back and see what they bought. Go ahead and check on the boy. I will see you in the morning."

"Okay, Grandmother. Goodnight."

I was already in bed, covered up, when DiAngelo came up and pushed me over.

"Move over, Rocco."

He sat down on the edge of the bed.

"I wanted to thank you, again," he said.

"No need. I will get free carwashes when I grow up."

"Are you going to stay here that long?" DiAngelo wanted to know.

"You don't want me to?"

"Yes, I sure do. I want my baby to be around you and learn all the ways."

"Are you kidding? You told me that my ways were weird."

"Well, that was when I first met you and didn't understand them."

"Tomorrow is your last day to stay home, then you got to go to work every day. You better wear a warm coat. Do you have a Carhartt?"

"No."

"I will buy you one."

"No, you're not. I just told you a few minutes ago you have to stop spending your money."

"I know, I know, Angelo. I can't wait until summer and feel that warm breeze again."

"Are you really that cold?"

"Yes, ever since."

"Ever since what, Rocco?"

"Mom had to stay in town for a few nights while Hadie was in the hospital, and Pa made me sleep on the porch. It was cold; and ever since then, the least bit of cold air makes me feel chilled."

"Oh, my. I thought it was just the change in the weather. You are sensitive to cold air."

"Well, I don't know about all that; I just get cold when it blows on me."

DiAngelo started to hug me, but pulled up short.

"You're still all wet."

"I didn't pee the bed!" I protested.

"Well, what happened, Rocco?"

"I don't know."

DiAngelo went to the door and yelled down the stairs, "Grandmother, have Miss Maria bring you up here."

When Mrs. Sandra arrived to our bedroom, she asked, "What is it?"

"He's all wet and says he didn't pee the bed. But his hair and head are wet, and his bed where he is lying is soaked."

"Get me a thermometer, DiAngelo." Looking back to me, she said, "Boy, we have been letting you run too much with your brother in this cold. Open up." She put the thermometer in my mouth under my tongue and said, "Don't bite it." In a few minutes she pulled out the thermometer and said, "DiAngelo, call for Dr. Bill. Tell him to come at once."

"No, I am fine. Today is a happy day," I replied.

"Go now, DiAngelo!"

When I heard DiAngelo coming back up the stairs, Mrs. Faye and Evett were with him.

"Look who has caught a cold," Evett said. "I kept telling you to stay in and not follow your brother everywhere."

"He is croupy and sweating, Faye," Mrs. Sandra told her daughter.

"I didn't pee the bed," I said again.

"I know, good boy," Mrs. Sandra said. "You are just sweating. It's okay."

"I didn't pee the bed! I don't need a whipping," I insisted.

"Honey, no one is going to whip you. It's okay," Mrs. Sandra tried to console me.

"It's come on him so fast with no early signs," DiAngelo tried to explain.

"DiAngelo, just how long has he been sweating?" Mrs. Sandra wanted to know.

"Well, I came up here; and he was already all wet."

"Run a tub of water; he is delirious," Mrs. Sandra instructed DiAngelo.

"He can't have cold water."

"Why?"

"His pa made him sleep on the porch, and he gets cold easier now."

"Dear Lord, where was this boy's mother when this was going on?"

"She was in town with her sister in the hospital."

"Dr. Bill is here," Evett announced.

"Well, how is this little guy?" Dr. Bill wanted to know.

"Something is wrong with him, Dr. Bill. He is sweaty and cold and burning up with a fever. Now, DiAngelo said he was made to sleep outside on a porch when he lived in Kentucky, so now he gets chilled easier."

"Yes, that sometimes happens when you get frostbite," Dr. Bill explained, "but I don't see any signs of that. Let me take a closer look at him if you all will step out."

A few minutes later, Dr. Bill opened the bedroom door back up and said, "Okay, you all can come back in. I need to do some blood work on him Monday."

"I can't go Monday," I weakly protested. "Angelo has to work at his new job."

Dr. Bill asked, "Did you give him anything to drink?"

"Yes, I gave him some orange juice," DiAngelo answered.

"I think what we may have here is a cold child with diabetes," Dr. Bill spoke.

"Really?" asked Mrs. Faye.

"Yes, the orange juice sent his sugar levels back up. I will know more Monday."

"I will bring him to the office Monday," Mrs. Faye offered.

"Are you sure, Mother?"

"Yes, I will be fine. Just let Mr. Scott know how to get there."

"Mrs. Faye, did you buy me something at the store?" I managed to ask.

They all laughed as they said "Yes" in unison.

"I bought you some new thermal underwear to keep you warm," Mrs. Faye responded.

"Long johns . . . I needed them, Mrs. Faye. Thank you. But I have to get up now and get out of these sheets; they stink."

I got up and went and showered while Mrs. Faye made up a fresh bed for me and talked to Dr. Bill.

"I think I need some food," I said to Mrs. Faye when I emerged from the bathroom.

"Why is he still shaking?" Mrs. Faye asked.

"His sugar levels are still on the low side. If you give him some food and soda, it will bring them up," Dr. Bill explained.

"No red sauce, please," I quietly requested.

"Want some taters?" DiAngelo asked with a smile.

Miss Maria went and made me a sandwich and brought some chips with it. I had a soda like Angelo liked to drink.

"He's going to be bouncing off the wall in a few minutes from all the sugar," Mrs. Faye remarked.

That night they kept coming and checking on me. While DiAngelo and I slept, I kept feeling Mrs. Sandra feeling my head and kissing it. I was safe at last and getting ready to meet my real father. What would that bring? How would he like me? I could only wonder.

Chapter 12

On Monday morning, DiAngelo was up at seven o'clock to get ready for work, and I was getting ready for another doctor appointment. Mrs. Faye was still happy dancing around and placing new things all over the house. DiAngelo and I went down to breakfast, and all of us sat down except Evett; she had gone to school already.

"Good morning, Mrs. Faye, Mrs. Sandra," I greeted them.

"Morning, Rocco. How do you feel this morning?" Mrs. Faye responded.

"I am great, Ma'am."

"Good, we will go see Dr. Bill. Then I want to get you a warmer coat and some warm cocoa at the mall."

"Mrs. Sandra, are you going, also?" I asked.

"No, I better stay here. I have something I need to do."

"Angelo needs a warmer coat, too, Mrs. Faye, or he is gonna get a cold at the carwash."

"Well, we will look for one for him, also."

"I want him to have a Carhartt so he will always be warm," I suggested. "Who's gonna help me with the lessons after the tutor leaves?" I wondered aloud.

"I will," Faye quickly responded. "I am a much better teacher than DiAngelo."

"But you don't make good jokes like he does."

"You really love your brother, don't you?"

"Nope."

Suddenly DiAngelo spoke up, "Hey, you better love me!"

"I do; I was teasing, but don't tell anyone."

"Young men," Mrs. Faye started, "I have something to ask of you. When your father gets here, we are going to play a joke on him. We are not going to tell him that I know that Rocco is his son. Can you play that joke, Rocco?"

"Sure, I will pretend that big mouth Angelo never did tell you."

"All right, Mother, we will pretend if that will make your joke work," DiAngelo answered while giving his mother a strange look.

"Angelo has to work . . . ha, ha. And I get to stay home and have ice cream for my sore throat."

DiAngelo looked at me and said, "I wonder when his voice is going to go out."

He laughed.

"Tell everyone at work I said 'Hi' and that I will see them soon."

"Okay, I will. I am going to get donuts and coffee for everyone on my way in."

"I want a donut, also," I complained.

"No, you don't. You cannot still be hungry."

"Mrs. Faye, can we get me a donut when we go to the doctor's?"

"Sure, we can as soon as we get out of Dr. Bill's office," she answered.

I looked over at DiAngelo and grinned. He just shook his head.

"You have him as spoiled as Grandmother has . . . and even Evett spoils him!"

"So, go to work and leave us to have a good time . . . just Rocco and I," Mrs. Faye said.

I walked with DiAngelo to the door and said, "Be careful, Brother. I will be here when you get home."

"Are you okay, Rocco?"

"Yeah, I just haven't been without you for all these months."

DiAngelo laughed.

"You're going to miss me . . . that's so nice," he responded tauntingly.

"Shut up and stop teasing me, Angelo."

"Okay. I will bring you something if you will listen to Mother and do what she says. Deal?"

"Deal!"

I think it was as hard for DiAngelo to leave me as it was for me to say goodbye to him. He went out the door. I went back into the dining room, and the door came back open.

"Oh, I forgot . . . don't let him go by himself at the mall, and hang onto him."

"DiAngelo, he will be fine. Now, go to work," Mrs. Faye pushed.

"Bye, Brother," I said once again.

"Bye, Rocco. See you soon."

"How many days until his father gets here?" Mrs. Sandra asked.

"Three," Mrs. Faye answered, "and I can't wait."

"I think I can wait; I am scared," I said.

"Why?" asked Mrs. Sandra.

"Mrs. Liza said he was the bad son, and all I've heard are bad things about him."

"Did Mrs. Liza say anything else?" Mrs. Sandra prompted.

"That me and Mikie will run the family one day with love and make better leaders than her two sons."

"She did?"

"Yes, and she gave me this ring."

"Can I see it?"

"Yes, but I can't take it off or I won't be safe."

When she held my hand up to the light to better see the ring, she said, "Oh, this is great . . . and Mikie has the other one?"

"Yes, he's my best friend and cousin. Angelo is my best friend and brother. He got to talk to Mrs. Liza when we went for Mr. Creek's going-home party. When no one was listening, I asked if she could get Angelo a ring like mine and Mikie's; and she asked me if I trusted him with all my heart."

"What did you say?" asked Mrs. Faye.

"I said the same bond that Mikie and I have, I also have with Angelo and that he swears to always protect me. She is going to get Angelo a ring made just like ours, but don't tell anyone; it is a surprise from our grandmother."

"Oh, I won't. Who else knows about the rings?"

"Just you know what they mean," I explained to Mrs. Sandra. "Uncle Marco told me what Mrs. Liza said. So, you, Uncle Marco, me, and Mikie are the only ones who know."

"Okay. Well, when your father is here, maybe it would be best if you didn't wear the ring."

"How come, Mrs. Sandra?"

"He might try to take it from you. Give it to DiAngelo to hide it for you."

"Okay, I will."

*****

We went to see Dr. Bill, and he took some blood out of my arm.

He said, "You are a very good soldier. Are you feeling better today?"

"Yes, I sure am. I didn't mean for them to drag you out to our house on a cold night like the other night."

"It's okay. I have been the Pettrachini family doctor since DiAngelo was born."

"Now, you are my doctor, also."

"Okay," Mrs. Faye spoke up, "let's get to the mall and pick out some coats."

"Not so fast," Dr. Bill interjected. "He is going to have to eat foods that are low in carbohydrates. I will have the nurse mail a list to you, Faye."

"Okay. You have a nice place here, Bill . . . it's a lot nicer than your old office," Mrs. Faye offered.

"Yes, I think so, too," he answered.

"Okay, bye. We have to go get Angelo a coat," I announced.

We returned to the car, and Mr. Scott was there waiting to let us in the back seat. I wondered why they needed this car if Angelo had a truck and Mrs. Faye never went out. Why did they have Mr. Scott? There was no need for a driver, but I was glad that he kept the car warm for us.

At the mall Mrs. Faye bought me the warmest coat I had ever had. It was the kind that made one look like an Eskimo. The hood had real fur in it and kept my face and the top of my head warm. It easily slipped over my brace.

We sat on a bench for a while and watched the folks walk by as we drank hot cocoa. When we got ready to leave, Mr. Scott picked us up right at the door.

"Want to go see Angelo and drop off his new coat so he won't get cold?" I offered.

"We better not," Mrs. Faye responded. "He will be busy learning the ins and outs of his business, so we will give it to him tonight."

"Okay, deal. I am kinda tired, anyways, Mrs. Faye. Maybe I can go home and take a nap. Will you turn on the tv for me upstairs?"

"Sure," she answered simply.

"Angelo always turns it to cartoons for me, and he goes to sleep. Maybe that will work for me, too."

When we got home, Mrs. Faye turned on the tv; and I lay in bed for a while. I was thirsty, so I went downstairs but didn't see anyone. I went into the piano room. There were Mrs. Faye and Mrs. Sandra, sitting in the two chairs, talking.

"What are you guys doing in my piano room?" I asked.

They smiled, and Mrs. Sandra answered, "May we borrow it? We are comfortable here."

"Yes, but make sure you use the coasters under the cups."

"We will, Sir Rocco."

I went back upstairs, watched the funny cartoons for a bit, and was soon fast asleep.

"Rocco, wake up. It's four o'clock, and you slept the day away."

"Angelo, hi," I responded as I wiped the sleep from my eyes.

"Hi, Buckaroo. Did you miss me?"

"Yup."

"Look what I brought you."

He handed me a microphone.

"What's this?"

"It goes with this," DiAngelo explained. He stepped aside to reveal a large speaker. "Now you can be a singer for real with your own mic and everything."

"For real?"

"Yes, and tonight I want you to practice your favorite song and sing it for Father when he gets here."

"Okay, I will try."

"Let's go eat. Grandmother also has a surprise for you."

When we got to the dining room, Mrs. Sandra had cooked a roast with taters and carrots, along with some of her great cornbread. There was even a sweet tater pie. I had a tall glass of milk.

"Dear Mrs. Sandra, you been cooking all day. Look at all this great-smelling food."

She smiled and said, "I thought you might be ready for some real food, boy."

I ate like I was at home and enjoyed every bit of it. Then I crumbled some cornbread in my milk and went to town on that.

"What are you doing, Buckaroo?" DiAngelo wondered.

"This is sweet milk. Try it."

"No, thanks."

Mrs. Sandra leaned over and I fed her a bite of it. She loved it.

"That is really good that way, Rocco," she commented.

"I know. All we need now is Mikie and Mom, and I would have my whole family . . . all of you and all of them."

Mrs. Faye said, "Maybe Marco and his family can come

and bring your mom this summer; and we will have a great big picnic, swim, and open up the entire house."

"There's more to this house?" I asked.

"Yes, there are two more bedrooms on each side of the house," Mrs. Faye explained.

"Dang, that's eight bedrooms."

"Yes, you counted good, Buckaroo . . . all on your own."

"Evett, tell Smarty here I can count to 100."

Evett responded, "That's higher than DiAngelo can count."

We all laughed . . . even he did.

"After a hard day at work, I come home; and you guys pick on me like this."

"Did you get wet?" I asked.

"Yes . . . and cold."

"Show him what we got him, Mom."

Everyone was quiet for a minute.

"I mean, Mrs. Faye, show him . . . he's going to like it. Tipper has one like it; it's a Carhartt."

DiAngelo tried on the jacket, and it fit just right.

"Thanks, Buckaroo. I love it."

"I like my speaker and microphone, too. Are they a Christmas gift?"

"Yes. I beat Santa up and took it from him."

"No, you didn't. Rudolph would poop on your head if you did that."

DiAngelo laughed so hard that the great big table shook. Every time he would think about it again, he would start laughing all over.

"I am going to teach the baby to laugh like Angelo laughs. I love it when he laughs. It makes me laugh. It's so funny," I said. "Can we have some sweet tater pie, now?"

"Sure," Mrs. Sandra answered. "I haven't cooked in years; it is good to see people eat my cooking."

"Well, you sure didn't forget how to do it. It is the best I have had in a long time."

"Thank you, boy. It means a lot to me."

"I better go call my mom if we are going to practice some songs after supper. I will see you all in my piano room after I talk to Mom."

And I was off.

*****

"Okay, Buckaroo, are you ready to sing me a song?" DiAngelo blurted out as he walked into the piano room. He stopped suddenly and lowered his voice, "Oh, I'm sorry; I didn't know you were still on the phone."

"Mom, is Mikie over there with them?" DiAngelo heard me ask.

"Yes, honey, he went with them today. That's why I'm here: Hadie went to be by Marco's side."

"How come you didn't call, Mom? She is Angelo's grandmother, also."

"Well, I figured that it was up to Marco and Ray. I am just staying here running the grill for Hadie."

"Do you have my bed made, Mom, for when I come to visit you?"

"Yes, and I have a surprise for you."

"What is it, Mom?"

"Well, really I have a *few* surprises for you. You will see when you get home."

"Maybe after Christmas Angelo will bring me for a few

days. I am learning a lot. I can count to 100 and spell a lot of things!"

"Good!" Mom sounded proud of me. "You learn all these things, and you can teach Mom; we will live happily ever after."

"Okay, Mom. I am going to get off here and tell Angelo about dear Mrs. Liza."

"Okay. I love you lots and lots, baby."

"Me, too, Mom. Goodbye," I said before hanging up the phone.

"What's wrong with my grandmother?" DiAngelo inquired, concern edging his voice.

"She has taken sick and had a heart attack. Uncle Marco and Aunt Hadie are there at the hospital with her," I responded.

"Nice of them to let me know," DiAngelo remarked with a slight sarcasm to his tone.

"I told Mom someone should have called you, and she said that was up to Marco and Ray."

"So, my father must know, already."

"I reckon. Poor Mrs. Liza. I love her; she is always so kind to me."

"Well, she is our grandmother; you *should* have loved her," DiAngelo practically admonished me.

"Do you think she knows I am Ray's son?"

"Sure, she did. She lived there with Marco."

"Oh, that's right. That's why she . . ." my voice trailed off.

"What, Rocco?"

"That's why she always hugged and kissed on me," I hurriedly finished what I had started.

"Well, she never did me; I don't think she likes me."

"You were all the way up here. She *does* like you. Remember, she patted your face and kissed you while we were up there for Mr. Creek's going-home party. If Mrs. Liza don't like someone, she just stares at them." I paused a moment before looking up at DiAngelo and remarking, "Angelo, I don't want another going-home party; I am tired of them."

Mrs. Sandra and Mrs. Faye walked in as DiAngelo and I were finishing our conversation. "Poor boy, it's okay. We all have to go some time," Mrs. Sandra said.

"So, you knew Mrs. Liza?" I quizzed Mrs. Sandra.

"Sure, I did. We used to shop together when our kids were tiny, but she never wanted to speak English. I would tell her things in Italian, like Uncle Marco does."

"Yeah," I responded. "He tells her what I say."

Mrs. Faye spoke up, "She lived here with us for a few years after her husband died. Then, she went to live with Marco when the fighting between your father and I got so bad."

DiAngelo remarked, "I don't remember that; I must have been real small."

"Yes, you were; and she would laugh at you all the time and hold onto you like someone was going to steal you. She and Daniel would dance all night at dances and go for long walks," Mrs. Faye continued, looking off in the distance as she recalled former days.

"My grandfather's name was Daniel?" I asked.

"Yes, why?" Mrs. Faye quizzed.

"That is my middle name: Rocco Daniel Brooks."

"No shit!" DiAngelo exclaimed.

"Angelo, we're talking about the sick and dead . . . stop cussing!"

"Yes, Sir Rocco."

"Anyway, wanna take a ride and say goodbye to Mrs. Liza?" I turned to Mrs. Faye. "Can we, Mrs. Faye?"

"I don't know. I don't think you should just be popping up at a time like this at Marco's."

"Popping up? I am his family; Angelo and I both are. Anyway, I have my own house we can stay at."

"Mother, it is okay. We will be back before Father gets here; I promise."

Mrs. Faye simply nodded her head.

DiAngelo and I bounded up the stairs and packed our things. We hurried to put our things into his truck.

DiAngelo spoke up, "Are you sure you want to stay at your own house, Rocco?"

"Oh, I didn't think about remembering Pa lying there in his own blood as he died from your gun." After thinking about it a moment, I answered, "Yes, I can do that; I will be okay. But what about your job at the carwash?" I added as DiAngelo drove out of the driveway and headed south.

"I already called them and told them to go ahead with things; I will be back in town in a few days. That's the good thing about being the boss," he explained as he smiled at me.

"Shoot! I forgot to bring the presents," I lamented.

"See, that's why you need a big brother to remember things. They're all packed up and in the back."

"Thanks, Brother. I have to remember to get something nice for Miss Maria for wrapping them for me. I had a lot of things to wrap."

"You sure did! I think you outdid Santa Claus!"

"I bought Mom and Mikie a lot of stuff, and it's going to be the best Christmas ever."

"What did you get last year for Christmas?" DiAngelo asked me.

"I got some peppermint candy, some walnuts, and a few

oranges and apples; and Mr. Creek gave me some nice, warm socks from the store. Mikie got me a new shirt and jeans."

"Thank God for Mikie!" DiAngelo responded.

"What do you mean?"

"I mean he got you some nice stuff; otherwise, you would have had only walnuts and oranges."

"Well, that was the best my mom could do. She did it from her heart, Angelo; and that's what counts."

"I am sorry; I didn't mean any disrespect to your mom. I really like her."

"Yes, my mom is good and would give you the shirt off her back. Before she had me, all she had was Aunt Hadie to love her."

"Who is the youngest . . . she or Hadie?"

"Mom is the older sister, and she used to take care of Aunt Hadie. Mom is 34; Aunt Hadie is 28. I heard Mom talking to Pa one day. She said Aunt Hadie had run off to be with Marco and that she did good for herself. My mom stayed with her mom till she was 26 and then ran out of the patch and went to Aunt Hadie's and Uncle Marco's."

"The patch?" DiAngelo asked. "What is that?"

"Mom and Aunt Hadie lived in the clover patch across the road from Mr. Creek's land. It sits way off the road. Mom showed me one time. It is a shack with no bathroom, and the moss had grown completely over it from the willows draping over it. The sun could not get in. I was scared there, and we never went back to see it again. I think Mom was missing her mom and went there to say 'Hi.'"

"Damn twilight zone."

"What?"

"Nothing," DiAngelo answered. "It's just that there's

a story for everyone in Kentucky. Do you know how Uncle Marco ended up there, anyway?"

"No, do you?"

"Rocco, if I knew, I wouldn't have had to ask you, now, would I?"

"Are you getting tired, Angelo? Because you always get grumpy when you get tired. Even Evett says that."

"Yes, a bit, I suppose."

"Well, I will go to sleep over here and mind my own business. Where's the pillow you brought?"

"Behind the seat . . . and don't pee on it!"

"I don't pee the bed! Shut up, Angelo!"

"Goodnight, Buckaroo."

When I woke up, the radio was going. DiAngelo had the window open a tad so he could stay awake, and I could smell those cigarettes burning.

"Stinky, you been smoking in the truck."

"I didn't want to wake you up by stopping and getting out."

"Angelo likes me; Angelo likes me," I said in a sing-song fashion.

"Shut up, Rocco, and go back to sleep."

"Nope. I am awake for the rest of the trip."

"That's good. Show me Mr. Creek's road again."

"We're here already?" I exclaimed.

"You slept six hours, snoring and everything over there. It is 5:30 in the morning."

"Mom will be awake and getting breakfast. You can eat and then get some sleep," I suggested.

We drove up to Mr. Creek's house, and Mom had the living room light on.

"Look," I said, "I knew she would be awake."

I got out and went to the door. A lot of things were going on in my head: this was Mr. Creek's house . . . this is mine and Mom's house . . . a bunch of bad memories about DiAngelo's shooting my pa.

I started knocking. I finally heard a timid "Who is it?"

"Santa Claus. Now, open up! I can't get through the fireplace."

The door swung open, and Mom got me and wouldn't let me go. She took to crying and held me a long time right there on the front porch.

"Merry Christmas, Mom."

"Baby, this is the best gift I ever got in my life! Get in here and let Mom see you."

She just stood there in the living room light, looking at me.

"I think you have grown a foot!"

"Mom, I have not; I am still as short as you."

DiAngelo rapped lightly on the door that was still open.

Mom said, "Boy, get in here." When DiAngelo came in, Mom bear hugged him, also, and said, "Thanks for bringing him home."

"You're welcome. We wanted to see you and Mrs. Liza before she passes. I was going to bring him home Christmas night, but we decided to come earlier."

"Well, I'm glad you did."

"Mom," I started, "your tree is real pretty . . . and look at all the presents! Who are they for?"

"They're for my baby."

"Where did you get all the money?"

"Well, that's the surprise. Come here and look. It has gotten light outside."

"What are we looking at?" I inquired.

"You don't see it?"

"No, Mom, I don't see anything."

"That's what I mean. Pa's house is gone!"

"Where did it go?"

"I had it torn down after you left. The folks bought the land, and I said I wanted the house torn down so we would never have to look at it again."

"You mean they send you a check every three months like they're doing for me?" I pressed.

"Nope. I got all mine up front. Just look here." Mom handed me a savings book. "I put half of it in your account and half in mine. After they seen how much coal was in Mr. Creek's back 40, they really wanted the land."

"Have they been getting a lot of coal out of there?" I asked her.

"You will see in about an hour. In the meantime, are you boys hungry?"

"Yes, and my brother needs some rest."

It kinda got quiet for a minute when I referred to DiAngelo as my brother. Mom gave me a strange look . . . almost a look of hurt.

"Mom, don't look at me like that. I am not ashamed of Angelo, and he's not ashamed of me. We're all one family now. His mom is very kind to me, and you are kind to him. Him and I have a bond . . . a brother's bond . . . him, Mikie, and me."

"Well, you and I have a bond," Mom said.

"Yes, Mom, like our bond . . . I would do anything for you and you for me. That's how it is with us boys."

"Like your Aunt Hadie and me," Mom added. "But does Faye know you are Ray's child?" Mom wanted to know.

"Yes, she does. Angelo told her, and she is even kinder to me. She has learned the ways and is a kind woman. She even bought me stuff, and she watches over me while I am learning the book ways . . . but I only have one mom . . . and that's you!"

"Baby, Mom loves you a bushel and a peck and a hug around the neck."

"Want to have Christmas now?" I asked excitedly.

"Sure. I will just open the grill a few minutes late."

Angelo returned to the truck and brought in all the gifts I bought. Mom opened her gifts. I noticed there was one for her that I didn't know from whom it was. She slowly opened it. It was the most beautiful sweater. Mom loved it and started to kiss me.

"Mom, I didn't get that for you."

I noticed a Christmas card tucked into the sweater. I pulled it out and handed it to Mom.

"Dear Mrs. Brooks,

Christmas this year has been the best that I have ever had. Rocco has taught us the meaning of not only Christmas, but also of the meaning of life. I wanted to thank you for sharing with us your very special and loving child. May God bless you and keep you safe in his arms.

Love,
Faye"

Mom's eyes had filled with tears.

"I have a gift for her and one for Mrs. Sandra, also," she said softly.

"You do, Mom?"

"Yes, there under the tree. I wanted to thank them for taking good care of you."

I opened my gifts. Mom had the nicest things for me. She gave DiAngelo a shirt and some jeans and smell-good stuff. Mom also bought him a necklace of gold with a ring on it.

"Look, Angelo, a ring! Let me see."

"Mrs. Liza got it for him. She wanted me to give it to him for some reason," Mom explained.

"Angelo, it is a family ring just like Mikie's and mine!" Suddenly, I said, "Oh, Mrs. Liza. I have to hurry and see her; she is leaving. Hurry, let's go!"

"You better listen to the boy; he knows things," she told DiAngelo. "He got that from my mom."

"Come on, Mom. We will drop you off at the grill."

We gathered our coats and headed out.

"I almost forgot that your father is in town, DiAngelo," Mom said. "He is over at Marco's, as well."

"My father is in Kentucky?" DiAngelo responded, somewhat surprised.

"Yes, he got in last night."

"Mom, you can't tell him Mrs. Faye knows our secret," I instructed.

"Baby, Mom doesn't plan on seeing him; but if I do, I will be sure not to tell him."

"Do you hate him, Mom?"

"No, baby, Mom doesn't hate anyone. He helped get you into this world. How could I hate him?"

"Well, maybe he will be gone before we get there. Angelo, are you okay?"

"Yes, just tired; it has been a long trip."

"We will go see Mrs. Liza off and come back and go to bed and wait for Mom to get home."

"Yes, you better not leave without seeing Mom, you hear me?" Mom broke back in.

"I am glad you are rich, also, Mom. I don't have to worry about you anymore. Life is getting better and better."

"Okay, here we are. Get back home as soon as you can. DiAngelo, watch my baby; and don't let him get hurt by no one."

"I will, Mrs. Dean," DiAngelo answered.

"I am trusting you," she added firmly as she stared into his eyes for emphasis.

"I know . . . so are a whole lot of other people."

We went into the hospital, and DiAngelo asked for Mrs. Pettrachini's room.

"CCU," the lady behind a counter answered. "Are you friends or family?" she asked.

"Family."

"Oh, wait. A block has been placed on all visitors."

"By whom?" DiAngelo asked. "I am her grandson."

The lady replied, "By her son."

"I am her grandson," DiAngelo repeated, "and I will see her now. Call Marco down here right now."

Marco soon showed up.

"Hi, boys, come this way."

"Why did you do that, Marco, . . . have us blocked from seeing Grandmother?" DiAngelo pressed.

"I had no block put on Mother's room; what are you talking about?"

"It must have been the bad son," I said.

"Hush, Rocco," Marco said. "We better hurry; Mrs. Liza is leaving."

When we got to the room, there he was in all his glory: Mr. Ray Pettrachini sitting by the window and talking on his phone. I walked over to Mrs. Liza's bed, and she was resting her eyes.

"She is unconscious," Mikie said.

I leaned over the still form and said softly, "Mrs. Liza, it's me, Rocco. I know you can hear me. Remember when I got hurt, I could hear Mom and Aunt Hadie? I came back to tell you something, and Uncle Marco said those words in Italian to you for me. I wanted you to know that I always loved you and wanted to thank you for being so kind to Mikie and me. See the man by the door? Don't be afraid of him. When he gets closer, you will see that it is your husband, Daniel. Remember, Mrs. Liza, I told you about it? When I get to the other side, I will see you again. Angelo is here, also, and Mikie. We are all here."

Mrs. Liza opened her eyes and said something in Italian. She rubbed my face gently and then went on to Heaven. Mrs. Liza was gone to her Maker.

Uncle Marco hugged me into his side, and Mikie was on the other side. We cried, and DiAngelo stood at the foot of the bed. Mikie and me hugged and cried some for Mrs. Liza and some because we were so glad to see each other.

"When did you get in, Rocco?" Mikie asked.

"We got in just a little while ago."

"Can you come to my house today?"

Uncle Marco offered, "We will be doing some business at home, so why don't you go to Rocco's house instead, Mikie?"

"Yes, we have business to attend to and don't want a bunch of kids running around," a voice from behind us spoke.

We turned and looked at Ray.

He continued, "Reunions are for the living, not the dead."

He came over, shook my hand, and said, "Hi, I am Ray, your Uncle Marco's brother."

"I know who you are," I answered matter-of-factly.

There seemed to be a roiling in my stomach, and I couldn't figure it out. I had waited so long to see my real father; and yet, I was angry.

"Who am I if you think you know so much?" Ray asked me sarcastically.

"You are Ray Pettrachini. You are Angelo's and my father."

"His name is *Di*Angelo," Ray corrected me.

"I also know his name, but I am surprised that you remembered it."

"Well, you ungrateful little brat!" Ray spat out.

DiAngelo had been mostly quiet up to this point.

"Rocco, I am glad you got to see Grandmother in time; she knew you were here after all," DiAngelo said.

"What was it she said, Uncle Marco, before she passed away?" I asked.

"She told you that you are a good boy and to take care of her family," Uncle Marco answered.

"How can an eight-year-old, smart-mouthed kid take care of a family?" Ray threw the question out into the air, not expecting an answer back.

"He's almost nine," Mikie responded with an edge of attitude.

"So, it will be okay if Mikie goes with us to my house?"

"Yes, Aunt Hadie said we will come and get you boys for supper."

"Good!" I answered. "You can open your gifts before I go back home to Michigan, Mikie."

Chapter 13

Ray spoke up again, "*This* is your home, little boy. I will ride home with my son as we take my mother's body back to Michigan to be laid to rest next to my father."

"I promised Mrs. Faye I would go back; she is teaching me how to read and write," I protested.

"Rocco," DiAngelo broke in, "I will handle this with Father." Then, looking to Ray, he continued, "Rocco is going back with me; he is a part of my family. If you choose not to have him as a part of your family, that is your business. But for our home in Holland, we love him; and he will be a part of our family."

"You have no home except I give you one," Ray said pointedly, looking straight at DiAngelo. "The home in Holland belongs to Marco and myself, and he has made himself a home in these damn woods for years. Remember that, sons."

"I don't care if we have to live in the streets," DiAngelo answered. "Rocco is going back with me; he is my brother."

"Very well. He can stay long enough to learn to read and write . . . and then he is out! And . . . I hope you don't call him your brother in front of your mother. She would die of hurt and disgrace if anyone knew."

DiAngelo and I walked to the truck and got on our way to Mr. Creek's house.

"Rocco, you sure know how to handle yourself when you have to. I am proud of you."

"He holds that house over me because he knows I love you and Mrs. Faye and everyone," I responded. "'Do as I say or I will throw you out,' I said in my best Ray impersonation. When I get back, I will buy us a house, and he can have that ol' house!"

Mikie spoke, "Rocco, are you okay?"

"I am better than okay. I have you and Angelo here with me; I don't need a pa."

However, before I knew it, I was crying; I was so hurt.

"Buckaroo, it's okay. Who needs him? I will work and make us a home when we get back."

"Yes, Rocco," chimed in Mikie, "who needs him? We have each other . . . you, DiAngelo, and me."

I knew Mikie threw DiAngelo's name in there to let me know he was getting used to the fact that I had another best friend and a brother.

"Where are they going to have Mrs. Liza's going-home party?" I asked.

"Well, I think that will be in Michigan at her parish in Holland," DiAngelo answered.

"Wait . . . that means you and Uncle Marco will be coming to Michigan, Mikie," I said excitedly. "You can meet Evett and Mrs. Faye and Mrs. Sandra and everyone!"

When we got to the house, I went to see if Mom had a bed made up. There was a set of twin beds Mom had bought for me and Mikie to sleep in. I guessed after all the years that Mikie was not allowed to come to my house because of Pa, Mom figured it was his turn to come and stay with us. She had matching bedspreads and curtains and everything, waiting for me to come home.

I said, "Mikie, look what Mom has gone and done. She got us beds alike."

Mikie opened his gifts that I bought him and said, "Geez, Rocco, all these gifts are for me?"

"Yes, for all the years you bought me gifts. Now, I can buy you some. I love you, Mikie."

We squinted our eyes at each other.

Aunt Hadie did as she said she would and came to take us to her place for supper. Mom piddled in the grill, while everyone else got ready to eat.

"Where is Mom?" I asked. "She has to eat with us."

Uncle Marco looked at Aunt Hadie and said, "Go get your sister."

My mom came in looking all shy and sat next to me. DiAngelo sat on the other side of me, and Ray was right across from us with Mikie and Marco on either side of him. Aunt Hadie was to the other side of Mom on our side of the table. Mikie sat looking at me, smiling from ear-to-ear.

"Look at all this food!" I exclaimed.

Mom had cooked a ham and some taters and, of course, cornbread for me. Aunt Hadie had made some lasagna for the red-sauce eaters.

"Mikie," I began, "Mrs. Faye said that this summer maybe you, Uncle Marco, and everyone will come to Michigan and that we can have a swimming party. Mom, she said for you to come, too."

"Well, if Hadie goes, I will have to stay here and look after the grill."

It felt good to me that I had just invited my mom to go to

Mr. Ray's house for a week of rest and relaxation. I never took my eyes off him; I wanted to see his face and his reactions.

"Well, Mom, you can have someone else stay here to look after the grill and come and see Mrs. Faye's beautiful home. The lake is great; we can swim there and have the best picnic . . . right, Angelo?"

I turned and looked at DiAngelo as I finished my question.

"Yes. Mother said it would be a party to remember," DiAngelo responded.

"And oh, Mikie! Guess what!" I bubbled.

"What, Rocco?"

"I am going to be an uncle!"

"You are? To who?"

"My brother, DiAngelo, is getting ready to have a baby. We are going to have a wedding party for him and Evett in February."

"Well, there's a lot of that spending that's going to stop. I have been getting bills like crazy from the Holland house," Ray snorted.

DiAngelo came into the conversation, "Father, it's about time that Mother gets out of the house and go on shopping trips with the other ladies. For years she stayed in that big house and never even went Christmas shopping. You've saved a lot of money for the last nine years; and now that she is going to be a grandmother, she is all-out happy and buying everything. I also want to name my son Rocco if we have a boy."

Mr. Ray's face got redder by the minute, and he seemed as if he was about to erupt.

"The wedding will be the greatest," DiAngelo continued.

"She has ordered all the fancy things and says this will be a wedding that folks will talk about for a long time."

I looked over at Uncle Marco. He seemed to know what we were doing and had a smile on his face . . . actually, a kind of smirk.

"Well, how does my son plan on supporting a wife and a child at the age of barely 18? You are still a child yourself with no money except what I give you," Ray proclaimed.

"Maybe I will take after my father and just leave them to support themselves while I go on to do whatever it is I want to do," DiAngelo flung at him.

"That is a lie . . . a bald-faced lie! I never left anyone to support themselves, DiAngelo. If that is what you were told, it is a lie!"

"Is it, Father? Is it a lie? Rocco, how many presents did you ever get from your father on your birthday? How many times did you get school clothes? How many times if not for Aunt Hadie would you have gone to bed hungry?" Turning back to Ray, DiAngelo continued, "No, Father, it is not a lie; you did take care of me, send me things, and made sure I was fed well; but I would have rather had a father who loved me and showed me he loved me . . . but for Rocco, you did nothing. You turned your head and walked away and left him and Mrs. Dean to fend for themselves."

"How dare you talk to me like that! How dare you talk about things you know nothing about! After your grandmother is buried, I want you out of that house in Holland; then you can also see what it is like to take care of yourself," Ray seethed.

"My pleasure, Father. I will have my wife, Evett, and Rocco right with me . . . and Mother and Grandmother; you will have no one."

"How will you be able to get a house?" Ray wanted to know. "You have nothing unless I give it to you."

"That is where you are wrong, Father. I will use my business as collateral to buy a home."

"What business?" Ray asked, almost mockingly.

"The one you would not help me get. Yes, Father, I got it; and it's all paid for. I will support my family and do what is right because as many people that are here at this table, if you wrap them up altogether, they would still not make a fourth of the person Rocco is . . . and that includes you, Father!"

"Well, I see you have made your stand, and it is with your brother; but as far as your mother moving with you, she will do as I say. I am her husband."

"We will see, Father; we will see."

"Well, it looks as if the oldest of the three children has grown up and is ready to spread his wings and fly," Uncle Marco observed out loud.

"Marco, please take care of your own family business; this is mine," Ray retorted.

"Father," DiAngelo continued, "it seems that Uncle Marco has taken care of his family business and most of yours: he has taken Rocco under his wing and helped raise him with good manners and a kind heart. He raised not one son, but two. Mother and me also helped, and the boy has a great mother who loves him enough to give him up for a season that he might learn and have more in life than what you ever have given him."

"I am tired of this conversation," Ray whined. "It is really starting to bore me. But remember, I am the oldest Pettrachini now; I am the head of this family. Now that Mother is gone, a lot of things are going to change; and a lot of purse strings are going to be cut to start with."

"We have enough to start over;" DiAngelo responded, "so, if you think we are under your control because of money, you are wrong, Father. Uncle Marco has never received a penny from the family money, and he took great care of Grandmother. Your money means nothing to us."

"Okay, I mean it. I want you to shut your mouth now, DiAngelo . . . right now!"

"Excuse me, please," DiAngelo responded, "it seems I have been sent to my room. Father, do you even know where my bedroom is . . . matter of fact, do you know *anything* about me?"

"Marco! Marco, please shut him up; I am getting angry! He has said enough," Ray all but pleaded.

"DiAngelo," Uncle Marco started, "I do think you have made your views quite clear. I do need to clear up one misunderstanding: Rocco was raised with my son, but his teaching and his ways were learned from his mother and my wife. Him and Mikie are both great kids, and they have taught us a lot. They are gifts sent from Heaven.

"I must say I am very impressed by DiAngelo's love and concern for his brother," Uncle Marco continued. "It touches my heart. I wish I could have had a relationship with you, Ray, like that."

"Well, aren't you just the loving uncle, Marco? Everyone seems to adore you . . . even my own son," Ray couldn't help but respond.

"I do, too . . . I love Uncle Marco and Mikie!" I added to the mix.

I squinted my eyes over to Mikie.

Ray noticed and said sarcastically, "Does the boy have eye problems? Why does he keep squinting them like that?"

Everyone simply stared at him in disbelief at his caustic attitude.

"Anyway," Ray continued, "I have the church and funeral home ready for Mother's return. They will have everything ready. The attorneys will meet with us at the house in Holland after burial. Then I will be on my way back to Italy."

"Do you have another family over there, Father?" DiAngelo asked pointedly.

"Maybe I do," Ray answered flippantly.

This made DiAngelo so angry that he got up from the table, said "Excuse me," and went outside.

"I think I made him mad," Ray said, almost with pride.

"I think he went to smoke one of those stinky cigarettes. Mikie and me don't smoke. Mom said good boys don't smoke," I said.

Suddenly, looking at Mom, Ray asked, "Dean, how have you been?"

Mom stared at him in disbelief for a minute before answering, "Well, I guess I don't have to say all the things that I have been aching to say to you, Ray Pettrachini. Your own son said word-for-word what I wanted to say. I don't hate you."

"Well, I would hate me if I were you."

"Ray, that's what makes me a better person than you. I was a lonely woman, and you took advantage of a bad time in my life. You lied to get what you wanted and left. But you left me with the best part of you. Rocco is the best son anyone could ask for."

"Thanks, Mom," I said as I stood up and went to her and kissed her cheek. "Mikie and me are going to check on Angelo."

I looked at Mikie as I said it and tossed my head in the direction DiAngelo had left the room. We found DiAngelo standing by his truck.

He looked up at me and asked, "Can we leave tonight, Rocco? I just want to get us home safe and sound and be able to sleep in our own beds."

"Sure, Angelo. I will go tell Mom goodbye, and we can leave. Can Mikie come with us?"

"If Uncle Marco says it is okay, it is fine with me."

"Angelo, are you okay?"

"No, I am not okay."

"Mikie, go ask if you can go home with us," I prompted him.

"Okay," Mikie excitedly answered, "but don't leave till I go ask."

"Angelo, you are not hurt by him, are you? He didn't say anything mean to you."

"No, I am hurt because of how he treats you so badly."

"Silly, don't you know every dog has his day? This man can't do anything to me that pa hasn't already done. I am not scared of him. Love comes in time. You remember when you took me the first time?"

"Yes."

"You didn't love me; we had to get to know each other and be with each other."

"But he has a cold heart, and I don't like it."

"Brother, are you mad because he has a cold heart for me or for you?"

DiAngelo looked at me as if I had just looked into his heart and soul . . . as if I had reached deep inside him, pulled out a broken heart, and held it out in my hand.

I said, "Let's fix it; let's fix your broken heart."

"I don't know how."

I bowed my head and said, "Lord, it's me again. I got a problem. My brother is hurting bad inside. He needs a new heart . . . one that don't hate. Teach him to love and be truthful at the same time; teach him to know who he is and stand tall and smile at the world, no matter who loves him and who don't. Teach him to love himself. Thank you for doing this for me, Jesus. I will talk to you later. Goodnight."

Then I looked up at DiAngelo.

"Angelo, dig down and bring forth your happiness and laughter. Show the world who you are and where you are going. Stop looking at all the bad; look at the good things in your life."

"My Buckaroo, thank you for loving me and teaching me the good and right ways and for being my brother and friend. I love you."

"I love you, my brother."

"I can go! I can go! Father said!" Mikie exploded out of the house. "Father says I can go if you will drive safe and slow."

"Well, maybe you better take the bus, Mikie," DiAngelo said and the three of us laughed.

"We have to get Mom home and get my gifts," I pushed.

On the way to Mom's, she put her arm around me and hugged me up against her.

She whispered, "I am proud of you, the little man you have become. I am proud to be your mom."

"I am proud to be your son."

After packing up my gifts, I kissed my dear mom goodbye; and we were off again on my way to my other home. Mikie and I talked about everything from school to Evett and went back and forth about the things in each state.

"Todd is being okay," Mikie offered. "But he still wants to show off and call me 'Whop' and 'Greaser' and trip me every now and then."

"Angelo will teach you to fight, also," I promised him.

"This is so great: both my friends and brothers . . . pizons."

"Pizons? What does that mean?" I asked him.

"We are pizons. In Italian it means a friend who sticks closer than a brother. It is a bond between friends that no one can understand. It is from one heart to another without words."

"Then the three of us are pizons from the heart," I observed.

DiAngelo said, "I love that word. It is what I have been looking for. It is a word my soul understands."

*****

As we drove into Holland, it was dusk.

"Look at all the lights! Everything looks bright up here," Mikie said.

"Wait till you see the lake behind the house. It's big . . . right, Angelo?"

"Yes," DiAngelo answered, "and deep, so I have to teach you to swim before I can take you out there."

As DiAngelo put on the blinker to turn in toward the gate, Mikie exclaimed, "My goodness . . . what is this?"

"This is where I live with my brother."

“You’ve got to be kidding, Rocco! This is bigger than our school at home.”

DiAngelo started laughing.

“Nothing to laugh about, Angelo. It is the truth,” I agreed with Mikie.

“Are you two teasing me? Your school is this small?” DiAngelo asked.

“No, your house is that big!” Mikie answered.

DiAngelo stopped at the front door to make it easier to bring things in.

“It’s about time you got home,” Mrs. Faye greeted us with a smile.

I ran to her and hugged her.

“How is my boy?” she asked me.

I couldn’t let her go. It all came out all over her as the tears that had built up inside me for so long . . . the hurt, the going-home parties, more hurt . . . flooded down my cheeks. I cried until she was soaking wet. Finally, she took me to Mrs. Sandra to the piano room.

“What happened?” she asked tenderly after she had sat me down in one of the chairs.

“Faye, just give him a chance to get it out. He doesn’t need to talk if he doesn’t feel like it,” Mrs. Sandra said in a soothing voice.

Mrs. Sandra stood next to me and rubbed my head as Mrs. Faye continued to hold me as years of pent-up pain flowed through my eyes.

“Buckaroo, aren’t you going to help us unpack?” DiAngelo asked as he stuck his head into the piano room.

“DiAngelo, leave us,” Mrs. Faye said.

I heard the door softly shut so Mikie could not see me crying.

After what seemed like hours, Mrs. Sandra said, "Okay, boy, that's enough." She handed me her hankie and continued, "You tell Mrs. Faye and me what happened."

"Don't tell Angelo I was hurt by his father, okay?"

"Okay," they said in unison, "but tell us what happened."

"He said I can't live here with you, and then he agreed to let me come back long enough to learn to read. Now, he is mad and said Angelo has to get out, also. Now we have to get us a new house. He said you can't live with us. I am going to miss you both. Now, I don't have Mom or you. Angelo made him real mad and told him off bad . . . right at Uncle Marco's table! I have made a mess for you all."

"Oh, boy, it's not your fault," Mrs. Sandra said.

Mrs. Faye went to the door, opened it, and screamed, "DiAngelo, get in here!"

DiAngelo had taken Mikie upstairs. He came back down and stood there quietly as Mrs. Faye just looked at him. She stepped back to allow him to walk into the room.

"Is this all true?" Mrs. Faye asked him, motioning toward me.

"Yes, Mother."

"You have to move, and I can't go with you . . . is that what he said?"

"Yes, Mother; it was bad."

"All of this was said in front of this child? I thought I told you to look out for him; he didn't need to hear all that. I am very disappointed in you. He was just getting on his feet, and you have allowed him to be knocked back down."

"Mother, it just happened so fast. We were going to have supper together, and it all went crazy."

"Well, no one will be moving from this house . . . is that clear?"

"Yes, Ma'am," answered DiAngelo.

"Rocco?" Mrs. Faye directed at me.

"Yes, Ma'am; but he's going to be mad if we don't get out."

"Oh, I will take care of Ray, believe me. Did you keep our secret?"

"Yes. I never said you knew he was my father; and Angelo didn't, either."

"Mother, what are you up to?" DiAngelo quizzed.

"Then he made Angelo mad when he said he might have another family in Italy," I inserted.

"Good Lord, Rocco, do you have to tell it all?" DiAngelo scolded me.

"Well, she asked." Turning back to Mrs. Faye, I continued in the same breath, "Mrs. Faye, I have something Mom sent to you and Mrs. Sandra. I will go get it."

"Rocco, who is that boy who came with you?" Mrs. Sandra inquired.

"Mrs. Sandra, that is Mikie, Uncle Marco's boy. I will fetch him when I get your gifts, but only one gift you can open now."

I went and got a few gifts that my mom had sent with me, and I took Mikie to the piano room with me.

"Mikie, this is Mrs. Faye, and this is Mrs. Sandra," I introduced him.

"Nice to meet you both," he greeted them.

"And you, also," Mrs. Sandra responded.

"Mrs. Sandra says you look just like your father," I offered.

Mikie smiled and said, "We all three do."

DiAngelo let out one of his geddy-up laughs.

Mrs. Faye opened her gift from mom. It was a quilt.

"Oh, that's beautiful! Where did she buy it from?" she inquired.

"I don't know, Mrs. Faye," I answered. "Mikie said she sewed it while she was working; her and Mom sewed it together."

"Are you kidding me?" Mrs. Faye asked in astonishment.

There were angels in each corner; and in the middle was a big angel. The note pinned to the quilt said, "Thank you for being my son's angels."

Mrs. Sandra opened hers next, and it was exactly the same, stitch for stitch.

"Looks like there are a lot of angels in this family," she observed.

"Yes," Mrs. Faye said, "and one devil about to be dethroned."

*****

We woke up early.

Mikie said, "Rocco! Rocco, get up! I hear something."

"It's just the planes. They fly over the lake and go to the airport," I explained.

"Oh, it sounded like a coal truck at first. You should see how many loaded trucks come off your road to the busy road."

"I hope lots and lots . . . so I can go to college. The tutor teaches me some class called history, and I love that one the best. But he says I need to be tested for dyslexia."

"What does that mean?" Mikie wanted to know.

"It means I read things wrong . . . sometimes backwards . . . and numbers go backwards, too."

"You don't have to be tested for that. I can tell them you are," Mikie offered. "When I would help you with math, you would say the right thing, but write it down backwards."

"Well, the tutor says if I would slow down and concentrate, I might get it right. It helps that I don't have to hear you tapping your pencil all the time."

At that, we both laughed.

"Do you like it here, Rocco, or do you want to come home now?"

"It's hard, Mikie. I want to live with my brother; and I want you here, also . . . it's kinda like I miss you if I am here, and I would miss him if I was there."

"Well, who do you like the bestest?" Mikie pressed.

"I don't."

"What, Rocco?"

"I don't like Angelo any more than I like you; it's both the same."

"But, Rocco . . ."

"But what?"

"I have known you all my life. It should be me."

"I know, but he has a different bond with me; he is my brother . . . it's more like a pa. He is right here watching over me like your pa does for you; and since I never had a good one, I like it. It feels right."

"He is like a pa to you, Rocco?"

"Yeah, a fun pa . . . and Evett is nice. I will introduce you to her at breakfast, and I also want to show you something. It won't hurt you."

I took Mikie to the bathroom and said, "Look," as I turned on the shower. The water came down, and his eyes got big.

Mikie said, "I would drown in there."

"No, Mikie, you don't let the water get in your mouth. It just sprays over you like Angelo's carwash does."

"I'm not going in there," he said.

"Yes, you are Mikie. It is called a shower."

"No way, Rocco! I am not going in there!"

"Mikie, put your hand under it. See, it's like rain. It doesn't hurt."

He put his hand under the stream of water and said, "It don't beat you; it feels good. Okay, I will try it," he finally agreed.

He took off his clothes and jumped in. We talked while he took his first shower in the city.

"Get that soap, lather up, and let the water get the dirt off," I instructed.

"Hey, I am not dirty; I took a bath yesterday."

"Make sure you let the soap get on those stinky feet."

We laughed and laughed.

"What are you two doing?" DiAngelo barged in on the fun.

"Good morning, Angelo," I answered. "I have to stay here while he tries and takes his first shower. He is a baby and thinks he will drown."

"I ain't no baby, Rocco. I heard that."

"Skeeter, hurry up so we won't be late for breakfast."

DiAngelo asked, "Do you know if Mother and Grandmother are awake yet?"

"Nope. We just got up. Did you sleep with Evett last night? You better be good; it's not February, yet."

"Okay, Buckaroo, I will try," he said as he laughed.

"Evett, get up!" I screamed through the bathroom door.

I heard her moan, "I'm awake."

"Breakfast going to get cold with all this sleeping going on," I added loudly.

Evett came in the bathroom and said, "Just when we got you trained to sleep to 8:00, now you're back up at 6:00, again."

"Rise and shine, pretty 'Vett," I said as cheerily as I could.

"Rocco, I love you; but you and Angelo get out of this bathroom."

Just about that time Mikie stepped out of the shower naked as a jaybird. Evett gasped. Mikie almost broke his neck trying to get back in the shower, covering up with the shower curtain.

"Evett, meet our cousin, Mikie," DiAngelo offered while extending a hand toward Mikie with the shower curtain clasped around his body. "Say 'Hi,' Mikie," he continued.

"Hi, Evett," Mikie answered timidly.

"Can all this wait until I use the restroom?" Evett asked.

DiAngelo threw a towel to Mikie and told him to wrap up. We walked out of the bathroom, laughing at Mikie.

"It's not funny! It's not funny," Mikie complained.

"Yes, it is!" I responded. "Evett saw you naked . . . and the way you almost fell backwards into the shower with your butt showing!"

"She is pretty . . . just like you said, Rocco."

"Rocco, were you telling stories about my wife-to-be?" DiAngelo asked with a mock sternness in his voice.

"Yes, I told Mikie how pretty she is and how she takes me to the mall and stuff like that."

We waited for Evett to get done. We then finished our showering and went to breakfast.

On the way downstairs, DiAngelo said, "You better have gotten your feet clean, Mikie. I smelled those shoes all the way into Evett's room!" DiAngelo teased.

We laughed, and Mikie snarled up his nose and said, "No, that was Rocco's feet!"

We walked in the dining room, laughing. There sat Ray in Mrs. Faye's chair. We all stopped in our tracks and just stared.

"How did he get here so fast?" I whispered to DiAngelo.

"Rocco, hush!"

Chapter 14

Coming up behind us was Mrs. Sandra and Mrs. Faye. We all just stood there and continued to stare. We didn't know where to sit; our routine had been disrupted.

"Ray, please remove yourself from my seat," Mrs. Faye said as she whirred past us.

"I am head of this table," he stated.

"Do it at the other end of the table; that is my seat," Mrs. Faye repeated.

I was surprised to see Ray get up, get his toast and coffee, and go to the other end of the dining room table. We sat in our usual seats, me and DiAngelo on each side of Mrs. Faye and Mrs. Sandra to my right. We put Mikie on the other side of Mrs. Sandra, and across was Evett next to DiAngelo. Father sat all the way at the other end of the dining room table by himself.

"Good morning, Faye," he said with a hint of sarcasm.

"Morning, Ray," she stiffly responded.

"I had the housekeeper get our breakfast ready. I hope you don't mind," Ray said.

"Matter of fact, I do. Our menus were made out last night. When Miss Maria came to me and said you had changed the menus, I took the liberty of changing them back."

"So, you knew I was here," he stated rather than asked.

"Mrs. Sandra, am I having eggs and taters or not?" I inquired.

"Yes, boy, our food will be here in a minute."

"Mikie, you want some eggs and taters . . . I mean potatoes?"

"Potatoes? That's funny," he answered. "You said potatoes."

"That's what they call them up here; so, shut up, Mikie."

Mikie's face lost its smile when I told him to shut up.

"Rocco, we don't tell guests to shut up," Mrs. Faye scolded.

"Yes, Ma'am, but Mikie is not a guest. So, can I tell him to shut up?"

DiAngelo burst out laughing. He then looked up at Ray.

"Father, good morning."

"Oh, you're talking to me again?"

"Sure. I want you to meet my wife-to-be. This is Evett; Evett, this is my father."

"Good morning, sir," Evett greeted him.

"Good morning. No 'sir' needed. I am Ray. Welcome to my family."

"Thank you," Evett answered.

Mrs. Faye's eyes rolled so far it made her head tilt, and she breathed heavily enough for the whole house to hear.

The gate buzzer suddenly went off.

"I'll get it," DiAngelo announced.

He let Uncle Marco and Aunt Hadie through the gate. They were the first of several they were expecting for Mrs. Liza's funeral later in the day.

When Uncle Marco and Aunt Hadie entered the house, they were bundled up as though they were in Alaska. Miss

Maria took their coats. They came into the dining room and greeted everyone with a "Good morning."

"Come, sit down here, Father," Mikie yelled.

When Aunt Hadie got to Mikie, she hugged and kissed him as though she hadn't seen him in years. She took the seat next to him, and Uncle Marco sat next to her.

"My side of the table has more folks than yours, DiAngelo," Mikie taunted.

Everyone laughed at him.

"Mother, Grandmother, this is Aunt Hadie," DiAngelo introduced.

The two ladies nodded their heads in acknowledgement and said, "Good morning."

"Good morning, ladies," Aunt Hadie responded.

"Where are my manners? I am sorry, Mrs. Sandra." Uncle Marco said as he got up and went over and kissed her on the cheek.

"Well, it's been a long time, Marco. Nice to see you and your family."

"Thank you, Ma'am."

Uncle Marco went to Mrs. Faye next.

"Hello, Faye," he greeted her as he shook her hand.

"Good morning, Marco," she simply said, but I could see her hand shaking like a leaf.

When she noticed she still had his hand, she quickly dropped it.

"I will have Miss Maria cook you some breakfast," Mrs. Faye offered.

"I can help cook," Aunt Hadie offered to ease the burden on Miss Maria.

"We hire help to bear our burdens in the north, Mrs. Hadie," Ray spoke up.

Everyone at the whole table looked at Ray with contempt.

"Well, I am from the south; so, I will help," Aunt Hadie said with insistence.

She excused herself and went with Miss Maria.

As we chatted about the weather and the snow that was coming down quite heavily, someone remarked that they had heard a storm was moving in. Mikie and I talked with DiAngelo and Evett as Uncle Marco and Ray talked at their end of the table.

"Mrs. Faye?" I said.

"Yes, Rocco," she answered.

"Will they have music at the church for Mrs. Liza?"

Everyone at the table became quiet.

"Not as lovely as the way you sing, I am sure," she answered.

"Mrs. Faye, do you know the preacher who is talking?"

"Ray, who is doing the service for your mother?" Mrs. Faye ventured on my behalf.

"He doesn't need to know all that, Faye," Ray snapped.

"Well, I do!" she snapped back.

"Father Steve," Ray finally answered impatiently.

"Father Steve," she repeated to me. "He was the priest who married DiAngelo's father and myself," Mrs. Faye explained to me.

"He should have prayed about it first before he went and done that," I replied.

Mrs. Faye smiled knowingly, while Ray raised his eyebrows at me. DiAngelo laughed.

"Buckaroo, you are a joy this morning," he said.

The gate buzzer went off again, and DiAngelo volunteered to answer it. Soon, a man, tall and thin, with a woman about the age of Mrs. Sandra came in.

"Good morning to you all," the woman greeted everyone as she stepped into the dining room.

"Good morning, Aunt Susan. Good morning, Tiny," several greeted them.

Mikie and me burst out laughing.

"They call him Tiny, as tall as he is?" I whispered to Mrs. Sandra.

She patted my arm to hush me, but I couldn't stop laughing; it was too funny.

Aunt Susan and Tiny took seats next to Evett on DiAngelo's side of the table.

DiAngelo announced, "Two more for my side of the table." He winked at me.

"So what? Still four to five, my win," I insisted.

"Not so fast," DiAngelo warned. "Let's see who else shows up."

"I am sorry to hear about your mother. I talked to her not two nights before she passed, and she was fine," Aunt Susan offered.

"Oh, you are the one who always called Mrs. Liza . . . and talked to her on the phone?" I asked.

"Yes, I am . . . and you must be Rocco," she answered. "And that's Mikie," she added as she nodded her head toward him.

"Yes. How did you know?"

"Liza always spoke of you boys."

"Her name is *Mrs.* Liza," I corrected her.

"Of course. I am sorry. My sister loved her grandchildren

very much . . . and look at this young man, DiAngelo Pettrachini."

"Hello, Aunt Susan. How are you?"

"I am fine, thank you. Your grandmother insisted I be here today or I would have stayed in my warm house and sent my love to her in my prayers."

We ate our breakfast and then changed into our church clothes. When we went outside, there were four big, black cars to carry everyone to the church. Ray separated all of us. I was to go with Uncle Marco and Aunt Hadie and Mikie. Evett and DiAngelo were in one car, and Tiny and his mom in one by themselves. Ray and Mrs. Faye got in the last one.

"Rocco, where are you going?" Mrs. Faye called to me.

"Mr. Ray told me to go with Marco."

"No, you will ride with Ray and me."

"Yes, Ma'am."

As I climbed into the last car, Ray looked at Mrs. Faye.

"Why is he here with us?"

"Because I want him near me so I can look over him."

"You mean, make him behave himself, don't you?"

"No, he is a very well-behaved child. I said I want him to ride with us so I can look over him," she repeated with evenness.

"Very well," Ray answered with a little bit of meekness stealing into his voice.

Mrs. Faye and I sat on one side of the car, and Ray sat on the opposite side. He kept looking at us, listening to us talk about our lives, soaking it all in.

"Rocco, I want you to be seated with Mother and me when we get to the church," Mrs. Faye instructed me.

"Who has Mrs. Sandra? Who is she riding with?" I wanted to know.

"She is with DiAngelo and Evett."

"We should have rode with them, Mrs. Faye."

"Does he have an opinion about everything?" Ray asked, impatience creeping back into his voice.

I didn't ever have too much to say to Ray; I would just look at him. I wasn't afraid of him . . . it was more of an ignoring thing. The rest of the folks would get him if he got too mean with me, like DiAngelo had done back in Kentucky. So, I let them fight my battles for me and kept my thoughts and words mostly to myself when he would make remarks.

"He *is* very opinionated," Mrs. Faye responded. "That's what we love about him."

"Or is it that you now have Marco's child with you that makes you love him so much?" Ray pressed.

Mrs. Faye stared at him with contempt. She brought me closer to her side.

"Do not speak to me at all until we have a meeting at home after we lay your dear mother to rest."

"Faye, I have let your short and rude comments go long enough. Now, tell me what it is that is bothering you."

Mrs. Faye continued looking out the window and didn't answer.

"Don't talk to her, and we mean it! Don't talk to me, either," I spouted.

"Why do you have such contempt for me, Rocco? Right from the start, you didn't like me."

"You should have been with Mrs. Liza on her dying bed. Instead, you were on the phone talking; and you ain't even supposed to use those phones in the hospital. Didn't you read?"

Ray laughed, and it was just like DiAngelo's laugh. I couldn't believe it.

"I thought *you* were the one who didn't know how to read."

"Angelo told me what it meant. It had a picture of a phone right on the sign with a slash through it."

"I saw it," he said.

"I know you did. You have to obey the laws of the land like everyone else."

"What were *you* doing at the hospital, anyway?" Ray pushed.

Mrs. Faye broke in, "Like you don't know what this boy has been through. Just leave him alone."

"Listen, Faye, all I know is I got a call from Marco. He said this child needed somewhere to hide out. He said nothing about him needing medical attention or I probably wouldn't have agreed. Those bills are still coming in, and they're not cheap ones!"

"You wouldn't have agreed to our helping this child, Ray?"

"No, I wouldn't have," he said as he looked at Mrs. Faye evenly.

"Well my Superman cast didn't cost anything. Dr. Bill let me borrow it. I can pay my own medical bills, anyway!" I responded adamantly.

"Good!" Ray answered. "I will have them sent back to the Holland house," he said laughingly as he sat back in his seat and rearranged himself haughtily.

"Ray, please do yourself a favor and shut up," Mrs. Faye strongly suggested.

"I am not used to people giving me such remarks. The women in Italy don't speak to their husbands like this."

"Dear Lord, help me," Faye prayed out loud.

"Amen!" I added.

The service was nice and short. They then carried Mrs. Liza to the cemetery. As they lowered her casket into the ground, My Aunt Hadie started to sing as Mikie and Uncle Marco cried. She held my hand and together we sang to Mrs. Liza . . . but this time, I sang loudly, and no one could hush me. There was no pa to say "Shut up." That day, when I sang, I did it from my heart to my friend. It carried her all the way to Heaven and set her at the Lord's feet.

I looked over at my folks, and they were all crying. I don't know what those Catholics were feeling, but they were sure sending Mrs. Liza off with half of their hearts.

We walked back to the big, black cars in the snow.

Aunt Hadie said, "Thank you for helping me send Liza off to the Father."

"You're welcome, Aunt Hadie."

"You are quite the singer now, little guy."

"Angelo did it; he got me a speaker and a microphone set so I can sing for them."

"I will have to remember to tell your mom that."

"Tell her I don't sing quiet any more, and tell her I love and miss her."

When we got back to the house, things were kinda quiet; we were all sitting in our own individual, little groups. Miss Maria had laid out some snacks for folks to eat on while they talked about Mrs. Liza. I stuck pretty close to DiAngelo and Mrs. Faye. Mrs. Sandra seemed to be having a good time with

Mrs. Susan talking about the good, ol' days. Her son kept mostly to himself, but kept watching everyone in the room.

"Angelo?" I said.

He kept talking to Evett.

"Angelo?" I said louder.

"What, Buckaroo? I am talking."

"I know, but it is I important."

"What, then?"

"Your mom and dad are going to have a meeting."

"What kind of meeting?"

"I don't know, but she said soon as we get home, she wanted Ray in the study with me."

"No kidding?"

"Can you go with me? I am scared."

"Maybe they just want to talk to you, Rocco. It will be okay."

"He said he is mad about my doctor bills and that if he knew I was sick, he wouldn't have let me come and hide out here. He told Mrs. Faye the reason she loved me was because I am Marco's son."

"Oh, crap! Father just hung himself."

"I think you are right because she asked the Lord to help her. She said, 'Dear Lord, help me.'"

"I think she was trying to contain herself, and she was asking the Lord to help her stay calm until later."

"See, I do need you to go with me. I think they are gonna argue bad this time . . . not like yours and Evett's kind of arguments."

"I think you're right."

Just then Mrs. Faye approached us.

"DiAngelo," Mrs. Faye started.

"Yes, Mother?"

"Take Rocco and go into the study right now."

"Mother, are you sure this is the right time?"

"Do it now, DiAngelo."

"Yes, Mother."

"Angelo, see what I mean? She is mad on the inside, and I think she is going to blow like a whistle on a train," I told him.

We were almost to the door, and I heard Mrs. Faye call out, "Ray, darling, can I see you for a minute?"

"Yes, dear."

They always put on a show for the folks as though they were really happily married, and he was just away taking care of his father's businesses.

When Ray joined us in the study, Mrs. Faye was sitting at his desk, in his chair.

She said, "Sit down, Ray."

I was standing next to DiAngelo, but I was holding onto a belt loop in his jeans. I knew in my heart all hell was about to break loose.

"Rocco, dear," Mrs. Faye said looking directly at me.

"Yes, Ma'am?"

"I want you to remember one thing during this meeting, okay?" I nodded my head as she continued, "I love you with all my heart, and this has nothing to do about you or that I think you have been bad, okay?"

"Yes, Ma'am."

"Ray, you sorry son-of-a-snake-in-the-grass. I am going to file papers of separation and take all the money I can from you. You will keep supporting me and Rocco for the rest of our lives, do you understand? As far as you holding this house over these boys' heads, no one is leaving . . . not our son or your son. Do you hear me?"

Mr. Ray sat there for a few minutes, then started in a seething voice, "Faye, if you ever call me those names again, I will slap you down, do *you* understand?"

"I mean no disgrace to your dear mother, but as soon as your business here is over, you return to Italy and never come back. I am not going to divorce you because of the church, but separation papers will keep you as far away from these boys and me as possible."

"Faye, I have one son; and that is our boy, DiAngelo. He is the only son I have."

"Well, I have *two* sons. Rocco is my second one. We will set the guidelines now: you are to send money every week to us. He will live a good and happy life here with his brother and me."

"Faye, why don't you really say what is on your mind? Why do you care if this boy goes back south or falls off the face of the earth?"

"Because you think he is Marco's son, that's why. You have said that to me two times today. I know Rocco is not Marco's son, but *yours*. However, I wish I would have had these two sons by Marco. There . . . are you happy that I have finally said it?"

Ray's eyes were as large as dinner plates.

Faye continued, "Yes, I was in love . . . deeply in love with Marco, and you raped me on my way home from church that night. I had to marry you because that is what I was taught: I had to marry the first man I was with. Instead of marrying Marco, I broke his heart and sent him away. He would have raised DiAngelo; I know he would have. He is more of a man than you will ever be."

I felt DiAngelo's belt loop pull on my finger, and it brought him backwards, away from killing his father.

Mrs. Faye looked suddenly at DiAngelo.

"No, DiAngelo!"

He backed off.

"We could have had a good life, Faye, back then but you just couldn't get over Marco. Your love was alive in you for only him, and you never gave us a chance."

"How was I supposed to love you, Ray? Tell me, damn it! Tell me! You took away from me the only man I ever loved. The big Ray Pettrachini takes what he wants, never thinking about anyone else."

"Not only am I not sending a penny home, I am selling this house and everything in it. Maybe you can be a cook at Aunt Hadie's Grill with his mother," he answered threateningly, jerking his head toward me as he spoke.

He laughed a bitter and fake laugh.

"So, am I to understand that you have no interest in this boy whatsoever and you are not going to help me finish raising him?"

"I couldn't care less about this boy or his mother. Matter of fact, I couldn't care less about *you*!"

It was a good thing there was a knock on the study door right at that time because I felt that tug, harder this time, but he eased up when Uncle Marco came in.

"Yes, Marco, what is it?" Mrs. Faye asked him.

"The attorneys are here."

"Bring them in here, please, Marco."

"Faye, could you please remove yourself from my desk?

However, I do want you to hear what you have just given away. I want to see your face."

Mrs. Faye took on a rather somber look and got up from his desk.

"Boys, we will be fine," she said to us. "We will start life over again with our new family and the new baby."

She hugged us both.

I said, "Thanks for trying, Mrs. Faye, but I am going to buy us a new house myself for Angelo and me."

"That's right, Buckaroo, and live happily ever after."

He hugged me to his side. I felt in my heart I could finally let go of his belt loop now, and I was glad because my finger was red and numb.

There were not only one or two, but there were five attorneys who came into the room.

"Damn! You brought your assistants with you," Ray remarked as he came from behind his desk to shake their hands.

"Angelo," I whispered as I tapped on his leg, "there's Mr. Hamson, that lawyer guy from Kentucky. Remember him?"

"I do. Now, hush. See what they say."

The eldest of the five said, "Do I have all parties involved in the will gathered here?"

"Well, we don't know. We have no idea what's in Mother's will," Uncle Marco answered him.

"I need a Susan Masterzo, a Rocco Brooks, a Mikie Pettrachini, a Marco Pettrachini, a Ray Pettrachini, and a DiAngelo Pettrachini."

"Yes, all accounted for," Ray answered importantly. "Good to see you all the way from Italy, Antonio," he added.

"Thank you, Ray. Your mother contacted me about five years ago and had me come see her."

"You never mentioned that to me."

"Your mother and father were my clients, Ray. I worked for *them*."

"I will remember your loyalties and with whom they were with," Ray answered with a threatening hint.

"Let's continue," the eldest man said, throwing off Ray's barb. "To my sons," he started reading from several pages in his hand, "I have always been disappointed with your actions to one another, the hatred that is in you for each other, the mean and evil things you did to each other, even as children and continue to this day. I have prayed daily for you to come together as a family. You have broken my heart and my Daniel's heart. I leave neither of you anything except for the $10 allowance that started your arguing a long time ago. It was the first time you hated each other, and that seed grew bigger and bigger to the point where I have not seen my prodigal son for eight years at the time of this writing.

"The love that I wish for you two has been passed onto my two grandsons, Mikie and Rocco. They love and adore each other and will be the ones to keep my family together in the future. They will never let money or any other human being come between them. They are the real Pettrachinis.

"So, to my grandson, DiAngelo, I leave a sum of $100,000 to be given to him at the age of 21."

"Yes!" DiAngelo quietly let out. He was so excited.

"Stupid boy, she left you nothing or next to nothing," Ray snarled. "You do not know her holdings."

"So! I am thankful for whatever she left me, Father."

"Can we continue?" the lawyer interrupted.

"Please do," Ray waved his hand at him impatiently.

"I do not need to divide the rest," the lawyer continued reading, "for if Rocco has one thing, then Mikie would have it, also; and if Mikie has one thing, then Rocco also has it. To these two I leave the following:

"In Italy: I leave to them the home and the vineyards on the north, south, east, and west of that said property. I leave the 14 businesses in Italy to them to be overlooked by one, said Antonio Farelli. I leave to them the businesses in Michigan, the restaurant chain in Grand Rapids, and the house in Holland. The money from said businesses will be deposited into one account, overseen by Mr. Hamson of Kentucky. The remaining $7million in my account will also be transferred to that account.

"Children, do what is right and take care of my family with love. Respect each other; teach them how to love and be as kind as you are. You are children sent to us from Heaven to heal Daniel's and my family. I love you. Mrs. Liza Pettrachini."

"I will contest this to my grave," Ray said bitterly.

"No need to waste your time, Ray. Your mother has had this done for a long time. No court will believe she was crazy. You men have done this to yourself. Are there any other questions?"

"Hang on, all of you," I spoke up. "I need to talk to Mikie somewhere alone."

I looked at Mikie. He was smiling. We went to my piano room.

"Mikie . . ."

"You don't have to say it Rocco. I already know."

"Know what?"

"You want to split with DiAngelo and give him more than what Grandmother said, right?"

"Well, I know that is in my heart, also; and we can share right down the middle. We have more than enough. But, Mikie, you are better at math than I am. Are we rich, yet?"

"We haven't gotten to millions yet in school, but I think we are," he answered.

We squinted at each other.

"So, you're okay with sharing?"

"If he means that much to you, then one day I hope to love him like that, also," Mikie responded.

We hugged and shook on it and went back into the study. Once we sat back down in the study, I looked over to Mikie.

I said, "Mikie?"

"Yes, Rocco."

"Do you like grapes?"

The whole room of lawyers and all our folks laughed . . . except Ray.

"We need to change a few things of how Mrs. Liza wrote them in the will," I started.

"You can't," the tall man said. "It was your Grandmother's wishes. It must be done as she stipulated."

"So, is it Mikie's and my money now?"

"Yes."

"Then, Mikie and I want to share it right down the middle with DiAngelo Pettrachini, my brother."

Marco leaned over and whispered to Ray, "This is exactly why Mother has chosen these two."

Aunt Susan spoke up, "Yes, she knew that's what you would do, Rocco. My sister knew who to trust her family with. She knew you and Mikie would share with DiAngelo. I was to give you this paper if you didn't share it with DiAngelo and have it split three ways. It is an amendment to the will in case you didn't. That's why she requested I be here today. Today you have made all of us happy, and my sister and Daniel in Heaven are very happy right now."

Aunt Susan then handed me two books the size of picture albums.

"What are these?" I asked.

"One is a book of pictures of your family dating back to the early 1900s. She wanted you to have them. Under the pictures I wrote their names for you to see who they are and how they are related to you.

"The other book is at Marco's house," she continued, "so make sure you get it. Do you understand, Marco?" she asked as she looked at Uncle Marco.

"Yes, Ma'am."

"That other book is a business bank account. All moneys are being transferred to this account as we speak. The *only* name who can pull out money is yours, Rocco, even though you split it into three . . . you are the overseer of it to run the family with."

When Susan finished, she looked at the group of attorneys.

"Good day, gentlemen," she said, dismissing them.

"Thank you all for helping us with the paperwork," I said to them.

They turned and shook hands with Mikie, DiAngelo, and then me.

Mrs. Susan saw the group out the front door. Her son helped her put on her coat, and they left, as well.

"Marco, Mother has put us in quite an awkward position

here. What are we going to do?" Ray quietly asked as he sidled up to Marco.

"We are going to follow Mother's wishes and learn from it," Marco answered simply.

"I am not kissing an eight-year-old's ass to get my father's money, believe that."

Mrs. Faye then spoke up, looking directly at Ray, "Can you please get out of Mr. Rocco's chair and let him have his desk?"

"See, Angelo, Mrs. Liza loved you as much as she did Mikie and me."

"I guess she did, Buckaroo."

"Then why are you sad?"

"I didn't do right by her. I never went and seen her, and I really never knew my grandmother."

"Well, she still loved you."

"And," DiAngelo continued, "you little guys, thank you for splitting with me. You really didn't have to but you did it, anyways, all on your own."

"We love you, Angelo," I said.

"Yeah, we love you, I guess," Mikie added.

"Marco, wake up, man! She left us without a penny. What are we going to do?" I overheard Ray press.

"No, she didn't" I argued. "She gave $10 for each of you . . . which was nice of her."

DiAngelo had one of us standing on each side of him as he said, "Yes, Father, she did leave you each $10. That was nice of her."

And he let out one of those laughs as the three of us walked out the door together.

Chapter 15

DiAngelo said, “I am going to tell Evett the good news.”

“I am going to find Mrs. Faye and check on her,” I responded.

“I am going to get my mom out of that kitchen for the rest of the day,” Mikie said.

We took to our separate ways.

I knocked on Mrs. Faye's bedroom door.

“Come in,” she instructed.

As I entered, I noticed Mrs. Faye was packing a suitcase.

“Where are you going, Mrs. Faye?” I asked as alarm crept into my body.

“Well, this is no longer our house; it belongs to you and Mikie now.”

“Mrs. Faye, this is a family home, and you're my family.”

“Rocco, you have more money than anything; you can hire staff to help you with the upkeep of the house and property.”

“You don't love me anymore?” I asked.

“You know I do, Rocco. What kind of question is that?”

“Then I need you to be my standby mom. I don't want to live here without you and Mrs. Sandra.”

Mrs. Faye continued her packing silently.

“I am telling if you don't stop that packing,” I said as threateningly as I could.

Mrs. Faye smiled and said, "Boy, I love you."

I stormed out of her bedroom and ran to DiAngelo.

"Hurry!" I said. "Come, I need you!"

"What is it, Rocco?" he replied, concern creeping into his voice.

"Hi, Evett," I inserted to be polite.

"We are rich," Evett said dreamily.

"I know. Isn't it great?" I quickly answered.

DiAngelo broke in, "Will you tell me what's wrong, Rocco?"

"Mother . . . I mean Mrs. Faye . . . is packing her things and moving. Go tell her 'No,' Angelo. Come on now before she leaves."

DiAngelo and I went together to Mrs. Faye room.

Walking in, DiAngelo said, "Mother, why do you have Rocco so fired up? Where are you going?"

"I'm not sure yet."

"Mother, I am a Pettrachini, and so are you; this is our home, as always."

I added, "Even more now! We own this house, and Ray can never throw us out, Mrs. Faye . . . never! This is your house still and not his; we will live here happily ever after."

DiAngelo continued, "Mother, don't break his heart. He loves you; we need you! Right, Rocco?"

"Yes! I need Mrs. Faye to keep teaching me. I will be a rich dummy if she leaves."

We all hugged.

Finally, Mrs. Faye quietly said, "You are rich, but by no means are you a dummy," as she kept one hand on my shoulder and looked directly into my eyes.

Just then Ray walked into the room.

"Well, isn't this sweet . . . my sons hugging on their mother?" he taunted.

"Oh, *now* he is your son?" Mrs. Faye asked. Just before the lawyers came, you said he was nothing to you."

"I know what I said, Faye. I was just saying that to heal your wounds, Rocco. Come and hug your father."

I said, "Okay," as I turned and hugged DiAngelo. "I have the best father of all of you. I don't need you, Ray Pettrachini; I have Angelo, Mrs. Faye, my mom, Mrs. Sandra, and Mikie." Then, trying to lighten the air, I suggested, "Let's go sing, want to? I will get Mrs. Sandra, and we will sing."

DiAngelo laughed and said, "Maybe later. We really haven't had anything to eat, yet."

"Mrs. Faye and Mrs. Sandra always feed me really well. I couldn't eat if they weren't here; I would die," I replied.

"See, Mother," DiAngelo looked back to his mother, "you are needed by all of us."

"Where are you going, Faye? Why are you packing?" Ray suddenly asked as he realized what was happening.

"I was thinking about taking my sons to show them their home and vineyards that their grandmother left them," she answered.

"Can Mikie go with us, Mrs. Faye?" I quickly asked.

"That is *my* house; I am going back as soon as I can," Ray said with the first real hint of fear in his voice.

DiAngelo turned to Ray and said, "We will have to vote on it, Father, and see what Mikie and Rocco say."

"Angelo?" I piped up.

"Yes, Rocco?"

"I don't think Mrs. Liza would like us mistreating him; I don't feel right about that in my heart. Let's let him stay there, and you can figure out how much to pay him for helping run the businesses. It is the right thing to do."

Ray looked at me with an almost pleading look and said with the little heart he had left, "If I was the kind of man that Marco is and could stand children around me, I would be proud to be yours and DiAngelo's father; but I can't stand either one of you. So, come and find me when you're over 21 years old."

"Can we vote on when he should go back to Italy?" I asked, looking up at DiAngelo.

"Yes, Buckaroo. My vote is 15 minutes ago."

I looked at Mrs. Faye and said, "Your vote as the head of this house?"

"Twenty years ago!" She headed toward her bedroom door as she threw over her shoulder, "And, Ray, don't *ever* come back to *my* home!"

"Let's go eat; I am hungry!" I quickly suggested.

"Me, too," DiAngelo chimed in. "Come on, Father, we can give you some food, I guess."

After we all ate, Ray was off to Italy. He came into my life that fast and left just as fast. A part of me thought why didn't he just stay and try to work it out, but another part of me said some folks just aren't meant to be fathers . . . and Ray Pettrachini was one of those folks.

Mikie and Uncle Marco and Aunt Hadie went back home, and I am sure the first thing Aunt Hadie told Mom was that we were rich . . . but I really hope she didn't forget to tell Mom I could sing loud!

*****

They say things in life come in threes. That year I had three deaths: Mr. Creek, Pa, and my dear Mrs. Liza. However, the start of the good threes is that DiAngelo and Evett were having a baby.

After Uncle Marco and Aunt Hadie got home, I got a call from Mikie; and it seemed I was gonna be a cousin two times: Aunt Hadie was going to have a baby, too! Mikie was happy as all get out, and I am sure my mom was dancing around and getting ready to be an aunt again.

Soon, it was time for a wedding. DiAngelo's and Evett's wedding was small, and very few people attended. I asked DiAngelo why there weren't many people there, and he said Evett didn't want folks seeing her getting married with such a big stomach.

DiAngelo moved back into his room with Evett, and I stayed in my room. I heard Mrs. Faye suggest that they move me over one room so the baby's nursery could be next to Evett's room.

It didn't seem to change life any now that we had a mess load of money; there was already everything we needed and more to keep us happy at the house.

I only had to make one decision: Ray called and wanted $100,000 to buy some new equipment for the vineyards. DiAngelo and I made out a check to him. About three weeks later, he called again, wanting to sell the north vineyard, saying that it had bad soil and the crops had used up all the minerals.

DiAngelo said it didn't sound right, so we called the lawyer, Mr. Hamson, to find out more. The lawyer discovered no new equipment was needed or purchased and that it was really Ray who intended to buy the vineyard. In fact, it was discovered Ray asked the $100,000 from us to buy our land. Then he would have the north vineyard all to himself.

DiAngelo called Ray.

After arguing several minutes, DiAngelo said, "Father, one more try like that, and I will have you thrown out of the Italy home and force you to pay back the money with interest."

It had been several months since that phone call, and we had heard nothing more from Ray since. DiAngelo had suggested I stop giving Ray any money from that point on other than his regular salary.

"But, Angelo, what if his salary isn't enough to make ends meet for him?" I asked.

"Then I guess he will not spend more than he makes," DiAngelo answered.

We had not used any from the family account, and DiAngelo's carwash was going well. I started receiving money from the coal company, and DiAngelo couldn't believe they hauled that much coal out of there. Over the previous three months, he figured I had earned $240 per truck at about 15 trucks per day. In addition, he made out a check for $125,000 and paid me back for the money I had used to purchase the carwash. Anything Mrs. Faye and Evett bought for the baby and things like that came out of DiAngelo's carwash money.

On the last page in the checkbook was a blank page. DiAngelo kept records in three categories on the page with each of our names at the top of a column. Mikie's and my columns didn't show any money coming out. DiAngelo's column showed the money he gave me for the carwash. He said that way he could keep up with who was spending the money. If I needed to write a check, it came out of my money that Mr. Creek had given me.

DiAngelo complained we had too many bank books. I had the coal mining book; then there was the private one from Mr. Creek, the one Mom gave to me, and the one from Mrs. Liza with which to run the family.

"Do you know how much money you have, Rocco?" DiAngelo asked me one day.

"Nope."

So, he took the balance from each bank book and added them up.

"Altogether, Rocco, you have $53million," he informed me with astonishment edging his voice.

"Why do you think Mikie hasn't spent any money, yet?" I asked DiAngelo one day.

"Remember, no one can get the money out unless you sign the check, Rocco," he responded.

"You mean they might be doing without?"

"I don't know. Uncle Marco and Aunt Hadie would never say if they were in need. You know his pride."

"I want to call them, Angelo."

DiAngelo dialed their number and handed me the phone.

"Aunt Hadie's Grill," a female voice answered.

"Hi, Aunt Hadie. How are you?"

"Boy, I am fine. Good to hear from you! I will get Mikie."

"No, Aunt Hadie. I need to talk to Uncle Marco first, please."

"Oh, okay," she quickly answered. "But you better talk to Mikie, too."

"Oh, I will. I have some catching up to do with Mikie."

"Ok," Aunt Hadie responded, "hang on, boy."

Uncle Marco got on the phone.

"Rocco, are you okay?"

"Yes, sir."

"Well, I didn't expect you to ask to speak to me. I thought something must be wrong with you."

"No," I said. "I need to talk to you."

"Well, go ahead, boy."

"Do you have money?" I inquired of him.

"Why do you ask that?"

"Well, Mikie hasn't sent for any money, and I was wondering if you needed any of it. It's just sitting there in the bank."

"That money belongs to the grandkids, not me," Uncle Marco explained.

"Well, I don't think you would tell me if you have any needs, would you?"

"I am fine, Rocco; but thanks for thinking of us. You ready to talk to Mikie, yet?"

"Yes, sir, I guess; but I need to talk to Aunt Hadie first."

"Okay, Rocco. Talk to you later."

With that, Uncle Marco handed the phone to Aunt Hadie.

"Aunt Hadie," I started. "You are my mom's only sister, and I want the truth. Are there any bills not paid at your house that I could help with to make it easier on Uncle Marco, Mikie, and you?"

"Boy, why do you ask?" she quizzed.

"That's what Uncle Marco asked. I have a feeling there are bills that need to be paid, and you and Uncle Marco are not being plain-faced with me. Do I need to call Mom?"

"No . . . no, Rocco." Aunt Hadie took a deep breath and let it out slowly before she continued, "We got a foreclosure on our home, the grill, and the gas station. They are going to take it all if business doesn't pick up."

"Why hasn't Mikie sent for money?"

"He doesn't know about it; your uncle didn't want to tell him. He is too prideful to speak of it to Mikie."

"Aunt Hadie, I will call Mr. Hamson right away and have this taken care of for you. We don't have to tell Mikie if you don't want to, but tell Uncle Marco not to worry."

"Rocco, I am not sure I should have aired our problems; Marco might get mad."

"Aunt Hadie, I am sure if you told Mom, she would have taken care of it for you."

"I know my sister would have done that, but I didn't want to bother her with it. It is our problem." Aunt Hadie paused, then started again with excitement in her voice, "I guess since I am going to be in trouble for gossiping anyway, I have good news, also."

"What's that, Aunt Hadie?"

"Do you remember Mr. White?"

"Yes . . . Mr. White from church. He always sat by himself; he didn't have a wife. A real nice man, he is. I liked him."

"Well, he isn't sitting by himself at church any longer; he is sitting with your mom."

"With my mom? Why?"

"Because he likes her, and your mom likes him."

"They're courting?" I asked with excitement growing in my heart.

"Well, no . . . well, yeah . . . a bit. Are you upset, Rocco?"

"Shoot no! I am glad Mom likes him. He is really nice, and I won't have to worry about her with him. He prays and everything."

"I am so glad you agree to it."

"I will call her right after I get off and talk to her about it,"

I responded. "Tell Mikie I can't talk to him right now, but I will call him later. I need to call Mr. Hamson."

"Rocco, what are you going to do?" Aunt Hadie pressed.

"I am going to have all that paid off so Uncle Marco can start fresh with no bills."

"Oh, boy, you can't do that! I thought maybe you would just get us caught up."

"I can do what I want with this money," I started. "It's family money, and Uncle Marco is my family. I am sure Angelo would agree. Just don't tell Uncle Marco until it's done with. I don't want him interfering with it and saying 'No.'"

"Okay, boy, I won't. And God bless you for this."

"He already blessed me so I *could* do this, Aunt Hadie. I will call back in a few days. Tell Mikie I love him."

"Okay, will do. Take care, boy. Goodbye."

I went to find DiAngelo.

"Angelo, can you help me?"

"Sure," DiAngelo answered. "What's up?"

"You know that lawyer, Mr. Hamson?"

"Yes."

"Can you call him for me?"

"Why, Rocco?"

"We are going to pay off Uncle Marco's bills so he can start new."

"Wait a minute, Buckaroo. Who asked you to do this?"

"No one."

"Are you sure, Rocco?"

"Yes, I am sure. I had to drag it out of Aunt Hadie. Uncle Marco told me everything was okay, but Aunt Hadie told me they are getting foreclosed on. I don't want you telling anyone . . . not even Mikie, okay?"

"Well, let's call and see how much we need."

DiAngelo soon had Mr. Hamson on the phone and asked him to find out how much it would take to pay off Uncle Marco's home and businesses. It only took a few minutes for Mr. Hamson to call DiAngelo back and inform him that $79,000 would take care of everything for them.

"Is that all, Mr. Hamson? Are you sure?" DiAngelo asked him. "Okay, Rocco wants you to take that much out of the account and pay it off for them. Thank you, Mr. Hamson, and good day."

DiAngelo sensed there was something about the transaction that Rocco was not quite happy about.

"Buckaroo," DiAngelo started, "it was only $79,000. Things in Kentucky are cheaper than here in Michigan."

"Yes," I responded, "but why didn't you ask me first which account I wanted to use?"

"Well, I thought that was what you wanted."

"I wanted to take it out of Mr. Creek's money."

"Didn't I tell you that was for college?" DiAngelo questioned. "Besides, we can split the $79,000 three ways out of the family account."

"You would do that for my Uncle Marco?" I asked.

"Remember, he was my uncle first."

"Angelo, what would I do without you? First, Ray cheated me; and you caught it. Now, you help me with this with a better plan than I had. Thank you."

"What are big brothers for?" DiAngelo said as he play-punched my shoulder.

"Okay. I have to call Mom and tease her."

"Why?" DiAngelo wanted to know.

"She has a boyfriend. His name is Mr. White, and I know him. He is a good guy."

"It's about time your mom had better luck with men."

"You can say that again, Angelo."

I soon had Mom on the phone.

"Mom, hi!" I greeted her.

"Hi, baby. How are you?"

"I am good. I just heard the weirdest thing."

"What's that?"

"That my mom is courting Mr. White." I paused a moment before saying in a sing-song fashion, "Mom has a boyfriend . . . Mom has a boyfriend."

"Who told you?"

I repeated, "Mom has a boyfriend . . . Mom has a boyfriend."

"Hush, boy, and listen. I was going to tell you in person when you came home, but I guess folks are already talking."

"No, Mom, just Aunt Hadie . . . because she is so happy for you."

"You're not mad or hurt, are you?" Mom wanted to know.

"Heck, no. I think it is great. So, now you won't be all alone and sitting on that big porch all by yourself . . . but he can borrow my chair only till I get home."

"Okay, deal. He is a very nice man."

"I know, Mom. That's why I am happy. He always said 'Hi' to me, and he knows how to pray and everything."

"Yes, he does." Then Mom changed the subject, "Aunt Hadie is going to have a baby."

"Looks like things are going great," I replied.

"They are, baby. We have had enough sadness to last us a whole lifetime, and it is time to be happy."

"Yes, Mom . . . and you know what else?"

"What, baby?"

"I am not mad anymore at you or Uncle Marco; I love you just the same now. There's no more anger in me at all, and I just want you to know that and that I love you more than anything in the world."

"You swear . . . that there's no more anger . . . not even a tinch?"

"Not even a tinch, Mom, I swear."

And at that moment, I knew my mom had been set free. I had been set free.

"Now, you had better not be crying on this great day, Mom," I mock scolded her.

"I know, baby. I am just glad to hear you say those words. Mom loves you more than chocolate cake."

"I love you more than your cornbread, Mom."

"Baby, are you coming home?"

"After Evett has the baby, I am coming home for a week."

"Good! I can't wait. Love you, baby."

"Night, Mom."

We hung up.

"You know, I better call Mikie back," I said to myself more than to DiAngelo.

"Buckaroo, you are going to go bankrupt using that phone so much."

"Really, Angelo?"

He roared with laughter.

"No, I was teasing. You could buy the phone company if you wanted to."

"Okay, Angelo, I'm getting you when I get off this phone," I mockingly threatened.

"Aunt Hadie's Grill," I heard once again.

"Hi, Aunt Hadie. It's me again. I didn't feel right not talking to Mikie."

"That's good because he got quiet and said he didn't want to talk to you."

"I wanted to get this taken care of for Uncle Marco."

"What did they say, Rocco?" Aunt Hadie pressed.

Since it was DiAngelo who had talked to Mr. Hamson, I looked at him and asked, "What did they say about the foreclosure on Uncle Marco, Angelo?"

"The foreclosure will be canceled and the deed sent to them first thing tomorrow," DiAngelo was happy to announce.

"Did you hear that, Aunt Hadie?" I asked.

"Yes, boy, I did."

"So, take what money you have and buy you something nice and tell your baby I said 'Hi.'"

"Boy, you are silly," Aunt Hadie said, laughing.

"What are you going to call her?"

"Her?" Aunt Hadie asked.

"Yes, you are having a girl this time, I think."

"Thank goodness," Aunt Hadie said with relief in her voice. "You boys wore me out."

"Aunt Hadie, we didn't."

"Let me get my other knucklehead on the phone for you," she said before the phone went silent.

"Hi, Rocco," Mikie said rather sullenly.

"Mikie, how are you?"

"Good. I didn't think you wanted to talk to me, so I said I didn't want to talk to you."

"I had something I had to do real fast. So, I called you back when I finished it. How have you been?"

"I am okay. They're here listening by the phone."

"Tell them to get. I have to talk to you."

I heard Mikie turn away from the phone and say, "Rocco said to get so we can talk." Then, turning back into the phone he said, "Okay, they're gone, Rocco. I miss you bad, Rocco . . . worse now than before . . . after being up there and having fun laughing and having my best friend back."

"It's okay, Mikie. I am coming home in the spring, and it's already March. So, we can have spring break together and go shopping and everything. Mikie, do you need any money?"

"Yes, I think I do. Send me $20 in case I want something and maybe buy Father something."

"Okay. I will put it in the mail tomorrow, I promise. Why didn't you tell me you needed some money before now?"

"I keep forgetting we are rich, and then it hits me: I have money! Then, I forget again."

"Mikie, you know how we never hide anything from each other?"

"Yup."

"I sent some money to pay off everything for Uncle Marco. Is that okay?"

"That's a good idea, Rocco."

"He owes the bank $79,000, and we all three are gonna split it, okay?"

"Reckon I need to just take it out of my share; after all, he is my father."

"Well, we wanted to do it, also. This way it makes Angelo look closer to our bunch, okay?"

"But you can't tell Uncle Marco until after he gets his mail. They are paying it off now, so you will get to see his face when he opens the mail tomorrow at four o'clock. Tell me how he smiles."

"Rocco, you're not going to stop until you make us one big, happy family, are you?"

"Nope. That was Mrs. Liza's wish, remember?"

"I love you, Rocco."

"I love you, my friend. Goodnight."

I went over, sat down on the couch, and just sat there thinking. DiAngelo came over and flopped down and put his stinky feet in my face.

"Smell," he said.

"Nasty!" I yelled as I grabbed his feet and held on for dear life to his tall leg and tickled him and tickled him. He laughed so hard, he couldn't fight back. Finally, he fell to the floor. I kept up, and he slung his foot away, sending me flying away and landing on my back. I just lay there for a minute as pain shot to my head.

"Oh, my God," DiAngelo exclaimed. "Are you okay?"

He scrambled to my side.

"No, I think you killed me."

Mrs. Faye came running in.

"What's going on here?" she wanted to know. When she saw me lying on the floor, she pressed, "DiAngelo, did you push him down?"

"No . . . well, yeah . . . but by accident!"

I looked at Mrs. Faye and put my sad face on as I said, "Angelo tried to kill me. Now, my back really hurts."

"Poor baby," she responded as she got down on the floor to check me over.

I looked over her at DiAngelo and smiled.

"You big faker! Mother, look at him; he's laughing because you got after me."

"Shut up, you overgrown ape; and help me get up," I demanded of DiAngelo.

"I will get you up, all right."

With one swoop, DiAngelo got me up by my brace, took me to the couch, and began tickling my feet.

"See how it feels?"

I laughed until Mrs. Faye said to DiAngelo, "Stop before you really hurt him."

"Yeah, you grape ape, stop before you hurt me."

"You want some more?" he pushed as he pretended to be a wrestler off the tv. "No one can beat me up; I am the king, Jerry Lowler."

Mrs. Faye and I just stared at him, then we looked at each other before bursting out laughing.

"We better call Dr. Bill and get him some of those pills they give me to sleep. I think he has gone stupid," I told Mrs. Faye.

"Who you calling stupid? I will throw you over the ring ropes, and you will cry," DiAngelo threatened.

However, I noticed DiAngelo was doing this without a smile; for real, he was trying to be a wrestler.

Mrs. Faye said, "You better stick to working at the carwash and stay safe."

We both laughed at him as he walked off.

"I think he needs to pick on someone his own size," Mrs. Faye observed.

"Yeah, go find Godzilla and wrestle with him," I yelled at DiAngelo's back.

Suddenly, DiAngelo turned in his tracks and started jogging toward us.

Mrs. Faye grabbed me and said, “Hurry! He’s going to get us!”

We ran and hid from him.

“Get out from under that bed, you big chicken,” DiAngelo demanded. “I won’t get you, I promise.”

“Angelo, how did you know I was under there?” I asked him.

“I could smell your nasty feet,” he answered.

“Uh-uh, I smelt them, and they don’t stink,” I responded.

“Yuck! Stop smelling your own feet, Rocco. Smell mine, instead,” he said as put his nasty feet in my face again.

“Stop it! Are you bored or something? Go to work!”

“Nope! I am aggravating you all night tonight. Evett is tired and told me to come in here with you.”

“Did you put your nasty feet in her face?”

DiAngelo laughed as he responded, “No, she would divorce me if I did. This is guy’s play . . . only guys can do this. The girls don’t like it.”

Chapter 16

DiAngelo went to work every day. I went to the study for lessons. Evett went to school. That was what life was like for the next few weeks. I always looked forward to supper so we could all sit and talk and be home at the same time.

Evett was as big as a barn, ready to deliver any day; DiAngelo ate every time she did, so he was getting big, also.

"Buckaroo, come down here; I have something for you," DiAngelo yelled up the stairs.

"What is it, Angelo?" I inquired.

"A new heater."

I went downstairs all bundled up in a sweater and another sweater pulled over that one.

"Rocco, you are going to burn up with all those clothes on."

"No, I am just right to keep warm." As I stepped off the last step I asked, "Angelo, what did you bring me?"

Out from under his coat, DiAngelo pulled a puppy.

"Do you like it?" he asked, excitedly.

"Nope. Get it out of here," I answered.

I walked to the dining room; but no one was there, yet.

DiAngelo followed me.

"Rocco, don't walk away from me; that is rude. I was talking to you."

"I don't want another dog."

"We don't have any dogs; this is the first one," DiAngelo explained.

"I had a dog before. I don't want another one. Now, leave me alone about it."

"Well, we're keeping it," DiAngelo replied adamantly.

"Go ahead; just keep it away from me."

"I have never seen you so mean. What's wrong with you?"

"Angelo, thanks, but no thanks. I don't want it. Save it for the baby."

"No, I got it for you."

I walked up to the puppy and patted its head.

"There. Now, are you happy? It's a nice dog. Go put it in the garage."

"He's not staying in the garage; he's staying with you. Now, take him. I got him for you," he demanded as he held out the puppy to me.

"I don't want it. *You* take it!"

"DiAngelo, what do you have?" Mrs. Faye asked as she walked into the dining room.

"Angelo has a puppy. He's making me take it, and I don't want it. Hey, Mrs. Faye, you can have it. Here, take it," I insisted as I took the puppy from DiAngelo and held it out to her.

"I don't want it; just take it to the garage," Mrs. Faye reacted.

"Mother, that's where he gets his sassiness from. I got Rocco a gift, and he doesn't want it," DiAngelo complained.

"Well, then leave him be if he doesn't want it. Maybe he doesn't like dogs," she remarked.

"You two are impossible!" DiAngelo all but spat out.

He walked upstairs, and I heard Evett say, "Get that thing off my bed. Where did you get it?"

"I got it for Rocco," I heard DiAngelo answer, "but he doesn't want it."

Mrs. Faye and I talked at the table.

"I think we hurt DiAngelo's feelings," she started. "Why don't you like dogs, Rocco?"

"If I tell you, you can't tell Angelo. I don't want him loving me because he feels sorry for me. I don't tell him bad things from down home."

"Okay, I won't," promised Mrs. Faye.

"I had a puppy. Uncle Marco gave it to me. One of his customers were giving some away, and he got me one. I loved it. I named him Keyo, and he would sit down at Mr. Creek's house during the day and wait for me to come up the road from school. He would jump all over me; he would be so glad to see me. I really loved him. He was something I could talk to and love."

"What happened to him, Rocco?"

"One day, I got to Mr. Creek's, and he didn't come to meet me. I told Mom I wondered where Keyo was. I took to looking for him, and over by the barn was a small tree sapling. He was dangling there from a wire. He was only high enough that his little feet would keep touching the ground just enough to get a little air. It made him suffer that much more. I got my dog off the wire, gave him a burial, and told him I would never have another dog . . . just him."

"Dear Lord, Rocco. Are you kidding me?"

"No, Ma'am. That's why I don't want the dog. If I take

another dog, then I would have lied to him . . . but I *do* want this dog . . . because Angelo bought him for me."

"Well, do you think your little dog would want you to be sad and not give another little dog some love?" Mrs. Faye prodded.

"I don't know, Mrs. Faye. A promise is a promise."

"Maybe we should just think about it and not talk any more about the dog. You stay here; I am going to speak to DiAngelo. I will be right back. Keep Mother company."

"I will, Mrs. Faye."

As Mrs. Faye arrived at DiAngelo's and Evett's bedroom, she spoke up, "DiAngelo, I need to speak to you in private, please."

"Yes, Mother."

The two went back downstairs and into the study. Mrs. Faye closed the doors.

"Did you know there are many more things that Rocco hasn't told us about . . . about his time living in Kentucky? I even wonder where his pa is, as he calls him."

"He is missing, and Mrs. Dean divorced him. He left them, and no one has seen him since."

"Well, I think the boy may need some counseling to get all this out in the open and get over it. Did you know his pa hung his dog?"

"What?" DiAngelo exclaimed.

"I am not supposed to tell you but yes, and he had to get it down and bury it. The way the man did it was evil. He let the poor dog touch the ground just enough to keep it alive longer and suffer more. I am never letting him go back there . . . never!"

"So, that's why he doesn't want the dog," DiAngelo surmised.

"He really *does* want it," Mrs. Faye started, but he promised his dog he would never have another one."

"Well, maybe I will keep the dog near me and see where it goes. Maybe he will warm up to it . . . but no counseling. He has a higher power to keep him safe," DiAngelo suggested.

"Okay, DiAngelo, whatever. Just be kind to him about it and try to understand."

"Mother, I didn't know. I would never hurt him, you know that."

"Let's go eat," Mrs. Faye prompted him.

DiAngelo walked into the dining room with the dog under his arm.

Evett looked up and said, "Yuck!"

"I am going to bathe him after supper; so, Evett, calm down," DiAngelo said. "I will need someone to hold him for me while I soap him up."

"Okay, I will help," I volunteered, "but I still don't want him."

"Okay, deal, Rocco."

"Mrs. Sandra, are you okay?" I asked as I turned toward her. "You have been quiet for the last few nights."

"Yes, Rocco, I am fine. It's just everyone has been busy, and we have no family time much anymore."

"I know it, and I don't like it, either."

"Well, the baby will be here in a few days, and I will be taking some time off work. Evett is going to need me," DiAngelo offered.

We all said, "Good!"

After we ate, we went and bathed the dog. When DiAngelo

finished, the puppy shook water all over us like a shower, but I don't think DiAngelo really minded it.

"Rocco, I think he is from the south; he is always cold like you," DiAngelo started.

"Where did you get him?" I wanted to know.

"He was behind the carwash in the cold, whimpering; and I heard him."

"I wonder if you heard me and brought me here," I said to DiAngelo.

"Your God brought you into my life, Rocco; and I will always be thankful to him for that."

"Well, then maybe God sent this little dog to us, reckon?"

"I think he did, Rocco. He knew you are the best one to tend to it, make him eat, sleep, and get better . . . fix him like you fixed me."

Looking back, I think my brother, DiAngelo, was preparing me for the change that was about to come. He would be busy with the new baby and his job and didn't want me to be alone.

We dried off the dog, and he jumped into my lap. From then on, he followed me around everywhere and wanted to go outside a lot. Mrs. Faye made everyone else take him out so I wouldn't get chilled. At bedtime, all I had to do was say, "Night-night," and he would run as fast as he could to the bedroom and go to sleep with me.

*****

"Rocco, wake up!" DiAngelo said sharply as he gave me a shake. "Evett is going to have the baby, and you have to stay with Grandmother. So, be good and listen well. I will see you after she has the baby."

"Is Mrs. Faye going with you?" I asked.

"Yes, so take care of things around here, and be a strong little guy."

"Okay, Angelo. I love you. Bring home a cute baby, not an ugly one."

"How can he be ugly when I am the father?"

My brother leaned down and kissed my head.

"Say a prayer for us."

"Are we going to the hospital or am I going to have the baby here?" Evett said from her room.

"I better get going," DiAngelo said. "Love you, Rocco."

"Okay, see you later, Angelo."

I rolled back over and said, "Lord, be with Evett," and went right back to sleep.

When I finally woke up for the day, DiAngelo was already home.

"Keyo, get up! Let's go eat," I told my companion as I ruffled his furry head.

We went downstairs.

When I saw DiAngelo, I simply asked, "Boy or girl?"

"It's a boy . . . a fine-looking boy. He weighs five pounds, two ounces and is 21 inches long," DiAngelo gave the statistics with pride.

"Who does he look like . . . you or Evett?" I inquired.

"He looks like both of us."

"When does she get to bring him home?"

"Tomorrow if all keeps going well."

"Already?" I said with surprise. "That was fast!"

"Yes, we have to tell all the folks and send some pictures."

"Angelo, can you let my dog outside to pee and poop?"

"Sure. Then I am going to bed . . . after I call the service and have them ready to send out a nurse."

"A nurse? For what?" I inquired.

"To help take care of the baby and teach us," DiAngelo responded.

"Mrs. Sandra is here . . . and Mrs. Faye. We don't need a nurse. They gave birth to their kids and to you."

"That's right, Rocco, you tell him," Mrs. Faye agreed, almost scolding.

She had been standing behind me listening to our conversation.

"Well, it will make it better for Evett for a few days," DiAngelo tried to explain.

"Well, if that's what you want . . . the baby to know strangers before he knows us . . . so be it," I replied.

"Good, because I just went through this with Mother. I don't want to explain it all to you."

"Good, because I don't want to hear it. But, good job . . . now, there are three boys and three girls in the house. Now, we're even," I deduced.

"Yes, I thought about that," responded DiAngelo. "Want some taters for breakfast?"

"No, I would like some pancakes and bacon," I replied.

"Mrs. Faye said no syrup for you."

"Yes, I ordered some oatmeal, toast, and a cup of cocoa for your breakfast. More oats for the blood," Mrs. Faye interjected.

"Yuck! Maybe Mrs. Sandra will sneak me some of her food," I suggested.

"We just love you and want you to be healthy, so will you do it for me . . . eat those oats?" Mrs. Faye pushed.

"Yes, Ma'am. Come on, Keyo, let's go eat some oats while they all eat bacon and pancakes," I lamented.

DiAngelo said as he hugged me, "Poor baby . . . don't get no taters."

As we walked into the dining room, I said, "Mrs. Sandra, we got a baby . . . a boy!"

"I know. Isn't it great?"

"I hope he looks like Evett and not him," I spouted off as I jammed my elbow into DiAngelo's side.

"Buckaroo, I think sometimes you wait until I am tired and then push the wrong buttons just for fun."

"That's what brothers are for," I taunted.

"After we eat, I have to call Father and tell him he is a Grandfather," DiAngelo announced.

"Tell him he can see the baby in 21 years as he wishes," Mrs. Faye suggested. "Rocco, this might be the thing that changes a father's heart."

"Might be . . . if he had one," I replied.

"A boy after my own heart," Mrs. Faye responded.

"I have to call Aunt Hadie, Uncle Marco, and Mom to tell them Evett has had the baby. What did you name him?" I asked as I looked at DiAngelo.

"We named him Rocco."

"Oh no, you didn't name him my name."

DiAngelo tore up laughing and said, "Are you the only Rocco in the world?"

"In this world, I am. Now, what did you really name him?" I pressed.

"I named him Alexander Rocco Pettrachini."

"Now, I like that. He is named after me but not his first name. Thank you, my brother."

"You're welcome . . . and since he is named after you, you get to change all the poopie diapers."

"No, I ain't, Angelo!"

"Oh, yes, you are, Buckaroo."

"So, we have a nurse to do that . . . ha, ha."

"Oh, now you like the idea of a nurse?"

The next day Evett and the baby came home in a long, white car. DiAngelo carried the baby.

Evett said, "Hi, Rocco. Did you miss me?"

"Yes, I sure did, Evett. I couldn't sleep without you here."

DiAngelo broke in, "Look what I have, Rocco."

He held the nicest looking boy I had ever seen.

"He looks like us, Angelo."

"Yes, I think so, also."

Evett said, "I am going to lie down, and she left us with the baby. DiAngelo sat me in the dining room chair and put the baby in my arms. He slept right there, good as gold.

"Be quiet, Keyo," I instructed the pup, "the baby is sleeping."

Keyo lay down right next to my chair; and when the baby would even whimper, he would look at him, then at me.

"Rocco, that's the most he has slept since he came into this world; I think he likes you," DiAngelo observed.

"I am still not changing poopie diapers."

Mrs. Sandra said, "I think we will all have to take our turn to change a few diapers."

"I can't wait for him to walk, run, and play tag with me," I said.

"He's almost like your little brother, Rocco. You have to teach him the good and right ways and watch out for him," DiAngelo commented.

"I know. I am going to teach him to laugh like you . . . and never let him get hurt . . . and never make him be quiet."

"He is going to be the first one of us to have a good father."

"Also, an uncle . . . to make sure that he has a good father," I added.

Over the next few days Evett left the care of the baby to the nurse and us. She suffered from postpartum depression: even though she loved the baby, she didn't want much to do with him. DiAngelo and I took turns holding him, and Mrs. Faye would feed him so she could make sure he was burped well and didn't get a belly ache. After a few days, the nurse left; and I never saw her again.

"Alex" held my finger as I talked to him; and the only time he had to poop, it seemed, was when I held him. DiAngelo got a kick out of it.

"It's not funny, Angelo . . . first, I had to smell your stinky feet, and now I am smelling his nasty poop all the time."

"Poor Buckaroo, don't you know he feels safe with you already? He is at ease with you; so, that's when he goes number two."

"Well, okay, then. I guess I don't mind."

Uncle Marco, Aunt Hadie, and Mom were so pleased with the pictures of Alex we sent them.

"Bring him down soon so we can see him," Mom suggested.

"And we need to have him dedicated," I added.

"What's that, Rocco?" DiAngelo asked.

"Brother Wallace prays for him, gives him to the Lord, and asks the Lord to look over him and protect him."

"Well, I guess we better have that done, then," DiAngelo agreed.

"Well not when he is ten years old, Angelo; so, make it fast so he can get covered."

"You are serious . . . you want us to take him to Brother Wallace to have him dedicated?"

"Yes, when you take me home for spring break. Make Evett get him ready, and we will take him . . . Mrs. Faye and Mrs. Sandra . . . all of us!"

Mrs. Faye responded, "Okay, if it is important to you, we will go, also; but we will stay in a hotel."

"You're gonna hurt the folks' feelings doing that," I tried to explain. "You and Mrs. Sandra can stay with my mom. Angelo and Evett can stay with Uncle Marco and Aunt Hadie," I planned out.

"Where are you going to stay?" Mrs. Faye wondered.

"The dog and me are going to sleep in Mikie's room and talk all night!"

The ride to Kentucky seemed not so long this time; we were all talking and carrying on like old times. Evett was the only quiet one; she just looked out the window most of the time, not talking . . . just there.

We got to Kentucky, got Mrs. Sandra and Mrs. Faye settled at my mom's house, and the rest of us went to Uncle Marco's. Evett and DiAngelo sat at the table talking with Aunt Hadie who was getting bigger by the minute. Mom, Mrs. Faye, and Mrs. Sandra finally showed up; and we all sat at the same table and had supper like one, big family.

I didn't know what Mom and Mrs. Faye said to each other at her house, but they were best friends by the time they got to Aunt Hadie's house. They acted like they had known each other forever. It did my heart good to see my moms talking and liking each other.

We got dressed and went to Saturday night church. Brother Wallace smiled as I walked in.

Brother Wallace said, "I heard you were bringing folks to get dedicated."

"I wanted our new baby, Alex, dedicated by you, Brother, and no one else," I said.

"Thank you, Rocco. Are you going to sing for us?"

"I think I might."

"Okay, good!"

He went to shaking the hands of all my folks. It was like going into the church with a mob of folks.

Sister Linda called me up front and asked, "Rocco, what are you going to sing?"

"'Just a Closer Walk with Thee,'" I answered.

"In the key of D, right?"

"No, I sing loud now."

Mrs. Sandra had overheard our conversation and offered, "Tell her to play in B sharp for you."

After Brother Wallace got all the folks inside and settled, he prayed and told the story of how Moses went to live with other folks who were not his family. However, he pointed out that when it came right down to it, Moses was still a Jew.

"We are all one thing to God: we are all His children," Brother Wallace explained.

Then Brother Wallace called up DiAngelo and Evett with the baby. He told them to raise him right and always put the Lord their God first in their lives. He put some oil on the baby's head and prayed for God to always watch over him. He held the baby in the air as he prayed for him.

Sister Linda motioned for me to come to the front and handed me a microphone, but I didn't need one. She started to play, and I sang loud and clear. Mrs. Faye and Mom stood together and held hands as their faces glowed with pride.

After I finished the song, I said, "One more favor, please, Brother Wallace: will you please pray for Evett? She has not been feeling well after the baby, and she needs a healing from the Father."

"Come here, Evett, and see what God can do," Brother Wallace said to her gently.

DiAngelo walked Evett back to the front, next to Brother Wallace. He started praying, and Evett went to crying quiet.

Brother Wallace said, "I pray for her hormones to come back in line and let her flow with a renewed spirit."

Everyone sang while Evett and DiAngelo went back to their seat. Mrs. Sandra placed the baby back into Evett's arms. She held him and began loving on him.

I don't know what happened that night, but I know Evett has loved and held that baby ever since. I think she got touched that night.

The next day while everyone was packing up to leave me there in Kentucky while they went back home, I felt a little twinge in my belly.

"Mrs. Faye, you make sure you get Angelo to come back and get me on the Saturday of next week, okay?"

"I sure will, and I am going to miss you."

"I am going to miss you, also, Mrs. Faye."

Uncle Marco and Aunt Hadie hugged them all, and I stood there as Mom hugged and kissed them all goodbye, also. DiAngelo came to me and hugged me.

"Be good or I will save all the poopie diapers and put them under your bed," he threatened.

We laughed; but in our hearts, we were not laughing. Mr. Scott closed the car doors, and they were gone.

Mikie jumped up and said, "What's for supper? I am hungry!"

*****

Mom and I walked up to Mr. Creek's big porch where Mikie and Aunt Hadie were sitting.

"Where have you two been?" Aunt Hadie asked. "I was starting to get worried."

"We went for a walk," Mom answered.

"Dean, did you have him over there by that clover patch?"

"He wanted to go, so I took him to see where I was born and raised."

Mikie piped up, "I want to see, also!"

"No, you don't, boy; now, go play," Aunt Hadie responded.

Mikie and I went inside while Mom sat down in the place Mikie had just vacated. I got some water.

Mikie said, "Look what I have. I hope you're not mad, but I traded Tom at school my camping knife for this one."

He pulled out a switchblade as long as a small butcher knife.

"Mikie, you had better be careful with that one," I warned. "I think it will take your fingers plum off. Why did he trade down for it?"

"Well, this one was his brother's; and he took it and traded it."

"They gonna come and want it back . . . wait and see."

"I hope not. Look . . ."

He had it open before he had it out of his pocket and was ready to stab something.

"You are as bad with those knives as Angelo is with his guns. Now, put it up before Mom sees it."

"Father wants you to come for supper tonight . . . just you and I. Our moms are going shopping together," Mikie suddenly changed the subject.

"That will be fun . . . just us guys," I responded.

We went back outside.

"Look, your house is gone!" Mikie exclaimed, pointing to where Pa's house once stood.

"Mikie, *this* is my house. Pa's house is gone; Mom had it torn down."

"Oh, that's right. I forgot," he laughed.

We went over to the line where they were digging coal and watched as they loaded up the next truck and drove it off somewhere.

"Dang, that's a lot of coal back there," Mikie said.

"I know," I replied and squinted my eyes at him.

"You gonna spend a few nights up here, Mikie?"

"Yes, Mom said I could. I didn't bring my clothes this time, but I have them ready."

"Aunt Hadie is really getting big," I said.

"She only has two more months, and she will have the baby. We have all the stuff ready. Everything is going good. She hired a new lady to help Aunt Dean while she is off."

"Good," I replied. "I don't want my mom working too hard. I wish you all would just come up north and live."

"Well, we wish you would just come home!"

We looked at each other and knew it was a draw.

"We better head back up to your house, Mikie."

"Reckon when we grow up we can do something fun and just hang out and swim and ride bikes?" Mikie wondered aloud.

"Well, Brother Wallace says we have to keep our hands busy, that idle hands are the devil's workshop," I answered.

"They will be busy . . . drinking, eating, and having fun."

"I think it means we still need to work."

"We were about to holler for you all. Where you been?" Aunt Hadie quizzed us as we approached the porch.

"We went up to see them dig for coal."

"Well, you better not get too close to the drills."

"We won't," we promised.

"Let's watch some tv, Mikie."

"Only soap operas are on now," Mikie complained. "You know that, Rocco."

"Oh, yeah. Up north we have about a hundred channels, and there are cartoons on everywhere."

"Well, Rocco, we're not up north."

"Dang, Mikie," I replied, "who stole your cookies today?"

"Nobody. I am just tired of you always saying 'up north,' 'up north.' I wish you would just go get your things and come back home and forget about 'up north.'"

"What you mean is forget about Angelo, Evett, and all my other folks."

"*We're* your folks; we've always been your folks," Mikie lamented. "You have been gone almost a year; it's time to come home."

"Mikie, I am doing my best to get better and learn at the same time. The doctors say I might even have to have back surgery. I might not be able to walk if I don't listen. All I would need is for Todd to trip me and break it altogether."

"Well, you better hurry up and get better. I am tired of this. We need you at home as much as they need you."

Suddenly a man ran up to the porch, yelling and waving his arms, "Mrs. Hadie! Mrs. Hadie! Come quick! The grill and gas station are on fire! Marco's trying to put it out, but there are flames everywhere!"

"Oh my, Dean, let's go!" she screamed.

We all got into the car, and Aunt Hadie drove faster than I ever saw her drive before. She pulled the car right into the gas station, and everyone started yelling for her to get out of there, that the pumps were going to blow.

"Where is Marco? Where is my husband?" Aunt Hadie frantically ran around, asking everyone in sight.

Mom took Mikie and me back to the road. We could feel the heat, and everyone was screaming at the sight of the inferno. Aunt Hadie continued screaming for Uncle Marco.

As the flames grew bigger, the folks grabbed her and dragged her back to the road. Just as the biggest flames went even higher, Uncle Marco came running to her out of the smoke with a box in his hands. He placed it in Aunt Hadie's hands and then turned back to watch the flames. He was covered in smoke. His face was so black, I couldn't even tell it was Uncle Marco. I held to Mikie's arm; we were both so scared as we stood and watched the flames.

"Marco, I love you," Aunt Hadie kept screaming over and over as she kissed him and cried.

By the time the fire department arrived, the gas station and grill were burned down to the ground. All that was left were the memories of the place where Mom had worked and by which she fed us.

Aunt Hadie hung onto Uncle Marco and kept repeating, "Thank God, thank God, my Marco is safe!"

Chapter 17

Uncle Marco and Aunt Hadie came and stayed with Mom that night. Mom and I went into town and bought some clothes for everyone and more food at the Winn Dixie store before going back home.

We all took baths while Mom and Aunt Hadie started cooking. Then each one of them took a bath while the other one continued with the cooking. At suppertime it was kind of quiet as the ladies served us and sat down. Before we ate, Aunt Hadie suggested we pray.

"Dear Lord, thank you for this food and a place to stay, but I want to thank you the most for keeping my Marco safe in the fire. Thank you from all of my heart. I will never stop loving you for keeping him safe, Amen."

We started to eat when Uncle Marco spoke, "Hadie, I can't do this again."

"Do what, dear?"

"I can't build it back up. There are the new ways, the bigger stations: Shell, Marathon . . . and now they have food in them, also. We will go broke trying to make a living in this business. It's all I know how to do."

"Marco," Aunt Hadie replied, "I don't know anything else 'cepting to take orders and cook."

I coughed, and they looked at me.

"Yes, Rocco?"

"We are Pettrachinis. Some of us are married to them, and some of us are born to them . . . and we *are* them. Some of us has borne their children, and some of us are their children. We are a strong family made from grapes and land. I am from Mrs. Liza's blood . . . and so are you, Uncle Marco and Mikie. Our grandfather built businesses all over Italy and came here and made more businesses. That was your father and mother, Uncle Marco. Are you weaker than them? Are you weaker than Ray Pettrachini?

"I have more money to start again, and we have coal-mining money. You helped my mom for years. You let her live with you when she came out of the clover patch. You have always been kind to me, Uncle Marco Pettrachini. Now, sit up and take note. Now, it's time for the family to help you, and you will accept.

"There is a house next to us in Holland. You can have a new start there. We own businesses in Michigan, some in Grand Rapids. There are restaurants, Aunt Hadie, if you want to work. We would want for nothing."

"What about my sister?" Aunt Hadie asked.

"My mom will be with you, right in the same house with you or in my house next to you. We are family, and we are the Pettrachini family. Mikie will be right with me, and we will live happily ever after on the lake."

Uncle Marco looked at me and said, "You are my mother all over again. I think she left you her guts and strength. Father left you his will to survive and his determination."

"Hey, don't give it all to him. I have some of that Pettrachini in me, you know," Mikie piped up.

We all laughed at Mikie, and I looked over at him and squinted.

"Let's vote . . . like we do at Mrs. Faye's house!" I suggested.

I looked at Aunt Hadie. She said, "Yes!" Mom said, "I don't know." Mikie gave a loud "Yes!" Uncle Marco lowered his eyes and said, "I don't know."

"It looks like the vote goes to me," I offered, "and I say 'Yes'! Well, Aunt Hadie, it looks like you win!"

"After all these years, I am going back to Holland," she said as she relaxed back into her chair and smiled.

"We will have two new babies. We have to get Aunt Hadie settled and the baby stuff all bought before she gets ready to have the baby," Mom said, planning out loud. "I just hope you know what you are doing, Rocco."

"When it comes to my family, I am not a kid. I pray every night for God to help me do what is good and teach me the business ways."

I walked to the phone and dialed my other home.

"Hi, Miss Maria," I greeted the voice at the other end. "How are you? Good. Listen, is Angelo home? Thank you."

DiAngelo's voice came over the line, loud and clear, "Rocco? I just called a few minutes ago, but there was no answer at the grill. Is everything okay? Is Aunt Hadie and the baby okay?"

"Angelo, the grill and gas station just burnt to the ground, but we are all safe now. I need you, Angelo," I said as I began to feel tears welling up behind my eyes.

"Of course, Rocco! Anything!"

"My family is coming home with me, and I want you to go over to that house next door . . the one you wanted for you and Evett someday. Tell the man you want to buy it, and don't let him hogwash you; get it for as cheap as you can. When you get the price as low as he will go, call me. Write the check out, and have it ready for me to sign. Okay, Brother?"

"Yes, but I think there's enough room here in this house for everyone if they want to just live here."

"We better not, but let me ask Uncle Marco what he thinks. Hang on."

I turned to Uncle Marco and said, "We can get the house next door, but Angelo says you can live with us if you want to. It's up to you, but I think you would be more comfortable in your own home, especially with the new baby."

Uncle Marco looked at Aunt Hadie and began circling his hand on her back.

"This is your decision," he said softly.

Aunt Hadie looked at Rocco and said, "Rocco, we want the house."

I turned back to the phone and said, "Angelo, we want the house next door. After you buy it, take the money out of mine and Mikie's columns in the checkbook, okay?"

"All right," DiAngelo responded, "I will work on it right now."

"May I talk to Mrs. Faye?" I asked DiAngelo.

"Yes. Hang on."

Mrs. Faye's voice came across the line, "Rocco, I was listening. Is everyone okay?"

"Yes, Ma'am, we are all fine; but the folks will need to stay with us for a few days until they can get settled in the house next door. Is it okay with you?"

"Rocco, you know it is okay, but thank you so much for asking."

"Mrs. Faye, you are the lady of our home; and Aunt Hadie and Mom will be the ladies of Uncle Marco's home. Tell Angelo to hurry and call me back. I love you, Mrs. Faye."

"I love you, also, Rocco. Goodnight."

As I hung up the phone, I turned and looked at the table, and the folks could not believe I was their little Rocco.

"Boy, where did you learn all that from . . . the tutor?" Mom asked me.

"No, Mom. I was there that day when Aunt Hadie was making a deal with someone when she and Uncle Marco bought the grill. She asked him if he could pay the folks working at the grill until she got on her feet; then she would take over paying them. The word is haggle; Aunt Hadie haggled a deal with the folks."

"Boy, I know what the word means," Mom interrupted.

"Dean, let him speak," Aunt Hadie admonished. "Those are the words I used, word-for-word . . . but how did you know that is what I asked him?"

"I was there, Aunt Hadie."

"But you and Mikie were on the counter in little jumper seats when I said those words. You couldn't possibly remember that! You were only nine months old."

"I remember it like yesterday," I replied. "I remember after the man left that you cried and told Uncle Marco that you hoped you had made the right decision. He hugged you and told you that you had nothing to lose. He kissed your forehead and hugged you to himself again."

Mom spoke up, "Okay, Rocco, why don't you and Mikie go play."

Aunt Hadie looked at Mom with wide eyes and said, "But, Dean, how did he know?"

"He gets it from my mom. Now, let it go; and let's start planning a trip."

Mikie and I were in the living room, and we were happy.

"Mikie, you are going to live closer to me now than ever . . . right next door!" I exclaimed.

"Is it the one with the yellow garage or the brick one?" Mikie wanted to know.

"The brick one. You seen it?"

"Yes, when I was looking out your window, I could see it. It's every bit as big as DiAngelo's house."

"I know," I responded, "but I want to surprise Aunt Hadie and Mom, so don't say anything."

I went back to the kitchen. Just as I started to pick up the phone to dial, it rang.

"Hey, Buckaroo, looks like I am going to need some more teaching. I didn't get it for less, but I did get him to leave all the furniture! Did I do good?" he laughed.

"You did even better than good! I forgot about furniture."

"Okay, tell Uncle Marco it is theirs. They will be moving out in the next week or so."

"Did you take it out of the two columns in the checkbook?" I inquired.

"Yes, but I split it three ways, also."

"Angelo Pettrachini, I love you, you big, feet-smeller. How is Alex doing?"

"I think he misses you. He hasn't pooped in two days."

"Angelo, shut up."

"Tell Uncle Marco I will bring the truck, and Mr. Scott will also drive so the ladies can ride home comfortably."

"You mean tell him now?" I asked.

"No. We are leaving in about 15 minutes to come and get you; so, wait until then. You know how Uncle Marco is."

"Okay, I will. Be careful. I love you."

"I love you, too, Buckaroo."

"Well, it looks like we are going to be neighbors, Uncle Marco! And Angelo got them to leave the furniture!" I announced.

"That's good because we don't have any now," Uncle Marco responded somewhat dejectedly.

"Uncle Marco, please try to look at this as a blessing . . . a new start."

"Rocco, I don't have $10 to start over with."

"You have me and Mikie, and we have lots of ten-dollar bills!"

"We sure do, Father," Mikie joined in, "and more every day going into our bank book. That's what DiAngelo told me."

"Your grandmother left that money to you boys."

"She left it to us to take care of the family with, and that's what we are doing," I countered.

"Did DiAngelo sound mad?" Uncle Marco wanted to know.

"Heck, no . . . and guess what?"

"He is coming right now with the truck and the limo so the ladies can ride in comfort."

I couldn't keep the secret any longer.

"Are you kidding me, Rocco?" Uncle Marco all but shouted.

"No, Uncle Marco. He took part of his money and bought you that house just like Mikie and me. He loves you and respects you, also."

"Well, if he is on his way, we better get to bed and get up early to get some things done," he suggested.

Mom and Aunt Hadie were already busy making up beds. Mom gave Aunt Hadie and Uncle Marco her bed, and she slept on the couch. Mikie and me slept in our twin beds that Mom had just bought us.

"Mom, wait till you see your new home; it's nice, and you will never have to worry about me again. I will be right next door to you."

"Good!" she responded. "Then Mom can cook you some cornbread every day."

"Night, Mom."

"Night, baby."

By the time Mikie and I woke up the next morning, there was a man there talking to Uncle Marco. He was an insurance man. He handed Uncle Marco a check.

"This will be more than enough to cover the business and your home."

Once the man left, Uncle Marco turned to me and held up the check.

"This is for $150,000," he said. "Rocco, I will be able to give you your money back . . . the money you sent to pay the places off."

"Uncle Marco, you are going to put that in the bank for you, Aunt Hadie, and the baby. Mikie and me have enough money, and no one needs to know that you have it. Who are you going to sell your land to?"

"Rocco, you are a brain! I forgot about the land," he said as he rummaged in his wallet, looking for a phone number. "Dean! Hadie! Come here," he called out.

"Yes, Marco?" Aunt Hadie answered.

"Dean, can I stay on for a few days here in your house?"

"Sure, but we can wait on you . . . whatever you need to get done," Mom offered.

"No, DiAngelo is already on his way. I will send you all ahead with him, and I will be up in a few days."

Aunt Hadie replied, "Marco, I don't know about this. Why do you want to stay?"

Right then Uncle Marco picked me up and twirled me around in the air.

"This young man," started Uncle Marco, "just reminded me of our land. Do you remember the Exxon folks who wanted to buy it a few years back and build a station there?"

"Yes, of course, I remember. And I remember you told him 'No.'"

"Well, now I am telling them 'Yes'!"

"Can you put me down now, Uncle Marco?" I asked as the room stayed spinning.

"Yes, boy. I love you and Mikie so much."

He got on the phone, and we had to be quiet while he talked with the "Exxon folks."

Mikie and I handed Mom boxes and papers as she packed a few of her things.

"Mom, you don't need this stuff. The house will have everything you need," I offered.

"Some of this stuff has meaning to me, and I want to take it with me," she responded.

She placed some of the pretty plates in paper, wrapped them carefully, and set them in a box.

"Those are just like the plate DiAngelo threw out the window in Michigan," I observed.

"Yes, baby, it goes with this set."

"You mean that plate was from Mr. Creek's father's house?

Oh, I remember: your mom used to bring food home to you on that plate when you were a little girl."

Mom smiled as she said, "You catch everything, don't you?"

"We will have to clean the new house, so take that bleach and the soap," Mom instructed me.

"Mom, we will not have to clean that house. There is a lady named Mrs. Ruth there who cooks for the Hamiltons and runs the house for them."

"Boy, did you say 'Hamiltons'?" Uncle Marco quizzed.

"Yes, Uncle Marco. Why?"

"Is that the house you bought for us?"

"Are you mad about something, Uncle Marco?"

"No, but I thought you bought one of the smaller houses on the road."

"I told you we were going to be neighbors."

"But, Rocco, it is too much. You have to tell them you changed your mind."

Aunt Hadie had come into the room just as Uncle Marco made the last remark.

"What did the boy do, Marco?" she asked with concern edging her voice.

"He bought the biggest house on the lake!"

"Even bigger than your old house, Marco?"

"Yes, Hadie!"

"Good," she responded, "so, we are better off now than when you came to Kentucky!"

He just looked at her, and I don't think he could figure out what she meant.

"She is saying you are going back richer than when you left," I explained. "What did the Exxon folks say?"

"They said they would buy the land if I tore down everything on it. I agreed to doze it down if they would haul it all away."

"So, it is a deal?" I asked.

"Yes," he answered.

One could have heard a pin drop when I informed them I had already made arrangements for the buildings to be bulldozed into a heap.

"They are faxing papers today to Mr. Hamson's office. All I have to do is sign them, and they will send a check," Uncle Marco explained.

"Looks like today is Uncle Marco Day!" I exclaimed.

He smiled for the first time in several days as he said, "Yes, things are going great for us today. We are Pettrachini!" He winked at me.

*****

"Wake up, Buckaroo! I'm here!" DiAngelo's voice broke through my sleep from the front yard.

A smile stole across my face as I jumped up, ran outside, and hugged my brother. It was the first time I had gone three days without him in the last year.

"Dang, boy, did you miss me?"

"I sure did, Brother. I sure did!"

"Everyone in Michigan can't wait until you get home."

"Even you?"

"Even me . . . you feet-smeller."

Mikie came outside and joined us.

He hit DiAngelo on the arm and said, "Hey, Yank, what took you so long?"

"We drove 70 all the way here, Mikie, while you were snug in your bed, sleeping. So, what do you mean what took us so long, you knucklehead?"

Mikie burst out laughing.

"You're right, Rocco. When he gets tired, he is a bear."

We all laughed.

Mikie added, "Poor DiAngelo is a baby!"

"Hi, DiAngelo!" Uncle Marco spouted as he walked outside. "Was it a long trip?"

"Not too bad, Uncle Marco, but I could use a few hours of sleep before we head back."

"That's great. You and Mr. Scott come in and eat some breakfast. I have some business to take care of. I will take these boys, so it will be quiet."

"I am staying here with Angelo," I protested.

"No, you're not; you're going with Mikie and me. The boy needs to sleep!"

I looked at DiAngelo and waited for him to overrule Uncle Marco, but it didn't happen.

He simply said, "After I sleep, you can ride with me into town and on the way back home, too . . . just you and I."

"Okay." Then I added, "Damn it!"

"Rocco, didn't I tell you about that word?" Uncle Marco questioned sternly.

"Yes, Uncle Marco. I'm sorry."

We all went back inside. Mom had DiAngelo's and Mr. Scott's beds all ready. She pulled the shades so it would be darker, turned on a fan, and instructed us to stay out. DiAngelo looked at me before lying down and smiled ear-to-ear.

"Come here and hug me before someone catches you in here," he said.

I hugged my brother and said, "I guess you really do need some sleep. I will be quiet and leave you be."

"Okay," he answered, "but don't let me sleep too long. I want to get back on the road."

"I won't, Brother."

Mikie and I went into town with Uncle Marco to the lawyer's office.

"Mr. Hamson, did anything come for me over the fax line?" Uncle Marco asked him.

"Yes, about two hours ago," he replied. "It's ready for your signature, and then I can fax it back to them."

"Mr. Hamson, we will be going up north to live, but I will still need you to look over my affairs here," Uncle Marco explained. After further explaining the deal he made with the Exxon folks, he asked Mr. Hamson, "What will I need to wrap this up now?"

"Just those papers you already signed; they will do the transfer of the deed and send it to you," Mr. Hamson responded.

A lady walked into the office and said, "Mr. Hamson, there is someone on the phone with questions regarding Mr. Pettrachini," she announced, nodding her head toward Uncle Marco.

Mr. Hamson picked up his phone and pushed a button.

"Yes, he is here right now." He looked at Marco and stated, "Marco, they need your account number to deposit the funds for the sale of your place or they can mail you a check."

"No," Uncle Marco answered, "give them Rocco's account number."

Uncle Marco looked at me indicating he wanted me to answer Mr. Hamson with the account number. I sent him back a dirty look. He snapped his finger at me to stop it. Once I gave him my account number, we went back outside.

I asked Uncle Marco, "What did you do that for?"

"Because I wanted to, and I am older than you. That's why."

He smiled at me.

"So, I am going to buy you a new car when we get to Michigan," I stated matter-of-factly.

"Ha ha," Uncle Marco mocked. "Boy, you are something else. I don't want or need a new car. Your Aunt Hadie and me are just fine now; we have money to take care of ourselves just fine."

"Good. Then, Mikie and I are going to buy ourselves something if everybody else has what they need."

"What are we going to buy, Rocco?" Mikie quizzed.

"I don't know, yet; but it's our turn," he ended by winking at me.

"I want a new bike and some uhhhh . . . uhhhh . . . some . . . some . . ."

Uncle Marco piped in, "You don't even know what you want. You're trying to make up something."

We all laughed.

"What do you want, Rocco?"

"Mikie, I don't think I need anything, but we will find something that we're gonna get once we get home. I do know I am going to have that fence torn down in between your house and mine, so I can get to your house easily," I prompted.

"I was wondering how you two were going to get back and forth to see each other," Uncle Marco wondered out loud. "I thought I remembered a fence being between those two properties."

"That way we will have the biggest backyard in the whole state!" I said excitedly. "Mikie and me can play tag, swim, and there's a thing that you can throw and catch . . . it flies through the air . . . it's called a fizz-bee, I think," I added.

"It's called a frisbee, Rocco . . . a frisbee," Uncle Marco corrected.

"Thanks, Uncle Marco. A frisbee. You can stand in your yard, and me in mine; and we throw it to each other."

"Well, I still want a bike, also," Mikie said.

"Okay, a bike and a frisbee. I think we can do that."

We laughed, and I asked Uncle Marco, "Are you going to take us out on the boat?"

"What boat, Rocco?" Mikie questioned.

"Mikie, we have a boathouse and some boats. In the summer a warm breeze blows all over you and warms you up, doesn't it, Uncle Marco?"

"Yes, and I remember the sun going down on the lake . . . the pretty orange sky over the lake," he answered.

"We can cook out. There's cheeseburgers, hot dogs on the grill, tater chips, and pop like Angelo drinks."

"Well, you two will be drinking lots of water," Uncle Marco said, eyeing Mikie knowingly.

"Yes, Father," Mikie answered.

"There will be two babies running around. And you know what, Mikie?"

"What, Rocco?"

"Your sister and Alex are going to be the same age, like you and me. We are both eight, and they're both going to be one together."

"I can't wait for you to have a sister, Mikie. I love my

brother. He is the best thing. He keeps up after me and watches me . . . and everything."

"You said he is like a pa, Rocco."

"Yeah, Mikie . . . but he ain't my pa; he just acts like one. He just loves me like one."

"Now, we both have someone who loves us like that."

Uncle Marco just listened as we talked; I think he was eavesdropping.

"Mrs. Faye is great, also."

"Does she cook for you?" Mikie wanted to know.

"No, you remember Miss Maria cooks for us. This lady, Mrs. Ruth, is gonna cook for you all. She is the nicest lady. She sat outside and talked to me forever one day in the summer while she snapped some green beans. She made some chocolate eclairs . . . the best in the world . . . brought them to the fence, and gave them to me. She is my friend; and now, I can see her more over at your house."

"Is there anyone that you don't know, Rocco?"

"A whole lot of folks up there I don't know. Tipper at Angelo's carwash is from Kentucky, also. He is nice, and I am going to go to church with him when things get settled . . . if they ever do."

When we got back to the house, Mom and Aunt Hadie were on the porch.

Mom warned, "You boys stay out here and let DiAngelo sleep."

"He told me to wake him up and not let him sleep too long, Mom."

"Well, I think you better get used to having a mom again and start listening to me. Now, get over here and sit down."

"I think I am going to do what Angelo asked me to do," I objected.

It was a standoff. I was afraid to go in, and she was afraid to push me; so, we just looked defiantly at each other.

"You know the Bible says to honor your mother; that means listen and obey," Mom started.

"What you really mean is you make me do what you want and when you want me to do it."

"Where did you get that smart mouth, Rocco?" she asked. "Now, sit down. You'll *not* be waking that boy up!"

"That's all you had to say; you didn't have to throw the Bible in there to make me do what you said," I complained.

"I think my family has him spoiled," Uncle Marco observed.

That made me madder than a bobtail cat having to look for its supper on an empty belly.

"You mean your family loves me."

"There is a difference in loving and spoiling, Mr. Smarty," Uncle Marco insisted.

"Mrs. Faye and Mrs. Sandra love me; Evett and Angelo . . . they all love me, Uncle Marco."

"I am sure they do, but I am also sure they let you have your way and give you whatever you want. Now, you need to tell your mom that you're sorry for not listening to her."

"I will not!"

Right then, Aunt Hadie spoke up, "Mikie, let's go for a small walk."

They left.

"Now, you tell your mother that you are sorry," Uncle Marco picked the battle back up.

"Nope, I ain't saying it. I didn't do anything wrong . . . just trying to do what Angelo told me to do. He said for me to wake him up when I got home, and that's what I was going to do."

"But then your mom told you to let him sleep."

"Well, Angelo is my boss."

"Boy, you have taken a leave of your senses; your mom is your boss. Now, tell her you are sorry."

Before I could say "No" again, Uncle Marco had pulled his belt out of his loops. I had seen him bust Mikie a few times with it, and I knew what was coming.

"Are you going to say you're sorry?" he asked, giving me another chance.

"No, I am not; I was doing what I was told to do by Angelo."

Uncle Marco strapped my legs as he held up my arms.

"Now, say it!"

"I will not!"

He strapped me again.

"You better stop it, Uncle Marco . . . I mean it. I'm telling Angelo when he wakes up, damn it!"

He strapped me again and again. I think it made him mad because I wouldn't cry.

With the last hit, DiAngelo interrupted, "Uncle Marco, that's enough. Let him be."

"DiAngelo, he was disrespecting his mom and wouldn't say he was sorry," Uncle Marco explained.

"Didn't you tell me to wake you up when I got home?" I asked DiAngelo.

"Yes, I did," he answered as he looked at Uncle Marco eye-to-eye.

"My mom said I couldn't wake you up and told me to sit down."

"Tell him the rest, Rocco," Uncle Marco insisted, ". . . that when your mom told you not to wake up DiAngelo you said DiAngelo is your boss."

"And he said I was spoiled," I lamented.

"Okay, listen," DiAngelo began, "we're all tired, and Uncle Marco has been through a lot the last few days, but you have to listen to your mom. *She* is your boss. I was just watching over you. You also have to listen to her, Rocco. Do you understand?"

"Yes. Just take me home, Angelo. I want to go to Mrs. Faye's."

"Rocco," DiAngelo added, "you also have to listen to your Uncle Marco."

After a short pause, DiAngelo turned to Uncle Marco.

"Uncle Marco, don't hit him again with a belt. As long as I am alive on the face of this earth, don't ever hit him with a belt again. His back is just about to heal and is inline again. The beating he got and being pushed off the porch did a lot of damage all over his body from his lower back to his brain. He has a fracture in his skull; they're still trying to figure out how to fix that. So, never hit him again. We talk to him and explain how things need to be, but we don't whip him. He's had enough of those to last a lifetime."

"Very well, but you had better talk to him about his mom and set things right, DiAngelo. She will *not* be disrespected!" Uncle Marco answered sternly.

"Baby, come to Mom," my mother said.

DiAngelo pushed me toward her.

"What, Mom?"

"I didn't mean to get you into trouble; I just wanted DiAngelo to get a little more rest than he thinks he needs. We have a long ride ahead of us."

"Okay, I would have understood that."

"Well, I guess Mom just didn't think of doing it that way. We will try it for a while. When I tell you something to do, I will tell you why we are doing it that way. Friends?"

"Yes," I answered. "Uncle Marco, friends?"

"Yes."

DiAngelo asked, "So, are we ready to get on the road?"

"Angelo, I have to go find Mikie and Aunt Hadie. I will be right back."

I went to the back where they were digging coal, and I saw Aunt Hadie and Mikie working their way back down the hill.

"We are ready to go," I yelled out, waving them in with my arm. "Are you all ready?"

"Did Father beat you, Rocco?"

"No."

"I think he did, Rocco."

"He just strapped me with his belt . . . not a real beating like pa's beatings."

"I bet my father is hurt that he had to whip you to make you mind."

"I was trying to mind; Angelo told me to wake him up."

"I think you have too many folks now, Rocco. They all want to be your boss, and you don't know who to listen to."

"Well, I better listen to my mom, Uncle Marco, and Aunt Hadie from now on . . . I can guarantee that."

Chapter 18

Aunt Hadie, Mikie, and I walked up onto the porch. The others went on into the house. I looked at Uncle Marco.

"You're still the best uncle in the world."

"Come here; sit next to me," he offered. I sat down on the porch swing as he continued, "Boy, you know I love you. I didn't know that your pa had beat you so bad or I would have come and got you from there. You could have lived with me and Hadie. I never knew how bad it was for you."

I looked over and realized Uncle Marco had tears falling down his face.

"Uncle Marco, it's not your fault. He told me I had better not tell anyone. So, to keep my mom safe, I didn't tell no one . . . not even Mikie . . . and look, God sent me Angelo to watch over me and care for me."

"That He did," Uncle Marco agreed. "I think DiAngelo would kill me or anyone else over you . . . anyone who ever tried to harm you would have to kill him first."

"DiAngelo fought his mother, his father, and even Evett over me; there is a bond that can never be broken. Mikie is safe with us, also. DiAngelo would kill over Mikie because he knows Mikie is my heart.

"Uncle Marco," I continued, "it's a different life in Michigan. I don't ever think about Pa or him trying to kill me.

I never think about him bleeding and dying right in front of me. I never think of bad things. They're all good for me up there . . . but I always missed something, and I think now that you and the folks are going to be there, I will never come back here. I will never talk about Pa or the things he did to me. It's in the past. We have a long life ahead of us. So, when we leave here today with my mom and all of you, I get to start a new life."

"But, Rocco," Uncle Marco inserted, "you have to talk about it to someone and let it out. You are getting hard. You didn't even cry when I whipped you."

"I cried enough on Mrs. Faye one night to soak her clothes after Ray said I was nothing to him. I buried two of my folks this year besides Pa. Uncle Marco, I don't have any more tears."

"Rocco, you are growing up fast . . . way too fast, and now you are the head of this family. I think my mother was wrong expecting so much of you. You handled getting me out of trouble two times already and more for the rest of the family. I just want you to be happy without trying to always look out for us all. Just relax and have a good life . . . you and Mikie are just kids."

"I will try, Uncle Marco, after I get us all out of here and away from the memories, the hard times, and the hurts. Life is good for me in Michigan. I don't have to recall any of this. Then I can be a kid."

"Okay, Rocco, but I am going to make sure you try."

"Let's go and make our getaway, Uncle Marco, and live happily ever after."

Seeing he got all his business taken care of in one day, Uncle Marco drove his truck with Mikie riding with him.

Angelo and I rode in his truck, and the ladies rode in style in the long limo. I could only imagine what was going on in their country heads.

"Rocco, are you okay, Buckaroo?"

"Yes. Uncle Marco was just trying to talk to me, telling me the same thing that you did when you first came and got me."

"What's that?" DiAngelo questioned.

"That I needed to let you and him worry about the grown-up things and try to relax and just be a kid: play and swim and enjoy life for a while."

"I agree, Buckaroo. It's your turn to be a kid. You have helped us all; now, let us let you have a childhood."

"How did you know I was going to love this dog?" I asked DiAngelo as I roughed up the puppy's ears as he sat in the seat next to me.

"Because you have so much love in you, and it took some of the hardness away that was growing. You can love now and not be afraid of being hurt by any of us. You taught us how to love like Grandmother said. Now, let us show you what we have learned."

"Only if you say it, you feet-smeller."

"Okay, I can, Mr. Rocco Daniel Brooks. I love you with all my heart, and you are the best brother in the world . . . a warm soul in a cold world."

"You cheated. That's what Mrs. Sandra says to me: 'You are a warm soul in this cold world.' Now, make up your own saying about me."

"Okay, I will have to think of one myself. Why are you so geddy-up happy, Rocco?"

"Because soon as you cross over the Kentucky line, I will never think about this place again as long as I live. I will have all of my folks and never have to hurt again. Even in my heart, I will never think about this place. I will hide it deep down and never let it come back. I have you, Evett, and Mrs. Faye and Mrs. Sandra; and all my folks are near me. No one can ever hurt me. We will have new babies this year to make our family grow bigger and have to buy the house on the other side of us, too," I pondered out loud.

"Dang, Rocco. You have our whole lives laid out."

"As long as I have you, Angelo, I am strong. Don't ever leave us. Promise?"

"Buckaroo, I promise that with all my heart forever . . . you and Evett and myself."

"You forgot Alex."

"Oh, yeah, and the little pooper."

We both laughed as we went under the "Welcome to Ohio" sign. I hoped everyone in all the cars were laughing like me and DiAngelo were laughing.

We arrived in Michigan, and it looked like a caravan of gypsies moving in. There were two trucks and a limo pulled up in front of the house, and Mr. Scott started bringing the ladies to the door. When DiAngelo opened the door to the house, we all went in and stood in the foyer of the big house. It seemed different this time: my mom and the lady of the house were now friends, and I didn't feel any twinge in my stomach about their being in the same house. It seemed neither of them wanted Ray Pettrachini as a husband so there was no envy over him between them.

"You all made it home safe!" I heard Mrs. Faye say as she and Mrs. Sandra emerged from the dining room.

I hugged them both, and they went to hugging and shaking the folks' hands.

"Come on in," Mrs. Faye urged everyone.

We went into the dining room where they were about to have supper. We each took our normal seats where Mom sat next to me and Mrs. Sandra took her seat to my left.

"Boy, I am glad to see you! Are you doing well?" Mrs. Sandra asked.

"Yes, Mrs. Sandra; and I missed you a lot!" I replied.

I looked over to Evett and the baby.

"Evett, can I see him? I have missed him a lot, also."

"Sure, Rocco," she answered. "I am glad you are home. He's all yours."

"Hey, little buddy," I said as I took Alex in my arms. "You 'member me? It's your Uncle Rocco, and I brought you something."

I unwrapped a blanket; and it had his initials, A.R.P., and little blue things sewed all around it. Uncle Marco and Aunt Hadie watched as I talked to the baby.

"Your baby will be here soon," I said to Aunt Hadie.

"Yes, and I have to find a doctor and get ready to deliver."

Mrs. Faye spoke up, "We have the best doctor, and you can go see him, Hadie, if you would like. We also have plenty of baby things to go through. Everything is going to be great!"

Aunt Hadie looked at her and with grateful eyes said, "Thank you so much."

"Dean, how are you? Welcome to Michigan!" Mrs. Faye said, looking at my mom.

"Thank you. It's a bit cold up here. We had Easter flowers blooming down home already."

"It won't last much longer."

Then she was off to tell Miss Maria we were ready for supper. She came back from the kitchen with a lot of things for the red sauce eaters and a lot of other things for Mrs. Sandra and me. There was a good mix of just about everything on the table. DiAngelo ate cole slaw with lasagna, and everyone looked at him strangely for his choice of groupings.

"What?" he asked everyone, looking around the table. "It's good! I like cole slaw, and I like lasagna, so they're both good together."

There was a lot of chitchat, and finally Uncle Marco spoke up, "We did not know the Hamiltons were moving."

"Yes, and because of that, Miss Maria has help tonight," Mrs. Faye responded. "Mrs. Ruth came and stayed with us tonight and helped cook. She has made all the other food, and Miss Maria cooked the Italian food."

"Mrs. Ruth is here?" asked Uncle Marco.

"Yes! She is in the kitchen."

"Mrs. Ruthie, come here, please," I yelled out.

"Boy, you are not supposed to scream at the table," Mom scolded me.

"It's okay, Mom. DiAngelo does it all the time."

Mrs. Ruth came out from the kitchen and said, "Yes?"

"Mrs. Ruth, I want you to meet all my folks. This is my mom, Uncle Marco, Aunt Hadie, and Mikie is over there," I introduced them one-by-one, indicating them with my hand. I continued, "And Mikie there is going to be your worst to take care of!"

I squinted at him.

Mrs. Ruth quietly said, "Hall-ow. Nice to meet you."

Everyone said "Hi," and she started to leave.

"Where are you going, Mrs. Ruthie?" I asked. "You don't have to be shy. Come eat with us. We have two chairs left, one for you and one for Miss Maria. We are having a party!"

I looked at Mrs. Sandra, and she smiled at me.

"It's okay, Rocco, if that's what you want."

DiAngelo said, "Look at all the food . . . country food and Italian food!"

Uncle Marco asked, "Mrs. Ruth, how long have you been with the Hamiltons? I remember you from when I was a young adult and you over there running the whole house while running after three teenagers while their parents were out of the country."

"I have been with them 20-something years," she responded in a thick accent.

"Well, we sure have been blessed to have you stay with us."

"Thank you, sir," she responded. Then looking at Aunt Hadie's large belly, she asked, "Mama, when should we prepare the child's room?"

"Well we have to shop for such things first."

"No, Ma'am," she quickly responded. "There has been a nursery over there before, and the furnishings are still in the attic. We need to clean them up and restore them," she added.

"See, Rocco? We do need the bleach and soap that I told you to bring," Mom said with a knowing smile.

"Good thinking, Mom."

Then another thought popped into my mind.

"Where are we all going to sleep?" I directed the question to Mrs. Faye.

"Mrs. Ruth says the Hamilton house is already empty of their private things, and they have already left for Russia."

"Already?" I asked.

"Yes, they were already in the process of moving," Mrs.

Ruth responded, “when Mr. DiAngelo came that night to offer to buy the house.”

Mikie all but jumped out of his seat with exuberance as he announced, “We could move in tonight, then!”

“Yes, the house is all yours, Mr. Mikie,” Mrs. Ruth answered laughingly.

“You don’t have to call me Mr. I am just plain Mikie,” he offered with a smile on his face.

We finished eating, and Mrs. Faye said, “Do we dare go over there this late?”

“It’s only six o’clock, Mother. I think it would be okay,” DiAngelo offered.

“I’m going with Mrs. Sandra,” I said, “so she can keep me warm. If we’re walking over there, she needs her furry coat; and I help her walk.”

“Yes, Rocco, you do. You’re such a good and loving boy.”

I could tell by the faces of my folks from down home that they were thinking that I was as spoiled as DiAngelo and that Mrs. Faye and Mrs. Sandra were guilty of doing the spoiling.

“Have Scott shovel us a path, DiAngelo, so we won’t get all wet and cold walking over there. Then Ruth can lead the way,” Mrs. Faye instructed.

When it was time to cross over to the Hamilton house, Mrs. Ruth did, indeed, lead the way. There was a wooden gate between the two homes. The walk was already shoveled and cleared for us. There were 11 of us walking over there to see the house that we had bought.

We walked through the garage attached to the house and up the few steps to the inside of the house. It was warm as could be. We found ourselves in the back of the house. We walked through a great big kitchen. A bedroom was next to it, and Mrs. Ruth informed us that the room was the helper's living quarters.

As we left that room, we went into the dining room. It was bigger than the one at DiAngelo's house; Mikie was right. It had a bright chandelier, and their table sat 20 on the sides and had two head chairs.

"Mom, look!" I said quietly to her. "You can put your good plates in there."

I pointed to a beautiful hutch standing against the wall. It matched the long dining table and chairs.

"Yes, Rocco, that will keep you from dropping them," she commented.

I looked over at DiAngelo in amazement at the grand house.

Their floor was a lot like ours, but not as cold as the one in our house. There was a fireplace that went all the way through the ceiling. The living room was great big with a huge screen tv . . . like at the movies.

"Mikie, we can watch a lot of cartoons on this one."

"We sure can!"

His eyes were big like a raccoon's as he took in the bigness of the house.

The study was done in red mahogany, and they had a library where there were hundreds of books.

"Mrs. Sandra, they don't have a piano room like me."

"Yes, there is another room over here," she answered as she drew me to it.

The room was so big, it had two doors. Mrs. Sandra opened both doors grandly, revealing the biggest piano I had ever seen. There were couches and chairs and another fireplace.

The one wall was nothing but windows that overlooked the lake; the scene was beautiful.

DiAngelo spoke up, "Grandmother, play something."

She went to the piano bench and sat down. She placed her hands just above the beautiful, ivory keys and softly began playing. The notes were clear . . . all of them. She played my new song that I learned. She stopped playing and looked at me.

"Sing it, boy."

When I started, it carried all over that great big house with echoes, because there was no one in the house moving about. My mom and Mrs. Sandra smiled from ear to ear.

Mikie spoke out, "Dang, Rocco! I didn't know you could sing that loud."

"DiAngelo gave me a speaker," I said with pride.

"Well you don't need it; you almost busted my ears!"

Mrs. Ruth added, "I could hear you sing sometimes, and it makes me feel God all over me and causes His peace to fill my soul."

"Ruth, do you know the Lord?" Mom asked.

"Yes, Him and I are friends, Mrs. Dean."

"Good! We will be great friends in the kitchen cooking together: Hadie, you, and me."

I think my mom was letting Mrs. Ruth know she was planning on doing some cooking in her house.

"That would be great to have someone in the kitchen cooking like Mrs. Ruth. Tell them about the eclairs you make," I insisted.

"I will do better than that; I will make some for you, Rocco."

"Only one," Mrs. Sandra cautioned. "We have to watch his sugar levels."

"Yes, Faye, you will have to teach me what he can eat and what he can't when he is over here," my mom said.

"Damn it!" I said half under my breath.

The whole bunch of folks turned and looked at me.

"What was that for?" Mrs. Faye asked, none too happy at my choice of words.

"I was going to sneak over here when Mrs. Faye wouldn't let me have sugar and eat it over here. Now you all messed up my plan," I complained.

Everyone started to laugh.

Mrs. Sandra said, "Boy, you are allowed to have a bit here and there, so she can make them when your levels are down."

"Oh, thank you, Mrs. Sandra. I love you!"

"He loves anyone who gives him his way," Uncle Marco remarked.

"Mikie, let's go find your bedroom," I suggested.

"Okay!"

"Mrs. Ruth, is there a bedroom with two beds? Mikie has stinky feet!"

Mikie and I walked out of the piano room all hugged up. The house had eight bedrooms, but they were bigger; and the room with two beds had two full-sized beds in them with its own, separate bathroom.

The room that Mikie and I picked out was the master bedroom, so DiAngelo said, "I think this is Uncle Marco's and Aunt Hadie's bedroom."

"Aren't we gonna split them all up like we did at our house . . . the older folks over there and us younger ones over here?" I asked him.

"Well, that's up to them, Rocco."

"You knuckleheads, you can't be all the way over here by yourself; you will tear the place down!" Aunt Hadie said as she walked up behind us.

"Yes, Aunt Hadie," I gave in.

"Not if we put Dean on this side with them," Uncle Marco suggested. "They can have this bedroom; it looks out over the lake the best. They are boys and need to see."

"Yes, Marco," Aunt Hadie agreed.

On the other side of the stairs, there was their room . . . just as big, but with a king-sized bed and a bathroom right off it. On the other side of them they were going to make the baby's room.

Even at this, there were still two extra bedrooms on each side, like our house.

"That can be Angelo's room when Evett kicks him out of our house," I offered.

He burst out laughing and said, "Can't I stay in your room anymore?"

"Yes, you can, Brother, if Evett kicks you out."

Mikie stared at him incredulously and started to say, "No." He caught himself just in time.

"You sleep in the piano room if she does," he offered instead. "Okay?"

"Okay, deal," DiAngelo answered.

We all went back downstairs. They had decided to stay there that night. The lights went on all over the house, and they had to learn their way around a few times.

"Rocco, are you staying here tonight?" Mikie asked.

"Well, I better give my back a rest and sleep in my own bed. I will stay here tomorrow night after you learn all the good hiding spots for us . . . but, Mikie, call me in about 20 minutes so we can talk."

"Okay."

We squinted at each other. My folks and I got our coats on and made our way back over to our house, leaving the others to get used to their new home. I went right into the piano room and fell on the couch.

"Rocco, are you okay?" Mrs. Faye asked with concern in her voice.

"Yes, but I am glad to be home!"

Mrs. Faye hugged me and said, "Boy, we love you; and I am glad that you are going to be living with us over here."

"This is our home. Angelo and me can never be apart. I can never leave him. He is my only brother, and I can't sleep well without you and Mrs. Sandra."

DiAngelo overheard the conversation and laughed.

"Boy," he said, "you can sleep anywhere. I have heard you snore while we drive in the truck."

"So? Shut up, grape ape; and smell my feet," I taunted him.

We went upstairs to our rooms, and it wasn't long before Mikie was on the phone telling me more and more about his big, new home.

"I am glad you like it, Mikie. Now, hang up and sleep well. Is Mom there?"

"Aunt Dean is unpacking. I will go get her."

When I heard her voice on the line, I said, "Mom, I just wanted to say 'Hi' and see what you were doing."

"Rocco, this house is so big over here. I don't have to share a bathroom! I can put all my stuff out, and it's not in anyone's way. I love it here!"

"Wait till you see the water in the morning, Mom, and sit and have coffee in the dining room and look out. I will be over as soon as I get up. I love you, Mom."

"I love you, too, baby. Night."

*****

"Rocco, get up! It's time to eat breakfast," DiAngelo urged me.

"Angelo, what time is it? It is still dark out," I grumbled.

"It's time for the uncle to feed his nephew; he is hungry and needs you."

I turned over in my bed with a groan. DiAngelo was holding Alex.

"Here, let me have him, and go get his bottle."

I put the baby under the blankets and talked to him. He just lay there . . . not crying but listening to me as I talked to him.

"Alex, I love you."

Angelo returned with the bottle and handed it to me.

"You feed him while I go back to sleep," DiAngelo instructed.

"No way! You feed him and let me sleep."

"Buckaroo, I am tired. Come on, please feed him," DiAngelo pleaded.

"You're a baby yourself, Angelo."

He laughed. I fed the little guy, and he burped really loud for his dad.

"He sounds like you, Angelo."

"Tell Uncle Rocco you need your diaper changed, too, because you pooped."

"Angelo, no, he didn't. Stop lying to me."

"I think he is going to love you more than he loves me, Rocco."

"That's because I am the best-looking Pettrachini."

"No, you're not; you have a big head, Rocco."

"Why don't you go to bed, and put this baby back in his crib?" I suggested, looking up at DiAngelo.

"You already have him back to sleep?"

"Yes, he just don't like smelling your feet. He wanted his uncle."

"Thanks, Buckaroo. I really am tired after all that driving the last couple of days."

"Wait. You owe me $4 babysitting fee."

"Right now, I would gladly pay it. Thanks for getting him to sleep. See you a little later, Brother."

When the real morning came, I went downstairs and had breakfast with Mrs. Faye and Mrs. Sandra.

"Where are Evett and DiAngelo?" Mrs. Faye inquired.

"They're still sleeping. Alex kept them awake. I know: I had to calm him by feeding him and get him back to sleep earlier this morning."

"Did you get enough sleep, Rocco?"

"Yes, Ma'am, I am just dragging this morning. Maybe I can have some pancakes and syrup?"

"Oh, Rocco, I give up. You can have them . . . but just today."

"Thanks, Mrs. Faye. I feel better already."

We laughed.

"Are you going to go over and see your mom and Mikie?"

"Yes, after I wake up more and eat. I am going over there

and wake all of them up. I might go over before I shower and scare 'em."

"Scare them?" Mrs. Faye repeated questioningly.

"Yes. Angelo says I look like a monster with my hair all over the place."

"No, you don't. DiAngelo better leave you alone or I am going to get him."

"Get him, Mrs. Faye; and tell him to stop teasing me."

"Well, I think you like it when your brother teases."

"Yeah, I reckon I do."

Mrs. Sandra walked into the dining room.

"Mrs. Sandra, if you could have anything, what would it be?" I quizzed.

"Well, I am a very blessed woman. I have no needs. I have good health, a great family, and as much laughter as one can handle since you came to this house."

"Well, you sure are hard to buy for."

"I just can't think of anything," she replied.

"I can help with that, Rocco," Mrs. Faye interrupted. "I know just what Mother needs."

"Good!" I answered. "Mrs. Faye, let's go to the mall."

"Okay, we will go soon."

"Okay, I am done eating; and I'm going to wake the folks up. I will be back in a bit."

"You come and let me bundle you up before you go out there in the cold."

"Yes, Ma'am."

Soon I stood, bundled. Mrs. Faye helped me put on my boots, and then I went outside, through the gate, and over to my mom's house.

"Good morning, Mrs. Ruth," I said as I went in.

"Good morning, Rocco," she cheerily returned my greeting as she bustled around the kitchen working on breakfast. "How are you?"

"I am well, but I am going to wake up the folks."

"You're too late, I'm afraid," she responded with a chuckle. "They were up at 5 a.m. and even beat me awake."

"My mom always gets up like that."

"Did she used to cook breakfast for you?" Mrs. Ruth inquired.

"Yes, on most days."

I went into the dining room. Uncle Marco, Aunt Hadie, and Mom were at one end of the table, just sitting there having coffee and looking out at the snow on Lake Michigan.

"Well, look who's awake! Good morning!" Mom greeted me.

"Good morning, Mom, Aunt, and Uncle."

"Did you sleep good, baby?"

"Yes, Mom. Did you?"

"Yes, but I stayed in bed too long; I slept until 5:15."

"Too early up here; we sleep till eight, Mom; you beat the chickens up!"

"There are some chickens out there?"

"No, Mom; it's a saying."

"Oh, okay."

"Where's Mikie?" I asked them.

"He's still sleeping, and it's about time for him to get up. Go get him awake, Rocco," Aunt Hadie suggested.

"Okay, Aunt Hadie, I will if I can remember how to get to him."

They laughed.

On my way out of the dining room, Uncle Marco reached out and grabbed me.

"Did you forget something?" he wanted to know. "You're not so old that I don't want my good-morning hug."

I hugged Uncle Marco tightly and said, "There!"

I was off to get Mikie.

I sneaked into Mikie's room, jumped on his bed, and screamed as loudly as I could, "Get him, Monster!"

Mikie jumped almost straight out of the bed. He sat there momentarily, trying to collect his wits.

"Rocco," Mikie whined, "that's not nice. You know I just got here last night."

I laughed until I almost peed myself. The more I laughed, the angrier he got.

"Okay, I am sorry," I fake apologized. "Your mom said for you to come down to breakfast. It's almost 9 o'clock."

"Really? It is?"

"Yup. Now get up, Skeeter; and let's go see this big house in the daytime."

Mikie got out of bed and washed his face. We then raced down the steps to the dining room.

"You two sound like a herd of cattle!" Mom exclaimed.

"It was Mikie thumping; I was just running." Turning to Uncle Marco, I said, "I am going to the mall today. Can Mikie go?"

"Well, I think so," Uncle Marco started. "Hadie, you didn't have anything for him to do, did you?"

"No; he's been good, so he can go."

"I am going to buy us coats just alike and some boots so he won't get wet and cold. Then we're going to the toy store and buy whatever we want. Did you all need anything?"

Mom answered, "Buy some of those warm pretzels you always talk about."

"Okay, I will, Mom. I will get Aunt Hadie some, too."

"Did you forget me, Rocco?" Uncle Marco piped up.

"No, Uncle Marco. You haven't been good; so, you don't get any."

Mikie spoke up, "I will get you one, Father."

"Oh, Son, Rocco has learned to play jokes. It's okay; he was kidding me."

"No, I wasn't," I contradicted him with a straight face.

Then I burst out laughing.

"Rocco, you are getting to be just like DiAngelo," Mikie commented.

"He is getting to be just like me every day. I teach him to be good and to love."

"And he teaches you to say bad words," Mikie quickly added.

"Mikie, I don't say bad words on purpose; they just come out when I get mad."

"Well, then, you sure get mad a lot."

"Okay, go upstairs and shower," I told Mikie. "I will go home. You come over when you get done. Bye, Mom, Aunt Hadie. See you in a bit."

"Hey! Where's Mom's sugar?" Mom threw out.

"In your coffee," I answered and watched for her reaction.

I finally walked over and gave my mom a kiss on her cheek. She laughed. On my way out I said goodbye to my friend, Mrs. Ruth, and went back home.

"Mrs. Faye!" I called out.

"In here, Rocco," came her answer.

"Can Mikie go with me to the mall today and get a coat and some boots . . . and I need four pretzels."

"Sure, I don't care."

"Mrs. Sandra, do you want to come?" I urged her.

"I think I will go this time."

"Really, Mother?" Mrs. Faye inquired.

"Yes, Faye, I think I want to go with you today."

"Great!" I enthusiastically responded. "My two favorite women and my cousin going with me to the mall today!"

I was off to shower.

"Hurry up, Stinky! I have to shower before the baby starts screaming again," DiAngelo yelled through the bathroom door.

"Get out of here! I was here first," I flung at him.

"Well, I will shave while you shower."

"And don't forget to brush your teeth; you smell like a cigarette."

"Boy, I haven't smoked in a week; I stopped smoking."

"Well, good for you. Can Mikie and me have them, then?"

"No, you can't."

"I seen them lying in the garage; you didn't stop," I plainly accused.

"Rocco, I did stop; those were from before."

"Then throw them away, and then you can say you stopped."

"Well, I might need them if Evett keeps griping and arguing."

"Chew some 'backer and leave the cigarettes alone, then."

"Some what?" DiAngelo pressed.

"Chewing 'backer," I clarified.

"Are you trying to say chewing tobacco?"

"Yes, damn it! Chewing 'backer."

"Okay, Rocco, you better stop cussing. You are getting me in all kinds of trouble with that."

"Okay, I will try and stop cussing if you stop smoking. When Evett gets on you, just think of something besides the cigarettes; see if that works."

"Do I really smell that bad?"

"Nope."

"Then why do you hate it so bad?"

"I seen on the tv that folks die from smoking, and Alex and me won't have you if you go to the Father."

I dried off in the shower, wrapped the towel around me, and stepped out.

"Rocco," DiAngelo started as he continued with his shaving, "don't worry; I won't die."

"Everyone is dying; I don't want to be left here . . . me and Alex . . . by ourselves."

"Okay, I will do it for you two. I won't smoke again."

"Thanks, Angelo . . . and I won't cuss anymore."

"Okay, deal. Now, get out of here so I can shower and then go eat."

Later in the morning we loaded up the car to head for the mall. Mikie and I played and laughed all the way.

Mrs. Faye said, "You two boys are getting bigger by the day."

"I have to get big so my brother will stop getting the best of me. Mikie and I are going to gang up on him and tickle his feet till he pees his pants . . . like Alex does."

"Oh, dear," Mrs. Sandra said as she rolled her eyes.

Mr. Scott let us out at the entrance to the mall, and we went in. We soon had purchased Mikie a coat and boots, and then we went to the toy store. We walked up and down the aisles looking for something that might catch our eye. Suddenly . . . there it was: a racecar track with Hot Wheels cars.

I grabbed Mikie's sleeve and pulled him closer to me, whispering into his ear, "Mikie, let's get two of them and hook them together to have the biggest one ever!"

We could assemble the track so the cars would go through the charger, then speed up, lasting until it got to the second charger where they would get enough power to get back to the first charger again. 'Round and 'round the cars would go indefinitely.

When we arrived home, we decided to assemble our new track on the big living room floor where that great big tv was. It kept us busy several hours.

Chapter 19

The tutor started coming to Uncle Marco's house and teaching Mikie and me there because there was more room. A lot of the books we needed were already in the library.

Mom and Aunt Hadie spent some of their time teaching Mrs. Faye and Mrs. Sandra how to sew and stitch a quilt together. Uncle Marco took to going to work with DiAngelo. Mrs. Faye took care of Alex while Evett finished school on Tuesdays and Thursdays. Mikie and I started going to the YMCA to learn to swim. We started making new friends there.

Mom insisted Mr. Scott take us all to church on Sunday mornings and on Wednesday nights, but she would wait until everyone was in before she would get out of the big car and go in. She said she didn't want to "show off."

Aunt Hadie finally had her baby girl; she was cute as a button. They named her Makayla Jade Pettrachini. We now had a baby in each house—only two months apart in age—to keep us laughing, changing diapers, and making bottles.

Evett studied hard for her tests. During those times Mikie and I had to be quiet and help care for Alex.

In June it was warm enough to start having picnics. Both houses would grill. We put out tables long enough at which all of us could sit. Life was good and quiet as we fit into our new lives on Lake Michigan.

We rode in the boats, lay in the sun, and Mikie finally got his new bike. We rode up and down the long driveway, never getting too far from Uncle Marco or DiAngelo. The warm breeze kept me warm.

Mom and the rest of the ladies finished about 20 quilts that winter. They set up a stand at an arts and crafts show to sell them. Their quilts all sold, and they gave the money to the church to buy new hymnals.

Mom and Mrs. Faye became close. They canned jellies and crafted and sold other homemade items.

Mom and I were asked to sing frequently. We never got to simply sit in church; we always were asked to sing.

Life continued like this through the next five years.

Mikie and I had learned a lot. I hit 14 two months before Mikie did; and by that time, I was out of my brace.

Mrs. Sandra had gotten to the place where she could hardly see. I offered her my shoulder to hold onto and walked her to the dock. We would sit, and I would tell her what everyone was doing. That summer she told me stories of Italy over and over again . . . about her growing up and how she loved to run and play. I think life took Mrs. Sandra back to her happy days, and she enjoyed telling me about them.

DiAngelo had purchased a few more carwashes. He and Uncle Marco went in as partners on the last two.

The "babies" were already five years old and running all over the place.

"Uncle Rocco! Uncle Rocco, look!" Alex would yell at me when he did something he thought was funny. He wouldn't stop until I responded with "Good trick!"

Evett was still going to school, learning how to teach.

Mom and Aunt Hadie loved their nice lives on the lake. It was as if we had this part of the world all to ourselves.

Mikie was a better swimmer than any of us; he was like a fish. Even when he wasn't in the water, he enjoyed just looking at it. Mom commented that she believed Mikie would sleep on the water if only his mother would let him.

"Rocco, it's as if the water calms me; each sound is different. I love it here," he told me one day.

We continued our swimming lessons at the YMCA. I noticed Mikie spending more time with a certain girl who was also taking swimming lessons there.

"I see you have a girlfriend at the YMCA," I remarked. "She is pretty."

"She swims with us in our swimming class, Rocco," he remarked, rolling his eyes at me. "Her name is Audrey Debree."

"I know who she is, but I think she likes you."

"Really, Rocco?" Mikie responded as he perked up.

"Yup. Maybe you should ask her to the movies. We will have Mr. Scott take us. You can sit with her by yourself; I will sit somewhere else."

Mikie liked the idea, so we made it happen.

On the way home that night, I looked at the girl and asked her, "Can Mikie have your phone number?"

"Sure," she answered and went to writing it down on a piece of paper. She handed it to Mikie as we pulled up to drop her off at her house.

"Dang, Rocco! I can't believe you asked her for her number. Thanks!"

"What are best friends for?" I asked as I smiled at him.

*****

"Rocco, get ready! We are going to be late for dinner," DiAngelo urged me. "It's Mrs. Ruth's turn to cook, so the kin folks are coming over here with some 'possum and fatback, and we gonna dance around the backyard."

"Angelo, why are you making fun of my mom and them? You never have made fun of my folks," I agonized.

"Oh, calm down. It was just a joke, Rocco."

"Well, it wasn't very funny, and I don't appreciate it."

"Dang, Mr. Rocco, who stole your cookies?"

"I guess the same one who stole my 'possum," I said flippantly and walked away from him.

"All right, I told you a hundred times to stop walking away like that when someone is speaking to you. I was only teasing."

"What did you do now, DiAngelo, the Great?" Evett asked as she walked into my bedroom holding Alex's hand.

"Nothing. Rocco is just being a baby."

We all went to the dining room where the folks were already assembled. Alex wiggled his hand out of his mother's hand and ran up to Makayla.

"Look!" he exclaimed to her as he showed her his new Captain America figure.

She grabbed the figure from Alex and exclaimed, "Pooed his pants."

Aunt Hadie said sternly, "Girl, he didn't poop his pants; now, give it back!"

Mom leaned over and kissed my cheek as I sat in my chair. It didn't feel the same at mealtime any more ever since Mrs. Sandra had started taking her meals in her room. After each supper, Mrs. Faye and I would take Mrs. Sandra's food up and have a "second supper" there with her. I would tell her all about our first supper. A part of my heart was missing as I sat at the table.

"Mikie," I started, "I need your help with some of this homework. The tutor went too fast today, and I didn't catch it all."

Mrs. Faye spoke up, "Maybe we should get another tutor to help more with your studies, Rocco."

"I don't know, Mother Faye. This is just getting too hard for me."

As time went on, I had learned to call Mrs. Faye my mother, and Mom was my mom. I think everyone became accustomed to it because nothing was ever said about it, and I never brought it up.

"Well, maybe if you stop worrying about everything else and study . . . keep your mind on what he is saying . . . it won't be too hard for you," DiAngelo said in an almost superior tone.

"Well, thank you, Mr. Pettrachini. I will keep that in mind."

"What is wrong with you two tonight?" Uncle Marco inserted. "I have caught not a few bad looks between the two of you."

"Nothing, Uncle Marco," I replied sullenly.

"Yes, nothing, Uncle Marco," DiAngelo agreed.

"Just that Angelo is trying to be a comedian these days. I don't like his damn jokes," I added.

"Yes, damn it!" Alex repeated.

"Don't say that, Alex," I scolded.

"Well, why shouldn't he say it?" DiAngelo threw at me. "His uncle says it."

"Angelo, are you going to keep your mouth running all night? Now, it's enough. Let it go."

"Yes, DiAngelo, let it go," Evett spoke up.

"I knew you would agree with him," DiAngelo accused. "You always do."

"Okay, do I have to put you in a corner . . . both of you?" Mrs. Faye asked.

"No, you don't," DiAngelo responded. "Come here, Rocco, and let's speak in the other room."

As we went out, the whole table followed us with their eyes. We walked into the piano room and closed the door.

"Okay, you tell me what's wrong," DiAngelo started. "Even you have made jokes of the folks down south and where you came from. Now, when I do it, you are all bent out of shape."

"I don't know," Rocco started slowly. "I have felt angry all day, and you were the first one who said something."

"Why have you been angry, Rocco?"

"I don't know; I feel something. I don't know what it is."

"You haven't spoken like that since you were a kid," DiAngelo observed.

"Angelo, I am sorry for being mean to you . . . but look."

I showed him my hand. It was shaking.

"I am cold all the time."

"Are you feeling all right? Did Mother check your blood sugar?"

"Yes, and everything is normal."

"Then what's wrong?"

"I don't know."

I scooted over next to DiAngelo and leaned against him.

"And it's getting worse." I quietly added.

"Do you want me to take you to see Dr. Bill?"

"Maybe, because I really feel sick to my stomach like I am going to puke."

"Maybe I should get Mother," DiAngelo offered.

"No, she has her hands full with Mrs. Sandra. If it doesn't go away, we will go see Dr. Bill tomorrow. Deal?"

"Deal, but I think I should keep you home tomorrow, and I will stay home with you."

Just then a pain shot through my stomach that doubled me over as I let out an agonizing groan. At the same time the gate buzzer rang.

"Dear Lord, Rocco," DiAngelo stood over me. "Are you okay?"

All my supper came flowing out of me like a faucet had been turned on.

DiAngelo started screaming, "Miss Maria! Mrs. Ruth! Come here!"

DiAngelo left to go find them. The other folks came into the piano room and tried to figure out why I was sick.

Alex kept repeating, "Rocco is sick; Rocco is sick."

"Yes, get over here with me in case he pukes again," DiAngelo said as he returned to the piano room and heard Alex's sing-song chant.

Miss Maria and Mrs. Ruth arrived and began wetting my head. Mom sat next to me.

"Boy, are you okay?"

"Mom, I feel something."

The gate buzzer went off a second time.

"Would someone see who's out there?" DiAngelo asked impatiently.

Uncle Marco went and buzzed someone in.

"Your father is here and on his way up the drive," he announced.

When those words came out of Uncle Marco's mouth, the pain vanished.

My mom remarked, "*That* is what he feels," as she tossed her head in the direction of the gate.

"Mother Faye, go to Mrs. Sandra and tell her I will be there in a minute."

"She is all right, Rocco. I want to stay with you."

"No, go to her and tell her to wait a few minutes before she leaves."

"Leaves?" Mrs. Faye questioned. "Rocco, I don't think she is going anywhere."

Miss Maria and Mrs. Ruth cleaned me up quickly. By the time I got to the foyer, Ray Pettrachini walked in the door. DiAngelo had me by the arm, and we were headed for Mrs. Sandra's room. We both just looked at him and kept walking.

"No 'Hi' or 'Welcome home' from you two?"

Marco shook his head to him to hush him, and we continued on our way to say goodbye to Mrs. Sandra. As we went into Mrs. Sandra's bedroom, she smiled at me and held out her hand for me to come to her.

"Did you hear the footsteps, boy?"

"Yes, Mrs. Sandra, I heard them."

I burst out crying and fell to her bed.

"Oh, boy, don't cry for Mis. Sandra; I am going to a better place."

"Thank you, Mrs. Sandra, for loving me. Thank you for being my grandmother."

She kissed DiAngelo goodbye and then me.

"Thank you for fixing my family, my angel," she softly spoke and closed her eyes as she went to the Father.

I screamed as loudly as I could, "No! No, Mrs. Sandra! No, don't go!"

When I opened my mouth again, a scream that lasted forever filled my ears. I think Holland and all the fish in Lake Michigan stood still for that hurtful scream. I passed out.

When I woke up, my mom and Aunt Hadie were tending to me, and I was in my bed. They were washing my face with a cool, wet cloth.

"Mom, I had a dream. Mrs. Sandra passed away," I weakly said.

"Boy, it was not a dream; she went home to the Father."

"That means Ray is here, also?"

"Yes, he is downstairs with Marco and the children."

Tears spilled over my cheeks once again and wouldn't stop.

"Where is Mother Faye and Angelo?" I asked between deep sobs.

"You had better wash your face and be strong," Mom advised.

"No, Mom. I am not going to do that. I don't want to wash my face and be strong. I want Mrs. Sandra back."

"Boy, you have dealt with death better than all of us. In the bad days, you keep the strength. Sing for her."

"No, I am never singing again. She loved me from day one; she kept me warm; she prayed for me; she loved me when no one else would up here. She was the first to let me cry. I loved Mrs. Sandra with all my heart. Now, let me up."

"Dean," Aunt Hadie responded, "let him up; and let him deal with it the way he needs to."

"Always I have to be strong and take care of everyone," I

grieved. "I don't dare cry and let folks see. I am only human, Mom. God didn't have to take her from me."

"Hadie, I think he has lost his mind Go shut the door," Mom instructed.

"No, you better not shut that door. I don't care who hears me . . . Ray, Marco . . . or anyone! I don't care!" I screamed. "Now, get!"

"Dean, maybe we should go and let him pull himself together on his own," Aunt Hadie offered.

"I am not pulling myself together, and I am not burying one more. You better not let anyone take her; I mean it. No one is taking Mrs. Sandra!"

"Rocco, can we come in?" DiAngelo said as he entered the room.

I could see he had been crying, as well. He asked the ladies to leave. Then, he grabbed me; and we cried and cried.

"Not Mrs. Sandra," I sobbed into DiAngelo's shoulder. "Not her, Angelo. I need her to love me . . . not her! Anyone but her and you. I can't be strong this time."

DiAngelo's tears flooded over my head and face; and my tears flooded over his chest.

"I will do it, Brother. I will be the strong one this time for you and Mother. I will bear this hurt; I will look after you both."

I moved away from DiAngelo and looked up at him.

"Where is Mother, Angelo?"

"She is downstairs in the piano room, waiting for the funeral home to come and get Grandmother."

"We had better wash up, Angelo, so I can go see her and make sure she is okay."

As we washed up side-by-side, I looked over to DiAngelo and said, "This is my hell, isn't it?"

"What, Rocco?"

"This is my hell right here: loving folks and burying them; loving folks and burying them. Angelo, I am 14 years old. I have buried and sang, buried and sang. This is my hell . . . sending folks to Father God. Each time, they take a part of me with them. There's no more for me to send. I can't do this again. After this time, I can't do it again."

"Rocco, it's the love that you put in the folks. You put all of your heart into loving them. We have been blessed to have been loved by you. The one thing Grandmother knew, she told me, was that we had to love you back to replace all the love that you give out."

"Mrs. Sandra said that?"

I started crying again.

"She gave me that saying that I was a warm soul in a cold world, and I will never forget it."

"Buckaroo, I think we have to wash our faces again," DiAngelo suggested.

Mrs. Sandra had been gone only an hour, and my brother and I had red streaks running down our faces from the tears we had already shed.

We went to the piano room but Mrs. Faye wasn't there; so, we went to the dining room. Only Uncle Marco, Ray, and Mrs. Faye were there; the others had gone home. I was sure they weren't asleep.

"Was that you that let out that blood-curdling scream?" my father asked me.

I looked at him and said with all my heart, "Ray, if you mess with me during this time, you will have a bullet planted in between those eyes of yours. Write that on your arm lest you forget it."

Marco responded, "I think the boy means that, Ray. You would do well to keep quiet and let him mourn Mrs. Sandra."

I walked toward Mother Faye. We stared at each other, our hearts melting, as I approached her.

I fell into her arms and said, "Mother, I am sorry; I am not strong this time."

"Rocco, you don't have to be strong this time. If anyone loved Mother, it was you. She had your heart and soul. The way that you would lead her around, tell her things, feed her, and let her see through your eyes these last few years, Mother loved you with all her heart . . . both of you."

"Mr. Rocco, would you like anything to drink or eat?" Miss Maria softly spoke to me as she placed a hand on my back.

"No, thank you, Miss Maria."

"Rocco, please try to eat. I think your lunch is all gone. Do you still feel sick?" Mrs. Faye pressed.

"No, Mother Faye, the feeling is gone."

I looked over at Uncle Marco.

"Is my mom mad at me?" I asked him.

"No, why?" he replied.

"I told her and Aunt Hadie to get."

Ray interrupted, "Yeah, we know. We all heard it."

"Mother Faye, please make him go away. Please."

I turned to DiAngelo who had just entered the dining room.

"Angelo, please take him to the airport. I don't want to see him right now. Please."

"Rocco, we can't just make him leave," DiAngelo tried to explain. "He is our father."

I slammed my fist on the table and said, "For 14 damn years he has not been my father, and I don't need him now. I don't need or want his comments. I don't want to look at him, and I don't want to hear his voice." Looking at Ray, I continued, "Now leave us alone to hurt and bury Mrs. Sandra in peace!"

I was so mad I started to cry again.

Mrs. Faye spoke, "DiAngelo, come with us."

She hugged me to her side, and we walked into the study with DiAngelo following.

"Rocco, sit here next to me and let's talk." After we sat down, Mrs. Faye continued, "Tell me, Rocco, tell me what is wrong."

Through my tears I said, "Mother, he is looking at us."

"What, Rocco? I don't understand."

"He is looking at Angelo and me while we hurt; he is enjoying it."

"No, Rocco, I am sure he's not . . . surely not at a time like this."

"Yes, he is, Mother Faye. I can feel it. He's filling his soul with our pain. He never cried for his own mother. Do you remember Mrs. Liza's funeral? He was laughing and talking to the folks. He has no soul, Mother Faye; and I can't fight him now. What is he doing here anyway?"

"We don't know. We were upstairs as you were."

"Mother Faye, I was sick because I felt him. I knew Mrs. Sandra was going home."

"Mother, he was fine until about the time Father hit the gate buzzer," DiAngelo inserted. "I don't know how this works in him, but he always knows things."

Mrs. Faye just looked at the floor, wondering what to do.

"I wish Dean was here," she finally said. "She says the boy gets this gift from her mother."

"My mom told you about my 'feelings,' Mother Faye?"

"Yes, Rocco, she did; and my mother said it was God keeping you safe."

"Dear Mrs. Sandra," I said as dry sobs still escaped me now and then, "I am going to miss her."

"Well," Mrs. Faye started, "I think I am going to say a prayer for you until we can talk to your mom."

She said a Catholic prayer over me, and I said, "Dear Lord, please keep me safe. Let me feel you. Please give me love instead of hate, Amen."

"Does that mean you're not going to shoot Father in the head?" DiAngelo asked.

Suddenly the gate buzzer rang.

Mrs. Faye stood up and said, "why don't you go next door until they're done here, Rocco? I will send DiAngelo to come get you when they're done."

"You will be okay without me, Mother Faye?" I asked.

"Yes, DiAngelo is here with me. You go see your mom, and don't forget to tell her you're sorry for telling her to 'Get.' Now, you hug me with all your heart."

I hugged Mrs. Faye, kissed her cheek, and said, "I love you."

"I love you, also," she replied. "We will see you in a few minutes."

I knew there were folks on their way up to the house to take away my dear Mrs. Sandra. I walked by and said, "Uncle Marco, I am going over to your house."

I looked at Ray and walked away.

Mom and Aunt Hadie were sitting at the table.

Mrs. Ruth asked, "Do you want anything?"

"Yes, Ma'am, I would like a cup of coffee with a few ice cubes in it, please."

"Rocco, you are going to drink that coffee?" Mom asked.

"Yes, Mom; and I am sorry for telling you two ladies 'Get.'"

While tears ran down my face yet again, my mom sat and held my hand.

"She was the grandmother you never had, boy. It's okay. We understand."

"Mom, I don't know why it is different this time. I know she is with Father God, but I can't feel happy."

"Baby, it's because you loved her so much that your heart is broken this time. You wanted her to stay more than you wanted her to go with God; but now she can see in Heaven, and she is no longer sick. Aren't you happy for her?"

"Yes, Mom. Now she can play that piano for the folks in Heaven, sing, and live happily ever after. Mom, you're so sweet; but I don't have to have the 'happily ever after' anymore. I am 14."

"Well, I said we were going to live happily ever after; and look at us, Rocco, we are happy."

"That's true, Mom. You were right. Mom, I need to talk to you and Aunt Hadie about something."

"What's that, boy?"

"I got sick tonight. I think it was because Ray was here, and I knew it beforehand. How do I know these things?"

"Well," Mom started, "my mom used to know things. She would get what we call 'feelings.' She would know when death and bad things were fixing to happen, and she would know how to fix them."

"Dean," Aunt Hadie interrupted. "why are you telling him all that? Don't you think he's been through enough today?"

"Yes, I do, but he is asking."

"Mrs. Sandra said it was God's way to keep me safe," I explained. "Is that right, Mom?"

"Yes, I think it is. I think God watches over you."

"Mom, why can't my soul love Ray? Why do I feel so much yuck for him?"

"Son, listen to Mom real good. When a person hurts you so much, you just don't want to be around him . . . like when we would go to Hadie's and have fun away from Pa, remember?"

"Yes."

"Well, that's what it is with you and Ray. We were all settled here having fun and a new life, and you're just afraid he will ruin it."

"If you say that's what it is, Mom, okay; but I *knew* he was here."

"Well, maybe he will be gone in a few days . . . but you listen to Mom: you be happy for Mrs. Sandra, and don't be begrudging her for leaving. She is doing great and can walk on her own now. She is seeing streets of gold. So, don't go and let Ray see your hurt. Not for this. You be happy at her going-home party."

"Mom, I will try."

DiAngelo tapped on the window and waved for me to come home.

"Okay, Mom, I guess they're done taking Mrs. Sandra. I am going home. I love you both. Tell Mikie I will see him in the morning."

I kissed them both and left.

"Buckaroo, how are you?" DiAngelo asked as I met up with him outside.

"Just tired, Angelo. Can you bring Alex to see me before you go to bed?"

"I have a better plan than that," was all he answered.

I got into the house and said loudly, "Mother Faye, guess what?"

"What, Rocco?"

"My Mrs. Sandra is in Heaven. She is seeing the folks; she is young with your daddy; and she can play that piano all over Heaven. So, I ain't begrudging that she took off and left me. I am happy for her; and she is playing music with the angels, waiting for me. That's where my Mrs. Sandra is: she is with Mrs. Liza talking about us and how they both loved Angelo and me."

"Is this boy a priest?" Ray asked, laughing.

"No, but put all that in your soul, Ray; and eat on some happiness instead of our hurt," I answered him. "We are going to be fine, Mother Faye . . . Angelo and me. This will not kill us; we are Pettrachini. We have Mrs. Liza's blood flowing in us. Your father gave me his strength and determination. Mikie and Angelo and I are the true Pettrachinis."

I looked back to Ray as I spoke, "I will not give you an ounce of my soul to even hate you. Now, what is it exactly that you are here for?"

"I have come home to resign. I will not be running the Italy companies any longer. While you all sit here and live like kings and queens, I do all the work over there."

"That's fine. Angelo, sell them all. Sell them to the lowest bidder. Sell the house, the vineyards, the companies . . . sell *everything*!"

Ray looked at Uncle Marco.

"Marco, are you going to stand for this?"

"Rocco," Uncle Marco said, hoping to get Rocco to understand, "those businesses are the family's moneymakers."

"Uncle Marco, we have more money than we need now. Angelo, help me here."

"Buckaroo, I have to agree with Uncle Marco. Those businesses keep things paid for and going. Think of all the people who would be without jobs if we sell."

Ray broke in, "I will continue to run the businesses if you open the accounts to me."

"To buy some new bikes for your kids over there, dear Father?" I spat out.

Ray's face went blank, and he was at a loss for words.

"Oh, come now, Father. You're not ashamed of your life in Italy, are you?" I pushed. "Tell us how you have a 17-year-old son and a 12-year-old daughter in Italy. Tell DiAngelo. Tell Mother Faye. Tell Uncle Marco. Tell them, you creep!"

"This has gone far enough for tonight," Ray put in. "Mother is tired and upset."

"Like you care, Ray. Tell them now!"

"Wait, how can he have a son 17 years old, Rocco? You are mistaken." DiAngelo put in.

"Oh, no, I am not. I asked Mr. Hamson to send someone to see how Father was doing . . . if he had enough money to live on because I felt bad for him. Even more than you did, Angelo, I wanted to make sure he had what he needed, remember? I was the stupid one who cared."

"Well, that's true; Rocco was worried about you, Father," DiAngelo said emphatically.

"Tell them Ray . . . and stop calling him 'Father,' Angelo," I pushed even harder.

Ray took a sip of his coffee as he stared at me over the top of his cup with hatred in his eyes.

"Never mind, Ray. I will show them myself," I said matter-of-factly.

I went to the piano room. From the back of the piano I pulled out a folder. When I returned, Ray was standing to his feet.

"No, sit, Ray," I commanded him. "The day I got these, I stopped talking about you. I stopped wanting you for a father, Ray."

I pulled out an 8x10 photo of Ray and his children in Italy, all hugged up and playing in the yard. I handed it to DiAngelo who looked at it and handed it to Mrs. Faye and then onto Uncle Marco.

"Another?" I asked. "Splendid!"

I handed DiAngelo another picture of Ray and his supposed wife hugging, the little girl standing by him holding his leg.

"Oh, and another?" I inquired.

I started to pull out another photo.

"No, that's quite enough," DiAngelo tried to stop me.

"No, this one is for you, my brother. Your mother is tired and upset."

I pulled out the last photo. It was of Ray and his son standing by a red sports car, the boy kissing his father on the cheek. After that picture circulated around, Uncle Marco handed the photos to Ray.

Mrs. Faye said in her most classy voice, "Ray, you take a good picture these days."

Chapter 20

"I still don't understand; how does he have a kid 17 years old?" DiAngelo revisited the question in his mind.

"Damn, Angelo! How old are you?"

"23."

"And how old am I?"

"14," Angelo answered.

"Ray, tell them right now," I demanded.

"No, you are doing a great job; go ahead and finish the tale."

"Mother Faye, I am sorry," I apologized before embarking on news that was sure to hurt her.

"Don't be, my number two son. . . I never loved him anyway. Tell it," Mrs. Faye insisted.

"It seems while your father was in Grand Rapids working," I began, "he had a girlfriend. Her name was Jessica Turner, and they had a child together. You were five, Angelo. The child's name is Vincent Pettrachini. He wanted to fly his new little family to Italy, but first made a stop to tell his mother and brother goodbye. That's when he met my mother. He stayed and had an affair of sorts and they had me. Then he and his other family went away to Italy and, in time, had a daughter. I forget her name. But get this: he gave them his name, while I had to settle for Hank's last name, Brooks."

"Why do you say his girlfriend's name as past tense?" DiAngelo wanted to know.

"She died last year after a long battle with cancer. Right, Ray?"

"Yes, God bless her soul," Ray said, almost sounding sad.

"Yes, bless her soul for putting up with you for all these years," Mrs. Faye snapped and then laughed. "I was really going to discipline Rocco later for calling you a creep, but he is right: you are one! He always wanted to name our daughter—if we ever had one—Jessica."

"So, you see, Angelo, when he told us to come and find him after we were 21, he implied it was because he didn't like kids. But that wasn't true; he just didn't want *us*. These pictures show how devoted he is to them and how much he loves them."

I looked around the room, then continued, "So, as far as me opening the bank book to you, dear Father, I would never do that. This money is to take care of *this* family, not for you to squander away on a woman, kids, and even more women. I will call Antonio Ferrelli and have him find a man to run the businesses over there if that's what Uncle Marco and Angelo want, but I have to talk to Mikie in the morning. The four of us will vote on it."

"Rocco, you will not have to hate me for very much longer. You are wrong: in my own way, I loved DiAngelo. And the first day I met you, I loved you. I loved the way your eyes shine . . . like my father's did. You remember, Marco?"

"Yes, I do," Uncle Marco simply answered.

"He would always get things done . . . Father would! You remind me of him, always spouting that he was a Pettrachini . . . loving his name. I think he would say it just to hear his name. Pettrachini . . . Pettrachini. Your mouth runs, non-stop . . . just like his, telling the way things were going to be. Always living a standard that has been set for you by some higher power. I could never live up to his and Mother's standards . . . always in Marco's shadow, the good son.

"So, I fell in love with Jessica," Ray continued. "We had a life together. I could be me with her and not have to ever be judged by Mother's or Father's standards. Like Mother said, she never loved me.

"Your mom," he said, looking directly at me, "was a good woman. That's why I stayed so long. I could have loved her forever. I stayed until you were four months old, and then I had to make myself leave."

I looked Ray in the eye and said, "I think it got easier for you after the first time when you left Angelo."

"Rocco, you judge me . . . but didn't you do the same thing? Aren't you doing it now as we speak?"

"What are you talking about, Ray Pettrachini?" I pressed.

"You came here with DiAngelo and fell in love with him; he is the brother you never had. Then, Mrs. Sandra loved you; and Mother sitting right there called you her second son. They loved you; and yet your mom is next door and you live over here? Does she love you? You went where there was more love . . . yes?" Ray pushed as he ducked his head a little lower to look into my downcast eyes.

"No . . . I mean, yes . . . but I had Uncle Marco, Mikie, Aunt Hadie, my mom, the folks at church . . . who all love me. I came to these folks here to hide while I hurt." After a short pause, I asked, "And, besides, why did you call Angelo to come and get me? You didn't want me; you didn't even care to call and see if I was okay. You even said all those things . . . that if you had known how much it was going to cost for my doctor bills, you would have never agreed for me to come here."

"Yes, I did say that," Ray said. "I am sorry. I have said a lot of things to you I am sorry for. I should have never said I only had one son. When I got back to Italy and saw Vincent, I realized what I had done. I denied my other children, and I felt bad for saying those things to you."

"Yeah, I got the card from you saying how sorry you were," I retorted.

"Rocco, let your father speak to you. Drop the sarcasm," Uncle Marco admonished.

"Yes, Uncle Marco."

"I can't change the past with either you or DiAngelo, but I can truly apologize."

"Well, that's all good and dandy," I started, fighting to keep the sarcasm from creeping back into my voice, "but you're still not getting any money." I looked over at DiAngelo and continued, "If I have to, Mikie and I will vote as one."

DiAngelo laughed and said, "Buckaroo, I think I might make you the president of my companies . . . as tight as you are with that money. But I think I am with you, also, on this: no money, Father."

"Well, will you do me a favor?" Ray asked. "I want to be buried with my mother and father in our place in Holland Cemetery."

"Ray, you're too mean to die; stop the dramatics," Mrs. Faye retorted.

"No, Faye, the doctors have given me, at most, two months to live. I wanted the money to have the burial taken care of. Vincent is almost in college, and Rachelle is almost 13. I need the money to leave them something for after I am gone."

"Who is going to take care of them?" I asked Ray.

"I am not sure, Rocco. I haven't crossed that bridge, yet."

"Well, you can stay here until you go to the Father, if you need to. We will make sure the girl is taken care of . . . and the boy. We will see he gets money for his education," I offered.

"You would do this for me, Rocco?"

"Yes."

"I am not cleaning up another mess for you, Father, dying or not. I am not raising another one of your children," DiAngelo spat out.

By those words, it felt to me as if my brother had slit my throat with the knife Pa had in his hand that fateful day. Tears instantly gushed from my eyes as the hurt tore into my heart. I looked at DiAngelo . . . and he realized.

"No, Rocco, no! Not you! I didn't mean it like it sounded!"

I unsuccessfully tried to wipe the tears from my eyes as I turned to Ray, "Father, we will talk more tomorrow. Uncle Marco and myself will raise the girl. Aunt Hadie and Mom will look after her. She can live with my Uncle, can't she, Uncle Marco?"

"Yes, I will talk to Hadie, but I am sure she will agree that we will finish raising her for you, Ray."

"Father, she will never want for anything, I promise you. I will write it down in my soul. I will never consider her a 'mess to clean up.'"

I turned to leave.

"Goodnight."

I went over and kissed Mother Faye goodnight before starting upstairs.

"Rocco, wait!" DiAngelo insisted.

Mother Faye sternly said, "Let it go for tonight, DiAngelo."

*****

Before I could fall asleep, DiAngelo brought Alex into my room and said, "We are having a sleepover. Do you mind?"

"Really, DiAngelo? I am tired. Just let me spend a few minutes with him, then I need to get some sleep."

"What you're really saying is that you don't want to see me right now. That's what you're saying?"

"DiAngelo, we will talk about that in about 20 years. Let's just let it go; you said what was in your heart. The funny thing is, though, I thought I was looking after you. I thought we were looking out for each other. I didn't know I was a 'mess for you to clean up.'"

"Rocco, you must understand. I didn't mean it that way. I would give anything right now to have not said it."

"Well, like I said, we better just let it go, DiAngelo."

"Why are you calling me DiAngelo? You have always called me Angelo. Now, stop it."

"Isn't it funny: that you once yelled at me for calling you Angelo, and now you are yelling at me for *not* calling you Angelo? We are both tired and need to get through this loss and try to see your father through his time of need. Mother says we are having a one-day service tomorrow and a luncheon . . . no long, drawn-out, three-day ordeal."

"Well, I promised Alex we were having a sleepover, and you know I never break a promise," DiAngelo said.

"No, you break hearts."

Without taking his eyes from mine, DiAngelo said, "Alex, Uncle Rocco is tired. Maybe we should make it another night."

"No. You said we could sleep over here with Uncle Rocco. You promised," the boy whined.

"Yes, DiAngelo, you promised . . . so shall it be," I responded. "Alex, play the toot-toot for Uncle Rocco."

Alex acted as though he held a trombone. Moving the imaginary trombone slide, he yelled out, "Toot-toot."

"Good boy! That was great."

DiAngelo spoke up, "Tell Uncle Rocco what we're having for breakfast, Alex."

"We're having eggs and taters!" he all but screeched.

"Boy, where did you learn that word, 'taters'?"

"From Father. He says it is a wonderful word and would cheer you up," came Alex's response.

"Well, your father is right; you sure have cheered me up. Now, hug Uncle Rocco and go to sleep."

"Nope. We're staying up all night . . . just you, Father, and me."

"You and your father may be staying up all night, but I am going to sleep."

"You're no fun, Uncle Rocco."

"Yes, Rocco, you're no fun," DiAngelo taunted.

"Okay, I will stay up for a little while with you, Alex. What do you want to do?"

"Watch tv . . . or play pin the tail on the father—I mean, donkey . . . and camp. We also have to make a tent. Look, we have it here."

DiAngelo had brought in a tarp bigger than any tarp I had ever seen. He draped it over the posters on the beds; and there we sat, pretending for the child that we were camping.

"Well, I think your father should have at least brought some popcorn and juice boxes," I complained.

"Me, too, Uncle Rocco. He is cheap and don't buy any."

The boy had a way of talking just like me . . . I think it was because he had always been around me when DiAngelo was at work.

"I am not cheap; I bought some stuff for our camping trip. I wonder where he learned that from, Rocco?" he said as he pointedly looked at me.

So, DiAngelo was off to get the things that he didn't buy; and I was sure he was sacking the kitchen for anything fun to eat. Soon he returned with his arms full.

"Here is what I bought for the camping trip . . . and you think your father is cheap."

He tossed the items onto my bed. There were peanut butter and jelly sandwiches, cheese puffs, and pop.

"Great! Pop . . . maybe we can stay awake for the next three days," I tossed out.

"Rocco, chill out. We only camp once in a lifetime. Anyway, I brought you water. You can't have pop."

"Good little boys share their pop with their uncle who loves them with all his heart," I strongly hinted.

"I will share with you, Uncle Rocco."

"I know you will," I said as I looked over at my brother and smiled as wickedly as I knew how.

We played camping and ate before the bears could eat our food. Then we turned off the lights and had just a flashlight burning on the outside of the tarp.

"Uncle Rocco?" Alex timidly asked.

"Yes, Alex."

"Are you scared?"

"No, because your father is here; he will beat up any ol'

bad man and make him run far away from us. We won't ever have to be scared again."

"Oh, good. Goodnight, Uncle Rocco."

"Goodnight, Alex."

He went right off to sleep before I could count to ten.

"Rocco?"

"Yes, DiAngelo."

"Do you remember when you first came to live here and I would sleep over in the other bed to make you feel safe?"

"Yes, I do."

"I was the one who was really scared. Every night I would be awake until I couldn't hold my eyelids open any longer . . . from about the time I was about nine years old when Father left us until you came here to live."

"After all these years you are admitting this? I knew you were scared, and you used me as an excuse to sleep in my room."

"You knew?" DiAngelo asked incredulously.

"Yes, I knew . . . but I was watching out for you. I also knew you had headaches all the time after you and Evett got married, the first year I came to live with you. That's why I would be quiet when you had them. Then there were the nights that you two argued and you would sneak into my room and be awake and leave before I woke up. Up until three weeks ago you did that, but I never spoke of it. I never wanted you to be embarrassed. Did you ever wonder who cleaned off your shoes . . . the mud you dragged in from the first carwash?"

"That was you?" DiAngelo's voice sounded genuinely surprised. "I thought Miss Maria did it."

"No, I wanted you to have nice, clean shoes; so, after you would go to bed, I would go and clean them off and polish them every night for you. For six years now I have been cleaning your shoes. Look under your pillow in the pillowcase. There's a four-leaf clover. I wanted you to sleep good; so, I kept it there. Did you think I loved you just because you killed Pa and made me safe? I love you because you are my brother; you are the only one I have. I am sorry if I messed up your life, DiAngelo."

"Rocco, you *made* my life. I was just mad at Father, again; and when you said we could take care of his children, it made me mad. You are kind to him, and he never even wanted us."

"DiAngelo, let it go, now. He can't hurt me anymore. If he loves us, he does; if not, he doesn't."

"Do you forgive me, Rocco, and love me the same?"

"I forgive you, DiAngelo."

"Rocco, after the service tomorrow, we need to talk to Father and see what his plans are," DiAngelo suggested. "Did you know the other kids are at a hotel here in Holland? Father left after you came upstairs to go be with them."

"DiAngelo," I started, "I am not worried about all that. Let's bury Mrs. Sandra in peace and handle business after that."

"Can you do me one more favor, Rocco?"

"Yes, Brother, if you will then shut up and go to sleep . . . anything."

"Please don't call me DiAngelo. It hurts every time you call me that."

"Okay, deal . . . as long as you don't call me a 'mess that you had to clean up' again, I won't call you anything except Angelo."

"Deal, Buckaroo."

"Can you do me just one more favor?" DiAngelo pushed his luck.

"Angelo, what is it?"

"Let's be careful where Father is concerned and see where he goes with this. Let's just leave the ball in his court, and you tell me if anything is out of the way."

"Brother, just stay near me a few days. You are smarter and can see things that he is up to. You saved me from my pa; save us both from our father."

*****

Bright and early the littlest camper was awake, trying to get everyone else awake.

"Uncle Rocco, did the bears come?" he wanted to know.

"No, good boy, the bears went to the hotel in town and slept there last night."

"That wasn't no bear; that was mean ol' Ray Pettrachini, and we don't like him . . . do we, Father?"

I looked at DiAngelo with wide eyes.

"Angelo, you really need to be careful what you say in front of him; he picks up everything . . . and I mean everything."

"You mean like 'damn' and 'shit,' Uncle Rocco?"

I looked at DiAngelo again with meaning in my eyes.

I continued, half under my breath, "Last week he asked me what 'stupid ass' meant. I asked him where he heard that, and he said, 'Father said it to Mother.'"

"Well, Rocco. She is a stupid ass sometimes. She is more concerned with school and getting a degree than she is with Alex and me. If it weren't for you and Mother keeping an eye over him, he would get no love and attention. We hardly ever kiss or hold hands anymore."

"You mean 'do everything'?"

"Rocco, I can't believe you remember that!" he exclaimed as he laughed so loud.

"Believe me, I remember, Brother."

"You were only eight years old; what was I supposed to say?"

"I guess you answered right. I knew there were some things you didn't do until you were married."

"Rocco, are you going to sing at Grandmother's service? I think it would mean a lot to Mother."

"I can't, Angelo . . . not this time."

"I guess we had all better go shower and get ready for this day."

DiAngelo took Alex and went to their room.

It seemed to me that my brother and his wife were at different points in their lives. He wanted more children; she wanted more education. I had always loved Evett; she was a good girl.

One time when I asked her why she was crying, she answered, "Rocco, I wanted to go to school and have fun . . . be with my friends. But I have become a wife and a mother way too early in life."

She made me promise her that I would take my time and enjoy life: see things and go places. I didn't know what she meant back then; but on this day, if I could go somewhere and be someone different, I would surely go. Mrs. Sandra's being gone just didn't seem right. I didn't know who I was going to tend to now . . . who was I going to love, and who was going to love me like Mrs. Sandra did?

"Rocco, you better get ready and stop daydreaming," DiAngelo said, breaking me out of my reverie.

We went downstairs, and little Mr. Alex would have no part of sitting on Evett's and Angelo's side of the table; he wanted to eat next to me.

"Well, if you're going to eat over there, then you better behave and eat all your food," DiAngelo warned him.

"Look, Alex, you have made your father sad; he misses you," I offered.

"So? I am going to sit in this seat from now on so you won't have to eat alone, Uncle Rocco."

It took me back to the day I left their side and went to sit with Mrs. Sandra so she wouldn't be alone.

"Sound familiar, Rocco?" Mrs. Faye asked.

As tears started running down my face once again, I said, "Yes, Mother Faye, I remember."

"Well, you sure were her sidekick; she loved you from day one."

"I just thank God that I had the time to get to know her and be her friend."

"Rocco, so many times you and my mother sang together. I would greatly appreciate it if you would sing at her service today."

"Mother Faye, I can't. Maybe my mom and Aunt Hadie will do it for me."

"Yes, they said they would if you wouldn't."

"Mother Faye, it's not that I won't . . . I can't."

"I understand, my number two son, but I want you to eat and get something in your stomach."

"I had a sandwich last night on our camping trip."

"Yeah, we had some pop and cheese puffs and some

peanut butter sandwiches!" Alex jumped up and down in his seat as he released the details.

"Pop, Rocco?" Mrs. Faye asked with raised eyebrows.

"Yes, Mother Faye. Since Alex likes to tell everything, I had a little of his pop."

DiAngelo started laughing.

"See how it feels, Rocco? Any time Mother wanted to know anything, she would simply smile and ask you. You never would lie to her," he taunted.

"So, what, Angelo? I would still tell on you if Mother asked anything."

"I doubt that, Rocco," Mrs. Faye interrupted. "You two are thick as thieves. The way you look out for each other is incredible."

"Well, he needs someone to look out for him. Not only did I get the looks in the family, I got the brains, also. It's not every eight-year-old who buys his brother his first carwash."

DiAngelo started laughing again.

"He was supposed to be shopping with Evett at the mall; and when he came back, he was all excited about something. Remember, Evett?" DiAngelo threw out.

"Yes, I remember," she answered, smiling. "He made me promise not to tell you. When that man came out and told me Rocco had just bought the place, I didn't know what to say or do."

"Rocco, you sure have brought a lot of joy to our lives," Mrs. Faye remarked.

"You all are talking like I am dead or something. Now, hush and let's talk about Ray before he gets here."

"Dear, I forgot all about him," Mrs. Faye said.

"I thought you had, Mother. Well, maybe we had better not speak of him; maybe he will go away," DiAngelo replied.

"Angelo, please. He is stealing your kindness by the mean things he has done to us. Let's be better than him and make Mrs. Sandra and Mrs. Liza proud of us."

"Rocco, I think we had better be careful of Ray's apologies and explanations. Be careful of his deathbed wishes and see what he is really up to," Mrs. Faye warned.

"See, Rocco? I told you Mother and I are on the same page regarding Ray. Let's just see where he goes with this."

"Good morning, everyone," Uncle Marco's cheery voice broke in.

"Good morning, Uncle Marco. We were just talking about Ray and his bad news."

"Faye, I don't wish any badness on my brother, and I hope this doesn't sound bad. But I can't really accept that he is dying. I think we would have known sooner. Please don't think bad of me, but I hope he doesn't have anything up his sleeve."

"Three to one, Rocco," DiAngelo spoke up quickly. "Uncle Marco, we don't think bad of you; we think he is up to something, also."

Evett piped up, "This family is warped to the max. Surely, the man wouldn't be that low to say he is dying only to just get money."

"Just give it to him, I say," I said emphatically.

"Rocco, have you lost your mind? What do you mean by 'just give it to him'?" DiAngelo responded.

"Give him the money, and maybe he will go away . . . or at least give him most of it. Keep some for us to live in comfort, and give him the rest," I countered. "Let's just bury Mrs. Sandra in peace."

"Faye, I'm sorry. I am so insensitive; please forgive me," Uncle Marco spoke up.

"Marco," she started, "my mother lived a good, long life and was a great woman. But we really need to be about business and see what Ray is really wanting."

"Mother Faye?"

"Yes, Rocco."

"Just call Antonio Ferrelli and see if there have been any unpaid doctor bills."

The entire table looked at me like I was a whiz kid, and I smiled because I knew what they were thinking.

DiAngelo responded, "Damn! Why didn't I think of that?"

"I told you I got all the brains in the bunch . . . along with Mother Faye, of course."

She laughed and said, "Yes! Thank you, Rocco."

While we finished eating, DiAngelo and Uncle Marco went to making phone calls and seeing what was going on with the Italy businesses, as well as how things were going with the transfer of deposits to the main account in Holland.

"Faye and Rocco, do you know what that man has done?" Uncle Marco started as he came back to the dining room to report on his findings thus far. "He has gone behind our backs and placed everything up for sale over there. He told Antonio that we were on our way to sign the papers and that he was doing this for us until we can get over there."

"Get Mikie! Hurry! Get Mom, Aunt Hadie, and Makayla!" I demanded.

"Rocco, what's wrong?" Mrs. Faye gasped.

"He is going to take them all so we will give him everything. Angelo, don't let Alex out of this room!"

Uncle Marco ran to the door, and there stood Ray.

"Ray, where did you come from?" Uncle Marco stammered in surprise.

"I was over at your house waiting for you to return. What's wrong, Marco? You seem rather upset."

"Nothing, really, Ray. It is just a bad time for us all," Uncle Marco was able to get out as he recovered from the surprise. "Let's just meet back here at three o'clock after the service. Faye has just asked everyone to leave her and the boys alone . . . even Evett and Alex have been sent upstairs. As you can see, Faye is beside herself with grief; and I don't think she wants to see you right now, either."

Ray tried to peer into the dining room at Faye.

"Okay, Marco, I will be back at 3:00 after the service."

He turned and left the house.

In a few minutes, Marco returned with the report that everyone was accounted for.

Mom walked up to me and placed her hand on my shoulder.

"Baby, are you okay?"

"Mom, Ray is here to do bad. I know what he is up to; I just know it in my heart."

"Rocco Daniel, hush for a minute. He asked Mikie to go with him to Holland to pick up some things. Your Aunt Hadie said he had to wait until Uncle Marco got home."

"See, I told you: he was going to take Mikie away from us."

I looked at Uncle Marco, and I could tell he was very angry . . . a quiet anger, but his expression wasn't quite right . . . it was a cold look, a look of hate and outrage. He didn't speak except for the required "Yes" or "No." I hadn't seen that look since DiAngelo had the same look when he protected me from Pa that day he had a knife and was going to kill me. DiAngelo had shot Pa, killed him, and then shot him again for good measure.

DiAngelo took over the talking for a few minutes, "Well, we have to have the service for Grandmother; and we must all pull together. Uncle Marco, you stay with Hadie and the kids; don't leave their sides. I will stay with Evett, Alex, and Rocco. We will all meet back here at 3:00 and confront Father with all this. But the women and children must stay guarded."

"We can't be everywhere, DiAngelo," Uncle Marco commented. "When we get back, the ladies and the children will have to go upstairs."

DiAngelo then got on the phone and called some folks. When we went to get into the limos for the service, there were men there to put us in and out of the cars and to walk with us. I went with Mother Faye. Standing by our car was Tipper who worked at the carwash.

"Tipper, you ain't no cop," I said.

He opened his suit jacket and said, "Yeah, but I know how to hunt," as he revealed a pistol tucked into his belt.

He patted my back for assurance and got Mother Faye and me into the car safely. I turned in time to see DiAngelo, Evett, and Alex get into the next car safely. Behind them I saw Uncle Marco's family. We all got to the church safely, and they walked us in and stood by the back door.

I whispered, "Mother Faye?"

"Yes, Rocco."

"This is ungodly that we can't rest our souls and minds long enough to mourn our loved one."

"I know, Rocco, but we have Mother in our hearts; and he can't steal that."

My family was strong, but I could feel their fear. They were worried . . . it was a strange worry. It was not an outside person who DiAngelo and Uncle Marco were keeping us away from; it was a member of our own family trying to hurt us.

Chapter 21

Mom walked past me on her way to the platform of the small church.

"Rocco," she simply said, but I knew immediately what she wanted when I saw the expression in her eyes toward me.

I dutifully followed her. The two of us met up with Aunt Hadie a little further down the aisle, and we proceeded to the front.

"No, Mom, I can't," I protested quietly.

"You can, and you will," she said in a tone that indicated I was not to cross her.

I looked back at Mother Faye and pleaded with my eyes. She only nodded for me to go ahead.

Mom grabbed my hand and whispered, "Do this for your loved one and for Mrs. Faye."

Mrs. Sandra's favorite song began to flow throughout the sanctuary. I thought I was going to die inside.

Mom and Aunt Hadie sang with me, and I was all right until I looked down and saw my Mrs. Sandra lying in her casket. That was the same time I got to the part of the song that Mrs. Sandra and I always sang together. I don't know how I managed, but I kept singing.

Mom and Aunt Hadie wept. There wasn't a dry eye in the house. I knew I had to keep singing even though every part of my being wanted to give in and quit. DiAngelo was sobbing, and Mother Faye was crying quiet. Mom took my hand once again; I felt her strength stream into me as I sang loudly.

Uncle Marco stood slightly behind DiAngelo with both his hands on DiAngelo's shoulders. Out of respect to Mrs. Sandra, he refused to sit during the whole service—something I hadn't seen since I left Kentucky. His tears flowed freely for he knew how much Mrs. Sandra loved him and wished he had been the one to marry her daughter.

After we finished the song, Mom and Aunt Hadie went and sat down. I took my seat by Mother Faye. She held my hand as I held DiAngelo's hand. The priest talked shortly, and we were once again off to the cars.

"Rocco, are you okay?"

"Yes, Mother, I am okay."

"Are you sure?"

"Yes, Mother."

DiAngelo decided to ride to the cemetery with us. Tipper was in the car with Evett.

The caravan of cars stopped at the side of the road; and we walked up a little hill. Once everyone was assembled, the graveside service began. When they started to lower Mrs. Sandra's body into the ground, Mom and Aunt Hadie sang a second song named "Heading Home."

Suddenly, I broke. Seeing her being placed into the ground was more than I could take. I began to cry without restraint as I yelled, "No! No!" DiAngelo ran and grabbed me, pulling me to him.

"Make them stop, Angelo!"

They continued to slowly lower the casket while I kept yelling "Stop!" When they threw the first bit of dirt onto the top of the casket, my legs felt numb. DiAngelo half carried and half dragged me all the way back to the car. I had faced several deaths and many going-home parties for people from the church. From the time I was big enough to walk, I had attended maybe 20 services; and they were all pretty much the same . . . but this one truly almost killed me.

We went home, and the ride was quiet. I just sat looking out the window.

"Rocco, you are too quiet; I am worried about you," DiAngelo softly said as he placed a hand on my shoulder.

"Don't be worried, Brother. I am thinking about business and my family."

When we arrived home, we went inside. Tipper went into the house with us and took the ladies and small children upstairs.

"Mikie, you and Rocco go upstairs, also," Uncle Marco instructed.

"Yes, Father. Come on, Rocco."

Just at that time, the gate buzzer rang, and DiAngelo hit it so it would open. Mikie went upstairs, and I followed him. He went into the room where everyone was gathered, but I went to my room to get a few things.

"I will be back in a minute, Mikie, but I need to talk to Uncle Marco."

I went back downstairs. As I descended the stairs, I saw the prettiest girl I thought I had ever seen. Her dark hair was in a twist all the way down her back; and her eyes, as she looked up the stairs at me, were big and brown. She kept her eyes on me as if she was studying me as much as I was studying her.

When I got to the bottom of the stairs, I said, "Hi, Rachelle."

"Hi, Rocco."

"You know my name, I see."

"Yes . . . and before you go in there," she started as she grabbed my arm and pulled me back, "you need to know that Father and my brother, Vincent, hate you and the rest of the family, as well."

I started back toward the study where the men were gathering. Mrs. Faye walked up beside me.

"Mother Faye, what are you doing down here? You're supposed to be upstairs. Rachelle here was just telling me to be careful . . . that her father hates us all; and her brother does, as well."

Mrs. Faye turned to Rachelle and said, "You are a very pretty girl; your mother must have been beautiful."

"Yes, Ma'am . . . and he was awful to her and to me."

"Rachelle, you listen to me," Mrs. Faye began. "Everything is going to be okay. Don't worry about us; we know what he is up to."

Mrs. Faye patted Rachelle's arm, giving emphasis to her words, as we walked in and found places to sit.

"Rocco, I thought I told you to stay upstairs," Uncle Marco said rather sternly.

"Mother Faye brought me in with her."

"Very well, then. You can stay."

Ray walked up to me with a tall young man next to him.

"Rocco, this is my son, Vincent."

"Nice to meet you, Rocco. Father has said a lot of good things about you."

I simply looked at Vincent in consternation.

Then I turned back to Ray and said, "Father, you really did feel badly for all the mean things that you said to me?"

"Yes, Son; I did."

"You see, Angelo," I began, looking at DiAngelo, "Father has a heart; and that's why I talked to Mikie about changing some things where he is concerned. I don't think the amount that you allowed him to have is right. Remember, Father, that I was the one worried about you?"

"Yes, Son."

"Well, Angelo can be mean and nasty at times; he's the one who said, 'You get what you get.' That's why Mikie and I voted to do something different so your last days can be good ones."

"You are so kind, Rocco . . . better than my firstborn," he replied, looking at DiAngelo with scorn.

"And I am better than your firstborn," Vincent spoke up as his father looked over at him.

Ray looked back to Rocco as he said, "Well, I am sure as time goes on, you will love Vincent like you do DiAngelo."

"Maybe more, Father; don't you think?" Vincent piped up.

"Maybe, Son . . . you can never tell."

"Well, I have overruled you, Angelo," I said as I turned more toward DiAngelo. "Mikie and I have decided to give Father a check for $1 million."

"Rocco!" DiAngelo yelled at me.

"DiAngelo, Grandmother left me in charge of this money. Write him the check so I can sign it."

"I will not!" DiAngelo said emphatically.

"No, he will not!" Uncle Marco chimed in.

"Marco, I don't really see what this has to do with you. My son is talking," Ray responded with a smirk on his face.

"Father," I said, "will you sign some papers giving us the girl so she won't be in the custody of strangers after you are gone?"

"Yes. I would appreciate your watching over her with the family money after I am gone . . . and what will you do for my son, Vincent?"

"I will fly him back to Italy or wherever he chooses to live. Since you have the home in Italy up for sale already, I think it should sell quickly."

Ray's entire demeanor changed.

"Yes, Father," I began again, "we know what you have done, and now Uncle Marco wants to talk to you."

"What is it, Marco?" Ray spat out.

"Ray, did you plan on taking my son from me? Kidnapping him? Holding him for ransom?"

"No, Marco! What makes you think I would want him? I don't even want the ones I have!"

"Father, how can you say things about me like that?" Vincent said with an apparent whine in his voice.

"Shut up, Vincent!"

"Ray, we want you to leave and never come back here," Uncle Marco said vehemently. "As of today, you have no brother or family in Michigan." Uncle Marco pulled out a gun and said, "I should kill you right now!"

"No, Uncle Marco," DiAngelo cried out. "Let me kill him . . . *please*!"

DiAngelo pulled out his gun. Now, two guns were pointed at Ray.

Mrs. Faye jumped up.

"No one is going to kill him; he is going to kill himself. Put the gun in his hand and help him pull the trigger," Mrs. Faye instructed.

Ray's eyes were crazed.

"You all are crazy!" he exclaimed. "Rocco, give me my

check, and I am out of here. I never want to see any of you again!" he yelled as he ran his hand back through his hair.

"Ray, when you get to where you are going, you write and let us know where you are," I strongly suggested.

"Rocco, don't give him a penny," a steady voice from behind me said.

I turned, and it was my mom.

"If you give it to him because you are scared and afraid of him, he will always be in your head; you will never be at peace. Son, listen to me and remember. Do you remember how afraid you were of the bad man? He was always in your head. You knew all along who the bad man was; you knew he was your pa, but you didn't want to face it. I don't care about the money; we have more than enough. I care about you! If you pay this bad man to leave us alone, he will be back for more and more because he knows you are kind and loving and that you are afraid of him."

"But, Mom, where will he live and how will he eat?" I objected.

"Son, Ray has made bad decisions all his life. There's one thing Ray can do, and that is look after himself."

I literally felt my shoulders drop. I already felt defeated by this man standing in front of me.

"I cannot make this decision," I stated. "Angelo, you and Marco make it."

"I think I would like to help make that decision," came a voice from the hallway.

Mikie walked in.

"Since it is my money, also, I think I will vote 'No.'"

DiAngelo said, "I say 'No.'"

Uncle Marco said, "No . . . but I will give you something to remember, Ray. Remember when we were in Italy and you were hanging out the window trying to get out and go with your friends when we were kids? I grabbed you and pulled you back in. I saved you from falling. But this time . . . this time, I will kill you if you ever come around my family again! That includes yours and Faye's kids. I will kill you, Ray . . . I swear on our Mother's grave.

"Now, I think Rocco is right. We are going to sell everything in Italy and keep our options open to the Michigan things. There are no businesses there for you to run and no home for you to live in."

"Okay, Marco," Ray spat out, "Plan B . . . where is the boy's pa, as they call him? Mr. Hamson says he never showed up. Did you and DiAngelo kill him? Maybe the police need to be notified and lock up both you and my ungrateful son."

"Rocco, tell him who killed your pa," Uncle Marco commanded.

"I don't want to," I stammered, wondering what Uncle Marco was up to.

"Go ahead and tell him," Mom urged.

"My friend Mr. Creek killed him and took him off in his truck. I don't even know where he took my pa, but Mr. Creek said they wouldn't ever find him because he burned him. He left a note saying he did it."

"Well, how convenient," Ray answered. "Looks like you all stick together, and you win. I will be leaving, but you can count on one thing: I *will* be back. You can't stop me from that! Let's go, Vincent."

Ray turned to exit the room, Vincent on his heels.

As they walked into the hallway, he ordered, "Rachelle, get your coat on."

"No, Father. I am not 21," Rachelle replied. "You told me to come and find you when I turned 21."

"Ray, for God's sake, sign her over to me," Mrs. Faye spoke up firmly. "Do at least one thing good and right."

"No, she's going with me," Ray answered.

"No, I am not, Father. I am staying with this lady and her son, Rocco. I like it here."

As they argued, I saw from the corner of my eye DiAngelo hand Tipper his gun. He sent him outside to his car.

"DiAngelo, will you promise me she will have the best life and want for nothing?" Ray inquired.

"I will, Father."

"Give me some paper," he ordered.

He began to write: "Faye Pettrachini has the right to make all decisions regarding Rachelle Pettrachini until further notice." He signed it "Ray Pettrachini, Father" and dated it.

"Good riddance to all of you until I come back for my victory!" Ray spewed.

"You didn't tell me they were all trash, Father. You only said the boys were."

Ray laughed uproariously at the joke.

Once the door closed behind them, Mrs. Faye turned to her family.

"Let's get back to being a family!"

The family members from upstairs came down the steps. Mrs. Faye put her arms around Rachelle's shoulders.

"I want everyone to meet the newest addition to the Pettrachini family. This is Rachelle," she announced.

Mikie grabbed my arm and pulled me back into the dining room.

His eyes were big and round as he asked, “Rocco, are you okay?”

“Sure, I am, Mikie.”

“Rocco, I know how much you wanted this to work out so you could have a father. It’s okay to hurt over this.”

“Mikie, it’s actually quite simple: he doesn’t love me. There’s nothing I can do about that.”

That day we mourned the loss of one great soul but found another. I didn’t think Rachelle could ever take the place of dear Mrs. Sandra, but she made the hurt a bit more tolerable . . . and Mrs. Faye now had the daughter she always wanted.

Sometime later, the gate buzzer rang. Momentarily, a policeman stood at the front door.

“I am sorry to inform you,” he said to Mrs. Faye and DiAngelo who answered the door, “but there has been a drive-by shooting on down the road. I’m afraid your husband and his son have been killed.”

Mrs. Faye’s hand involuntarily flew to her mouth as she looked at DiAngelo knowingly.

“Oh, my goodness,” was all she could get out before she choked on the words. She wiped at her non-existent tears for the benefit of the police officer.

“Once again, Mrs. Pettrachini, we are sorry for your loss. We’ve heard it’s been a difficult day for you and your family.”

“Thank you, sir. Goodnight,” she said softly as she closed the door.

She turned and leaned back against the door and just

looked at DiAngelo. She looked over at Rachelle who had just come out of the study.

"Rachelle, your father and brother were just killed in what looks to be a drive-by shooting on down the road somewhere," Mrs. Faye told her as she quickly walked up to her and put her arms around her.

Rachelle stiffened somewhat and pulled away from Mrs. Faye. Mrs. Faye could see real relief in the girl's face.

"Well, at least now Father will never be back to take me away."

"No, good girl. And I will always be here for you."

She put her arms around her again and hugged her. This time Rachelle accepted the hug.

*****

Many things change; and yet they stay the same. Uncle Marco wanted Mikie to learn and see more kids his age, so he decided he would attend the Catholic school. Seeing I was not of that faith, Mrs. Faye kept the tutor coming. He taught both Rachelle and me at our home.

Every day I would walk Mikie to the car and say goodbye to him. Each day I made sure no one was picking on him. He learned to be not so shy with this new bunch of kids and made many friends. It helped that the girl from the YMCA, Audrey, also went to the same school. Sometimes she came over to study with Mikie after school and would bring her brother, Chris, with her.

After their studies, we would all swim in the lake. Chris was the same age as Mikie and I. We had turned 15 the summer Mrs. Sandra died, and we were on our way to growing up.

Rachelle, when not with Mrs. Faye, would hang out with us, as well. She and Audrey became best of friends, even though Audrey was only 13, a few years younger than Rachelle. I believed Rachelle was a bit like me: quite mature for her age. No telling what life had dealt to her, living with Ray.

DiAngelo, Evett, and little Alex were all doing great. Alex would run and swim with Makayla. They both loved the water. When they were in the water, I could never really relax or be at ease because I would tend to them and worry about their safety by the water.

"Alex, you and Makayla get up here closer to me where I can watch you," I would tell them.

"Uncle Rocco, we can swim out here; Father said it was okay," Alex would argue.

"No, I want you up closer. Now, get over here!"

Alex would give me a "little Angelo" look, but would eventually do as he was told. Makayla, on the other hand, would say okay and just do it.

"Rocco, come on! Let's swim!" Mikie broke into my thoughts.

"Mikie, I can't; I got these brats. Go on and have fun. I will take them out of the water in a few minutes and take them to their moms."

Mikie was getting taller by the day, it seemed, and was almost as tall as Uncle Marco.

"Go have fun; we will watch the kids," I heard Mom say as she walked up behind me.

"Okay, Mom, but don't let them get too deep."

I ran out to a deeper area of the lake with Mikie, Audrey, Chris, and Rachelle.

"Chris, are you staying over at Mikie's house tonight?" I asked.

"No, you and Mikie are supposed to come over to my house," Chris responded. "We are going to sneak out later and go to the state park. A lot of us are camping over there. I am going to tell my dad I am at your house; you tell them you are at my house."

"You mean you want me to lie to Angelo?"

"Yes. You are 15 now. You and Mikie can come and have fun with us."

"Does Mikie know about this?" I inquired.

"Know about it?" Chris repeated. "It was his idea!"

I had heard how the other kids would go camping over at the state park. While their parents were busy, the kids would go and have fun in the water. After thinking it over a moment, I thought it could really be exciting.

"Okay, count me in," I stated.

"Cool! We will meet down the road from my place and walk to the lake about 5:00," Chris offered.

"Okay. Mikie and me will be there," I reaffirmed. "Where are we going to sleep for real?" I suddenly threw out.

"Dang, Rocco! You worry too much."

"Well, I just wanted to know."

"Probably on the beach. It is fun . . . you will see."

A few minutes later I called DiAngelo at his work.

"I am going with Mikie to spend the night over at Chris' house."

"Well, I guess it will be okay; but if you need me, you call."

"Okay, Brother. You stay home tonight and see after Alex."

"Of course, I will."

We hung up.

My brother had also taken up the habit of leaving around 9:00 p.m. after he put Alex to bed. He would come into my room and tell me to hold the fort down. I didn't know what was going on with him and Evett, but it wasn't good. He had taken up sleeping in the room on the other side of mine. Most of the time Alex would sleep in there or in my bed.

I gathered some shorts and extra things in a duffel bag and went next door.

"Mikie, are you ready to go?"

"Yeah. Hang on, I am coming."

Mom and Aunt Hadie looked at me knowingly.

"Rocco," Mom said, "you watch out for yourself and Mikie."

"I will, Mom. We are going to have fun and cook out over at Chris' house."

"Well, make sure to take clean undies in case of an emergency."

"Mom, stop it. We are only going down the road. There will be no emergency." Then in a loud voice I yelled, "Mikie! Come on! I'm leaving you if you don't come on."

"He has to do his hair over and over again till he gets it right, Rocco," Aunt Hadie commented laughing.

"Boy, did you get some cash to take with you?" Uncle Marco asked me.

"Yes, Uncle Marco," I answered impishly, "but you can give me some more if you want to."

"You're a mess, Rocco Daniel!" he laughed. "You boys had better behave yourselves, and I mean it!"

"Yes, sir, we will," I responded.

"Come on, Rocco," Mikie urged.

"Who are you rushing now? I have been here waiting for you for 30 minutes!"

Laughing, we grabbed our bags and went out of the house.

"Hurry!" Mikie pushed.

We hurried down the street as soon as we saw there were no cars coming. We didn't want anyone knowing we lived in the big houses on the lake. We crossed a yard, and we were on the beach.

"Chris said to meet him on his street," Mikie objected.

"I know, but we're going straight to the park and beach, instead," I replied.

When we finally arrived, it was dusk. Folks were leaving. We went to the top of a row of stairs, and Mikie indicated we should crouch behind some bushes. In the middle of a group of trees out in front of us there was a fire ring. It appeared folks had either camped there or partied there.

"Mikie, why are we hiding behind some bushes?" I wanted to know.

"So the cops won't get us; the park closes at 9:00."

"Well, we better get out of here, then."

"No, we're going to stay and have a party."

Mikie held up a bottle of something he had buried in his duffel bag.

"Here, take a drink," he offered.

"Uncle Marco is going to kill you!" I seethed between my teeth. "He's going to kill *me*!"

"No, he's not. I got it from DiAngelo's bar at your house and put it in my duffel bag last Tuesday when we had our big family supper."

"Angelo is going to beat us black and blue, Mikie, when he sees it's gone!"

"Are you going to have fun or not?" Mikie pushed.

"Yeah, but he's going to beat us . . . so, we might as well have fun before he does."

I grabbed the bottle and took a gulp of the vodka.

"It's good . . . right, Rocco?"

"No! It sure isn't!" I complained, screwing up my face.

"Here," Mikie offered.

He removed a glass from his duffel bag and a small bottle of orange juice. He put some orange juice in the glass, poured in some vodka, and stirred the mixture with his finger. He handed me the concoction.

"Now, try it," he prompted.

"Ewww, nasty!" I said as I curled my lips.

"It's okay; my finger is clean!"

I laughed.

We finally decided it was safe enough to walk out from behind the bushes.

As we walked to the group of gathering teens, I asked, "Where did you learn to drink, Mikie?"

"At Chris' house when I would spend the night there. His father has every kind of booze. We would drink a little of this and a little of that so He wouldn't miss it."

We drank a whole lot before Chris and Audrey showed up. Then another guy named Jerry and a Brian showed up. More folks kept coming. The more that came, the more booze there was.

"Try this one, Rocco," Chris handed me a bottle of something.

"Okay, Chris. Thanks, friend!"

We were drinking too much, I thought, when someone suggested we go swimming. We stumbled down the stairway to the beach, watching for cops. We went into the water, far into the lake. It was a nice, warm night; and the breeze felt good.

Mikie and Audrey were off by themselves while the rest of us talked and laughed. Brian told jokes; he was the funniest guy I had ever seen.

"So, Mikie's your cousin?" he asked me.

"Yes. I am Rocco. Nice to meet you."

"You, too, dude," he said as he started laughing.

"What's so funny?" I inquired.

"You said 'Nice to meet you.' It's just us here," he said as he swung his arm around indicating all of them at the party, "don't talk so formal."

I didn't know whether to take it as a compliment or pull up my sleeves and hit him.

Before I could make that decision, Brian continued, "It's okay. We will teach you how to talk right. We had to learn, also."

"Okay, then. Deal."

He laughed again and said, "Dude, where are you from?"

"Kentucky."

"Well, that explains it, then," he responded with a smirk.

"Give me another drink, funny guy," I stated.

"No, I think you have had enough for now, Rocco," Mikie's voice broke in.

"Mikie, get out of here. We're having fun getting drunk; and he's teaching me how to talk right."

"You talk fine, Rocco," Audrey piped up as she looked over at Brian.

I didn't think she liked Brian very much.

Several got up and started a fire. Soon, it was popping

and crackling. The music played loud, and most were dancing around the blazing fire.

Chapter 22

"Anyone bring any food?" Brian threw out.

"No, Brian, you should of ate before you came," someone called out.

"I got some crackers and cheese, Brian, if you want them," I offered.

"Rocco saves the day," Brian yelled out as he tore into the pack. "I'm still hungry," he lamented when he had finished off the last one.

"There's a party store by the entrance to the campground. Let's go, Rocco," Brian said as he grabbed my arm and pulled.

Brian and I took off. He got what he wanted, and I picked out a few things that looked good to me. We went to the counter to pay. Brian had $3, but the snacks he had picked up came to $7.

"Got any money?" he asked, looking up at me.

"Sure, I do," I quickly responded.

I pulled out a handful of money.

"Damn, dude! Where did you get the cash?"

"I got it out of my headboard at home."

"Dude, cash me in; and I will pay you back soon."

I didn't know what he was talking about, so I just looked at him with a puzzled look on my face.

"Lend me a few dollars for a few days," he insisted a little harder.

"Oh, okay."

I handed over $300 to him and put the rest away.

We paid the lady at the counter. When we went to leave, a man came around from behind the counter and grabbed Brian by his shirt.

"Are you going to pay for the things in your bag?"

"Get off me, you turtle-looking creep!" Brian yelled as he shrugged the man off.

"We will see," the man said. "Gina, call the police!"

"Brian, what did you take?" I insisted.

"Rocco, I just took some cigarettes and another bottle of wine."

Turning to the man who had Brian still cornered, I said, "Sir, please don't call the police. I didn't know he was stealing. I have money to pay for these things."

"You boys aren't old enough to buy cigarettes and wine."

"How old do you have to be?" I inquired.

"You have to be 21 . . . and neither one of you are no 21!"

"No, sir, I am not. I'm only 15."

"Okay, I will call your parents to come and get you rather than call the police," the man offered.

I handed the man DiAngelo's number. DiAngelo answered and told the man he would be right there.

"Now, Smarty," he started, looking at Brian, "what's your parents' number?"

"I don't have one; our phone has been disconnected."

"Well, if his father will take you home, then you can leave with them; if not, it is the police for you."

As the man stepped away, I looked at Brian and shook my head.

"Stupid, Brian! Why did you have to call him a turtle-looking creep? You made him mad," I seethed.

"Well, he *does* look like a turtle."

He doubled over and laughed and laughed.

"I don't know why you are laughing. Angelo is going to kill me."

"I am sorry, dude, to get you into trouble."

DiAngelo soon pulled up in his truck and came flying into the store.

"You were here stealing?" he yelled just before he slapped me across my face.

"No, I wasn't."

The man from the store spoke up, "No, he wasn't the one stealing; the other one was. Your boy tried to pay for the cigarettes and wine. I would keep your son away from this guy. He is nothing but trouble."

DiAngelo looked at Brian.

"Who are you, and how did you get with Rocco?" he demanded angrily.

"Angelo, can we go and speak outside?" I asked.

"No, we cannot."

DiAngelo looked back at the man from the store.

"Did you check their pockets?"

"No, we are not allowed to do that."

DiAngelo grabbed me by the neck and said, "Empty everything out."

"Angelo, I didn't steal!" I insisted.

"Now!" he screamed in my face.

I pulled out my money, my wallet, and my camping knife.

"You!" DiAngelo said, putting his finger in Brian's face. "What is your name?"

"Brian," he answered rather timidly.

"Brian, you empty your pockets, too."

"Dude, hang back," Brian demanded.

"I said *now* . . . or he calls the cops," DiAngelo retorted as he pointed at the man from the store.

From one pocket Brian pulled out the $300 I had given him and something called a roach clip. From his other pocket he pulled out some weed as he looked up at DiAngelo, pleading with his eyes.

"Oh, so you're a seller."

"Nope, I am a smoker," he answered and then laughed.

"Not with that kind of money on you," DiAngelo responded. "Maybe we *should* call the police," he suggested, looking at the man from the store.

"I gave him that money," I spoke up. "He asked me if I could cash him in, and I said 'Yeah.' So, leave him alone. Give him his money back right now and cash out."

"Dude, it's cool here. Thanks anyway, Rocco."

"You're welcome, Brian."

"Get to the truck, both of you," DiAngelo demanded.

Brian and I walked out.

"Here, Brian," I offered as I handed him the $300. "I had a good time. Thanks for making me laugh."

"Dude, it's okay. You're a happening dude."

"If I ever catch you around my brother, again, I will kill you," DiAngelo threatened. "Now, go back to the rock you crawled out from under."

It looked as though DiAngelo had hurt his feelings.

I said, "Brian, I will call you. Give your number to Mikie."

"Cool, dude. Give your brother a chill pill," he answered, laughing, as he walked off.

"Get in, Rocco, with your smelly self. You smell like a drunk," DiAngelo ordered.

"I don't know why you are being so mean; I was having fun," I lamented.

"This kind of 'fun' you don't need," DiAngelo scolded me. "Now, where is that Mikie at?"

"He's up to the beach at the park. Did you tell Mother I almost got locked up?"

"No, I didn't. I will tell her in the morning."

We rode in silence for a minute or two.

"Rocco, don't you realize you are in trouble here?" DiAngelo finally broke the silence.

"For what? I didn't do anything wrong. I didn't steal. I didn't know you had to be 21 to drink vodka."

"Where did you get the vodka . . . and you better not lie to me!"

"Okay, I won't lie."

"Then tell me."

"Nope."

"Oh, you won't lie, so you won't tell me at all . . . is that it? You are grounded."

"What's that mean?" I asked DiAngelo, screwing up my face in puzzlement.

"Oh, my God, what have we done to you? You are so spoiled that you have never had anything taken away from you when you've done badly."

"I have never done anything bad, and I didn't do anything bad tonight."

"Rocco, you lied, for one thing!"

"Well, that's true, Brother, but I didn't want to do that. I couldn't understand why I felt I had to lie. I could have just told you I was going to have fun at the beach."

My brother was getting angrier by the moment, but I couldn't understand why.

"So, tell me what I did bad besides telling a lie to you on where I was going to be. You do it every night at 9:00 after you put Alex to bed."

"Rocco, we are talking about you . . . a 15-year-old kid . . . not me; I am an adult. There's a big difference."

"We have to walk up the stairway at the park. That's where Mikie is."

"You go get him and bring him down now, and you better not work out any more lies with him. Never mind! Damn it! Show me where he is."

We hiked up the stairs and went to the group of trees. Mikie and Audrey were lying on a blanket, and they were naked as a jaybird. They covered up real fast when they saw DiAngelo.

"Mikie, get dressed now!" DiAngelo barked.

"I am going to go tell the folks," I said. "Bye."

"No, you're not, Rocco."

"Can you guys turn around so we can get dressed?" Mikie timidly asked.

We turned around, and DiAngelo said, "I can't believe this, Rocco. I am ashamed of you."

"Do you think they did 'everything'?" I ventured to ask.

"Rocco, will you listen to me? You are grounded!"

"Grounded from what?" I wanted to know.

"No watching tv, for starters."

I laughed.

"I don't watch tv, anyway," I countered.

"Well, I will think of something. That vodka has given you a smart mouth. I'd watch that, if I were you."

"All I said was 'I don't watch tv.'"

"You really don't understand what you have done wrong, do you?" DiAngelo asked incredulously.

"Nope . . . but I think you are mad for whatever it is."

"Okay, we can go," Mikie said.

Mikie kissed Audrey goodnight. We walked down the steps and got into DiAngelo's truck.

"Mikie, this is your fault," DiAngelo started in on him. "Rocco has never lied to me. You are teaching him things he shouldn't learn. Where are you learning all this yourself . . . sleeping with girls at the age of 15?"

"I wanted Rocco to have a good time and get away from that damn house and stop taking care of kids all the time . . . and just be with me: swim, laugh . . . is there anything wrong with that, Mr. DiAngelo?"

"No, but what if you drunks were to drown or something . . . or get hurt? Look, Rocco was giving his money to that thug!"

"Brian isn't a thug; I like him. Let him be," I protested.

"Where did you get the vodka?" DiAngelo seemed he wanted to pursue a different line of questioning. "Rocco wouldn't tell me. And you better not lie, Mikie."

The booze had really started to work on me; I think because the truck was moving.

"Tell Angelo the truth," I told Mikie.

"We bought a vodka company," he announced in grandiose style.

He laughed and laughed. As Mikie continued to laugh,

DiAngelo and I just sat there. DiAngelo was getting redder by the minute.

"You two think you're funny. Wait until I tell Uncle Marco."

"He is going to kill us . . . also Mikie," I said lamely.

"I don't care!" Mikie blurted. "At least I got you out of that house and let you have fun. He can kill me if he wants."

"I think we better stop," I suddenly said.

"Rocco, what's wrong?" DiAngelo asked, panic edging his voice.

"My vodka is saying 'Hi' to my mouth."

"You better not puke in my truck . . . I mean it, Rocco. I mean it!"

He pulled over. Just as I opened the door, it came flowing out of me like a waterfall.

"Mikie, look! There's our lunch!"

We were looking at the mess I had just made.

"Dang, Rocco! You ate a lot!" Mikie responded.

We held our stomachs as we laughed and laughed.

"If you two don't get back in the truck, I am leaving you both standing there," DiAngelo threatened.

"Good! We can go back to the beach and have some more fun," I suggested.

"Oh, your fun days are over with as of tonight."

"That's okay. We are going to have the party at our house next time, and you're not invited!"

DiAngelo said, "If you don't drink vodka, that would be fine."

"Really?" I asked. "Can Brian come? I love his jokes."

"If he doesn't steal anything, he can."

Mikie spoke up, "Let me get this right . . . you are saying

we can have our friends over, and you will leave Rocco alone to have fun and just be with us?"

"Yes, but no drinking; and the clothes stay on! Deal?"

"Deal," we both said in unison.

"I will have to talk to Uncle Marco, but tonight I think it would be best if you stay over at our house, Mikie, and sober up."

"A campout!" I suggested. "I am getting Alex."

"Rocco, if you wake him up, you're staying up with him. Mikie, go in and get to bed. We will be back. My brother and me are going for a ride."

"Okay, but stop and get some food," Mikie interjected.

"Okay, I will."

We let Mikie out, made sure he got in the house in one piece, and took off. DiAngelo sat quietly for a few minutes.

"Angelo, are you mad at me?" I ventured.

"Rocco, I don't know what to do with you. I want you to be a kid and have fun, but I want you safe, also. I can't watch out for you if you're running all over town."

"But I have never been out; I have never even stayed over to Mikie's. I stay at home all the time. He goes to school, and I can't go with him; I am lonely."

"I know, Brother. I have been thinking about it before all this. You need some kids your own age; but you need good kids, also."

"Can my friends come from church and we have a party? They're the only ones I know."

"Then you're surrounded with just one kind of friend; I need to talk to Mother about this."

"What did *you* do, Angelo?"

"I was lonely, too, until I met Evett at the beach. Then you came and was my friend."

"I never thought about that, Angelo. I am sorry."

"Sorry for what?"

"I understand now. You should have been out having fun and meeting friends. Instead, you were home always taking care of me. I understand now."

DiAngelo looked at me and said, "I think you do understand now, and I am doing the same thing to you. You are always taking care of Alex and doing the things I should be doing. I am taking your childhood away, but we are going to change all this."

"How, Brother?"

"No more of me rushing to get Alex asleep and running out at 9:00 p.m. for starters."

"Do you have a girlfriend, Angelo?"

"Why do you ask?"

"Evett is not sleeping in your bed, and I never see you kissing or holding hands."

"Rocco, there's good girls and bad girls. I love Evett; but when you're older, you will understand that men have needs. If the good girls don't do their duties as wives, men look elsewhere. Do you understand?"

"You mean you have a 'Jessica' like Father did?"

"Dear Lord, no! As of tonight, I am going to work things out with Evett and stop seeing the other girl."

"Angelo, thanks for telling me the truth. Can you tell me one more thing and trust me?"

"Yes. You know I trust you with my life."

"Did you have Father killed?"

"Rocco, stop that nonsense!"

"You didn't say 'Yes' or 'No.' Angelo, you said you would tell the truth. Now, do you trust me or not?"

The truck sat silent for what seemed an hour. DiAngelo fumbled with things in his glove box, cleaned out his sun visor, and was all-out fidgety.

"Can I tell you what I think happened? You can just listen, Angelo. That night when we forced Father to tell the truth and he said he would be back for his victory, you got scared and thought of him hurting me or Alex . . . any of us, for that matter . . . so you told Tipper to follow him and kill him. That way you would never have to be worried about him coming again. It was an end to your worst fear. So, instead of letting the one you loved a small amount to live, you saved the ones that you loved a great amount. Is that about right, Brother?"

"Rocco, he was my father for nine years of my life before he left. I couldn't let him take the life of you or my son. He was driven by hatred and greed."

"So, say it . . . get it over with, and let it go. Maybe it will help you get over the headaches and work on your marriage."

"Yes, Rocco. I had him killed by my gun. Tipper had his own gun, but I wanted it done with my gun . . . the same gun I killed your pa with . . . to protect you and the rest of the family."

"Angelo, are you going to kill Brian? Mikie? Anyone who tries to get in our lives? We kill them if they're not the way we want them to be? We have to trust that God will watch over us . . . not your gun. The killing must stop. We have buried three men: our father, brother, and Pa. It has to stop, Angelo . . . never again! Your soul has become hard from all this. Let it go now, and let's have a good life."

"Rocco, how do you see what's in my heart all the time?"

"Angelo, do you remember when I went upstairs with Mikie and then came back down?"

"Yes."

"I went and got my gun. I was going to kill him before I let him hurt you anymore and take a loved one away from us."

"You, Rocco?"

"Yes. I was going to follow him out and shoot him. When I seen you give your gun to Tipper, I just stood back. In a way, I also shot Father. I knew what you were doing, and I said nothing. I gave him no warning, and I have to live with this just as you do.

"I want to go to Italy and see Mrs. Liza's house before it is sold. Will you take me . . . just you and I? I want to see where we came from, and maybe it will let us know where we are going in life."

"Okay. I will make the arrangements . . . just you and I will go like on our trips back and forth to Kentucky. But unlike when you put things behind you when you left Kentucky, we have to come back, Rocco. We can escape this for a season, but we have to come back."

"Brother, you know me too well. I love you."

*****

DiAngelo talked to Uncle Marco about our having friends over from time to time. The last part of August had some nice weather, so we had our first party then . . . mostly with Mikie's friends, but also with a few of mine from church. The two worlds didn't combine very well, so soon the kids from the church wouldn't come anymore: some of Mikie's friends were kind of wild for their taste.

Being 15 is a very sensitive time. I was happy that Mikie had made friends and had himself a girlfriend, but I couldn't understand why my life wasn't falling into place like his had.

"Rocco, why aren't you outside with the other kids?" DiAngelo asked me at one of the parties.

"Angelo, all they want to do is drink and cuss. It isn't too much fun for me, even though Mikie is having a good time."

"Want to go with me in the truck?" he asked.

"Angelo, shut up."

"Well, every time that truck would even move when you were younger, you thought you had to go."

"Well, I will still go; let me get my wallet."

We jumped in the truck and took off. I can remember that day as if was yesterday. The windows were down, and our hair was blowing.

"Rocco?"

"Yeah?"

"I have a surprise for you if you smile."

"Okay."

"You never smile, Rocco. You look at people and always look through them as if you're looking through to their souls. Sometimes, it makes people feel uncomfortable. What are you seeing when you do that?"

"Their eyes."

"What?"

"I am looking at their eyes. You can tell what's in their hearts if you look into their eyes. I can see their pain or their joy . . . their excitement or their sorrow."

"Rocco, look in the mirror. What do you see in your eyes?"

"I don't want to play this game, Angelo. Let's talk about something else."

"No, I want to talk about this."

Just as he said that, he unfolded the visor in front of me and said, "Look. What do you see?"

"Stop, Angelo. I mean it."

"Yes, that's what I thought. I got too close, didn't I, Rocco? I got too close to that place that you have always pushed us all away from. Loving us all, taking care of everyone, but never letting anyone love you to the point where you really trust them . . . not ever letting anyone really know you. I want you to look right now and tell me what you see. Tell me, damn it! Now, Rocco, you tell me *now*!"

DiAngelo screamed the word, "now," like a mad man.

I said, "Caged."

"Now, tell me what does that mean?"

"Why are you doing this, Angelo? I love you."

"I love you, too, Brother, but you tell me . . . it's just you and me here."

"I can't breathe anymore, Angelo: I am everything to everyone. I am your Buckaroo; I am Mother Faye's number two son; I was Sandra's good boy; I am Mom's baby, Alex's Uncle Rocco, and Mikie's best friend and cousin. There's no more room for me to breathe."

"All that on top of what, Rocco? Tell me the rest."

"I can't tell anymore."

"The guilt is eating you alive, isn't it, Rocco . . . about Father, and Vincent, and your pa? All the pain from what he did to you . . . it's still in there, isn't it, Rocco? I thought by giving you a better life that you would forget about the old one; it has never gone away from you, has it?"

Right then I let my brother know that it was all in there, locked up in a secret room, lurking and occupying the corridors of my soul . . . afraid to tell anyone, but also afraid not to tell. It was slowly driving me crazy: a teenage child searching for answers and reasons for things that had no answers.

As the tears ran down my brother's face, he said, "We have to find a way for you to let it go. We have to find a way to help you. After we get back from Italy, I want you to see a friend of Dr. Bill's. I should have listened and taken you to see him years ago and let you talk and get it out."

"You mean a shrink?"

"Rocco, they are trained to help folks like you."

"Folks like me? What does that mean, Angelo? I am no different than you."

"No, I know that. They are there to help get you over the past and let you understand you have a future."

"Mrs. Liza gave me a future," I simply responded.

"You mean the money, Rocco? That's no future."

"No, you and Mikie can have it. She is going to help me."

"Rocco, what the hell are you saying?"

"I am going to stay in Italy for a season, learn to breathe again, and learn who I am. I don't need a shrink. I need some room. I need some air."

"You can't stay there without me."

"Yes, I can. You have Evett and Alex now to take care of. You can't be trekking all over with me, looking after me. I am going to school there with other kids . . . run, jump, and ride horses like Mrs. Sandra said. I am going to laugh and even maybe one day smile . . . maybe one day even learn to love myself like I love all of you."

"Rocco, this is crazy; you are barely 16. You can't just up, move, and live by yourself in another country."

"You are to tell no one anything except that we are going on vacation. Then you will return alone without me."

"I will not; they will kill me. All of your folks and Mother and Evett will not stand for this."

"Angelo, do you love me with all of your heart?"

"Of course, I do. You know that."

"Then I don't need you as a brother right now. You have been the closest thing to a father that I have ever had. Please be my friend right now and let me go so I can breathe . . . *please*!"

DiAngelo saw the tears had started and knew I had given it much thought.

"I will stay with you long enough to hire some help for the house, get you enrolled in school, and see that you have everything that you need. In three months, I will return to Italy to bring you back."

"Thank you, Brother. I love you. You will see this is what is meant to be. I know it; I can feel it."

I smiled for nearly the first time in seven years; it was a heart smile. I smiled, but behind that smile I knew in my heart that I would not be coming back in three months.

DiAngelo looked over at me and tousled my hair as he said, "We leave in two days. That was your surprise. He handed me our tickets to Italy in an envelope. Inside were also my passport and the things I would need to go to yet another home . . . a home where I could just be myself and learn to breathe.

Chapter 23

It had already been planned that we were to have a family supper over to Mother Faye's house. I was going to use this time to tell everyone that DiAngelo and I were going to Italy and that I would not be returning with him. The warm breeze blew through my hair, as I sat on the back deck, looking at the lake and filling my soul and mind with memories to recall later.

"Rocco?"

"Mom, I thought you were coming over in a bit for supper. You are early."

"I am but I wanted to talk to you first. Are you going to Italy for any other reason than a vacation?"

"Mom, you always know, don't you? You have some of that 'feeling' stuff in you, also."

"I have a bond with you. Being your mom, I know when something is wrong."

"No, really, Mom. I am just needing some air and some space."

"Rocco, do you want me to go with you to Italy?"

"No, Mom. I want you to stay here and look after Alex for DiAngelo and me. Just keep an eye open and keep him safe."

"You're not coming back with DiAngelo, are you, Son?"

She shocked me with her question, but I also knew I couldn't hold the truth back from her.

"No, Mom, I am not. Can you please just keep it to yourself . . . just you and I?"

"Yes, but I want you to call me every night before bed and let me know how you are doing."

"I will, Mom. It seems like we just got settled good here, and now I am leaving, again."

"But this time, you are not running away from hurt or pain; you'll always know there are folks here in Michigan who love you like I do."

"Sometimes, they love me too much, Mom."

"Mrs. Faye also knows you will be staying, so you might as well tell everyone tonight at supper the plans that you have."

"Yes, Mom, I guess you are right. I can't leave like I was planning on doing; I better tell the truth and tell everyone goodbye."

"Not goodbye, Son . . . just a hug and a see-you-soon . . . but I might also come and check on you from time to time."

"All the way over to Italy, Mom?"

"I can ride a plane to see you and make sure my baby is okay."

"Thanks for understanding, Mom. See you at supper."

My mom kissed my cheek, hugged me, and went back inside.

Alex came out and sat with me. We sat there just watching the boats on the water.

"Alex, Uncle Rocco is going to see another lake and make sure it is okay for us to swim in. When you come and see me, I will have it ready for us."

"How long will you be there, Uncle Rocco?"

"For a little while. Are you going to be a good, strong boy and take care of my brother for me?"

"Yes, I will take care of Father, and we can come and see you every night before bedtime."

"No, good boy, I will be in Italy . . . it is a long way away. But you can call me every day, and we can talk on the phone before your bedtime. Can I tell you a secret?"

"Just you and me, Uncle Rocco?"

"Yes, it is just for us. You know your father is kinda scared of the dark. You have to sleep in the other bed and watch out for him so he can sleep better."

"Okay," Alex agreed, "but I think you better come back home soon because I will miss you bad."

"You will miss Uncle Rocco for real?"

"Yes! I love you. No one makes cocoa like you, and no one loves me like you do."

"Yes, good boy, they do love you in their own way; they all love you like Uncle Rocco does . . . they're just not as fun as I am."

"I don't want you to go, Uncle Rocco. I want you to stay and be my friend."

"Well, who is going to get the lake ready for us if I don't go and get it ready? We won't be able to swim."

Alex sat and thought about that for a minute.

"Okay, but we could send Mikie to get it ready," he suggested.

"No, he would swim all the water away. You know how he likes to swim; and if he swims it all away, we won't be able to swim in it."

"Okay, but I better go. Oh, yeah, Father says it is suppertime."

"Okay," I said as I grabbed his hand, and we went into the dining room.

There was a sign that said "Bon Voyage, Rocco." They had planned a party for my going away.

Mother Faye stepped forward and said, "Come in, Rocco!"

"Mother Faye, you didn't have to have a party."

"It was actually DiAngelo's idea. He wants our last supper to be nice. There is a table loaded with all your favorite foods!"

The family members from next door filed in and looked around.

Little Miss Makayla said, "Rocco, you are going to Italy and be a big boy?"

"Well, yes, Miss Makayla . . . that is, I am going to finish up school there and learn some new things."

Mikie just looked at me with an almost scornful look.

We all sat down. Miss Maria and Mrs. Ruth started serving our supper.

Mikie finally spoke, "Let's have a toast to my best friend and cousin on a safe return."

He stood up and had a glass of wine in his hand.

"To Rocco, may you find a good life in Italy and be able to run and be free. May you find everything that your heart is looking for, and may you never forget your favorite cousin and best friend. I love you, Rocco!"

We clicked glasses and drank the wine. I squinted at Mikie, and he squinted back.

"Mother Faye, are you going to miss me?" I asked her.

"Like the air I breathe, number two son."

"Well, at least you will have Rachelle to keep you busy."

I looked over to her and smiled.

"Rocco, I want you to tell Sara Renee I said 'Hi' and that I love her."

"Okay, who is she; and where do I find her?"

"Oh, believe me, you will find her. Her father is Martin who does the handywork at the house in Italy."

"Are you sure you don't want to go with me?" I asked her.

"No, Rocco. I have nothing there. Just tell her I said 'Hi.'"

"Angelo, are you all packed and ready to go?" I asked him.

"Yes, we leave at 7:00 tonight, and our flight leaves at 9:00. Don't forget your passport."

"I won't, Brother. How long will it take to get there, Uncle Marco?"

"About 10 hours after you get out of the States."

"Me and Angelo are going to be tourists and see a few things before we actually get to the house."

"Rocco, here is the other book that my mother wanted you to have."

He handed me a well-worn book.

"I thought it burned with the gas station, Uncle Marco."

"No, when I went back into the house, I got my pictures and your book that Mother had left you. Aunt Hadie saved them all in a box."

"Thank you, Uncle Marco."

I accepted the book from him, laid it next to my plate, and finished my supper.

"I haven't been there in years and years," Uncle Marco said.

"Maybe you should go with me, Uncle Marco," I suggested.

"You are inviting everyone, Rocco; and this trip is for you and I," DiAngelo reminded me.

"Angelo, I know, but there is always room for one more."

"Yes, but there is not enough time to get another ticket."

"Uncle Marco, you come and see me soon . . . and bring that knucklehead with you."

Mikie smiled broadly at me and said, "I might have to come during winter break. Father can come with me then."

"Mikie, I am going to postpone the sale of the house and vineyards for a bit. Is that okay with you?"

"Sure. I don't care," he replied.

I looked at DiAngelo.

"Angelo, is it okay with you?"

"Yes, Uncle Marco and I talked about it, also; and we feel it can be our summer home in case we ever get the time to go."

"Evett, is the house close to where your parents moved?" I asked her.

"Kinda. Greece is a short way away, but we can travel to Athens when I come to see you."

"Dang, I am going to have a lot of visitors! Is someone going to bring Mom and Mother Faye?"

"We are coming in the spring . . . your mom, Rachelle, and myself," Mother Faye answered.

"For real, Mother Faye?"

"Yes, number two son. I always wanted to see it over there. I would never let DiAngelo go when he was growing up; but now I want to go, as well."

"Good! You, Mom, and Rachelle can come with Mikie and Uncle Marco and his family on spring break."

"That's what we are thinking," replied Mother Faye.

Mom sat through supper, mostly quiet and studying on all of it.

"Faye, you and Rachelle might have to go to Italy alone."

"Why is that, Mrs. Dean?" DiAngelo asked.

"If Rocco has it in his heart that he is staying there, I am going to stay there with him. I am not letting him stay for too long by himself without anyone looking over him."

"Well, I guess we will have to wait and see how he does over there," DiAngelo responded.

My mom looked at DiAngelo in the eye and said, "DiAngelo, I am his mom. I know what my son needs, and right now he needs some air and space. But I am also responsible for his safety. I will go where he is when the time is right."

"Yes, Mrs. Dean. I understand."

With that, Mrs. Ruth and Miss Maria began clearing the table. I didn't know if there was any hostility in my mom's words, but DiAngelo knew what my mom was saying and knew not to go any further with that conversation.

Everyone got up and started hugging DiAngelo and me. We were all packed, and I had my book Grandmother gave me.

"I am taking this on the plane so I can see what it is and whose pictures are in here," I announced.

"Rocco, bring it back safe; I didn't get a chance to make copies," Uncle Marco said.

"Yes, Uncle Marco," I answered as I hugged him.

My mom was next in line. She dragged me to the side.

"Baby, you say your prayers every day and think of Mom."

"I will, Mom . . . and I will call every night."

She hugged me and cried.

"Take care of yourself way over there."

"I will, Mom."

Mother Faye spoke up, "We had better let them get going or they're going to miss their plane." Hugging me, she added,

"Son, make me proud of you and bring yourself back safe. Remember all the things your mom has taught you."

She and Mom walked us to the door. DiAngelo and I gave one last "Goodbye," and we were on our way. We had to ride in the big car so DiAngelo wouldn't have to leave his truck at the airport.

DiAngelo let out a big breath and said, "Rocco, that was so hard, I almost changed my mind about going. Alex was crying and didn't want me to leave."

"I know, Brother, but we will hurry up and get you back soon."

We sat there in the quiet. When we got to the airport, Mr. Scott let us out at the door. We got out our luggage. Some men grabbed our bags and took them inside. There were so many folks there. We went to Gate 21 and showed them our paperwork. They let us on the plane, and we soon found our seats.

"Rocco, here we are," DiAngelo said now with some excitement in his voice. "Are you scared?"

"No, Brother. Hush!"

"You are scared; I can tell. This is your first time on a plane."

"Well, if it crashes, at least we will be together."

"Rocco, it's not going to crash; we will be fine."

"I know. Can you hush now for a few minutes?" I insisted.

"He laughed and said, "Okay. I will talk when we get up and on our way."

"Okay. Thank you, Brother . . . but before we play Quiet Mouse, I just want to say 'Thanks.'"

"You're welcome, Rocco. You're welcome."

Coming Soon!

Book Two - The Pettrachini Family Saga

Vineyards of Love

Made in the USA
Columbia, SC
02 June 2025

58837973R00243